WHY READERS LOVE FINE FINE FINE

My favorite thing about this book is how REAL it felt.
(And obvs because it was really, really hot, okay?)

@GREMLINKAIT

This book should come in a welcome package for every
romance reader who joins the Dead Parent Society.

@READINGANDGRIEVING

This isn't a grief story that tries to fix you; it's one that
sits with you until you can breathe again.

@TALESWITHATTICUS

READ REVIEWS

Also by CB Woods
Rift
Rebel
Risk
Courting Death & Desire

Visit cbwoods.net to read more

FINE
FINE
FINE

FINE FINE FINE

CB WOODS

To anyone who is sick and tired of being totally fine.

CONTENT WARNING

Fine Fine Fine is a love story for readers who know how it feels to lose something you can't get back, while being forced to smile through the mourning.

This story was originally written in the depths of grieving my mother and then revisited five years later—after a metric ton of therapy and a few hundred sunflowers. If substance use, grief, and depictions of the anxiety and depression that come with it are too heavy for you right now, I hope you'll come back when you're ready to be reminded that life moving on isn't always a betrayal.

Eventually, it's a gift.

—CB

ONE

When Hanna Stevens found herself with time to kill, she preferred to drown it in whiskey.

She checked the time on her phone as she caught the bartender's eye. He reached for the bottle of Maker's she'd put an impressive dent in and tipped it over once more.

4:17 PM.

She still had forty-three minutes to talk herself into attending her best friend's engagement party, despite the unfortunate guest list.

The bartender poured another two fingers' worth of whiskey over ice and slid it across the bar—the ancient wood as chipped as her outdated manicure—and she took a long, slow drag of it. The room swirled as the aged spirit pooled on her tongue and burned the whole way down.

Probably. She'd stopped feeling the sizzle at that point.

Hanna could have arrived at the Rodriguez house early and, in all honesty, probably *should* have. She'd accepted the sacred Maid of Honor role six months before and, thanks to her long-distance friendship, had skirted many of the obligatory duties. It was time she paid her dues in the form of fluffing rented linens and arranging grocery store flowers in thrifted glassware.

Instead, she'd cruised by the classically beige suburban home twice before deciding it was safer for her to let the rest of the attendees trickle in and take up space before she had to face anyone.

Sara had been perfectly understanding, of course.

Not that she had any choice.

Hanna found that the only—*only*—benefit of her mother's death the previous summer was the wide berth it earned her in social scenarios. Whether it was because they were kind and understood the special hell she was in, or because they simply couldn't think of something to say, she wasn't sure.

And it didn't really matter.

What did matter was that she maintained just enough of a buzz to convince everyone at the party she was *totally* fine without it feeling overly contrived. A task that would have been easier if the groom didn't share DNA with the former love of her life—and current nightmare ex—Logan.

She checked her phone once more and restlessly tapped her teeth, idly scrolling through Instagram.

Nope, still not blacked out, she thought as she sipped her glass.

The whiskey in her throat had burned away some of the anxiety, at least enough to convince her she could handle seeing Logan.

Hanna *loved* a whiskey buzz. Smooth, cozy, just witty enough to earn a laugh from the room but not enough to show her ass.

Tequila drunk, and she'd cry to the bartender about that bitch Logan had left her for.

Gin made her vomit.

Vodka... *oof.* Vodka turned her into a five-foot-nine woman scorned, looking for any and everything to incinerate.

No one liked Vodka Hanna.

But Whiskey Hanna? Whiskey Hanna was safe. Whiskey Hanna curled up in armchairs, reminiscing about the good old days she wasn't sure she'd ever even had. Whiskey Hanna hardly even remembered the way the funeral director smelled of cheap aftershave and Marlboros.

She set the glass back on the bar, twiddling at the rim absentmindedly and debating how much further she could push her buzz.

She didn't want to be the problem child at the party. She already knew she was in for a night of pained tongue-clicks that preceded asinine questions like, "How are you?" and "You hanging in there?"

And she was, beneath the anxiety, very excited to see her best friend, which was almost enough to override the dread tightening her spine. Sara had fled Phoenix for Silicon Valley the moment they graduated from college, and they'd survived on FaceTime and long weekends for the decade since.

It wasn't enough, but as ready as she was to see Sara, she just couldn't fathom sitting in a house full of people who knew her innermost pain while they attempted small talk—

"Hey, sorry, but are you Hanna?"

The low voice crawled over her shoulders and slid onto the stool beside her as his question hung in the air. Even sitting, she knew he was tall by the way his shoulders hunched to speak into her ear. He was wrapped in a dark pair of jeans and a button-down with sleeves shoved up over his elbows, revealing a canvas full of inky-black tattoos.

Wait a minute, she thought. She knew those tattoos.

Hanna cleared the whiskey simmering in her throat and turned to face him, tentatively asking, "Milo?"

"Okay, cool," he returned. "I thought that was you, but I was afraid to creep on a stranger."

He laughed and set his own half-drained glass next to hers as she wondered how long he'd been perched in the corner of the dive.

Hanna took a slow breath, the pleasant buzz she'd curated suddenly harder to think through.

She'd seen him in the occasional Instagram post over the years, lingering at the edges of Warriors games and movie nights. He was a childhood friend of Sara's fiancé, Matty, and the two had reunited when they both moved back up to the bay. If Sara's reports were reliable, he was as chronically single as he was devastatingly charming.

And Sara's reports were always reliable.

Milo's lips tilted into a lethal grin as Hanna stared for a moment too long.

Some kind of government entity should regulate that jawline, she thought. *It cannot be legal to wield something that sharp in public.*

"Sara said you'd be at the closest, grossest bar, and lo and behold."

Hanna flinched. "I bet she did." She watched as he sized her up with rich hazel-green eyes, his gaze bouncing between her and the final whispers of amber whiskey in her glass.

"Bourbon or scotch girl?"

She shrugged. "Right now? Or stranded on a desert island, and I can only bring one?"

He gestured to the glass. "Right now."

"Bourbon. Maker's. Keeping it simple, but I've actually been into Japanese whiskeys lately."

She wasn't sure why she felt the need to tell him that, but then again, she *was* three, maybe four whiskeys in before dinner, so it was harmless, considering.

4

Something in his eyes lit up.

"Hibiki?" he asked.

"Yeah," she mumbled, feeling a little less mysterious than she'd aimed for.

Hanna angled herself, keen to see more of his face, her legs swinging over one another in what she hoped was effortlessly casual and not a prelude to slipping off the stool.

"They're having a moment right now. All the rage in the city," he said.

"As much as I *love* small talk, I gotta ask. Why are you hiding here? Sara's mom get handsy and run you off?" Hanna looked around, her eyes landing on no fewer than seven geriatric men glued to sticky tables as they watched the singular television mounted in the corner. "Not exactly a hip destination."

She wouldn't have blamed him. Cami could be a *lot* for anyone, but especially a young, handsome man when she was three buttery chards to the wind.

Milo sighed. "I'm not supposed to say."

Jesus, the dimples.

Hanna hung her head forward. Of course, he was the designated groomsman sent to find her.

"Sara sent you."

"She did."

"She knew I'd be too early," Hanna mumbled.

"She did. And she wanted to make sure you had a ride." Milo pointed to her glass again, the gesture landing like an accusation.

"Thoughtful." She clicked her tongue.

Sara was never one for subtleties. From the moment Logan broke up with her, to the moment her mother died (granted, there weren't *many* moments between the two), Sara had pestered her relentlessly about coming out to drown her sorrows in Milo's dimples.

She'd gracefully given up on that after... well, everything.

Even if Hanna had been interested in something romantic with Milo, she had three very well-rehearsed reasons why she would rather throw herself into the Grand Canyon.

1. He lived in San Francisco.

This didn't require much thought—long distance was an absolute nonstarter, given how her long-term relationship with Logan imploded within weeks of him moving cross-country for work.

She wasn't doing that bullshit again.

Ever.

2. He was just, like, too hot.

Hanna was a woman of the early aughts and, as such, she'd worked for years to accept her body and love herself. But even with thousands of dollars invested in therapy, there was a line in her ambition.

Milo took that line, made sweet, sweet love to it, and never called it again.

Seeing him in person only reaffirmed her initial distrust of those dimples. He was massive, not in a yoked-gym-bro way, but in a Thor-was-probably-the-first-branch-of-his-family-tree way. His dark hair was long enough that she had to consciously make an effort not to reach out and touch a curl hanging at his jaw. The deep bronze set off his olive tan, perfectly complemented by earthy eyes that she was certain were capable of X-ray vision.

The kicker?

Just enough tattoos to push him firmly into Bad Boy™ territory, but a stable enough tech job and somewhat decent moral compass—again, if the rumors were to be believed—that barred him from full-blown mischief membership.

3. He knew too much.

There was one last reason—just a small one.

When her mom died after a rollercoaster diagnosis of late-stage cancer that no one saw coming, Hanna called Sara from the hospital parking lot. It was Wednesday, movie and wings night. Milo answered as Sara argued with Matty in the background. He'd caught the brunt of Hanna's shock and grief-fueled hysteria, and she simply refused to ever get to know him well enough to talk about it.

Every time she glanced at his unreasonably handsome face, she whooshed through the last year and found herself back in that parking lot, baking in the Phoenix sun as she screamed into the phone.

The devastation welled up in her chest again just at the sight of him—she couldn't invite any more suffering into her life.

She was maxed out on pain.

"Listen, if you don't think you can handle being in a confined space with me... you can always call an Uber." He smirked and a surprise fourth reason bubbled up.

4. Milo was entirely too aware of the aforementioned number two.

He flashed a cocky smile, earning a huff and an eyeroll from Hanna.

"I knew you'd be an arrogant bastard, you know that? You just have that *look*."

"I've heard that a time or two," he said, a low, rumbling laugh reverberating off the bar top.

Hanna reached into her purse and tossed a twenty down, drowning her final sips, and then reached for his glass. Milo covered her hand, the weight of his a shock to her very lonely system.

"I could have just bought you a drink. All you had to do was say please."

She leaned close to him, catching those green eyes with her own fiery stare.

"I'm bored."

She marched out of the bar and into the harsh evening sunset, her season-old espadrilles crunching in the gravel parking lot. Sara might have had a point in sending someone to collect her, after all. Her head swirled, and not entirely from the temperature.

She tapped across her phone, opening her Uber app and scrolling to find the Rodriguezes' address. The app thought, and then thought some more.

"Damn," she whispered. Was there really no one hanging around waiting to rescue a slightly bitter bridesmaid from her best friend's hot groomsman?

"Suns game," Milo said behind her.

Hanna spun, whipping her dark curls around as the rest of the parking lot followed on a delay. Everything wobbled. It occurred to her as the world resettled into a somewhat coherent image that she had not eaten since breakfast.

She glared. "What?"

"There's a Suns game. You're not getting a ride anytime soon."

"Then I'll walk," she huffed, starting off in the general direction of Sara's childhood home, only for her ankle to immediately roll.

Milo's hands caught her elbow, steadying her body, but boiling her blood. The muscles in his forearm flexed against her and she willed herself not to think about the way the veins pulled under black rivers of ink.

You're pathetic, she chastised herself.

"We got off on the wrong foot," Milo murmured. They both scrunched their noses at the pun. "Bad phrasing."

Hanna pulled her elbow from his grip, smoothing the coral ruffle of her sundress.

He waved toward his rental car. "If you'd like to drop your attitude, I'd *love* to take you to your best friend's engagement party now. And maybe get some food in your system."

Hanna stared for a few beats, wrestling with the asshole in her head who wanted to go another round or two. But the rumble in her stomach needed him more than she needed her pride.

She threw her hands up in defeat and followed him to a silver sedan, sliding gracelessly into the front seat. Her thighs stuck to the hot leather as the open back of her dress betrayed her, fusing her skin to the interior.

"Who gets leather in Arizona in May?" she asked. He didn't answer, which was probably for the best.

His forearm tensed as he reversed from the parking spot. Her eyes landed on the tattoos stretching across his skin while the beiges and oranges of suburban Phoenix blurred through the window. She noticed a clock, inked in gray and black shadows, that fell over the ten and six on its melting face.

"AM or PM?" she blurted.

"Hmm?"

"Your clock tattoo. Morning or night?"

Milo unleashed a smirk, glancing at her quickly as he wound through the Rodriguezes' picturesque subdivision.

Is he capable of another facial expression? she thought.

"AM."

Hanna nodded. "Cool."

"Cool?"

"Yep," she said. He stared ahead, likely waiting for a follow-up question, but she didn't feel the need to know more. "I'm not going to ask for the story." She heard how bratty it came off, but it was too late, and she was too drunk.

He shrugged. "I'm not going to tell it."

"Good," she said, folding her arms.

"Hanna," Milo sighed. "You're wasted. I can't let you go in there like this. We're still a little early. Please, let me get you something to eat."

Hanna shook her head, the lights on the dashboard blending into one large tunnel of color.

"No, no, no. I just need Cami's enchilada casserole. It heals all ailments, I swear."

She attempted a look to convey just how serious she was about her favorite comfort dish, but Milo was clearly skeptical as he slowed the car to a stop outside of a sprawling ranch-style home with a bubbling fountain in the front.

He cut off the engine, but before he could even swing his door open, Hanna was up and off, brushing quickly through the gate and reaching for the handle of the front door.

Any drunk confidence that propelled her through the yard had vanished by the time she got to the threshold, the sounds of a buzzing family gathering striking a chord somewhere in her memories.

Her fingers lingered on the bronze of the funeral home's bathroom door, the next room over humming with thoughts and prayers.

A wave of panic gripped her throat—not just about seeing Logan, but seeing *everyone*. She'd spent the last year holed up in her home like a hermit, dreading the day she'd have to make her public debut again.

The universe was cruel for shoving two of her biggest heart-breaks into one calendar year.

It *wasn't* Logan's fault her mom got sick and died two

months after he shattered her entire world. No one could have predicted it.

But still.

Who else was there to blame?

She hesitated for another moment, long enough for Milo to catch up to her.

"You ready for this, Arizona?"

She inhaled, holding the breath longer than necessary. He leaned around her and pushed the front door open, arching his brows.

"Fuck you," she muttered.

"Say please," he bit, his hand pushing against the small of her back and forcing her into the house.

TWO

The rich scent of Cami's kitchen hit Hanna like a slap on the ass after a game well played.

"You're heeeeeeeere!" Sara squealed, her arms capturing Hanna before she made it through the foyer and squeezing the ever-loving shit out of her.

Hanna's ribs crunched, but the human contact wasn't all that unwanted after months of cradling herself.

"I aaaaaam," she mimicked, matching the energy as best she could. She could tell by the soft pity in Sara's eyes that she wasn't even close.

"Oh my god, I have so much to show you. Mom and I have been busy this week! Come in! Come in! Oh, hey, Milo," Sara said, shuffling behind them to pull the front door closed. Her small frame looked practically miniature beside him, but Hanna knew Sara could take him no problem.

She was a spitfire.

Her highlighted hair glowed like a golden honey halo around her tan face, the curled ends sweeping just below her shoulders against a white lace dress. She looked like she had walked right out of the Engagement Party Pinterest board they'd curated years prior, long before Matty had even popped the question. They'd devoted hours to pinning photos and giggling in their dorm room.

"Thank you for your service," Sara whispered to Milo.

"I'm fine," Hanna insisted.

"I know!" Sara chirped, studying her friend. "Let's get you some food."

She must have looked worse than she felt.

Sara pulled her hand through the house and into the massive open kitchen where they used to talk about boys over waffles. Cami buzzed behind the island, shuffling dishes to make room for something in the oven.

"Hanna! My sweet girl," she cooed, sinking her into a wine-soaked hug. Hanna did everything she could to not let her mind wander to how similar hugging her felt to hugging her own mother, breathing through a deep pain in her side.

She'd gotten used to it—the ache in her muscles and bones at the smallest reminders of what she'd lost. The sudden vice-grip around her heart at a laugh that was too similar, or a pair of glasses that looked like her mom's.

"You're not eating enough," Cami chastised, poking at Hanna's hips.

"I came to remedy that!" She laughed it off, but it was always the first thing people commented on. What else was she supposed to say?

Oh yeah, don't mind my ribs, I just forget to feed myself ever since I lost the two loves of my life in one fell swoop. Thanks for calling me skinny, though!

A loaded plate plopped onto the island beside her as three sets of eyes landed on it, and then swished to Milo.

"Enchilada casserole," he said, shrugging and handing her a

fork. "And I'll take that." He reached for the glass of wine heading Hanna's way in the hand of one of Sara's aunts.

She glared, but picked up the fork all the same.

Fuck, she'd forgotten how good real food tasted.

"Where's Matty?" Hanna asked around her third bite. What she really wanted to ask was, "*Is his brother here? Has he mentioned me? Has New York's water made him uglier?*"

"He's helping Dad out back with the grill. Logan isn't here yet," Sara said, her tone decidedly neutral.

"I wasn't asking—"

"Just giving you the lay of the land," Sara said, moving a plate of burgers to the side. Her movements were identical to Cami's, as if they'd choreographed it.

"Milo, honey, could you take Berto that plate?" Cami asked, pointing a spoon at the burgers. He'd barely gotten out of the room before she turned her amber gaze toward Hanna. "Now you listen to me, little girl. If you don't sleep with that man, I will."

"Camila!" Sara gasped as Hanna pressed her hand to her chest, instantly sober. A scarlet flush climbed her throat as she laughed through her casserole.

"Cami, oh my *god!*"

"I'm serious, Hanna. I know you've been through hell and back, sweetheart, but you *deserve* those arms. Those eyes! Just think about it," Cami said.

Hanna reached for the casserole again.

"Okay, you two, I don't want to hear it this weekend. He lives in San Francisco! You think I'd ever be tempted to do long distance again?"

Cami leaned over the island. "You don't have to *marry* the man, Hanna! I just want to hear about anything you may or may not do with him, that's all." She raised her perfectly sculpted eyebrows as Sara's dad, Berto, burst into the room.

"Have you seen my sunglasses, mi amor?" Berto clicked the tongs in his hand and swept through the kitchen. "Well, would you look who's here!"

He set the tongs down and squeezed Hanna as she continued eating, his cologne drowning her senses. He pulled back and beamed.

"My second daughter has finally returned!"

"Hi, Berto," Hanna mumbled, fixing the collar on his fancy button-down—the one he wore for their college graduation, high school graduation, Lisa's funeral...

There it was again, that simmering panic just waiting for someone to crank the heat one notch higher.

"We don't see you enough, kiddo," Berto said, patting her shoulder. "You know, just because my daughter abandoned us for the West Coast Elite, doesn't mean you can't come by any time."

Sara glared. "Dad, Hanna doesn't want to hang out with a bunch of boomers."

"That's not true!" Hanna protested around a mouthful of tortilla. "I hear you and Cami are hanging out at the casino lately. My invite get lost in the mail?" She finished another bite, finally feeling like the alcohol in her system was evaporating.

"Lone Butte next weekend!" Berto tossed over his shoulder as he grabbed another set of tongs and placed a kiss on Cami's cheek. "You stay away from that groomsman."

Cami laughed, resting her hand on his cheek. "No promises."

"I used to have a jawline like that, believe it or not, girls!" Berto snapped his tongs once more and disappeared into the backyard.

A knock at the front door sent Sara and Hanna both into shades of pink. Sara started for the foyer as Hanna darted out of the kitchen and into the backyard, unwilling to see if a tall, lanky blonde stood behind the door.

She knew she couldn't put it off forever, but she could put it off for a few more minutes, and that was enough.

Hanna cut across the yard, passing the turquoise pool, and headed toward the fire pit. Twinkling patio lights crisscrossed overhead, glowing a warm amber as the sun dipped lower behind the Ahwatukee foothills.

She smiled politely at the relatives she recognized, grateful no one seemed ready to engage her as she caught the broad shoulders of the brother she still couldn't help but adore.

"Do my eyes deceive me, or is that Hanna Fuckin' Stevens in the flesh?" She hardly had time to brace herself before all six-foot-six of Matty wrapped around her, his beard tickling her ear.

His bright blue eyes, so similar to his older brother's, sparkled as he set her back on the ground.

Hanna often thought the heartbreak was worth it if it meant Matty and Sara met one another. There was no better match for Sara's petite, feisty nature than Matty's gentle giant ways. If it took her getting crushed by Logan to introduce them on a Thanksgiving weekend trip, so be it.

"I miss you, dude," Matty said, fishing through the assortment of bottles on Berto's outdoor bar. "When are you just going to give in and move up to the Bay?"

"Never. One finger on that pour. Started early."

He pulled a plastic cup and poured no less than two fingers' worth of something expensive for her.

Matty's fault, not hers.

He sighed. "Can't you work from anywhere?"

"Technically, sure." Hanna took a sip and reached for a few ice cubes. "But one of the most expensive cities in the world?

Pass. Plus, I just bought my house and I have *so* much work to do on it."

"Rent it out! Be a Cali landlord, Arizonans *love* that shit," Matty said. "You could live with us for free, come on."

Hanna's nose scrunched. It wasn't that she hated the idea— it was that she couldn't imagine leaving the last city her mother was alive in. If she moved to a new city, how would her mother know where to haunt her?

"Because every newlywed couple wants a sad, thirty-year-old roommate?"

"Thirty on the coast is like, twenty. You'd basically be aging backwards. And maybe a change of scenery isn't the worst idea," Matty said, his voice dropping on the last sentence. She followed him toward the fire pit, where Milo sat with another groomsman whose name she should have known from the group chat.

Brad. Brent?

"Milo, Brandon," Matty said, pointing at them respectively. "This is Hanna, she's Sara's childhood best friend and basically a sister to me. Act accordingly."

Brandon mumbled a greeting and went back to staring at his phone, the Suns game streaming across the screen. Hanna plopped onto the chair next to Milo, sipping her drink and trying to think of anything to say that would keep her from having to make conversation with Brandon.

"Sorry about earlier," Milo said.

She fought the urge to tell him he was flattering himself by thinking she would even remember any of the day, but she'd promised Sara to at least try being nice to their bridal party.

"Same," she offered.

"I mean it, I should have read the room. This probably isn't exactly a good time for you," Milo said softly.

Hanna turned, her eyebrow raised. "How do you mean?"

"I've known Matty since we were kids and, therefore, Logan," Milo explained. She resented the undercurrent in his tone that sounded like pity.

"Ah," she sighed.

One day, she was going to move to a city where *no one* knew her or looked at her like that. Somewhere new, where there were simply no ghosts at all.

Milo scanned the scene in the backyard. "How long's it been?"

"Hmm," Hanna pretended to mentally tally the months since their breakup, despite knowing exactly how long—nearly to the minute—it had been since she'd taken a full breath. "We're just hitting the one-year mark."

"Does it help knowing their mom *hates* the new girl?"

Hanna snorted. She couldn't help it. Marcia DeBrune was one of the nicest people on the planet. It was impossible to imagine her disliking anyone.

"No way."

"It's true." He grinned, leaning forward in his chair. "Sloane doesn't like game night or eat gluten."

"Oof," Hanna sighed. "Yeah, not the way to Midwestern Marcia's heart."

"And," he lowered his voice. "I heard Tucker growled at her when they went home for Christmas."

Hanna pressed her hand to her chest, feigning a gasp. Tucker, the family's golden retriever, who was all things fluffy and good, liked anyone who would make eye contact with him.

"Scandalous."

"Tragic," Milo said, shaking his head. A comfortable silence settled between them as Berto's yacht rock floated on the warm breeze. She cleared her throat.

"Thank you for saying that. I'm still absolutely ready to die, but it kind of helps."

"The good news is you don't have to dread it much longer," Milo said, nodding toward the house. She twisted in her seat, her vantage point offering her a perfect view of Logan coming through the patio door, his hand wrapped around the golden skin of Sloane, the new girl in question. She was short with caramel skin and perfectly placed highlights.

Hanna couldn't even remember the last time she'd had a haircut.

"Damn," Hanna muttered. "I was hoping she face-tuned her Instagram photos."

Milo coughed on his beer.

Sloane was hot and Hanna wasn't about to pretend otherwise. She also wasn't Hanna's enemy, as easy as it would have been to hate her.

No, the worst part about their breakup was that Logan hadn't cheated on her. He did it all on the up and up, the fucking bastard. She could still hear his throat tightening around the words on the phone.

"I don't know how to even say this, Hanna."

She flopped back on their bed, her brunette curls fanning out as her brows furrowed. He'd called her every night since moving to New York, but he'd missed last night.

"I, uh, god—"

"Just say it."

"I think I met someone."

Hanna bolted upright, the cotton bedspread bunching under her thigh.

"You think you met someone?"

"It's going to sound so fucking dumb—"

"It already sounds dumb!"

"Hanna, I am so, so sorry. I know it sounds crazy, and I hate that I'm even saying this, but you know me! I'm not the guy who cheats on his girlfriend on a whim. I would never do that to you.

But I met someone at work yesterday, and I just... I don't know. The feeling... it's not nothing. And I couldn't not say anything to you."

Hanna fought for a breath as their bedroom—her bedroom— fell away, plunging her into a black void.

"I think we just... we've been together since we were kids, Hanna."

"Here we go," she sighed. She pinched the skin on her leg, needing to be sure it was really happening. "We were too young, we've changed, it's not you, it's me!"

"Don't do that—"

"Don't do what? That's what you're about to say, isn't it?"

Logan took a deep breath. She wondered which of his suits he was peeling off after his workday.

"I'm sorry."

"Yeah," she breathed, her throat collapsing under the weight of the shock.

"Hanna—"

She hung up and turned her phone off. It was the last thing she'd hear him say for a year.

For months after that phone call, she'd wished she had caught him texting someone else, or that she'd seen him in someone's Instagram story, dripping over another woman in a swanky Manhattan bar. It would have been so much easier to hate him if he were a bad guy.

But Logan wasn't a villain, even if she was the victim.

Her eyes fixed on him as he cut a path across the patio, a baby-blue polo capping his nicer work pants. She wondered if Sloane had picked the shirt for him.

Hanna pulled herself out of the lounge chair and put on her bravest face.

"You want company? Logan doesn't like me, might be fun."

She tossed a glance at Milo, noting to dig into that piece of information later. "Go get 'em, tiger."

She smoothed the hem of her sundress and rolled her shoulders back. The threads of her muscles screamed in protest as she pushed herself across the yard and pasted on the same *No really! I'm fine!* smile she'd been wearing since the funeral.

If nothing else, her mother's death had given her a PhD in faking it. In the first few months, she had learned how to easily disarm anyone who knew what happened with the perfect blend of somber eyes and a hopeful nod to prevent them from asking the kind of questions that punched her in the gut and knocked the wind out of her.

You can do anything for fifteen minutes, she told herself, her espadrilles clicking onto the patio.

And she almost believed it.

She used every one of the twenty steps between them to get ahold of her breathing, all for two piercing blue eyes and a megawatt smile to send her heart rate through the roof as he turned toward her.

THREE

Hanna had forgotten how pretty he was.

Logan called out her name like it was a sacred prayer, and her skin flushed with a boiling red tint and thin layer of sweat. She crossed the final distance between them.

"Hey," she mumbled, resenting how feeble it sounded as she leaned in and hugged him. In all her imaginary dress rehearsals, she hadn't blocked a hug, and the motion threw her off her balance. She leaned into the momentum and did what none of the thirty sets of eyes on them expected—she hugged Sloane too.

She smelled even better than Hanna feared. Expensive.

"It's so nice to meet you," Hanna croaked.

"You too," Sloan managed, an unexpected sweetness in her tone. She rambled off the requisite small talking points as Hanna tried to manage her breathing.

She liked Phoenix, the sunsets are amazing, the heat is a lot, but at least it's dry!

Logan's eyes clung to the floor between them.

When Hanna had counted to one hundred in her head, she widened her bullshit smile and chirped, "I need to freshen up my drink!"

She turned, ready to dart back toward the bar, and patted herself on the back for surviving the first rip of the proverbial band-aid.

"I'll come with you," Logan said.

She groaned. *So close.* "No need!"

"We need drinks, anyway," he said.

We.

"Okay," she sighed. Logan walked silently beside her, the heat of Matty's stare lingering on her back as she busied herself with ice and liquors she wasn't actually interested in.

"How are you?"

She fought the urge to laugh. *How was she?*

Well-rehearsed. That's how she was.

"Fine. You?"

"Hanna," he snorted. He lowered his eyes to hers, a stinging within them she tried not to choke on. "How are you, really?"

She took a deep breath and a long sip of whatever strange cocktail she'd thrown together. It was not good. It did not matter.

"I'm surviving," she finally said.

Logan reached for two red Solo cups. "You haven't returned a single one of my calls."

"Correct."

"I've been worried about you."

Hanna rolled her eyes. "Don't do this, please. I don't need a white knight to worry about me."

Logan stepped closer. "You know what I mean. I knew Lisa for ten years—"

"Don't," she snapped. It was instant, the burning at the

23

back of her neck. The tears threatened to make a spectacle if she didn't get him the fuck away from her. "You don't get to do that."

"Hanna," he started, but she held up a hand.

"I can't do this here. It's not fair to Sara or your brother."

Logan blocked her path as she attempted to circumvent him.

"Then when? Can we meet up later? I'm here through the weekend."

She wanted to tell him absolutely not. She wanted to tell him to get fucked. But his eyes dropped into that boyish puppy-dog expression she knew so well.

"I don't know. I'll... I'll think about it."

"That's all I'm asking."

Hanna sighed again, the prickling in her spine crawling into a suffocating heat.

"That's not all you're asking," she said. She moved as quickly as she could to get inside without alarming the guests and headed toward the safety of Sara's childhood bedroom. Each step pushed her farther from the breakdown she felt coming, giving her the air she needed to stuff it all back down. She fell onto Sara's perfectly made bed, counting the boy band posters they'd stuck to the walls with putty in high school. Everything buzzing against her lips drifted back into the quiet hum she'd gotten used to, the white noise of her grief nearly comforting.

"Hanna?"

For a moment, she thought it was Sara's voice coming from the hallway, but it wasn't quite familiar.

Oh.

Sloane poked her head through the door and, for a brief second, Hanna considered how hard it would be to break the window to her right.

"Is it okay if I come in?"

"Uhhh, sure?" she replied, annoyed at her own betrayal. Sloane perched on the edge of Sara's desk and Hanna waited for her to speak.

She waited for a while.

Sloane's lips finally parted after a silence so painful she thought they both might implode.

"I just wanted to say that I'm sorry. About everything."

Hanna couldn't have stopped the bitter snort if she wanted to.

"Everything, huh? You invent glioblastomas, Sloane?"

Sloane twisted her lips and fumbled with the phone in her hand.

"I just, I feel bad. About the timing of it all. Logan is such a great guy—"

"Yeah. Super."

"He never wanted to hurt you. We were so careful about not letting anything happen between us."

Hanna pinched the bridge of her nose. "Very noble."

"And I guess I just wanted to clear the air between us. Since we're going to be spending quite a bit of time together this year. Logan was so heartbroken when your mom—"

All of the buzzing in Hanna's ears condensed with so much force that it ignited a fire at the base of her skull.

"Oh my fucking god, no."

Sloane shut up.

Hanna tried to breathe through the rising firestorm in her chest, but it was too late. Her anger was driving a bus heading for a cliff, and Sloane had just cut the brakes.

"Listen, Sloane. It's one thing to feel the need to defend Logan. I get it. He's a good guy. He didn't cheat on me. Yay!" Hanna slapped her thighs, rising from the bed and knotting her fists against her hem. "But what we're not going to do is talk about the literal worst thing that's ever happened to me with the close second. We are strangers. Actually? We're worse than strangers. We're before and after. I fully understand that there are many, *many* painful nights ahead for us, and I will be civil. I'm a grown woman. But you don't get to come in here and try to force me to feel bad for not including Logan in my mother's death."

Sloane's eyes widened, the implications of her comment registering. She held up her hands. "I didn't mean to—"

"No one ever does." Hanna was sick of comforting people who offended her. "Just please, *please* drop this. Logan is welcome to grieve my mother however he needs to, but he has to do it without me. He gave up that right when he dumped me and he has to live with that. I will not be taking on his guilt."

"Hanna—"

"That was a dismissal," Hanna hissed. Sloane shook her perfect fucking hair and slipped out of the door, her cheeks red.

Hanna pushed against her chest, the box of bad feelings she harbored there cracking open and leaking all over her lungs.

Fuck Sloane. Fuck Logan. Fuck brain cancer. Fuck weddings.

It became a mantra as her breathing spiraled out of control, her lips quivering as she tried to quell the misery crashing against her.

"What the hell," she whispered to herself, her head swimming. It was bad enough having to see them, but a coordinated attack? Diabolical.

She sat back on the edge of the bed, her knees giving out as the panic fully took over, a year's worth of rage spilling into her veins and rushing from head to toe.

Her nails dug into her palms. Sometimes she just needed to feel something to bring herself back to reality, but even the sting in her flesh didn't cut above the noise in her head.

Somewhere in her lizard brain, she registered the door opening, but she was beyond seeing through the static. Two bags of ice hit the floor on either side of her as a hand pressed against her chest.

"What are you—"

"Relax," Milo said. "I'm not making a move. Just trying to help. Count to ten for me."

Hanna attempted to grasp the number one, but it was just out of reach. Her hands came up, pushing away from him, but he kneeled on the carpet and leaned into her.

"Milo—"

"Don't waste breath being stubborn. Breathe into your stomach, not your throat." Milo pressed harder on her chest, applying a steady pressure. The touch grounded her as she inhaled, a wobble in the breath threatening to undo any progress it made.

"Another," he said, his voice soft.

Hanna held the next one at the peak, counting to five before letting it slip back out.

"One more."

The third breath was easier, releasing something in her head. She could hear dishes clinking together in the kitchen, the laughter of Cami and her sisters as they poured more wine. She could smell the beer on Milo's breath, mixed with a smoky amber cologne warmed by his pulse.

"Better?"

She nodded, the panic now replaced with a white-hot shame.

"You have a lot of panic attacks?" he asked, rocking back onto his heels. The air conditioning kicked on, rushing a cool breeze over her.

"Uh. No. Yeah. Sometimes," she said.

"It's normal to have them after a significant loss. Or two," he added.

Hanna avoided his gaze. The concern was too much. She could hear the echo in his voice on the phone eight months ago as she screamed for Sara.

"Thanks," she mumbled.

"Don't be embarrassed." His tone was so gentle that it somehow hurt more than if he had pointed and laughed.

"I'm not."

"Liar," Milo laughed. "After my dad died, I'd have panic attacks in the middle of class. It was brutal. Teenagers aren't very understanding."

Hanna fought back tears as her emotions circled one another, but they weren't on her behalf.

"High school?"

"Yeah," Milo said. He folded his arms as he stood and leaned against the desk, taking Sloane's place. "I was fifteen."

"Jesus," Hanna murmured. "At least I was through puberty. I'm so sorry."

She could see it, all that pain still sitting right under the surface of his skin, even fifteen years later. The realization unsettled her.

It never went away then.

Milo shrugged. "It gets easier."

"Does it?"

He sighed as his shoulders dropped. "I hate that I just said that. It used to piss me off. Because the truth is, it doesn't. It... changes. Gets more predictable, I guess."

Hanna stood, crossing the space and pulling his forearm between them, the clock resting between her fingers.

"Time of death?"

Milo smirked. "Yeah, not that you'd ever ask."

Hanna ran her thumb over the face of the clock, the ink

rippling beneath her touch. She dropped his arm and pushed the puff sleeve resting above her elbow back, revealing the black and gray wings of the butterfly tattoo she'd gotten just before the holidays.

"My mom had a butterfly tattoo. Felt appropriate."

Milo reached for the back of her elbow, bringing the artwork closer as he examined it.

"It's pretty."

Hanna pulled her sleeve down and reached for one of the bags of ice.

"Shitty club, huh?"

"The fucking worst." He cracked a smile and grabbed the other bag. "The t-shirts are kinda cool, though."

Hanna gasped. "You got a shirt! Did mine get lost in the mail?"

Milo nudged her as they left Sara's room. "I'll alert the council."

The ice chilled her hand, a welcome feeling after the hot flush of her panic attack.

"You coming out with us tonight?"

Hanna chewed on her bottom lip. "I don't know if I have round two of the Logan and Sloane show in me."

He shrugged, hauling the ice over his shoulder and sliding the glass door open. She trailed him into the backyard and made a concerted effort not to look for Logan while Milo opened the cooler and unwrapped his bag of ice.

"You're missing out. The hotel has Hibiki on tap. It's been a while since my initiation, but I believe..." Milo grunted as he snagged the second bag of ice from her and turned it over into the cooler, continuing, "That it's customary for a tenured Dead Parent Society member to buy new recruits a drink."

Hanna giggled, despite herself. Her eyes flickered between

his and Sloane, who laughed obnoxiously at something Matty said.

"Rain check?" she asked.

"Of course." Milo opened a can of soda. "That's the worst part about the Dead Parent Society. Membership never expires."

FOUR

Hanna sank further under the water with each buzz of her phone.

The bath water had gone cold an hour earlier, but she couldn't find it within herself to climb out. She leaned forward, flipping her phone over on the counter.

It was Logan. Again.

DO NOT ANSWER

Palomar at 10?

Hanna. Come on.

I really want to talk. Sloane told me what happened.

Okay. Well, I'll be here all night. Hopefully I'll see you.

Only Logan could think that talking about her dead mom at a trendy rooftop bar would appeal to her. She'd spent six hours making terrible small talk with Sara's family and avoiding his sad-boy eyes from across the yard. She couldn't devote any more energy to him.

Besides, she'd embarrassed herself enough for one day. She didn't need to add crying in public to the list.

She did, however, find the idea of crying in her bathtub with a glass of wine appealing—if only the tears would come. They seemed quick to threaten her with an appearance whenever she was around others, but the moment she was alone, it was like she was stuck.

Her phone buzzed again.

SARA

We're all at The Palomar. Come be my friend!

Ugh.

Logan was easy to ignore. But Sara? It was hard to pass up the temptation to get time with her without family members hovering and inquiring about wedding plans.

She sat up.

She'd hate herself in the morning if she didn't go. The guilt always ate her alive when she passed on something for no reason other than "ugh."

Hanna slipped out of the tub and toweled off, chugging water as her head began to tighten. A pair of well-worn black jeans and a tank top with a messy bun, and she didn't look half bad—at least not for a half-drunk, pathetic mess.

She downed a third glass of water before venturing from her little bungalow, rotting just like she was, and took the light rail downtown.

The hotel rose above the hot streets, teeming with post-Suns game-goers. Sara waited beneath the hotel awning, eyes glued to her phone, likely watching Hanna's location as she weaved through the city.

"Hanna!" Sara wrapped her arms around her friend, her

sweet vanilla honey scent warming Hanna. "I'm so sorry I barely got to see you at the party! Thanks for coming back out."

Hanna shrugged. "I'll put pants on for very few people in this life, but you're one of 'em, babe."

Sara laughed, the sound soothing Hanna's aching ribs, and she held the door open to the hotel lobby, scanning a key at the elevator. The doors had hardly closed before she attacked.

"Mom saw you getting ice with Milo."

"Is that what the kids are calling it these days?" Hanna muttered. Sara pulled her eyes away from the rows of elevator buttons and arched her brows. "I'm kidding. He asked for a hand."

"Because Milo can't lift two bags of ice?"

Hanna sighed. "It was nothing."

"Right." Sara rocked forward on her heels. "He's hot, though. I wasn't lying."

"You were not," Hanna allowed. "But nothing is going to happen."

"Okay!" Sara chirped. The sing-songy quality implied she didn't buy Hanna's resolve. She was much too confident.

The elevator doors scrolled back, depositing them into the chic bar in the middle of the city, surrounded by glassy buildings and the distant mountain ranges. The bar buzzed with a late-night crowd scattered between lush white lounge chairs and billowing curtains.

"Logan told me about Sloane," Sara said quietly as they weaved between patrons toward the bar.

"Yeah. That was... something," Hanna said, sliding onto a barstool. Sara ordered without having to ask. One whiskey ginger, one gin and tonic. Two limes.

"She felt bad," Sara said and pushed her card across the bar. "She thought she was being a girl's girl or whatever."

Hanna snorted. "Uh huh."

"Logan was *pissed*."

Hanna nodded.

"They had a huge fight after."

"Bummer, I missed it," Hanna said as a cocktail landed in front of her. She lifted the glass to cheers her best friend who watched her face with careful eyes.

"You're a good friend to put up with them for all of these stupid wedding events."

Dammit, there were those public tears again.

The thought that Hanna had been a good anything to anyone over that last year struck her in the chest. Sara—who had been on the first flight out when her mother got sick, who sent flowers weekly while she was in treatment, who cooked meals and held hands and wiped tears—thought Hanna, who hadn't returned a single call to anyone *except* Sara, was a good friend?

"I owe you," Hanna said. It was all she could say.

"Shit," Sara mumbled over her straw and pointed to Hanna's phone as it lit up with DO NOT ANSWER once again.

"Logan's been blowing me up for hours."

Sara closed her eyes and sighed. "He has a lot of feelings about your mom. Matty and I tried to tell him repeatedly not to involve you in them... but you know how he is."

She did. She knew how he was about everything.

Sara gave her a wicked grin, her eyes narrowing as a bit of gossip bubbled to her lips. They'd done their best to maintain the separation of church and state when it came to Logan, but Hanna had earned it.

"You should see how Marcia looks at her. Like she has two heads."

Hanna chuckled. "Ah, yes, Milo mentioned she doesn't eat gluten."

"Did he?" Sara asked without any attempt to hide her interest in pulling at the thread.

"He was trying to make me feel better."

"I've heard he's particularly talented at making women feel better," Sara cooed.

"Stop that. He was being nice. It was when Logan showed up with Sloane."

"Speak of the devil," Sara said, wincing. Logan appeared over Hanna's shoulder and slid onto the stool beside them. He'd changed into one of his old, faded college tees, and it clung to his biceps as he ordered a beer.

"Mind if I borrow Hanna?" he asked Sara, which only made Hanna even less interested in speaking with him.

"That's probably a question for her, no?" Sara returned. His jaw clenched, but Hanna felt no interest in making things easy on him. "I don't think she's up for talking tonight, Lo."

"She isn't!" Hanna chimed in, not that anyone had asked.

"Hanna," he pleaded. The tone was familiar—the same one he'd use to pacify her during arguments. "Just one conversation, and then I'll drop it."

Hanna hung her head forward and sipped her drink.

Just *one*. It felt like a DM from a girl she knew in high school trying to get her into their MLM. *Hey, boss babe! You have a few minutes to catch up?*

"One chance?" he begged again.

A chance at what? Crack a rib instead of just breaking her heart? Cut her kidney out and sell it on the black market to buy Sloane an engagement ring? God, the thought of him *marrying* her—

"Go find Matty, Lo," Sara said again.

"But—"

"I said no!" Hanna barked.

He swallowed, his hand reaching for her arm.

"Hanny—"

She slammed her glass down on the bar and stood, jerking her elbow from his grasp. She saw his mouth move, but she only heard her mother's voice. *Hanny! Hanny! Hanny!*

"I think I should go," she whispered to Sara, who frowned but understood. She patted Hanna's shoulder and kissed her cheek.

"Call me tomorrow?"

She nodded, pushing through the crowd and heading for the elevator, her eyes stinging as she mashed on the lobby floor. The doors moved inward, but a hand caught them before they could close.

A hand attached to a bevy of tattoos.

Fuck, she thought, wiping at her eyes as Milo stepped onto the elevator. He took in the scene before him, seeing her at her most deranged for what, the third time in one day?

"Hey."

"We have to stop meeting like this," she deadpanned, sniffling with her arms cradled around her body.

"Logan find you?"

She nodded. "I'm fine. It's fine. Everything is fine."

"You know, the third one really sold it," Milo said, shoving his hands into his pockets.

Hanna laughed, not hard enough to shift the tide inside her, but enough to take the edge off.

"I really will be okay. I just needed a minute away from... all of it. Usually I only have one breakdown per twenty-four-hour period."

Milo smiled. "Caught you on a hot streak."

"Something like that."

"I'm heading to the corner store to grab a few things, wanna come?"

The elevator hit the ground floor and opened to the quiet

lobby. Maybe it was that she'd already put hard pants on and hadn't gotten the return on her effort, or maybe it was the ridiculous way he smirked, but a walk didn't sound terrible.

Hanna followed him around the corner, the late spring night perfectly warm now that the sun had set. She trailed wordlessly behind him as he plucked things off the shelves—gum, two energy drinks, Advil, and a travel bottle of Tums.

He held the bottle up and shook it. "None of us are twenty-one anymore, but these assholes still drink like it. The heartburn is *killing* me."

Hanna smiled, her mind starting to quiet.

He asked the cashier for a pack of Marlboro Reds and a lighter, surprising her.

"What?"

"You don't smell like a smoker," she said.

He leaned toward her. "Paying attention, are we?"

She rolled her eyes.

"One of those, too," Milo said, pointing at a bucket of flowers on the back of the counter. The cashier plucked a bright yellow sunflower out of the water, beads dropping across the counter as Milo handed it to her. "Consider it an apology on Logan's behalf."

Hanna stared at the flower, twirling it in her hands, the ache in her chest opening up once again.

She followed him from the store on autopilot, stroking the soft silk of the petals, the light perfume bringing her back to weekly deliveries on her mother's bedside table.

Back at the hotel, they walked onto the elevator and Milo tapped the panel. Hanna breathed slowly as it lurched to life. She realized halfway down the hall of the seventeenth floor they were heading to his room. He swiped his key card, tossing his bag onto the bed and pulling off his shirt.

"It's fucking *hot* here," he muttered, pulling at the white tank top under his button-down to get some air. Hanna stayed perched at the doorway, rotating the flower in her hands as he fished through his bag for a t-shirt. He popped two Tums and held the bottle out to her, but she shook her head. She watched him peel the plastic off the pack of cigarettes and smack the carton against his palm, then tuck it into his back pocket.

"You good, Arizona?"

Hanna's eyes snapped to his, her head pounding. "Yeah."

"You wanna try again?"

She held up the flower, her fingertips brushing the soft fuzz on the stem.

"My mom loved sunflowers."

Milo winced. "Ah, shit—"

"You didn't know," she said.

"I feel like I'm just a walking trigger for you," he said, laughing.

"At least you're charming about it." She leaned against the doorframe, setting the flower on the desk by the door.

"I don't bite," he said and gestured to the rest of the room.

"That's not what I heard," she said, her eyes grazing over his. He glanced at her quickly and shoved his energy drinks into the mini fridge. A sinister grin tugged at his lips.

"I've had very few complaints, Hanna," he mumbled.

Milo slid between her and the door, making no small show of tapping her hip as he opened it and paused in the doorway. She caught her breath, unprepared for the contact. He turned toward her and lowered his voice.

"What's the saying? Don't knock it 'til you try it?"

He pulled her forward into the hall and reached behind her to close the door before making his way back toward the elevator, leaving her standing in front of his hotel room. She shook her head.

Cocky bastard.

She followed him through the hallway and into the elevator, the weight of the day starting to push her down again. Or perhaps it was the several gallons of whiskey she'd imbibed since three in the afternoon.

Who could say?

Hanna leaned against the wall as her phone started buzzing.

DO NOT ANSWER

I just wish we could have a mature conversation :(

"Nice," Hanna muttered, shoving the phone back in her pocket. It was the emoji that broke her, in the end, not the sentiment.

Her throat tightened and the heat of it stung her teeth. God, she was so over panicking. She was so over Logan. She was so over everyone.

"You good?" Milo asked, moving closer.

She was not good. She wasn't even neutral. She was in a downward spiral, and Milo's proximity was the final push. She leaned forward and brushed her fingertips against that ridiculous jawline, sending him back a foot.

"What are you—"

"You said not to knock it. I'm *trying it*," she hissed, leaning forward again. His eyes searched hers, unsure what to make of the advance. She walked her fingers down his neck, tapping stubbled muscles as she slid to his t-shirt. She could see the war waging within him. He was trying to decide between the smart thing and the booze whispering, *why the hell not.*

"Hanna," he said, a warning. She leaned closer, pushing up on her toes.

"Hmm?"

She lingered for a brief moment, giving him an out, and

39

exhaled. The up-close heat of him mingled with his cologne—a much more intoxicating blend than she'd prepared for—and she wondered if she would smell like him in the morning.

God, it was a bad idea.

But Cami would be proud.

Hanna moved a millimeter closer, his mouth hovering just a sudden stop away from hers. Before she could close the distance, he twisted away, darting to his side of the elevator and rubbing the back of his neck.

Hanna laughed. "All bark, no bite, huh?"

He glared. "You're drunk, Arizona."

She shrugged. "And you're not?"

"Not that drunk," he said.

"Ouch," Hanna whispered.

"That's not what I meant," he insisted as the elevator jolted toward the rooftop.

"Don't worry about it," she mumbled, staring at the panel of buttons as they flickered out, one by one, racing toward the bar. She drew in a stilted breath, her face flushing with that insufferable shame she couldn't seem to shake around him. She was stupid for even suggesting it; they'd both regret it for longer than the list of reasons she kept tucked in the back of her mind. And it wouldn't fix anything—

Before she could finish her thought, her back was pressed up against the ice-cold handrail attached, one tattooed arm pinned to the wall beside her head, the other pulling at her chin.

"You're a fucking mess," Milo whispered, his lips brushing her jaw.

"Assho—" she muttered, but he cut her off with a thumb on her lip. He leaned into her, their bodies pressed together as the elevator came to a halt.

"I didn't say I didn't like it."

"Milo—"

He grinned, his eyes sparkling as the doors slid open and he moved away from her.

"Can dish it out..."

He disappeared into the crowd, leaving her to wander in a daze to Sara. She leaned over a table and tasted Matty's martini.

"You're back!"

Hanna pursed her lips, the buzzing in her ears wildly different from what she'd felt earlier. Logan eyed her from across the table, but she happily ignored him and rested her fingertips on her lips, pretending to listen to Matty and... Brendon? Brandon? Shit.

Before she could ask Sara, the tattooed hand that had just pinned her against the elevator wall dropped a glass of golden whiskey between them.

"The Society welcomes you," Milo murmured before tucking himself into the other side of the table.

Sara didn't say one word, but her eyebrows certainly said plenty.

FIVE

"Show me the blue one again!"

Sara's voice did the high-pitched half-squeal thing it had always done when she was overly excited. Hanna set the phone on top of her dresser while Sara spread out over her couch in SoMa, a backdrop Hanna was intimately familiar with from their FaceTime dates.

She reached for the zipper at her back, sweating her ass off between the chiffon and taffeta gowns strewn across her bed. Plastic packages and packing slips adorned the floor as she shimmied out of Number Four.

"The light blue or the navy?" she clarified.

"The light—oh! You're home!" Matty caught Sara's attention off screen, her eyes lighting up as he tossed his keys on the counter.

Hanna kicked the pink floral A-line dress they'd firmly ruled out into the corner of her room and snatched the light blue silk from the back of an armchair. It was a slick fit that hugged her every curve, with a back on just that side of scandalous.

Sara and Matty chatted back and forth for a moment before a third voice rumbled over the call.

Milo.

Hanna sighed. It was Wednesday. Movie and wing night. She hadn't spoken to him after that night at the hotel two weeks earlier, but from what she could tell, thanks to a totally normal amount of social media stalking for a woman in her thirties, he'd started seeing some girl named something cool like Chloe.

Okay, not *like* Chloe.

Her name was exactly Chloe, and Hanna knew which art school she went to, the name of her labradoodle, and that she worked at the same software company as Milo.

All very normal things to know about someone she had touched once in an elevator.

Sara ran with her phone through their loft and set it down on the counter, the rustling of take-out bags buzzing over the speaker.

"Okay. Light blue is on!" Hanna called, yanking the zipper up the final half inch. The ceiling fell away and Sara's face popped back into view.

"Oh my *god*, yep. That's it. That's the one!" She darted through the kitchen and shoved her phone into Matty's hands. "Babe, what do you think? Is it the bridesmaids' dress? Tell Hanna how great she looks!"

Matty gripped the phone, half a wing sticking out of his mouth.

"Hi, Hanna! You look... very blue!"

Sara rolled her eyes and took the phone back.

"You look hot, dude. I'm almost tempted to put you in the pink one so you don't show me up."

Hanna laughed, picking at the neckline. "I don't know about the back," she mused, twisting to show Sara the drop. "It's a lot."

Sara shook her head, popping a wing in her mouth. "Nope. It's perfect. Matty's grandpa is officiating, it's not like we have to impress the clergy."

"But like, one wrong move on the dance floor and my tits are out, you know?" Hanna said, shimmying in her bedroom alone to demonstrate her fears.

Sara giggled and an off-screen voice called, "Then that's for sure the dress."

"See?" Sara said. "Milo approves. It's definitely the one."

Hanna groaned. What happened in the elevator was her own damn fault and nothing else, but she still couldn't help thinking about it.

Usually late at night.

After a cocktail.

She sighed. "Milo's approval is *exactly* what I'm afraid of."

"Lemme see," he said, his massive hand covering the screen before his face appeared. He'd let his stubble fill in over the last few weeks, which made him look even more like trouble. His eyebrows arched in confusion. "What are you talking about? You're completely covered."

"It's the back that's in question," Sara said. "Turn around, Han."

Hanna could have killed her.

She reluctantly twisted, flashing the open back as quickly as she could get away with.

"Oh," Milo mumbled through a bite of food. "Your grandpa have a heart condition, Matty?"

Matty had definitely checked out of the conversation immediately, but responded, "I don't think so?"

"Then I think it's the one. It's settled," Milo declared. A red heat washed over Hanna's skin and she hoped that any god that hadn't abandoned her over the last year was merciful enough to mute the color rendering across the screen.

"Amazing," Sara squealed. She grabbed the phone back and dipped into the bedroom, flopping onto the bed. "Now that the dress is handled, we just need to decide on a hotel for the bachelorette."

Hanna waved her hand. "I have it all planned. You just have to show up! Taylor and I are on top of things."

She scooped the pile of rejected dresses off her bed, tossing them onto her favorite depression chair. Sara listed off all of the restaurants she wanted to make sure they hit while in Vegas, and Hanna was *totally* listening, and not at all thinking about the Greek god in the next room over.

She should have stuck to her guns and never given him a second glance.

It wasn't that she expected anything after the elevator incident—she wasn't even sure he was sober enough to remember it —but she thought she might get at least a social media connection out of the damn thing. Her number was *right there* in the bridal party group chat.

She sighed as the embarrassment crept back in.

"I'm talking about the wedding too much, I'm sorry," Sara said.

"No! No, no, it's not you," Hanna assured her. She sat on the floor, stretching her back as she refocused her wandering mind. "I was just... it's not important."

Sara tilted her head and frowned.

Hanna could have sworn she was talking to Cami, thirty years younger. The thought pulled at another thread—would anyone remember her mother's facial expressions enough to think the same thing about her?

"Your stuff is always important to me, Hanna. I feel like we haven't talked about you in a while. Check in?"

Hanna inhaled slowly, chasing the burn of her previous thought. When Sara said 'you,' she could have meant 'your mom' or 'Logan,' but she had no idea she should have meant 'Milo.' All at once, Hanna realized how dramatic it all was.

Nothing happened.

"I mean. Sure. Logan stuff sucks, as per usual. He's been calling relentlessly since he was here. I haven't answered."

"Of course."

"Mom stuff sucks more." Hanna bit her lip. "I feel a little like I'll never take a full breath again. I think I'm just lonely," she confessed. "I'm in this house all by myself. I work from home. I never leave. Phoenix always felt like home because my mom and Logan were here, but now I'm the only one left."

Sara nodded, absorbing her words. That, right there, the *silence*, was why Hanna loved her best friend. She didn't need to fill it with platitudes or weird speculation. She could let the grief be what it was.

"What if you came out here for Memorial Day weekend? Would that be helpful or hurtful?"

Hanna considered this. She'd visited them a few times over the years, but it had been a while since she'd been out that way. She could use the coastal exposure.

"A long weekend could be nice..."

"Or just, like, sublet your house for the summer and come be my friend!" Sara tried not to look too eager.

Hanna could smell the desperation, but perhaps that was better than the smell of rotting drywall.

"The whole summer!" Hanna gasped.

"What? Like it's that crazy? We could get so much wedding planning done!"

Hanna twisted the other direction, her lower back popping as her eyes fell on the bronze sunflower bookend resting at the end of her shelf. Logan had given it to her mother for Christmas one year.

She hated that it was hers, but, in that moment, the sight of it felt like a push she needed.

"Okay."

"What?" Sara asked, her eyes wide. She'd posed the question a dozen times over the years. It was as common as asking about the weather or work.

"Okay," Hanna mumbled, the relief in her shoulders foreign. "I'll do it."

"Ohmyfuckinggod," Sara yelled.

"Are you good?" Matty burst into the bedroom, appearing over Sara's shoulders.

"Can I tell him?"

Hanna nodded, the light in her eyes irresistible.

"Hanna is going to stay with us for the summer."

Matty snatched the phone from his fiancée. "Don't play with me, Hanna."

"Only if you guys are sure I won't be in the way! It will make wedding planning easier, and I could use the shake-up. I have a friend who just lost her roommate. She could probably use a few months to figure her shit out."

And I'm not at all interested in hanging out in an apartment that occasionally has Adonis's cooler, tatted-up brother in the living room, she thought.

"How soon can you be here?" Sara asked.

"I'll look at flights tonight," Hanna answered.

"I JUST HAVE A QUESTION," Olivia said, tapping her pen to her lips in her signature *I'm about to fuck up your whole day* way that Hanna had grown to fear in their sessions.

"Hit me," she whispered.

"Why do you keep telling yourself that interacting with this Milo guy was nothing?"

"Because it *was* nothing."

Olivia scoffed. "You've spent the last six months lamenting the fact that you feel absolutely detached from this world, but the first time someone walks in and makes you feel *anything*, you're quick to dismiss it. I find that revealing."

Hanna chewed on the inside of her cheek. "Okay, but—"

"I just wonder if you're running *from* home, or running *to* someone."

"I'm not running at all," Hanna said quickly. "I'm temporarily relocating."

"Hmm," Olivia said, scribbling a sentence across her notepad. What Hanna would've paid to read through the pages upon pages of notes Olivia had taken since Hanna's mother had gotten sick. "You're avoiding my question."

"Can't the answer be yes, and?"

"It can," Olivia said. "But I worry how you'll cope in a new city without your typical routines."

Does it matter? Hanna thought. She'd never feel normal again, anyway. What did it matter which zipcode she was sad in?

"You do virtual sessions, right?"

Olivia gave her a half smile. That was the answer she was looking for. "Lucky for you, I'm also licensed in California."

"I'm going to make you regret that."

SIX

The plane had hardly taxied before Sara sent eight texts detailing how thrilled she was that Hanna had finally given in.

She'd planned a dinner for that night with her and Matty's closest friends and it took Hanna everything she had not to ask if Milo would be there.

Not that she cared.

Sara's apartment was a twenty-five-minute Uber ride away, right in the heart of SoMa. As the car glided to a stop on Brannan Street, Sara was already firing off comms.

Hanna hauled her suitcases from the trunk and stared up at the lofts she'd toured via FaceTime two years ago. It only took a few breaths to rehydrate her sun-dried desert heart, the humidity almost instantly curling the ends of her hair.

"Hanna!" She looked to the second floor of balconies hanging over the street. "We're coming down!"

Hanna didn't have much time to consider that "we" might not mean her and Matty before Sara and Milo stepped off the elevator and out of the lobby. A nervous flare shot up her spine as Sara ran toward her, scooping her into an embrace.

"I cannot believe you're actually here!"

"Me either!"

Sara released her and shoved her at Milo, who offered a tepid side hug that shut down absolutely *any* lingering what-ifs in her mind. At least it was quick and painless.

Milo grabbed one of her bags despite her protest and he was already calling the elevator by the time she processed his acquisition.

Sara prattled on about all the things she wanted to do that weekend once Hanna was settled in, but Hanna heard none of it. Standing beside Milo on an elevator in his home turf did something strange to her stomach.

She followed them off the elevator and down the hall where Sara stopped at unit three.

"And this is Milo's place!"

Milo's place? The hell?

"I didn't realize y'all were neighbors?" Hanna said, glancing between them. *Don't be weird, don't be weird, don't be weird.*

"We weren't. I just moved in a month ago."

As always, she had incredible timing.

"Did I not mention that?" Sara asked, her lips curling into a crooked smile.

"No," Hanna said, crossing the hall. "You didn't."

Sara took a few steps across the hall to her and Matty's unit and bumped open the front door with her hip, calling back to Milo as it swung inward.

"See you in twenty!"

Their loft smelled like a version of home to Hanna—one where she was nineteen in the ASU dorms and studying for finals while Sara chattered on the phone with Matty who lived a state away.

There was a small kitchen to the right overflowing with

plants sunbathing under the skylight above, but the real draw were the floor-to-ceiling windows that peered into a courtyard garden below. She remembered it from the tour—an instant seller.

"You're upstairs," she said. "Bathroom and bedroom are all yours!"

Hanna climbed the narrow iron staircase and slid open a large wooden door to reveal a small, but tasteful, guest room. Sara followed with Hanna's second suitcase in tow.

"I know it's not a lot," Sara said. "But by San Francisco standards, it's a flippin' mansion."

"It's perfect," Hanna breathed, her lungs loosening more with every second she spent in Sara's home. "I cannot tell you how happy I am to be here. I already feel... I don't know. Lighter."

Sara squeezed her arm and leaned against a small desk in the corner while Hanna rifled through her things. Sara pointed to a floral sundress at the top of the bag.

"That's perfect for where we're going tonight. But bring a jacket."

"A *jacket*," Hanna scoffed. "I'm here to enjoy the sub-triple digit weather."

Sara rolled her eyes. "Trust me. And I know it took a lot for you to come out here. I'm really proud of you for getting out of the house. I think it'll be so good for you!"

"We'll see how you feel in two weeks," Hanna laughed. She plucked a few more necessities out of her bag and arranged them across the desk. "So. Milo is your neighbor."

"Yes."

"You're diabolical."

Sara held up her hands. "I forgot!"

"You're full of shit."

"I didn't want to scare you off," Sara confessed. "But if you *happen* to get the dicking down of your life while you're here, so be it!"

Hanna glared. "There will be no dicking down."

"Hanna," Sara said, sitting on the edge of the desk. "We both spent our entire twenties with the same dumb boys. Matty is well trained, but I *need* to know. Do it for *me*."

"Pathetic," Hanna grumbled.

"I have to call Cami back about place settings. Can you change and then grab Milo?"

"*Pathetic,*" Hanna repeated. Sara shrugged as she left.

"See you in the lobby!"

Hanna spent more time than she normally would have on her hair, telling herself it was the nerves of meeting new people. She brushed her teeth and pulled the sundress over her head, the strappy back *way* too cute to hide under a jacket.

When she'd decidedly run out of distractions, she crossed the hallway, hovering outside unit three.

This is stupid, she told herself, forcing her fist up to rap on the door three times. She was about to go for a fourth when the door cracked open.

"Hey! Sara had to call her mom real quick. She said she'd meet us in the lobby."

Milo glanced at the door behind them.

"Perfect," he mumbled, checking his phone. "That means we have time to pre-game. Camila can *talk*."

"With or without a partner," Hanna agreed, following him into the apartment. His unit was nearly identical to Matty and Sara's in layout, but the smell was all new. There was no tidal wave of nostalgia, only a combination of whiskey and leather, mixed with a faint waft of weed coming through his patio door. Where Sara and Matty had photos of vacations and holidays, Milo had vinyl sleeves and movie posters. His apartment faced the street and Hanna figured it must have been where Sara was waiting for her.

He didn't ask if she wanted anything. Instead, he poured a few ounces of something from an unlabeled bottle over ice and handed it to her.

She pulled the bottle off the counter and examined it, only a hand-scrawled date on some masking tape to be found.

"Am I about to drink something you made in a toilet?"

Milo laughed. "Too good for prison style?"

She rolled her eyes as he took a long sip, confirming it was at least tolerable. He pushed his flannel sleeves over his elbows, the fabric flexing as he set the glass down.

"My friends work at a distillery over in Oakland. They're always making weird shit in specialty barrels. The flavor profiles are unique. This one was casked in an old rum barrel. Promise it hasn't touched a toilet bowl."

Hanna smelled it, the notes prickling against her nose. It hit like a typical whiskey, but there was something warmer in the depths of the scent. Spicier. Maybe the hint of an orange peel, or something citrusy. It was like inhaling a half-formed memory.

She took a sip.

"Yeah?" he asked.

"Goddamn," she said, exhaling. It was bright, warm—everything she loved about a good bourbon but with a surprising twist. It was smoother than it had any right to be with a certain darkness on the finish. "Jesus."

"I'll have to take you out there. They have this sour cherry mash cocktail, it's incredible in the summer."

He finished his glass and Hanna remembered that they did, actually, have somewhere to be, throwing hers back in another long pull.

"We should probably go," Hanna said. Milo nodded and

grabbed his wallet and keys from his counter as she opened the front door. His hand caught her elbow, pulling her back.

"Hey," he said, the low volume drawing her in. "I, uh—" he stopped.

For a second, she expected him to bring up the elevator incident directly, and she braced herself against the doorframe. She couldn't read a thing in his face, but after a few seconds, he picked the thread up again.

"I just wanted to say it's good you're out here. I haven't seen Sara this excited since they got engaged."

Hanna smiled. "Oh. Yeah. Good."

It was barely a whisper. He was too close to her. She could lean forward just another two inches and—

"Cami's probably done by now," he said, releasing her elbow.

"Right."

Hanna stepped out and waited while he locked up. She made sure to put as much distance between them as possible in the elevator to the lobby.

SHE WAS four dumplings away from a food coma.

Another swell of laughter careened over the table. Sara and Matty's friends were unsurprisingly lovely, and she regretted how many weekends she'd wasted alone in her crumbling fixer-upper.

The mysterious Chloe didn't appear until sometime between rounds three and four. Milo had long since given up on waiting for her outside, sliding into the seat beside Hanna and running his finger over the menu to point out all his favorites she should try.

Her eyes dropped to his phone as it buzzed against the

table. An unsaved number flashed across the screen, but there was a string of messages between them.

"Chloe's here," he mumbled, mostly to himself, and rose from the table. She focused on her cocktail and a story Matty's coworker spun about a board meeting they'd crashed, but she couldn't hold onto the sounds as a bouncing red head landed at the table.

She was even cooler in person.

It made sense that the universe would shove two people like Milo and Chloe together. She had that effortlessly cool vibe that Hanna once wished she could pull off, but her body's rejection of a nose piercing three times had sealed the deal for her. She was firmly on the tame side of that line.

The worst part about Chloe was that she was fucking hysterical. Everything she said dripped in charm and Hanna wanted to hate her, but it was simply impossible. She tried not to stare during dinner, but it was hard not to be drawn to two such beautiful people being beautiful together.

Chloe worked overtime to ask questions about Hanna's life, her job, and her favorite places to visit in Phoenix. She, once again, resisted the urge to stare as they said their goodbyes—a chaste kiss so brief she nearly missed it. It wasn't the hot and heavy exchange a new couple still insecure with one another might share—no. It was *comfortable*.

Sara led them down a few blocks to the pier, the wind whipping Hanna's hair into her face. She tried not to walk with Milo, but he seemed to take an interest in pointing out all their favorite hangouts on the way home.

"Chloe seems really sweet," Hanna said, wrapping her arms around herself.

"She is," Milo replied. "It's... casual," he added.

Hanna tucked that information somewhere between her ribs, letting it percolate through her body and spread a warmth that almost cut through the bay breeze tickling the back of her neck.

"Ah. Explains why you haven't saved her number," she blurted.

Milo's smile tilted. "She was texting me from her work phone. But noted that you're watching."

"No," Hanna protested. "Not watching. Just... observing."

"And that's completely different."

"Obviously," she said, chewing on her lower lip as they waited on a corner. "It's none of my business."

"Hey," he said, pulling her wrist toward him as Sara and Matty started across. "Are you freezing?"

"I'm f—"

"Fine, yeah, I know," Milo said smugly, sliding his flannel off his shoulders and draping it around hers. She drowned in the scent of him, the same as his apartment, but closer now. "You got a *lot* going on up there, huh Arizona?" He tapped the space between her eyes and she pulled back. "I've been where you are. It's a war zone. I just want it on the record that I'm not trying to add to that chaos."

Hanna wasn't sure what he was getting at, her head tilting as she thought as much. It must have read all too clearly in her eyes because he shook his head, his dark curls bouncing under the streetlight.

"If you need a friend, I'm a damn good one. If you need to flirt a little and push someone's buttons, I'm not opposed. I'm a grade-A distraction if that's what you want. But if you're going to be here all summer, I just want to get it out there now, I'm not a relationship guy."

Hanna's mouth opened, but closed again. Whatever she'd expected him to say, it wasn't that.

"And I don't mean that in a toxic fuck-boy way. I mean it in an I-never-want-to-leave-a-wife-and-three-kids-without-a-father way. I just find that friends with benefits is a better situation for someone like me." Milo rocked back on his heels, tracking Matty and Sara across the street. "But I like you. I think you're cool. A little fucked up, but I heard what I just said, so I'm not going to pretend I'm not in the same boat. So. That's where I'm at."

Hanna took his words in, but didn't process a single one of them. She'd never once had someone be so direct.

She pursed her lips. "You're either in a *lot* of therapy, or none, aren't you?"

"CBT, talk, and group," Milo said, a grin spreading over his lips. "I will always tell you exactly what I need, but not everyone can handle that."

"But Chloe can."

"For now," he said.

"I don't know what to make of any of that," Hanna admitted. "How many years until I can just communicate how I feel directly without every single feeling I've ever had rushing out in one long, verbal panic attack?"

Milo laughed, reaching forward and buttoning his shirt around her collarbones. His fingertips brushed her shoulder, the chill well and thoroughly gone from her muscles.

"How many therapists you got?" he asked.

"Just the one."

"Add a second and maybe we can talk," he murmured. He rested a hand on the small of her back, pushing her forward as the light shifted green.

"Milo?" she asked, watching Sara stare over her shoulder from half a block over.

"Arizona?"

"Friends with benefits—"

"You're not ready for that," Milo cut her off abruptly. "That's triple therapist territory."

Milo stuffed his hands in his pockets, bumping into her shoulder.

A strawberry-red blush crept over her neck. "Why do I feel like you're either going to be my best friend or the worst thing that's ever happened to me?"

He sucked a breath through his teeth.

"Only time will tell, huh?"

SEVEN

There is a scent to grief.

It's sterile, like a spilled bottle of nail polish remover on the kitchen table while waiting for a call from the doctor, or a whiff of hand sanitizer between gloves and morphine doses.

It lingers. You go blind to it in your own home, but suddenly, out in the world, it finds you, and the inside of your nostrils flare. The headache sets in.

Hanna woke to the sharp clinical fragrance of grief before she even opened her eyes on the June morning she'd been dreading for exactly one year. It had crawled toward her, hour by hour, the slow sting of scores kept invading her lower back and inching up her spine. It whispered, *Can you believe it? One whole year without her? Can you?*

She could not.

It had been a month since she'd escaped the onset of a Phoenix summer. Between all of the morning walks and lunch breaks and movie nights with the group—Sara, Matty, and more often than not, Milo and Chloe—she'd managed to condense the dread into small doses.

But she could not avoid it entirely.

Below her room, Sara clinked around in the kitchen before work, making her breakfast smoothie. Matty had surely already made his way out the door to the office. Hanna figured she only had to lay there for another twenty minutes—child's play—to successfully avoid Sara as well.

The thought of making eye contact with anyone who knew why she could hardly breathe sickened her.

She checked her phone, immediately regretting it.

People meant well, but that didn't make their messages any less overwhelming. She ignored ninety percent of them, but did choose to open an email from her boss who had kindly given her an out from work for the day. A novel from DO NOT ANSWER rolled in, and she was tempted to throw her phone into the Bay and never check it again. She settled for simply turning it off.

An hour later, Hanna had finally convinced herself to get out of bed, and dragged leggings, a pair of good walking shoes, and a flannel that did not belong to her over her slumped frame.

A walk could do wonders.

She forced herself not to look up at Milo's balcony as she passed below and ducked into the cafe where she'd spent every morning her first week in town. She slipped into a booth, staring out the window along 8th Street until an empty mug landed in front of her.

"You're late today," the server said.

"Slept in," Hanna mumbled.

"No work?"

"No," Hanna said. She forced a smile. "Not today."

The server filled her mug to the brim—no cream—and disappeared. Hanna knew she had about six minutes to herself before the server would reappear to take her breakfast order. Staring at the haze of steam curling over the white ceramic mug, she wondered what she should or should not attempt to do on the day of all days.

Olivia had warned her about the Big Days. Anniversaries, birthdays, Mother's Day—the pressure that came with them—all stretching and bending the lines on the calendar for attention. That day, she decided, she would make *no* plans. She would follow whatever compulsion entered her mind and let the universe guide her for a bit.

After another round of coffee and a dry but pleasant scone, she decided she was at risk of heart failure if she didn't shake off some of the caffeine. She wandered from the cafe, waiting for some sort of cosmic tug—from *her* or elsewhere. Anything that could be mistaken for a sign was on the table, but for the first half hour, it was mostly Bay breezes and morning commuters.

She passed a corner flower shop, the notes of a song her mother liked floating from the open door. Hanna stopped, a gentle smile pulling at her lips. She turned and entered the shop. Black and white marble tiles stretched beneath several antique dressers and tables holding overflowing bouquets and stems of roses and lilies.

"Good morning!" a voice chimed from under a desk painted teal, the edges peeling, but in a chic way.

"Morning," Hanna murmured, reaching out to stroke the pale pink petal of a rose.

"Looking for anything in particular?" A woman in her late fifties sprang up from the desk, a white canvas apron tied around her waist over a denim shirt. Her dark hair curled around her ears, lines crinkling at her eyes.

"I'm not sure," Hanna confessed. "Just something to brighten the day."

"Ah," the woman said, her eyes scanning her shop. "You know what, I have the most gorgeous arrangement in the back that hasn't found a home yet. I threw it together this morning. I must have known you'd come in."

Hanna felt a tingle in her shoulders, a certain *something* that tugged at her heart. The woman returned with a teal mason jar filled with seven sunny-yellow blooms.

She choked on a rush of emotion, her eyes narrowing against the tears.

"Are you alright, honey?" She set the mason jar on the desk, rounding it to reach for Hanna's shoulders.

"I'm fine!" she insisted, brushing the tears away. "Just a tough day. Could I come back for these later? I'll be out and about all day."

"Of course," the woman said. "I'll keep them in the back. I hope your day gets easier." She patted Hanna's shoulder once more. Hanna backed out of the shop and waited for the light to change on the corner.

There was a woman on her phone, chatting away to someone. Under her arm sat a canvas tote bag with a bouquet embroidered across it, sunflowers blooming over the side. All at once, Hanna's plans solidified for the day.

She followed the woman for a few blocks until she dipped into a small coffee shop next to an antique store tucked between office buildings. Hanna casually strolled in, unsure what she was looking for next. The floor creaked under her as she weaved through aisles of figurines, furniture, and books. She pushed her way to the back of the shop and flipped through rows of vinyl albums when a light breeze swept through her hair.

It pushed her gaze over her shoulder to the open door at the back of the shop, peering into an alley. As she contemplated her next move, a bicyclist streamed by wearing bright yellow shoes that spun in rapid circles.

Okay, then. Sometimes the universe doesn't scream, it whispers, and Hanna decided to accept proximal sunflowers in the form of yellow accessories.

She exited through the back door and down the alley. The bike raced too far ahead for her to catch up, but she decided the general spirit of her idea was enough, so she kept on in the general direction. She walked along Market for a while, passing by all the noisy shopping center traffic, and hoped that she was heading in a more interesting direction.

It took another ten minutes for Hanna to find the next clue in her endless scavenger hunt, but a little girl trailing behind her mom sported a bright yellow backpack with big sunflowers printed across the plastic.

They headed for the streetcar, as did Hanna.

They rode for about twenty minutes. When the sunflower backpack jumped off, she made her exit too. She was somewhere near the Painted Ladies, which seemed as good a place as any to stop and write a little.

She headed over to the park, enjoying the sun as it peered through gray fog and warmed the city. There were only a few other people scattered throughout the bike paths. She found a bench and made herself comfy for the foreseeable future.

Hanna pulled the navy journal from her bag she'd neglected over the previous few months. She'd started it when her mother was diagnosed, but things moved so quickly, she hadn't made the most of it. She flipped to the next blank page, after an entry dated around the holidays.

"Sorry, Mom," she whispered, fishing a pen from her bag. Right around Thanksgiving, her depression hit an all-time low, and she'd abandoned her letters to her mother entirely. It had been her first Christmas without Logan in ten years, and the first without her mother in thirty. She was lucky to have even showered during that time.

She'd lost all motivation to talk to *anyone* at that point, let alone someone who couldn't talk back.

She stared at the blank page for a good five minutes, unsure of what to say. She sank back. It was rare for Hanna to take time assessing her own feelings. Forget committing them to paper.

She battled back the temptation to list off all her grievances, deciding instead to make a list of the things going *right* in her life.

That was something she missed the most about her mother —she'd always been one to hold space for a rant, but it inevitably ended with the question Hanna had repeated to herself a thousand times in the year since losing her mom.

"Try again tomorrow?"

Of all the things she'd lost, her reminder that today is not forever was at the top of the list. Hanna touched her pen to her journal, surprised by how easy the words flowed from her.

1. I'm good at my job, good enough that they haven't fired me after a year of working from bed.

2. I bought my dream fixer-upper, largely thanks to life insurance money, but whatever. In this economy, a win is a win.

3. I can be in the same room as Logan without dying, though it's not much better.

4. I'm eating again. My curves have started to come back now that I live with people who don't miss meals.

5. I'm meeting new people and making new friends.

Hanna snorted. She did *not* include that one of those new

friends was a source of constant anxiety, but her mother didn't need to know who she thought about late at night.

6. I didn't die when you did.

That last point surprised Hanna a bit. It had rolled around in her mind, of course, that her life ended the moment her mother drew her final breath.

But it didn't.

It changed.

She did not die.

There had been many nights in the year following when she'd gotten into bed and hoped she would wake up and it had all been some sort of awful nightmare or, worse, that she wouldn't wake up at all. She wished more people talked about those ugly hours, the ones when slipping away to wherever your person went and confronting them face to ghostly face seemed better than waking up in the cold light of morning and continuing on.

A tear dropped onto her journal. She hadn't felt it fall.

Hanna was about to start number seven when someone crested the hill in front of her, a bright yellow bucket hat framing their face.

Off we go, she thought, shoving her journal back in her bag.

She followed them for long enough that she worried about being mistaken for a stalker, so she fell back to the other side of the street and put in her earbuds. She found the sad-girl playlist she'd been curating since college, through a lifetime of bad dates and Big-T traumas, and let it rub salt in her wounds for a few more blocks.

Twenty minutes later, her bucket hat-bearing guide darted into an apartment building.

Well, shit, Hanna thought, looking around for her next spot of sunshine.

She choked on a laugh when she glanced up and read the sign above her head. Tucked between The Roxie theater and a Money Mart, The Sunflower hovered over 16th Street. The windows glared in the midday sun of the hole-in-the-wall restaurant.

She debated if it was too early for lunch.

"Hanna?"

The hell? Hanna spun, a familiar figure hanging out under The Roxie's unlit neon sign, waving to her. Chloe, clad in tight, acid-washed jeans and a cropped t-shirt of a band Hanna had never heard of, darted forward from the shadows.

"Chloe?"

"How funny! Did Milo invite you?" She hugged Hanna quickly, her very cool perfume drowning her senses.

"Um, no, actually, I was just on a walk and ended up here."

"Crazy," Chloe said, her head tilting. "Well, hey, it must be meant to be! Milo and I are playing hooky and catching a matinee. You should join us!"

She looked *far* too earnest in her invitation.

"Oh no, that's okay, I don't want to crash..." She almost said 'your date,' but then remembered that Milo *doesn't do the dating thing.*

"No, seriously, it'll be fun! There's almost never anyone here midday. They play old movies during the week."

"Uh, well, I have to..." *You fucking idiot, Hanna, say literally anything!*

"Hanna?"

Welp, too late now, she thought, turning as Milo approached in a faded t-shirt while trying not to notice the way the cotton curled around his biceps.

She wished he hadn't seen her, wished she'd been clever

enough to escape. Chloe was a stranger. Hanna didn't care if Chloe thought she was insane. She could have bolted.

But Milo, in all aspects, was more complicated.

"Hey," Hanna breathed, the nerves in her throat clenching on the sound. Maybe a car would pop over the curb and take her out. At least then she could bitch about this to her mother's face.

"Look who I ran into!" Chloe announced. She bounced in a way that only added to her charm.

"What are you doing in The Mission?" Milo asked, shoving a hand in his pocket.

"Long story," Hanna mumbled.

Chloe chirped, "I invited her to join us!"

Milo's face curled in a mix of surprise and concern. "Oh, uh, cool. Yeah. Are you sure?"

Hanna wasn't sure who he was asking, but she resisted the urge to bark, "*No! No, I'm not sure! I actually want the street to open up and swallow me to the depths of hell!*"

Instead, she shrugged and whispered, "Totally."

"Did you tell her what we're seeing?" Milo asked Chloe.

"No, but you like the classics, right Hanna?"

Of course she fucking did. "I suppose so," she muttered.

"Great!" Chloe beamed.

"Great," Hanna repeated, her neck sweating. She followed them to the ticket booth as Milo awkwardly paid for three, despite her protests. Her head spun as they grabbed seats, Chloe placing Milo between them before bouncing back out of the theater for snacks.

Hanna glanced at her ticket stub.

Love Story.

Her stomach churned. Milo must have sensed the boiling anxiety in her chest. He leaned over and said quietly, "You don't have to stay for this."

"Uhhh, it's fine. I'm fine," Hanna insisted.

"One more and I'll believe it, Arizona." He smirked. "I can tell Chloe work called or something. She won't think twice."

Hanna took a long, deep breath. Before she could answer, her eyes dropped to his shirt, and she silently cursed her mother. The light off the screen illuminated the remnants of a sunflower field, a pale blue sky peeling from the top under half of a band name she remembered from the early aughts.

Her mother always did have a fucked up sense of humor.

She'd followed the sunflowers that far. She couldn't give up then.

Was it ideal? Hell no.

Was it better than crying in a park alone? Debatable.

She shook her head. "I'll be okay. But you have to do me a favor."

"Anything."

"If you see me crying, no you didn't." She grimaced and tried to translate it into a smile, but didn't quite make it.

Milo chuckled, a genuine smile breaking across that jaw of his.

"Fine, but if you see *me* crying, yes you did. I fucking *love* a public cry."

Hanna groaned, bracing herself for the next ninety minutes as the lights dimmed.

EIGHT

Each one of those ninety minutes passed very, *very* slowly.

But it wasn't a waste of time entirely. No, when the credits finally rolled, Hanna had a fresh list of newly discovered medical trauma for Olivia to help her sort through.

Productive.

When she finally checked her phone in the theater lobby while waiting for Chloe to leave the bathroom, she had thirty-two text messages and several missed calls. None of them seemed like anything she wanted to return. As they exited the theater, Chloe rambled on about how much she just *loved* old movies.

Hanna couldn't recall a single scene.

"I'm so glad we ran into you, Hanna! This was a great midday break," Chloe said, throwing her arms around Hanna's neck.

"Yes," Hanna said. "Great."

"I'll see you tomorrow," Chloe said to Milo, placing a kiss gently on his cheek before flitting off to wherever manic-pixie-dream-girls went to recharge in San Francisco.

"I am so, *so* sorry," Milo said before Chloe was even around the corner. He walked, and Hanna followed. She didn't care where they went, as long as they were moving.

"It's okay, she had no idea," Hanna said, waving her hand. *She meant well,* as people always did.

"You never actually told me how your mom died." Milo glanced up and down the street before crossing.

"You never told me how your dad died."

Milo shoved his hands in his pockets. "I'll show you mine if you show me yours?"

Hanna sighed. "Fine. But if I'm going to trauma dump on you, I need to be in a dark, grungy bar, not in direct sunlight where you can see me sad in high definition."

Milo stopped and thought about that for a second, checking his phone. It was still early in the day, but surely somewhere was open for the depressed.

He started walking again. "There's a place not far from here I like. Dingy, definitely accustomed to pretty women crying in the booths."

Hanna gasped dramatically. "You think I'm *pretty?*"

He rolled his eyes. "Don't be like that."

"Like what? *Gorgeous?*" Hanna batted her lashes, enjoying the moment of levity.

"I didn't say—"

"Stunning? Breathtaking?"

Milo threw his head back and laughed. "You're a real pain in the ass, you know that?"

She flipped her hair over her shoulder. "My god! Enough with the compliments, Milo! You're making me blush."

"Jesus Christ, now *I* need a drink," he mumbled, leading her around a corner and down another block before stopping abruptly at a thick, wooden door with a small sign in the window that read simply, LOUNGE.

The shift from the bright street to the near-black bar strained her eyes as they adjusted to the row of dim glass fixtures hanging over five crinkled vinyl booths. A shiny bar with ornate carvings on its corners lined the far wall. It looked like it had lived there for a century, and certainly smelled like that was the case too.

It was perfect.

A low hum from an ancient jukebox whispered seventies hits, a whining guitar running beneath Milo's instructions on where to sit before he glided to the bar and ordered for two.

It was only them and the bartender, the ideal situation for her impending breakdown.

"Starting a tab?" the bartender asked.

"Put it on the owner's," Milo quipped. The bartender rolled his eyes. Hanna guessed they were friends.

"They've got this bourbon just in from Texas you have to try," Milo said, plunking two glasses onto the table between them.

"You seem to think I'll like an awful lot of whiskeys," she said.

Milo arched a brow. "Have I steered you wrong yet?"

"Hmm, I guess not," she conceded and clinked the glass against his. She took a cautious sip, ice hitting her lips first, and tasted the sweet vanilla notes as they drifted downward. He was right, she did like it. "It's good."

"Told you."

Milo fell silent. She knew what he wanted to hear, but she needed at least a second drink to say it.

"You have to go first," she said.

"Me?"

"The person with the longest Dead Parent Society tenure goes first, duh." Hanna sipped more of her whiskey, trying to get a buzz going before she'd inevitably crash the mood.

"Damn, I must not have gotten my copy of the rules," Milo huffed.

"Well, we're not very good with follow-through at the DPS. Between the depression and the paperwork..."

"Too true," he groaned. He threw back half his bourbon and rolled up his sleeves. The motion reminded Hanna that she was, indeed, wearing his flannel shirt, and her face flushed to a deep scarlet. "Man, it's been a while since I told the full story. Where to start?"

His face contemplated which threads of the story to include, and she could tell he wasn't lying when he'd told her it never got better. She could see it in the way his jaw clenched around the words.

All the pain rushed to his green eyes in an instant, and she was looking at a fifteen-year-old boy, not a thirty-year-old man.

"Well, you know I was in high school. It was a week before Spring Break, we were in class and the teacher's phone rang. After all these years, that's what I remember most vividly. The look on her face when she told me they wanted me in the office and to bring my stuff."

Milo took a long sip of his drink.

"She wouldn't tell me why. I just assumed I was in trouble for something stupid. I was a bit of a problem child," he admitted. "Anyway, I walked into the office and my aunt was there. My dad's sister. She'd been crying, I could see it all over her face. The school counselor was there too. I knew at that point something was wrong, but I never would have guessed..."

Milo trailed off, swallowing as his eyes scanned the bar.

"They pulled me into this stupid room with glass windows. That's all I could think about. If anyone walked by, they'd see me fall apart. So I did my best to keep it together. Motorcycle accident," Milo said, his face reddening. "He was changing lanes on the highway and a truck didn't see him."

"Fuck," Hanna whispered. "That's awful."

"Yeah, I mean, it was quick. That's really all I have to hold onto, I guess."

"Tell me more about him," she said. "What was his name?"

Milo's lips dropped into the kind of smile she gave anyone who asked about her mom. It wasn't a pure thing, sparked by joy or nostalgia. It was the bitter release of the fear that she'd already answered the last question about her.

"Elias. Greek as hell, he grew up in Crete but moved here as a teenager. He was a really big guy, but super soft spoken. You had to lean in to hear him. But he was fucking *funny*. Not in that typical dad-joke way. You always knew if he was opening his mouth, it was going to be good."

Milo paused, laughing at something that crawled into his mind. She wanted to slip into it, live in the memory with him.

"I really resent him, you know? For being such a damned good dad. Thirty years ago, men didn't give a fuck about their kids, but he did. He was helpful around the house. He was *obsessed* with my mom."

"I feel like the only answer to this is 'as well as she could,' but how did she handle it all?"

Milo's face fell. "My poor mom. She had three teenage boys to deal with, and none of us made it easier on her. I think a piece of her died with him, you know? She just... she never really recovered. Still hasn't remarried. I think it just gutted her. It's better now, but those first five years were like living with a ghost."

Hanna nodded. "Does she date at all?"

"Oh," Milo sighed. "I don't know. I'm *sure* she does. But she's never introduced anyone, so maybe not?"

"How many girls have you brought home?" Hanna asked, a playful smile unfurling.

"Fair point," Milo said. "Either way, that's none of my business."

"And fifteen years and three therapists later, you're content to never engage in anything that might put you at risk of repeating your biggest trauma."

"Nailed it, Arizona."

"Are you the oldest?" she asked.

Milo's head tilted. "The baby, actually. Why?"

"You just give off a bit of a big brother thing," Hanna said.

Milo's forehead crinkled. "You think of me like a brother?"

"No," Hanna said. "Maybe."

"Unfortunate."

Hanna finished her whiskey. "Not that it matters, since you don't date."

"Right," he said. "You've successfully avoided your turn long enough."

Hanna exhaled, the breath shaky. "My turn." She pushed her empty glass to the end of the table. "Alright, well, you already know that I had just broken up with Logan, so the timing wasn't *ideal*. But one day, I was sitting in a meeting, and my phone kept blowing up. Over and over. I talked to my mom every single day, on the way to and from work, so if she was calling outside of that, I knew something was wrong before I even answered."

Hanna pushed down the creeping chill in her spine.

"It wasn't her, it was her coworker calling from her phone. She'd passed out in the middle of lunch. They took her to the emergency room for a laceration on her head, and her white blood cell count was through the roof."

She could hear the tears pooling on her tongue, building as she relived the worst weeks of her life. She'd never told the story out loud before.

"They did a CT scan, and it came back with mets on just

about every inch of her body. Honestly, every doctor we talked to was floored that she was still walking. She'd been losing weight for a month or two, but she was a woman in her fifties—she was always dieting. They thought the first tumor was a glioblastoma but, in the end, it didn't really matter. It had spread so badly, she'd probably been sick for months, maybe years. It was hard to trace it all."

"Shit," Milo whispered. He didn't say he was sorry, or that it must have been so hard. Like Sara, he understood the value of just sitting in the pain. Hanna tapped her hands against the table, willing the tears away.

"I still feel bad for the doctors. I could tell it was torture for them, having to try and stay positive for a young girl when her mother was defying death with every breath she took. There was one time—" Hanna surprised herself with a laugh that caught in her chest. "—she had a fever and, in chemo, that's a do-not-pass-go, do-not-collect-two-hundred-dollars, straight-to-the-ER thing. They asked her what she was in treatment for, and she told them she was just one big tumor and to stop asking stupid questions. The pain meds made her a little bitchy," Hanna added. "It was only eight weeks from the fainting to her dying."

"Hell of a ride," Milo said. He pushed against his chest, and she wondered for not the first time if they were doomed to always be walking triggers for one another's deepest pains.

"There's no winning that game," she said. "But I got time to say goodbye. I had time to have conversations no one ever wants to have. We got to go to the Grand Canyon together for a weekend and said all the things everyone is afraid to say." A sob bubbled up through her chest, unstoppable. "Sorry," she said.

"For... being sad about your dead mom? That shit doesn't scare me, Hanna."

She couldn't look at him.

"I mean it, Arizona. I can hold it. I've had *lots* of practice."

She ignored him, battling it back down. She'd had lots of practice in *that*. Maybe she'd brave that meltdown one day.

But not that day.

She held her breath for a second while the prickling settled.

"My mom was funny, too. Like your dad, not in the goofy-boomer-parent way. But just *truly* funny. Unlike your dad, however, no one would ever dare call Lisa soft-spoken. She was a fucking force. You knew when she entered a room and when she left. Sweet as hell, but she bit when necessary."

Milo smiled. "What about your dad?"

Hanna glanced at one of the neon signs on the wall as feelings much older and much less accessible to her made an appearance at the table. She tried to think of the last time she'd even talked to him.

"Ah, yeah, they divorced when I was pretty young. I'm sure it was hard for him in a way, but they hadn't spoken in like two decades."

Milo's lips twisted. "You keep your therapist *busy*, huh?"

"I believe I'm saved in her phone under Job Security." Her eyes snapped to the far end of the bar as the door swung inward and three older gentlemen strolled in, nodding at the bartender.

"It's been about a year, right?" Milo asked.

"Just about to the hour," she whispered.

"Goddammit, Hanna," Milo exhaled. "I'm torturing you. The movie, making you relive it. I'm so sorry."

She wiped a tear from the corner of her eye. "Hey, love means never having to say you're sorry, right?"

Milo dropped his eyes to hers. "I told you not to fall in love with me," he whispered dramatically.

Hanna blushed. "I was quoting the movie—"

"Relax," Milo chuckled. "I was referencing *A Walk to*

Remember. One sad terminal illness movie to another, I figured it would translate."

Hanna hesitated to confess, "I've never actually seen it."

Milo leaned his head back against the peeling vinyl behind him.

"Why would you have? It's only one of the most iconic love stories of our generation!"

"I missed my window!" she cried. "I never saw it as a kid and then the whole mom dying of cancer thing kind of put a damper on it. Plus, you just spoiled the ending."

"Nah," he shook his head, grinning against the edge of his glass. "When you're ready to stop doing this suppress-all-tears nonsense, you let me know. We're watching it."

"Gimme a few days to recover from *Love Story* Gate."

"Deal," he murmured and swiped her empty glass. "You got another round in ya?"

"Yeah," she said, shaking off the emotions clinging to her arms. He strode across the bar and she couldn't help herself— she watched the muscles beneath that damned T-shirt ripple.

"Where you been, hotshot?" One of the older men bellied up to the bar and clapped his hand on Milo's shoulder. She couldn't hear his reply, but it sparked a roar of laughter between them.

The bartender pointed to Hanna and asked a question to which Milo nodded. He plucked two more glasses off the back of the bar and filled them with something new.

"Your ma know you're seeing other women?" the man asked, moving his hand from Milo's shoulder to pinch the skin at the back of his neck. Milo batted him away playfully.

"Don't tell her she's prettier," he said, winking as he snagged the glasses and returned to the booth.

"Friends of yours?" Hanna asked, taking the whiskey from him.

"Kind of," Milo said, sliding back into the booth. "Uncles."

"Oh, seriously? Your family hangs out here?"

"Yeah," Milo said, leaning over the table and flashing a grin that would have stopped her heart if either of them was even remotely emotionally available. "I mean, I kind of own it."

Her eyes widened as she tried to do the mismatched career math in her head. As far as she knew, Milo worked for some tech company.

"What do you mean? Aren't you in sales?"

He leaned back, stretching an arm over the booth. "By day. But this was Dad's bar. It stayed in the family. That's my brother, Frankie." He pointed at the bartender, who waved briefly. Hanna gave him a good look and, had she done so sooner, she wouldn't have been so caught off guard. They had the same green eyes, the same sharp jaws. Frankie was a few years older and a few inches shorter, but they had the same warmth to them. "We all own it. Frankie runs it most of the time. Our older brother, Nikolas, is in LA with the wife and kids, so he's just an owner on paper. Mom lives in the apartment upstairs."

Her brows tucked together. "You marched me into your family bar without any warning?"

"Yeah," he said. "Why not?"

She thought about that for a second. Milo didn't owe her a damn thing, certainly not any explanations. They were barely friends, let alone something that warranted warnings. She glanced around the bar, family photos warming the walls above outdated furniture they'd never give up. Regulars poured in as the work day drew to a close.

She sipped her second whiskey.

"Tell me more about your mom," she said.

SHE WAS HALFWAY across the hall, leaving Milo at his own door, as she tried to beat Sara and Matty home so she could hide out again.

"Wait," he said.

She spun, apprehensively moving back toward him.

"You never told me how you ended up with Chloe earlier."

Her face flushed. It seemed so silly now. "It's kind of embarrassing and makes me sound a little crazy."

"Safe space," he said, the words bouncing off the hallway. Something about the earnestness in his eyes did her in.

"Okay. I think I told you my mom had a thing about sunflowers, yeah? I was having breakfast this morning and trying to figure out how to spend this stupid day, and I saw this flower shop—oh, shit. I forgot to go back and pick up my sunflowers." She chewed at the edge of her thumb. "Anyway, I started following sunflowers I saw around the city—or sunflower adjacent. And I ended up at The Roxie."

"The Sunflower has good food, we should try it sometime," he said.

"Noted," she said.

"That's not crazy, Hanna. I think it's nice." He folded his arms over his chest, leaning against the door frame.

"Day certainly could have been worse," she murmured.

"Wait! You forgot about me!" He pulled his shirt out, the crumbling silk screen graphics hardly counting. "You want to know something crazy?"

"Crazier than following sunflowers all over the city?"

"This was my dad's shirt," Milo said. "I found it in a box when I moved in here. I don't even listen to Stone Temple Pilots."

Hanna tilted her head, fighting the blush threatening to take over her entire face.

"Maybe your mom sent me to be your guardian angel."

"Alternatively, maybe you're a demon from hell."

Milo bounced his eyebrows, leaning in closer. "Yeah, yeah, you seemed so miserable hanging out with me today." He turned and pushed his door in halfway.

"Thanks," she said, drawing him back out.

"I told you I make a great distraction, Arizona. But make sure you don't stay distracted. Feeling like shit is a key part of the process."

Hanna saluted him as she backed away and shoved her shoulder into the front door of Sara and Matty's apartment.

"It seems like the *main* part of the process."

Milo laughed, the sound twisting something inside of her she'd rather have never known was there.

"HANNA!" Sara's voice echoed off the walls below as she closed the front door behind her.

Hanna popped her head out of the loft to see Sara holding a bouquet of sunflowers wrapped in kraft paper in one hand, and a second arrangement in the other. As Hanna raced down the stairs, she recognized the teal mason jar.

"Kind of rude of Milo to show me up like that," Sara muttered, pointing to the amber bottle beside the arrangement. "I grabbed these on the way home." She wiggled the bouquet in her hands.

"Add them in!" Hanna said, pulling the bottle from the kitchen counter. A handwritten label across the front read *The Lisa Anniversary Blend. Sweet as hell, bites when necessary.*

"Menace," Hanna whispered under her breath. Sara leaned over and giggled, unwrapping the flowers she'd picked up. "You're *so* in trouble," Sara said.

NINE

"Another?"

The server at the cafe across the street from the loft suspended her pot halfway between them. Hanna watched the burnt coffee grounds swirl at the bottom of the pot.

"Thanks," she said, folding her book and resting it on the table as she slid her mug closer. She'd been working all morning and finally had finally taken a break to read a bit.

"Hanna!" Her head snapped up, Chloe's fiery red hair barrelling toward her, Milo trailing closely behind.

"Oh, hey guys," Hanna said. Chloe slipped into the booth across from her. She reached for Hanna's book and flipped it over.

"Oh my god, I just finished this series. It's *so* good," Chloe said.

Milo slid into the booth next to Chloe, nudging her over the same way he did on the couch during movies and baseball games. They'd only left the same arrangement twelve hours ago, Chloe's feet tucked under her body as they'd passed boxes of wings back and forth. Hanna tried not to wonder if Chloe had gone home before showing back up for lunch.

Not that it was any of her business.

"I love it so far," Hanna said. "Sara ripped through them all in, like, two weeks."

"Can't blame her. You're just about to hit the *really* good parts," she giggled.

"Pervs," Milo said, stealing a sip of Hanna's coffee.

"I don't know how you two drink that diner coffee black," Chloe said, reaching for one of the stuck-together menus parked behind a decades-old napkin holder.

"It's the whiskey," Hanna said. "He's destroyed my taste buds since getting here."

"You two are just *so* tough," Chloe mocked. "I'm looking at the pastry case. Need anything?"

"Nah," Milo said.

"I was asking Hanna," Chloe replied.

"I'm good," Hanna said.

"We're not intruding on your date with a shadow daddy, are we?" Milo asked, snagging her book. He flipped it over and cracked it to a random page. Hanna blushed preemptively. It didn't matter what page he opened to. There was bound to be something on it she'd never have the courage to read out loud.

"Jesus," Milo gasped. It was rare to catch a pink blush on him, but whatever he read did the trick. He closed the book and set it back down on the table. "I didn't know you got down like that, Arizona."

"Yeah well, you wouldn't, would you?" she asked, raising a brow.

Whatever she'd awoken in him flashed across his eyes in a sparkling ignition. He leaned close, the heat of his breath on her neck.

"Whose fault is that? I told you, you're but a therapist away from a good time."

"Shut *up*," she groaned, pushing him back toward his side of the booth. "You're so full of shit."

"You've thought about it."

Maybe it was the caffeine rush, maybe it was the four chapters of smut she'd consumed before he sat down, but she bit.

"Aren't you here with your girlfriend?"

Milo shook his head. "I told you—"

"Yeah, yeah," she muttered. "Casual. It's all very Summer of Love."

He took another sip of her coffee, wrapping his hand around the mug.

"You know, a little oxytocin would do you a *world* of good."

"I get *plenty* of oxytocin, thank you," she muttered, attempting to pry her mug back from his hand.

"Sure," he said, lowering his voice as he pulled the mug back. "But does your vibrator tell you what a good, good girl you are?"

Her jaw fell open. She resented the laugh that rumbled through his chest.

"Oh, god," Chloe said as she returned. "What did the degenerate say to you?"

"Nothing," Milo said, smirking. He drained what was left of her coffee, waving down their server. "Can she get a fresh pot? This one was a little fried."

"No problem," the server said, flashing the kind of smile Hanna imagined every woman in San Francisco gave Milo.

"The coffee was *fine*," she protested.

"We're aiming higher than *fine*, Arizona," he said, scanning the menu. "You eat yet?"

"I'm just taking a quick break between calls."

"That's a no," Milo said to Chloe. The server returned,

setting a fresh mug of coffee down between them. "Can I get the breakfast sandwich, double bacon. She'll have the Denver omelet, extra bell pepper, if you could."

Hanna sighed. "Do you fucking study me?"

"He does," Chloe said. "He does it to everyone."

"Big Red here will do the French toast, no whipped cream... and it's June, so peak berry season, strawberries on top, please?" The server scribbled their order down before fading into the kitchen, no doubt forming conclusions about the three of them that amused Hanna.

"While we wait," Milo said, leaning back in the booth and pointing to the book. "I need one of you to explain knotting to me."

Hanna choked on her coffee, delighting him. Chloe smacked him on the arm, but gave him a charming wink.

"I'll draw you a diagram later."

"YOU LOOK CUTE!" Sara said, tapping Hanna's shoulder as she brushed behind her in the kitchen. "New dress?"

"New to me," Hanna said. "I went thrifting with Milo and Chloe yesterday."

Sara reached for a banana swinging from the hook behind her.

"Y'all fucking or what?"

Hanna coughed, her cheeks heating. "*They* are. I'm just third wheeling." Hanna left out the part about Milo offering to include her in the fucking portion of things. Sara would have never let that go. Not that she'd been thinking about it every second of every day—and not that every time she saw him she was halfway out of her clothes already.

"You'd probably just have to ask, knowing Milo," Sara said

as she scrolled through her phone. "This Vegas group chat is a mess. Think you can get everyone organized?"

Hanna nodded, snagging a piece of the banana. "I will. Tell Matty to send me his wishlist for dinner plans. I know he's already got a list in his notes app."

"Perfect," Sara chimed, setting her phone down and tilting her head. "You look really good, Han."

"It's just a dress," Hanna said.

"I mean, in general. You can tell you're sleeping better."

"I feel more like me," Hanna said, her voice tightening. "I am getting a little nervous about seeing Logan."

"I was wondering when we'd get there. Have you guys talked at all?"

"No," Hanna sighed. Not for his lack of trying.

"We'll spend most of the weekend with the girls," Sara said. "He'll hardly be there."

"You're right." And she knew Sara was, but her face still heated, her muscles unconvinced.

THE WAY the shadows intertwined in the early summer swathes of light over the courtyard brushed against a memory, one she thought she'd locked far enough away that it couldn't find her in a new city.

She'd spent those early warm days the year prior listening to aunts and uncles argue over floral arrangements and Bible readings in the hospice courtyard, as if any of them had been the one to sign their name on the stack of hospice paperwork confirming that they were, indeed, giving up. As if any of it even mattered.

Every time she signed her name on a receipt, the space

between her thumb and forefinger ached—it felt like condemning her mother all over again.

Whatever it was that lurked in the shadows seeped into her skin, bleeding into her veins and souring the day.

"Arizona!"

She closed her laptop halfway, straightening in the patio chair as Milo approached, dressed for the office. He'd left early that morning, and she'd seen him dart from the lobby as she left the diner with her coffee and bagel.

"You got lunch plans?"

Hanna didn't have a grip around the next five minutes.

"You buying?" she asked, sliding her laptop into her bag.

"If you pretend to be really interested in enterprise-grade infosec software, I can expense it."

She walked a few blocks with him as he ran her through all of the summer specials he was planning with Frankie, waiting for her approval on each of them. She nodded and hummed as he spoke, her mind stuck on the phone charger she'd left in the small office center of the hospice home. It had been one of the really good cords, not the flimsy shit.

She'd never get another one like it.

The restaurant air chilled her shoulders as they wound through wobbling tables. Her eyes stayed fixed on the vinyl coating between them, still thinking about all the things the hospice home had taken from her.

"Thanks, man," Milo said, and Hanna's eyes snapped away from his hands. "There she is." He chuckled as he handed the menu back to the waiter. Hanna hadn't even noticed he'd arrived.

"What did I order?" she asked.

"Caesar, fries, and a Diet Coke."

"You're useful to have around on the weird days, I'll give

you that," she muttered, shaking her head as if she might be able to loosen the muck clinging to her mind.

"You ever read The Body Keeps the Score?" Milo asked, unfolding the linen napkin on the table and laying it over his work pants.

"I'm a thirty-year-old woman," Hanna laughed. "Of course I've read it, long before the mom shit."

Milo held his hands up in surrender. "The first year is hard, but the second year is grieving the loss of a person *and* the loss of the last year of your life."

The waiter dropped two Diet Cokes on the table with the promise to return shortly.

"I just want to be on the other side of it all," she said, sipping her drink. "Like you."

Milo closed his eyes and laughed. "You've only seen the good days."

Her lips sloped. "Don't tell me that."

"I think year five was the hardest for me."

"Five!"

"Ten was really weird, too. Something about another five years just slipping away..."

She sighed, leaning back against the chair and twisting the paper wrapper from her straw between her fingers.

"This conversation is depressing me."

Milo rolled his eyes. "Your dead mom is depressing you. I'm only calling attention to it."

Hanna sat up straight, her ears ringing like he'd just punched her.

Lisa passed away. She lost her battle. Or Hanna's least favorite, *the lord called her home.*

No one ever called Lisa what she was—*dead.*

Milo set his drink down. "Hanna—sorry, the direct thing—"

A sharp laugh cut through her chest, the kind that had

edges and teeth. Her head spun with such a sudden lightness, such a *relief.* She was still laughing when a salad and a plate of fries appeared.

"Everyone avoids that word," she finally said, his eyes wide with concern. "I love that you don't."

"You gotta fight fucked up with fucked up," he said, reaching across the table and snagging a fry. Hanna slapped at his hand.

"I haven't even had one yet!"

"Fine, fine," he muttered, pulling his hand back. "But next time hit harder so I've got something to fantasize about later."

Hanna scoffed, her cheeks turning pink, but Milo moved on, unfazed as ever.

"What are you doing tonight?"

"Hmm," Hanna picked up a fry and pointed it at him. "Why? Chloe busy?"

"We're going to a friend's show, if you want to come."

Hanna, unfortunately, *had* fallen into the trap that was Chloe. She was fun to be around, even if Hanna frequently had dreams that she *was* her.

"What kind of show?"

"Cover band. Mostly nineties grunge."

She'd seen Sara fussing with a seating chart diagram on her laptop that morning. If she *were* at home, she'd likely get roped into the logistics of how to keep Logan as far away from her as possible, and that wasn't nearly as appealing.

"Yeah," she said. "Okay."

"I'll come grab you at eight-ish? Wear my flannel, it's very Cobain."

Hanna giggled and pushed her plate of fries toward him, her veins still buzzing with the high of not having to talk around the pain in her chest.

CHLOE LOOPED her arm through Hanna's as they waited in line for the bathroom.

The bar was beyond a dive, but in a charming way, or perhaps it was Chloe's proximity that made it appear so. The smoke scent clinging to the walls was as old as she was. There were more people on the stage than watching the band cycle through their renditions of Seattle's best, but they were having fun, so that was enough.

"They're getting better," Chloe said, nodding her head back toward the end of the bar where Milo stood guard over their table and drinks.

Hanna slipped into a warm smile, aided by the third Jack and Diet she'd ordered, much to Milo's disappointment. "I like the nostalgia of it all."

"*I* like that I have someone to wait in line with now," Chloe said, squeezing Hanna's elbow.

"Are you sure?" she asked. "I always worry I'm ruining date night for you guys."

Chloe snorted. "Hardly. Milo and I are just friends."

"Yeah, he's, uh, explained it to me a few times."

"It's bullshit, to be frank," she muttered, stepping forward as the bathroom door swung open. "But there's no convincing him he's going to live a long and miserable life."

Hanna bit the inside of her cheek. "It's hard. Once there's a number on the table to outlive... the idea of making it longer than your parent did is horrifying."

Chloe squeezed Hanna's arm. "I hope you don't mind that Milo told me about your mom. He wasn't happy about the whole *Love Story* thing."

"Oh," Hanna said, holding the door as Chloe stepped in. "It's okay. You didn't know!"

Chloe motioned her forward. "Here, we can trauma bond while we pee." Hanna stepped into the bathroom, locking the door behind her. It was the most intimacy she'd shared with someone in a long time, and she couldn't help but mentally rally against the fact that it was with Chloe and not the guy waiting for them.

"Milo and I met in group therapy as teenagers," she said, peeling off her jeans. Hanna traced phone numbers scribbled on the walls. "My sister and I were in a car accident in high school. Bitch died on me." She stood and washed her hands while Hanna took her turn. "I've forgiven her now, but took a good ten years of hating her first."

"That's awful," Hanna sighed. She always hated hearing it, but selfishly, it helped to know she wasn't alone.

"We reconnected when I started working with him. It's the only reason he hangs out with me—I already know his bullshit." She moved out of the way to let Hanna wash her hands, watching her in the mirror. "We haven't hooked up since you got here."

Hanna looked up from the sink, her eyes connecting with Chloe's.

"Really?"

"Just some trivia for you," Chloe said, a smirk pulling at her lips.

"Sorry—"

"Oh, I'm not telling you because I care! I've got plenty of other situationships to take up my time. I just thought you'd want to know." Chloe reached forward and smoothed Milo's collar over her neck. "Cool shirt."

Hanna laughed. "You didn't get it for him, did you?"

"No," she sighed, bumping the door with her hip and holding it for Hanna. "The flannels are all his dad's."

Chloe skipped toward the bar in the way she skipped toward everything, leaving Hanna to sweat under Milo's stare as she crossed back to him. The band took to the stage again, diving into another set of late-nineties hits, this time with a twang.

Hanna's heart beat as each chord plucked at memories within her. Her mother's permed hair bouncing in the kitchen as she did dishes and belted every word to every song that graced the country hits station, nowhere near the right key. She swallowed as she tried to tell herself it was okay—that it wasn't going to kill her to feel something, that it would pass.

"You good, Arizona?" Milo watched as she struggled to keep her lip from wobbling.

"Fine," she said, ignoring his unimpressed frown. His hand pressed into the small of her back, the warmth giving her something else entirely to hold onto.

Something even worse than the memories of her mother—the memories she'd never make with Milo.

"YOU'RE STILL HAVING A HARD DAY," Milo said, the words slipping over her shoulders and poking at bruises as they stepped onto the elevator.

He hit floor four, and she shrugged, silently proving his observation true.

"You wanna come in for a bit? Talk about it?"

A heavy breath tumbled away from her. "It's late."

"I knew it," he said, crossing his arms, his leather jacket squeaking against its own friction. The elevator opened and they stepped off. "You turn into a pumpkin at midnight."

"Caught me," she said.

His keys jingled as he fished them from his pocket and stopped at his door.

"You could come in and... not talk about it."

"Milo—"

"I didn't mean that! Unless—ow! Okay!" Hanna backed away, the satisfying swat of his arm too much contact for the tenor of the air. "But if you aren't ready to be alone yet, I'm still up."

"It was the song."

She hadn't planned on confessing it. She hadn't actually consciously realized she had anything to confess. There was just something about him that drew the truth from her.

"Song?" Milo unlocked his door and held it open for her. She took her place on his couch, the same one she'd curled into the night before for movie night, but the room felt different somehow. He dropped a glass in her hand before she even gathered the words to form her thoughts.

"The country one. What's her face?"

"Deana Carter?"

"Yes." Hanna sank into the leather, trying not to think of how many women before her had been held by its warmth. "My mom loved that song."

Milo leaned forward and poured her a decent gulp of one of his experimental bottles, the label only boasting numbers this time.

"My mom also went through a Strawberry Wine renaissance." He glanced around his apartment, a twist on his lips that sparked something in her nerves.

"What are you doing?" Hanna groaned as he took her glass out of her hand and set it on the coffee table. "Milo!"

He pulled on her fingers, lifting her from the couch as he said over his shoulder, "Hey, Siri, play Strawberry Wine."

"Milo, what the hell?" She dropped his hand, a knot forming in her stomach.

"It's exposure therapy," he said, swiping her hand once more. "We're building a tolerance."

The speakers jumped to life with the song's first twangs, the melancholy lilt pushing down on her shoulders.

She shook her head, her hair brushing against her shirt, every nerve on her neck alert.

"This is literal torture!"

He pulled her closer, wrapping a hand around her back and spinning her, his socks slipping over the concrete floor.

"You can handle it."

Every muscle in her body resisted his sway, locked in an iron defiance, certain she could not, in fact, handle it. Her face flushed and her heart pumped with a white-hot rage.

Milo hummed the first verse while he pushed and pulled, rocking her back and forth, her head reluctantly lolling side to side with the motion. She swallowed, irritated that he'd managed to make something so painful seem even remotely approachable.

He twirled her slowly and she rolled her eyes but played along, her breath catching in her throat at the arrival of the chorus. When it broke, Milo sang loudly—and poorly, which only added to the charm—bringing her in close to him. It was the warmth of his chest that finally thawed her frigid heart, melting away the anger and pain that protected something so much more frightening to have exposed.

Love.

She loved the way her mom fucked up the lyrics, no matter how many times they listened to it. She loved the way she couldn't pick a key. She loved watching her spin and twist in their kitchen, singing into a wooden spoon.

She loved that she could still hear her voice echoing in her mind, off-key and out of time.

"Don't leave me singing all alone, Arizona," Milo said between verses. The bridge approached—a big note her mother never even got close to leaving both their lips. Hanna broke. A laugh bubbled out of her, her forehead leaning on his shoulder, and he tightened his grip on her.

"There it is," he murmured, spinning her out and back in again.

When he caught her, her laugh cut short. Exposure therapy to her memories of her mother was one thing—exposure to the way it felt to dance in a half-lit living room after a night out was another entirely.

Milo held her stare, frozen with her, his fingers weaving into the sleeves of his flannel slung over her hips.

Her stomach rolled in on itself, queasy at the heat in her chest.

How long had it been since she'd felt that little flicker of something? Anything?

"All good?" he whispered.

Hanna forced a half smile, searching for any semblance of a thought to latch onto.

"It's just always so wild how it sneaks up on you. I heard the first few words and knew it was coming, told myself it was okay to let it kick me in the teeth, and then it took so long to crush me I thought maybe I'd—I don't know."

Milo listened, stroking the dark stubble on his neck as they stood, still entangled.

"Well, let me ask you a question. When did you stop loving your mom?"

Hanna's mouth fell agape. Milo had a lot of nerve, but the notion that there was even an ounce less of love within her sent the heat in her chest straight to her shoulders, pulling back and away from his hold.

"What? I didn't!"

He held up a hand and circled his fingers as he drank, urging her to follow the thought.

"I never will," she whispered.

"Then why do you have it in your head that there's this distant future someday when it won't take you to your knees? They're two sides of the same coin—the price of love *is* grief, Arizona."

Hanna sighed. "Hate that," she said, throat closing around the other words she wanted to use. "So I'm just supposed to live the rest of my life between breakdowns?"

"You can minimize the potential for them. That's what I do," Milo said. She was sure he thought he was being aloof, but she saw through the veneer of it.

Hanna laughed—and not with him.

"Coward."

Milo stepped back, tilting his head. "Excuse me?"

Hanna leaned back on her hip, grounding herself as she folded her arms.

"You're such a coward. I'm a fucking disaster, but at least I haven't closed myself off to the possibility that one day I might not be. You waltz around here like you're so well adjusted... but of course you are. You'll never have anything new to hurt you," Hanna said, shrugging her shoulders in an attempt to dispel some of the strain building in her muscles. Milo flopped back into his chair and took a long sip of his drink.

"Goddamn, Hanna. I'm just over here trying to be a good little grief counselor—"

She flinched. "But I didn't ask you to be. In fact, I've pretty much asked for the exact opposite—"

"Okay. See, this is exactly why..." Milo trailed off and set his glass on the coffee table.

She swallowed. "Why what?"

"Nothing."

"I should go," she mumbled. She brushed by him, seeing red when his hand caught hers once more. "Milo—"

"I'm sorry you had a hard night." It was the sincerity that crushed her most. The unwavering devotion to forcing her into eye contact, into conversation, into feelings that had claws. "I'm sorry if I made it harder."

She sighed. "I'll see you tomorrow, okay?"

He squeezed her hand, releasing it.

She battled the voice in her head that wished he hadn't the entire way back to her bed.

TEN

"Say hi to Berto for me!" Hanna said as Sara flashed her phone toward her from across the living room.

"Hanna! No wonder she hasn't accepted our casino night invites!"

"Happy Father's Day, Berty!" Hanna called, realizing she hadn't fired off her obligatory text to her own father. She sent it into the universe and frowned.

She wondered what Milo did on Father's Day. Sara finished her conversation with her dad, and Hanna asked, "Do you need anything? I gotta run a few errands."

"I don't think so! We're heading to brunch over at Tom and Marcia's... I'm assuming you'd rather die than come?"

"Correct!" Hanna replied, though she did miss them.

"They miss you, too," Sara said, reading her mind.

Hanna stared at her phone, and then the wall, and then an idea formed.

She pulled on her shoes and snagged her bag and sunglasses, heading toward the flower shop she'd never made it back to. Her hand hesitated on the handle, unsure if they'd be open on the holiday, but surely men got flowers on Father's Day?

"Sunflower girl!" the shopkeeper chimed. Her hair was swept up into a messy knot, a pale blue linen apron wrapped around her this time. "You're a few weeks too late," she said, winking.

"I was hoping you'd be open today. I got distracted before." Hanna strolled around the shop, two sets of shelves along the window lined with bottles of wine, chocolates, and San Francisco mementos. She wasn't sure what she was looking for, but she hoped it would jump at her.

"Not a super popular day for florists," the woman said. "But those shelves will be cleared by the end of the night."

"What do you recommend for someone who definitely won't be seeing their dad today?"

The woman crossed her arms, ambling around her desk and scanning the shelves.

"Because they don't want to, or because they desperately wish they could?" she asked.

"The latter."

"Something strong," she whispered. She ran her fingers over the dark bottles facing the street, a gold band set with a square emerald glinting on her left hand.

"Beautiful ring," Hanna noted.

"Thank you. My husband thought diamonds were boring. Ah, here we go, sunflower for the sunflower girl." She pulled a tall green bottle from the middle shelf, a golden sunflower painted on the side. The label was in another language.

"Is this wine?" Hanna asked.

"Of the gods," the woman said. "Ouzo. Greek liquor."

Hanna snorted. Every time she walked into that shop, the universe rewarded her.

"It's perfect."

"I'll wrap it up. You need anything else while you're here? Some sunshine?"

Hanna smiled. "I'll take whatever you've got." She'd need it today. She hadn't talked to Milo since their little row a few nights prior, and the regret had firmly set in.

She'd taken her pain out on him—pushed him away for the sin of seeing too clearly. It hadn't been fair.

The woman disappeared into the back of the shop and returned with a small bouquet of sunflowers and pale pink roses wrapped in lavender paper.

"You're in luck. It's buy a bottle, get a bouquet day."

Hanna laughed as she rang her up. She took the bottle and the flowers, wishing the florist well as she headed back to the lofts.

She hesitated outside of Milo's apartment, unsure if he'd want the intrusion. She left the bottle and flowers at the door, nearly making it back into the apartment before she heard him.

"Hanna?"

"Sorry," she mumbled. "I didn't want to bother you today, but I left you a little something." She pointed to the bottle at his feet. It looked much smaller in his hands than hers as he scooped up the bouquet. "The Greeks don't make whiskey, but the girl at the shop said this was a good option."

Milo looked at the label, then at her, a slight smile cracking across his face.

"Thanks."

"Anyway," she said. "If you need anything—"

"You wanna come in?"

Hanna looked back at her door. "Uh, sure? I don't want to intrude."

"And I don't want to drink alone," he said, wiggling the bottle in his hands.

"Okay," she relented. "Sure."

She slipped through his door, following him into the kitchen as he dug out two shot glasses from his bar cart. He popped the cork out of the bottle and poured two shots, setting the bottle to face her.

"Do you speak Greek, Hanna?"

"Not a lick," she laughed. His lips twisted into a half smile. "Do you?"

"Enough," he said.

"Does your mom?"

"No, Mom is a Cali girl through and through. Third generation in the Bay."

Milo fussed with the bottle, his eyes avoiding hers.

"How did they meet? Your parents?"

Milo snorted, the ghost of a good story crawling over him.

"Traffic school." He grabbed two glasses from his kitchen and filled them with water. "Mom taught it, Dad frequented it. He used to say every ticket after the first one was just so he could see her again."

"Expensive way to flirt."

Milo nodded. "No brunch with the DeBrunes today?"

Hanna laughed. "Absolutely not. No plans with your mom?"

"We'll have dinner with my grandpa and all the nieces and nephews."

She leaned against the counter, spinning the cork between her fingers.

"You have a big family?"

Milo closed his eyes, counting. "Seven grandkids just between my brothers. Can't even count the cousins."

"Aw," she said, running her finger over the edge of the shot glass. "Uncle Milo."

"Mi-wo to most of them. Alright. You ever had the nectar of the gods before?"

She shook her head.

"Close your eyes."

Hanna glared. "Why?"

"Ouzo is meant to be sipped slowly on a patio over the Mediterranean. Not in my shitty bachelor pad. We'll have to do some visualization. Close 'em."

Hanna squeezed her eyes shut, feeling vulnerable in front of him in a way she didn't completely dislike.

Milo spoke softly, in a sing-songy tone. "You're on your third course of feta-stuffed olives, the tzatziki is flowing, the sun is setting over the cliffs. A gorgeous Greek god is sitting across from you, feeding you grapes. His name is Milo," he whispered.

"You're ridiculous."

"Concentrate." He moved closer, the heat buzzing against her chest. "You there in your head?"

"Yes, Milo," she sighed.

"Great, take a sip."

Hanna lifted the shot glass to her lips, letting it roll over them slowly. The flavor was intense, herbal—incredibly complex. She opened her eyes as he shot his back, clearly more accustomed to the flavor profile.

"What do you think?"

"It's interesting," she said, taking a second sip. "Not at all what I expected."

"The gods will sneak up on you like that," he said, just inches from her.

Since meeting him, he'd teased her relentlessly—the suggestive comments, the long stares. In one month, she'd blushed more on account of him than she had over every other man she'd ever met combined. But the way he looked at her then— like she wasn't some project to work on, or a fawn left in the woods—did her in.

She could feel it in the way his fingers twitched against the countertop. Something had shifted. She wondered if he'd taste like ouzo, complex and bitter, but only for a moment before he'd warm her head to toe.

"I think it's time, Arizona," he whispered.

"What?" Her heart beat faster.

Milo's grin widened, and she worried he could hear it.

"It's time to destroy you," he said, tilting his head to the living room. "We're doing it. We're watching *A Walk to Remember*."

Hanna wanted to fight him, but she saw it, swimming in the mossy green of his eyes. He was well-therapized. He was as healed as he could be. But he was not invincible.

"Yeah," she said quietly. "Whatever you need."

Milo moved to his living room, leaving her breathless as he dropped to his knees in front of his bookshelf.

"Ah, ha," he exclaimed as he pulled a pink DVD case from the fray.

"Who in the hell still has a DVD player?" Hanna groaned.

"There's popcorn in the pantry," Milo mumbled.

"It's ten in the morning."

"And?" he asked.

Hanna shrugged. He had a point. She fished through his pantry—surprisingly well stocked for a man she'd only observed eating takeout or Sara's cooking—and tossed a bag of popcorn into the microwave. Two glasses clinked together in the living room as he mixed the ouzo with something bright yellow.

"Again, it's ten AM," Hanna called.

"Grab me some ice, will ya?"

She finished off her glass of water, largely in preparation for the cocktail she was about to imbibe, and filled the glass with ice as the microwave pop, pop, popped behind her. When it sounded its alarm, she dumped the contents into a bowl she found in his cabinet and set it on the coffee table.

"I didn't realize you did cocktails, too," she said.

"I own a whole-ass bar, Hanna."

"Fair." She giggled and crossed back toward him, but the laugh broke into something else. "Milo," she said, a lump bubbling in her throat as he set their drinks down and slipped the DVD into the tray.

"Yeah, Arizona," he returned, not taking his eyes off the DVD menu.

"I don't want to cry in front of you on Father's Day."

Milo stopped flipping through buttons and settings and turned to her. He dropped the remote to his side and tilted his head.

"Even as a gift to me? I'm *very* sad today."

"You're depraved!"

She flopped onto the couch and pulled at one of the fleece blankets he kept along the back. Milo leaned forward, forcing her to hold his gaze.

"You said whatever I need."

"And you need me to be a fucking baby?"

He grinned. "I *need* you to start processing all of your bull-shit, so that I can eventually fuck you senseless without worrying about breaking your heart, Hanna. Is that what you want to hear?"

She reared her head back, swallowing the outrage in her throat.

"I warned you," he said. "Direct."

Something about his demeanor brought a more direct question to her lips.

"Is that the only thing that's stopping you?"

"Yep," he said, turning back toward the TV to start the movie. "Would have made a move on you in Phoenix if I hadn't caught you hyperventilating three times in a six-hour period—"

"Fuck you!"

"Hanna, I am *trying*," he groaned, turning to her and looking her dead in the eyes as a very early two-thousands bassline blared from the speakers. "One good big-girl cry, and I'm all yours."

"You're insane."

"I'm regulated," he scoffed. "You're one tough talk away from shaving your head."

"Jesus, Milo!"

"Shh, you're going to miss the inciting incident. Very important context."

Hanna's lips parted. She had about a thousand other things she wanted to say, but the way he plopped onto the couch beside her and yanked half the blanket over his lap silenced her.

"What am I drinking?" she asked, the bright summery drink washing away the horror of her twisted nerves.

"I just threw some shit together."

Hanna arched a brow.

"I never said I was a *good* bartender. Now pay attention. This movie is sad as fuck, but the soundtrack is easily in the top ten early aughts rom-com soundtracks. Maybe top five."

Hanna tucked her feet beneath her as the movie rolled along, the angst a constant reminder of the conversation Milo had just so easily abandoned a moment earlier.

She tilted her head when things started to get interesting.

"God, Shane West was really something, huh?"

"Why am I not surprised you're into sad, brooding bad boys?" Milo teased.

"Don't flatter yourself." She set her glass on the coffee table and readjusted the blanket. "You're not even that good at brooding. Fire one of your therapists, and then maybe we can talk."

"I was talking about *you*," he said. "But noted."

"I don't brood!" she protested.

"You are actively brooding all over my couch."

"I'll leave," she threatened.

"Shh! You're going to miss a really good part. Real tear-jerker. Ugly-cry territory."

Hanna sank down beneath the blanket, mumbling without looking at him, "Watched pot."

He only chuckled, finally peeling his eyes off her. He checked back in every few minutes, the disappointment that she hadn't fallen apart visible as the movie progressed. It wasn't until they made it well past the twist, the arguing, and the admittedly hot kissing despite how chaste it all was that he looked over and frowned.

"Nothing?"

Hanna swallowed. "Nothing."

"She *died*!"

"People die all the time, Milo!" They both winced. "I told you. I'm *fine*."

"You are so far from fine it's diagnosable," Milo muttered, grabbing the empty popcorn bowl and glasses and taking them to the kitchen. She followed, setting her phone on the counter. "The star? The state line? The ring still on his finger at the end? Are you made of *stone*, woman?"

Hanna laughed, but her eyes didn't quite catch the light.

"I can't, okay?"

"Hanna—"

"Just, drop it, Milo." Her phone buzzed against the counter. DO NOT ANSWER. Milo glanced at the screen and raised his brows. She sighed. As if she needed to add another grief to the plate. Milo stood in her path, dropping those green eyes to hers.

"No one is this ironclad. If you let it go now, it won't sneak up on you later."

She held his gaze, ignoring the second call coming in.

"What if I start and never stop?" she asked, her voice wobbling. "I feel like I'll drown."

Milo nodded, moving closer to her, taking up space she hadn't filled in a year. She twisted her fingers into the hem of her shirt, trying to think of a clever way to escape him, but the burn at the back of her throat was relentless.

"Don't they teach you how to swim out there in the desert, Arizona?"

Her phone buzzed a third time, both their eyes landing on the screen. She ignored it, his hand hovering close to her hip. There, in the space between his fingers and her jeans, a truth lingered she hadn't seen before. He didn't just want to sleep with her. He might have told himself that, but he was genuinely *concerned* about her, and that was exponentially worse. Milo leaned into her, the amber of his cologne swirling around her head. It was hypnotizing.

He smelled like coming home after a late night at work, all the lights off except for one warm bulb over the stove, the one that never burns out. Her phone vibrated again.

"You gonna get that?" he asked, just an inch from her.

"No," Hanna whispered.

"Fucking *messy*," Milo mumbled, shaking his head as he closed the distance between them. He moved slowly, likely so as not to scare her off, but she knew the moment his lips hovered an inch from hers, they'd made a very bad, very stupid choice.

But *goddamn* did the static in the space between their skin feel good.

"Hanna!"

The anger in Matty's voice ripped them apart as he pounded on Milo's door, shaking it in its frame.

"Are you in there?"

Milo nudged her to the side, her cheeks pink, and opened the door. Matty flew into the kitchen, his face much redder than either of theirs.

"You!" He pointed at Hanna, Sara trailed behind, begging him to calm down.

"Me?" Hanna asked, confused.

Matty ran a hand through his hair, taking a deep breath.

"Does my brother know you're here?"

"I have no idea!" Hanna said.

Her phone buzzed against the counter again, and Matty snatched it.

"Who the hell is DO NOT ANSWER?"

Hanna frowned.

"Hanna!" Matty hissed.

She grabbed the phone from his hand. "You don't get to have an opinion on how I cope with your brother, okay?"

Milo stood behind Hanna, the contact sending another blush over her cheeks.

"What's the problem, man?"

"She never told Logan she moved!"

"I didn't *move*, I just temporarily relo—"

"Whatever you want to call it," Matty cut her off. "You didn't tell him, and guess who decided to surprise our parents for Father's Day and a week of job interviews in the city?"

"Shit," Milo said under his breath.

"He's driving down here *now* to stay with us and I was too much of a little bitch to tell him that my guest room is occupied by his ex-girlfriend!"

"Matty!" Hanna gasped.

Matty sighed. "You have to fix this."

"It's not Hanna's fault that Logan didn't think to ask first," Sara said, patting Matty's shoulder.

"I know," he groaned. "I know. I just *hate* how messy all of this is."

"Can't he stay with your parents?" Hanna asked.

"It's a two-hour drive into the city. He has interviews lined up all week."

Hanna chewed on her lip. "Why is he interviewing?"

Sara leaned toward her. "He, uh, quit his job."

"What?" Hanna and Milo said at the same time.

Sara waved her hands. "I didn't get the details."

Hanna's phone buzzed again in her hand. "Why is he blowing up my phone?"

"I don't know, but what a *perfect* opportunity to tell him you're here!" Matty quipped.

"Ahhh, fuck," Hanna grumbled. She stepped out of the kitchen and into the living room, answering the first call from Logan in over a year. "Hey?"

"Oh, Hanna, hey! Sorry, I'm used to getting your voicemail."

She laughed awkwardly.

"Listen, I'm glad I caught you. I'm in San Francisco for the week, and I've been thinking a lot about how we left things in Phoenix and the Vegas trip coming up. I really just wish we could clear the air."

"Okay," Hanna said, pinching the bridge of her nose.

"I don't want the entire bachelor party weekend to be us fighting. I was just thinking it could be fun if you came out for a few days and we... I don't know... broke the ice a little."

Hanna paced across Milo's living room, the traffic from the street below bubbling up and adding to her anxiety.

"Um. Well. Maybe?"

Logan's voice pitched up. "Really?"

"Yeah, I mean, I guess that's not the worst idea." She grimaced. It might have been the second-worst idea she'd had that day. She wasn't sure where it fell, her belt loops still warm with the whisper of Milo's touch.

"I can talk to Matty and Sara, I'm sure they're cool if I crash on their couch and you take the guest room."

"I... don't know about that, Logan."

"I'll be on my best behavior," he said, the tone of his voice a familiar velvet. "I'll give 'em a call, but look at flights."

"Uhhh yeah. Okay. I will. Bye!"

Hanna hung up before he could say anything else, turning back toward her audience as they all waited.

"He... wants me to come out to San Francisco for a few days so we can hash things out before Vegas."

Sara's brows arched, the red returning to Matty's face.

"He said he'll talk to you two tonight about me staying in the guest room."

Sara snorted. "Logan's really making a lot of assumptions, *Matthew*."

Hanna whispered, "He wants me to look at flights."

The air in the apartment tightened as eyes bounced back and forth. Matty groaned.

"And you just... didn't feel the need to mention you were already here?"

"I panicked!" Hanna said, throwing her hands up. "I don't know. I can't stay with him, Sara. You *know* that's a disaster waiting to happen. Can't he stay here?" Hanna pointed up Milo's stairs.

"Uh," Milo said. "Well, he could—"

"He won't," Matty said. A brief glance passed between them, clearly revisiting an old wound Hanna didn't understand.

"Then he can get a hotel!" Hanna cried. "He makes big boy Wall Street money!"

"Well, he *did*," Sara said.

"Okay," Hanna sighed. "You know what? It'll be fi—"

"You stay with me," Milo cut her off.

They all turned toward him, Hanna's chest tightening.

"Me?"

"Yeah, why not? We have fun together. You seem clean enough. Be my roomie, Arizona." Milo flashed a wicked grin, sending a bead of sweat rolling down her neck. She hadn't even processed the fact that moments ago their mouths had been nearly tangled up in one another, and now she was going to be his roommate?

Bad, stupid, dumb fucking decisions.

"That would actually work really well," Sara said.

A flush crawled Hanna's spine. She knew *why* he offered, and it certainly wasn't out of the goodness of his own heart.

"It would save us all a lot of Logan drama," Matty sighed.

"God, okay. Fine. Fine!" Hanna said, throwing her hands up.

"One more fine and I'll buy it," Milo said quietly, smirking.

"Alright, we've got, like, twenty minutes to get all your shit moved," Matty muttered, pulling Sara out of the apartment.

"You're a problem," Hanna hissed at him.

Milo grinned. "I'm merely benefiting from the universe's cruel sense of humor."

"Milo—"

"Can't this just be fun, Hanna? Don't you deserve that?"

She huffed. Maybe she did.

"Fine, I gotta go pack."

"Make sure you bring those green yoga pants you had on the other day," Milo said, laughing and smoothing his hair back.

"You're a *problem*," she said again as he followed her across the hall.

"You like it."

And that was, without a doubt, the biggest problem on her rapidly growing list.

ELEVEN

It was easier, they decided by committee, to spring Hanna on Logan at an early dinner.

In public.

DO NOT ANSWER

Did you block me on Instagram?

Hanna twisted her lips as Milo stole a handful of her fries. She'd forgotten she'd blocked him. He clearly hadn't checked recently.

She typed out a response in the interest of not arguing before he even arrived.

HANNA

Sorry.

DO NOT ANSWER

For blocking me or for this being the first text you've responded to in a year?

HANNA

Can you blame me???

DO NOT ANSWER

No, and I've been trying to tell you that. But you're too stubborn to even let me apologize.

"Yikes," Milo mumbled. She flipped her phone over and glared at him. "Sorry."

She whispered, "This is going to go so badly."

"I got it," Milo said. "Gimme." He held his hand out for her phone. Milo swiped across her screen for a moment and tapped on the keyboard. "There. He's blocked until he gets here. And now you have a new number to text."

She unlocked her screen, tapping on her most recent thread with a number saved as ALWAYS ANSWER.

HANNA

Thanks, Daddy.

"You're fucking gross," Hanna groaned.

"But you're laughing." He pointed at her with one of her fries. She hated herself for smiling. "A win is a win."

Her phone buzzed again.

ALWAYS ANSWER

Look up.

Hanna glanced from her phone to Milo's face.

ALWAYS ANSWER

Good girl.

Her face heated, annoyed that he had any effect on her, but especially that one. Milo laughed, draining his beer. He'd teased her a dozen times like that, but she was always ready for it. She'd gotten too comfortable.

She smirked as she tapped back a message.

HANNA

Want a titty pic?

Milo glanced at Sara and Matty, wrapped up in their own meals and discussing the details of Logan's impending residency in their home.

ALWAYS ANSWER

Do you need me to beg for it?

I will.

HANNA

As hot as you probably look on your knees, the first one's free.

Milo watched her hands intently as she swiped through her photos, searching for the one she had in mind. She fired it off, and watched his eyes as he opened the message, taking in every glorious inch of Matty's shirtless body from their most recent beach trip.

Milo squeezed his eyes shut, laughing quietly as he pressed his hand to his chest, clutching his non-existent pearls.

"Ice cold."

Sara's head snapped toward them. "What did she do?"

"You'd never believe me," Milo said, setting his phone face down on the table.

"Hey, weren't you supposed to go to your mom's for dinner?" Hanna asked, the chaos of the day settling.

Milo shrugged, about to say something, when Sara interrupted them.

"Look who's here!" Sara giggled nervously, nudging Hanna in the side as a tall, lanky blonde weaved his way through the crowded restaurant. He saw Matty first, but his eyes quickly scanned the table and landed on Hanna, looking as if someone had thrown a cold bucket of water on his head.

"What the fuck?" he said before he even sat down.

"Would you believe how quick the flight is from Phoenix?" she asked, clenching her jaw.

"What are you doing here?"

Hanna chewed on her lip. "You invited me!"

Logan's eyes narrowed. "Hanna."

"I got you your favorite beer!" she chirped, sliding the IPA across the table to him. Logan glared at Matty, but she quickly jumped in to defend him. "Don't be mad at him! I froze up earlier when you called. I've actually been out here since May—"

"May!"

"Yes. I... needed a change of scenery. But, I'm out of Matty and Sara's for the week, so we can both have our space!"

"Where are you—"

"She's staying with me," Milo said, not making eye contact with Logan.

"When did you even move back into the city?" Logan asked.

"Few weeks before Hanna." Milo reached for her Diet Coke and took a sip, holding up his hand as the waiter swept by. "Can we get another round, boss?"

"Guess I'm way out of the loop," Logan said, his eyes fixed on Hanna's hands as she twisted them around one another.

"Let's just enjoy dinner and then get back home, and you two can loop one another into oblivion, okay?" Sara said, pointing between Logan and Hanna.

He huffed a sigh, but they both nodded.

What Sara didn't know was that Hanna had a foot regularly tapping against hers under the table, completely distracting her from the pout forming on Logan's lips.

"WE'LL BE UP IN A MINUTE," Hanna said to Sara, releasing her hand as they stopped in the apartment lobby.

Milo tapped her hip and slipped behind her. "See ya, roomie."

Hanna waited for them to disappear before she turned to Logan, the nerves in her stomach tightening at a myriad of things. Sharing an apartment with Milo, being alone with Logan—it was all too much.

In the Uber home, she realized that she was actually *enjoying* herself in the city, and she wasn't about to let Logan mess that up for her.

"I don't want to fight with you," Hanna said, folding her arms and leaning against the wall in the apartment lobby. "I'm tired of being angry with you."

"I'm tired of you being angry with me, too," Logan joked. He added as her eyes flared, "Not that you don't have valid reasons."

"Sara mentioned something about your job?" She bit back the urge to ask about Sloane.

"Yeah," he said, rubbing the back of his neck. "I, uh, I wasn't doing well in New York."

"I'm sorry."

Logan chewed on the edge of his thumb. "I think it was too much change. You, Lisa..."

Hanna flinched.

"I just have some shit to figure out."

She drew in a slow breath, trying to calm the storm in her chest at just hearing him say her name.

"It was really fucked up hearing about it from Matthew," Logan whispered. She wrapped her arms around her chest, the cold shiver running over her spine stinging as it settled between her ribs. "I know I hurt you, Hanna, but that was cruel—"

"I didn't do it to hurt you," she said, her voice hollow.

"But you *did* hurt me, so where does that leave us?"

"It leaves us nowhere," she said. "Can't we just move on?" She knew even as it left her lips that it simply wasn't possible, but what if just that one time the universe granted her the ability to cast spells?

"That's not how it works. You can't just sweep all of that under the rug and hope it doesn't come back."

She bit her lip. "I don't know what you want from me."

"You're so fucking stubborn, Hanna, you know that?" Logan pushed off from the wall, heading for the elevator. "I can't even talk to you when you're like this."

"Then don't," Hanna said, throwing her hands up and pressing the call button. The door slid open and she stepped on, annoyed that they had to ride up three floors of painful silence.

He didn't want to smooth things over. He wanted to punish her for doing what she had to do to survive. Logan would never understand the agony she went through, completely alone, and it wasn't on her to explain. She tapped her foot, lightning building in her muscles as she bit back the worst kind of tears—angry ones—and she gripped the edge of her shirt. As soon as the door opened, she stomped off, leaving Logan to find his own way to Matty and Sara's.

Milo was waiting at the kitchen counter when she got to his apartment, and he watched her chest heave with a rage she'd never given space to.

Hanna dumped her shoes and bag at the door, the strap tangling in her hair and yanking on the strands.

"Fuck," she hissed, her skin on fire. She fussed with it for another second, only pulling the knot in her stomach into a tighter mess.

"Hanna," Milo murmured, grabbing her purse strap and gently untangling it from her hair. She pushed him away, shaking her hands to dispel the pain building in her veins.

"Sorry," she muttered, smoothing her hair and shirt.

"Don't apologize." Milo hung the bag on the hook beside the front door. "You okay?"

"No," she laughed. She was not okay, he knew she wasn't, everyone knew she wasn't. Logan's face burned in her mind, the pain written between the lines as he levied his grievances. The worst part about what he said was he was *right*. It had been cruel of her. She'd had every opportunity to tell him what was going on, and she'd been too angry, too *scared* to call him.

She'd wanted him to hurt the way she did, and she knew it, which was bad enough. But the fact that *he* knew it?

Devastating.

"Arizona?"

Hanna's eyes flickered to Milo's, still too green even in the dim kitchen lighting. He was standing exactly where she'd been mentally all night, in the space between a good decision and a bad one. A decade earlier, she might not have even realized how stupid it was, but wisdom had no bearing on her decision in the end.

She pushed herself forward, desperate to feel anything that wasn't her own self-loathing for just a minute. Milo caught her, his arms flexing around her waist as she crashed into him.

"Hanna—"

"I don't want to talk about it," she rasped, her hands winding into the hem of his shirt, searching for skin. "I want a distraction."

"Distraction?" he asked, his fingers tangling into her hair before she could even answer.

"You offered," she whispered, her voice tight with the guilt and shame she'd been burying for too long.

"I'm not protesting, just making sure we're clear on what this is and isn't," he said. His hand moved to her neck as he pushed her toward the kitchen. "For both our sakes," he added.

Her back touched the cold granite countertop, sending her arching into his hands. She drew in a shaky breath, wrestling with herself.

"You sure you can handle it?" Milo asked.

She laughed, leaning further into his hold, slipping under the current of him.

"Of course I'm not."

"Then we definitely shouldn't do this," he said. He ran his hand through her hair, bringing it back to cup her face and stroke her jaw with his thumb. His breath against her neck made it hard to form words. "Right?"

Hanna's eyes squeezed shut. She sucked a sharp breath in through her teeth. She'd already made the bad choice in her mind a million times.

Could it really be that much more harmful if he already occupied so much of her mind?

"Time box," she blurted, her heart jumping from her chest as his hips hit hers. "While I'm here, it's all on the table."

"All?" Milo asked, his dark brows knitting together.

"Okay, not *all*, but like, a lot," Hanna stipulated, his fingers tightening in her hair and sending a shock from her neck to her stomach. *Why are we still talking?* "But once I move back across the hall, we're done. Just friends."

Milo considered that. "Time box," he repeated. "I can do that."

He pressed further into her, sending her mind into space. For the first time in a year, she wasn't *thinking*, she was just *doing.* Milo's hand came to her hip, pushing at the hem of her shirt and crawling the soft skin beneath.

"Dirty talk?" he asked.

"Hmm?"

Milo nipped at the edge of her jaw. "Do you like dirty talk? Or are you into more of the slow, sensual, love-making shit? I like it both ways, just trying to gauge what you need right now." He ghosted a hand over her collarbones, pulling at the fabric of her top and slipping it over her head. His eyes dropped, darkening as he took her in.

Hanna pulled at his shirt, desperate to even the score. He was so warm beneath her touch—so responsive as she grazed his chest. Every touch was met with a low hum, like touching those lightning lamps at museums. Every brush zapped her fingertips and made her hair stand on end.

"I don't know what I need," she confessed, his lips dragging down her neck and to her shoulder.

It was stupid. So, so stupid. The anticipatory regret bubbled beside the lust in her stomach, blending into a sick need for him she resented.

"How about I push some buttons and you tell me what works?"

"Okay," she whispered. He snagged the final sound off her lips, parting them with his tongue, and whether or not it was stupid no longer mattered.

Nothing did.

Hanna let him in, thrilled to discover that the fantasies she'd had about his kissing abilities weren't even close to how attentive he actually was. It made sense, a man didn't look like Milo, talk like Milo, *smell* like Milo, and not kiss like a fucking professional. She'd gotten a preview, but his matinee performance didn't compare.

Milo was a slow plume of smoke blanketing every inch of

her as he burned away any thoughts of how risky it was. He melted into her, pulling and pushing and biting at all the right turns, destroying her in the most incredible ways.

"Fuck," she gasped in the brief break she got from his kiss, his lips curling around the encouragement.

"We'll get there, Arizona," Milo pressed into her skin, his fingers slipping under the clasp of her bra. She ran her hands over his back, enjoying the pleased sigh from his throat. The hooks popped free and he pulled the straps down, leaving her topless in his kitchen.

"Wow," he muttered, staring at her. Hanna leaned back, admiring the full range of his tattoos, taking up nearly his entire torso. She ran her fingers over swirled black ink, tracing the shapes of whiskey bottles and years and geometric patterns. One day, she'd take a more thorough look at them, but not then.

She needed *much* less space between them.

Hanna pulled him toward her, clashing their mouths together once again, his slow pursuit of her no longer the case. Milo moved quickly, hungrily against her as he gripped her breasts, pinching and pulling in time with his tongue. She rolled into the motion he set, her hips grinding against his as a hand pulled at the button of her jeans.

Losing her patience, she swatted his hand away and peeled them off herself. She tossed them on the kitchen floor and followed him to the living room, where he pulled her down to the couch, over his lap.

Hanna sank over him, hissing as she felt how badly he wanted her.

Milo grabbed both sides of her face, sucking her bottom lip between his teeth and biting gently, just enough to elicit a gasp from her as he bucked his hips into hers. She wished she'd pulled those damn shorts off before they crashed into the couch.

He dragged her hand up and placed it around his throat, squeezing her fingers around his stubbled flesh as he refocused his lips on hers. Her vision blurred at the edges when a low moan vibrated against her hand.

"Milo," she breathed, leaning back and sucking in any air she could. Two fingers dipped below the lace of her underwear, pulling at the waistband and searching for where she needed him most.

"How many times has this already happened in your head, Hanna?" he asked.

She wanted to lie—to tell him never, but the arch in her back as he found her center gave her away. He turned his lips loose on her breasts, everything wet and pinched and squeezed in a blur of praise and worship for her.

"Too many," she finally answered, moving her hips faster against him, the hard length beneath her twitching in response.

Milo pulled her hand up between them.

"Do you fuck these fingers and think of me?" he asked, his eyes half closed.

Hanna would have blushed if her entire body wasn't already cherry red, her lips parting and another gasp escaping as he ground into her. She nodded.

"Say it," Milo insisted.

"Yes," Hanna rasped, leaning into him. She drove herself down onto him, cursing those fucking basketball shorts as she circled her hips faster. Her knees slipped against the slick fabric.

"Hanna," Milo warned her. "Don't ruin the fun yet."

"Aw," she breathed. "What? You've also thought about this too many times?"

"I'm serious," he groaned, his hands pushing at her hips. Hanna didn't care. She didn't need him inside of her. She needed him to be at her mercy. She doubled her pace, the pressure sending wave after wave of blinding pleasure over her.

She pitched forward, running her tongue over the black ink at the base of his neck, higher, higher until she found the ridge of his ear, tucking it between her teeth. She wasn't as gentle as he'd been, and he only rewarded her for it with a muted whimper, his hands holding onto her hips for dear life.

"Hanna," Milo gasped. "I'm gonna—"

"Yes, you are," she whispered, releasing his earlobe. She could have gone with him, so drunk on the power of making someone like him finish before her clothes were even fully off. She squeezed his throat again, snagging his lips in a desperate kiss as he groaned against her. His head fell back against the couch, throat taut beneath her hold as he choked on her name.

A low laugh followed, a fire burning in his gaze that she hadn't had the pleasure of seeing before. Milo pushed her onto her back, falling over her. His hand pulled at her underwear, whipping them off and tossing them across the room.

"I'm going to make you pay for that," he said, finding her eyes as he kneaded the curves of her breasts.

"Promise?" Hanna asked. She tangled her hand in his dark hair and tugged lightly while he slipped from her neck to her stomach, carving a brazen trail into her skin.

"Unbelievable," Milo mumbled against her as he landed on her hips, biting at her hot skin, mottled with pink marks from his fingers. His hands wandered and he moved between her legs. She tensed against him, her knees clasping around his shoulders as he found a pace that blinded her.

For a moment, she forgot that their best friends—and her ex —were only feet across the hall. She quieted herself, resisting the urge to scream his name, his own moans against her thighs pushing her close to the edge. Her back tightened, the muscles squeezing against the pressure of his work.

If she'd been angry with anyone, she had no memory of it as the world crumbled into tomorrow's problems.

Her mind floated, any lingering thoughts eddying away with every movement of his mouth. Hanna's fingers dug into his scalp and she fell over the edge, her face flushing.

"Whoa," she managed, drawing another laugh from him as she propped herself up on her elbows.

"Yeah?" Milo asked. He grinned, wiping his hand over his mouth.

"Yeah," she sighed. Her chest heaved. She sat up as he pulled her into a softer kiss, so different from a moment ago.

"Sufficiently distracted?" he asked, running his hand behind her head.

"What?" she asked, her hands slipping over his basketball shorts, the wet fabric tightening something in her belly again.

He laughed. "I'll take that as a yes," Milo said.

"I wanted it to just be fine," Hanna groaned, covering her face. "That would have been easier."

"Please," Milo scoffed. He stood and grabbed her clothes, tossing them onto the couch. "You knew it was going to be so much better than that."

"I feared."

Milo dropped his eyes to hers and rested his hands on her knees.

"Me too, Hanna. But we'll be okay. Time box."

"Time box," she reaffirmed.

She rolled her eyes the moment she was up the stairs in his guest room, alone to grapple with the knowledge that there was no boundary strong enough to contain what she'd just had with him.

Idiots.

TWELVE

"You seem... chipper?" Olivia asked, her suspicion hardly an undercurrent as she leaned toward her computer.

Hanna adjusted the volume on the laptop, leaning closer so her therapist could note the exact runtime of her eyeroll.

"I'm having a nice time," Hanna said.

"That's great to hear." She tapped her pen on the edge of her lips. "Are you getting outside?"

"Yeah," she said, shrugging. "It's nice to be in such a walkable city."

"And there's nothing else contributing to the fact that you're grinning like a kid on Christmas?"

Hanna tried to ignore the sound of the coffee maker gurgling to life downstairs.

"I don't know. Maybe the humidity agrees with me."

Olivia nodded, her silence a condemnation all on its own.

Even she knew Hanna was an idiot.

"I think that's our time," Hanna said, stealing her line. She said her goodbyes and closed the laptop. The smell of coffee wafted up the stairs, and even though she'd slept decently for the first time in months, she craved the caffeine. She went to find a bra, but thought better of it as she pulled Milo's flannel over her bare skin, finding the shortest shorts she'd brought in her suitcase.

If they were going to abide by the time box, she needed to make the most of it.

She'd had coffee with Milo many, many times in her weeks in the city, but she'd never seen him fresh out of bed.

He was a morning person, dressed and ready for the day as she scrolled through no fewer than ten texts from Logan, each more desperate to apologize than the last.

Milo sat on the couch, reading emails on his laptop. A pair of thick black glasses rested on his nose.

"Morning, Clark," she said, passing through the living room. He chuckled.

"Coffee's in the kitchen," he said.

She rounded the counter, touching the petals on the sunflowers she'd brought him the day before. There was already a mug for her next to the coffee maker.

"What's on the schedule today?" she asked, sitting across from him in the worn leather chair Matty usually claimed.

He glanced at his screen. "Meetings most of the day. Sara mentioned something about pickleball, but I wasn't sure if you wanted to see Logan after last night..."

"Not particularly," Hanna mused. "I have back-to-back calls until lunchtime. I can run and grab us something if you're slammed?"

Milo smiled. "Can we *please* go back to that sandwich shop that did you dirty last week for redemption? I promise they don't usually fuck up."

Hanna rolled her eyes. "If there are pickles on mine again, I'm eating yours."

"Deal," he said, typing fervently.

"I'll have to talk to Logan at some point today," she said, pulling at a loose tendril from her bun. "And then... I guess I'm just waiting for you to let me suck your dick."

Milo coughed, pushing his laptop away from him.

"I can be direct, too," Hanna said.

Milo checked the time on his phone. "I've got twenty minutes."

Before he finished the sentence, she dropped to her knees, his legs spreading as she ran her hands over his thighs.

"Nope," he said, pulling her chin up to face him. "I need a little romance first." Hanna laughed, surprised that the *doesn't do relationships* guy was also the *needs to be sweet-talked* guy. She climbed over his lap, settling comfortably into him as his hands wandered her back. "Will I ever get my shirt back?" he asked.

"Looks better on me," she breathed, rolling her hips forward and running her fingers over his neck. She knew from the night before that he liked a little pressure there, and the widening of his eyes as she squeezed his throat only reconfirmed his preference.

"Looks best on the floor," he mumbled, pulling at the buttons. "I need to see those tits again, Arizona. I thought about them all night."

Hanna shrugged his shirt over her head, glad that her no-bra plotting paid off. He dropped to her chest immediately, his tongue circling every inch of flesh as he hardened under her. His hand slipped under her shorts, teasing the skin of her hips as she moaned into his mouth.

She rolled her hips against his again, a hiss escaping his lips.

"Romanced enough?" she whispered.

"No," he rumbled, his mouth catching hers. Her experience might have been limited, but she was certain no man on Earth kissed better than Milo. It was like he had some sort of venom dripping from his tongue, not crafted to kill, but to daze. Her head swirled as he parted her lips, coffee and peppermint blending into an intoxicating potion. He pushed up into her, the romance clearly taking effect.

Hanna slipped down his body as he lifted his hips and shimmied his pants and boxers off, tossing them onto the couch.

If he'd been a boyfriend, or even a potential boyfriend, Hanna might have spent more time teasing him and working him up, but that was one of the perks of their arrangement. It was about getting him off, not getting him hooked on her. Hanna stroked him twice, getting her bearings, before eagerly taking him into her mouth.

She'd thought about it as she drifted to sleep the night before—what he might taste like. What he might sound like on the edge of ruin. And par for the course, Milo did not disappoint.

"Shit, Hanna," Milo gasped, his hand wrapping around her hair and pulling as her tongue circled him. She shoved him deeper, addicted to the way his forearm flexed as he pushed her gently, setting the rhythm that worked best for him.

She watched the ink on his arm pulse and relax in time with her movements, his muffled moans growing in volume. The sound sent a fire through her—Logan had always been so *quiet*. She never knew if he was enjoying it or not. But Milo made no mystery about it, throwing his head back onto the couch and rasping filthy commentary to her increasing speed. She tucked her free hand between her legs, riding against herself at the insistence of her body. She couldn't resist the need for friction as he mumbled something about how well she took him.

"God, are you touching yourself?" Milo asked, his head snapping toward her. She moaned around him, her eyes locked on his.

"I want you to come with my cock in your mouth," he whispered. He pushed on the back of her head harder, her belly tightening at the sound of his pleasure. She moved her hand faster, but lost her control over her pace when his eyes found hers. She clenched around her own hand, the pressure driving her faster, harder as he squeezed her scalp. Hanna cried out against him, her vision exploding into stars at the way he bit his lip. "God, the look on your face. So fucking beautiful. Don't stop, Hanna, I'm right there."

She doubled down on her efforts, bringing her hand up, soaked in his name, to grip him even harder.

Milo finally stopped talking.

He grunted as he approached the edge, releasing the grip on her head and tapping her shoulder as a warning—one she happily ignored.

Hanna took everything he had to give her, his eyes closing as she beamed with a satisfactory smile. She stood, his chest heaving, but he pulled back on her hand.

"I guess I should have warned you before we decided to do this that I like to cuddle after," Milo said, dragging her onto his lap.

"Oh no," Hanna giggled. "The gorgeous man who wants no strings attached, god-tier sex, also wants me to feel human after? How terrible a fate."

He laughed, and she felt the sound absorb into her skin, warming her from the inside out.

"I have a dress fitting with Sara this afternoon," she said, peppering his neck with kisses. "But maybe after that I can make us dinner?"

"You cook?" Milo asked, his surprise offensive.

But then she realized, in all the weeks she'd been there—in the last *year*—she'd hardly cooked at all.

"I cook."

"Damn," Milo said. "Really putting the benefits in FWB."

"OKAY, just a little more in the waist and then I think it's perfect!"

The alterations manager scribbled a few more notes on her form and tapped Sara on the shoulder. She stood on a pedestal in the middle of a bridal shop in Lower Haight, twirling left and right in what was possibly the most incredible wedding gown ever made.

It was a little bohemian, a little timeless, a little sexy. All the things Sara had put on her list when they'd started shopping. Hanna held the phone up as Cami blubbered on Face-Time. Once the shop attendant added the lace veil, it was over.

"You look like a celebrity," Hanna said. Cami started anew in her tears—there was no way she was surviving the ceremony.

"Do I have to take it off?" Sara said, admiring her reflection.

"I think it's a bit much for happy hour," Hanna quipped as Sara hopped off the pedestal. The moment she disappeared from the frame, Cami launched into a line of questions about how she was liking San Francisco.

After a short silence, Cami said, "You know, I've gotta tell you, sweetheart, you're *glowing*."

Hanna blushed. She glanced at her face in the bottom of the screen. She wasn't wrong.

"I mean it! You look so healthy. It's nice."

"Thank you," she mumbled, averting her eyes from her own face on the call. *Time box, time box, time box.*

"Sara told me you're shacking up with that Milo boy."

Ah, so there *was* an ulterior motive to her compliment.

"Only for the week," Hanna said, running her fingers over a wall of lace samples.

"Berty said he's not allowed in the house again." Cami giggled. "You know, I always pictured you with someone like him. Tall, dark, moody."

"He's not that moody, the tattoos kind of misrepresent him. He's actually really sweet."

Cami's eyes lit up. "Is he now?"

Hanna sighed. "He lost his dad when he was a teenager, so he just kind of gets what I'm dealing with, you know?"

Cami dropped her voice. "Are you being safe?"

"Camila!" Hanna barked at the same time Sara rounded the dressing room corner.

"Mother!"

Hanna handed her the phone and she swiftly launched into rehearsal dinner logistics. When she hung up, she turned to Hanna.

"Oh my god, she's too much."

"I love her," Hanna said, shaking her head as they exited the bridal shop.

"We all love her, but Jesus." Sara eyed the shops across the street. "Are you though?"

"Am I what?" They strolled around the corner. "Greek or sushi?"

"Greek, and are you being *safe*?" Sara asked.

Hanna drew a deep breath and ripped off the bandaid.

"We're not having sex."

"Oh, shit," Sara said, throwing her head back and laughing. "I fully expected you to tell me to go fuck myself."

"Milo is a really good friend," Hanna said, holding the door open to a hole-in-the-wall restaurant teeming with blue and white flags. "It would be really stupid to complicate that." It *was* the truth.

"So, what? You're just... friends? Would you ever date him?"

"No," Hanna snorted. "Milo doesn't date."

Sara rolled her eyes. "And you don't do long distance."

"Exactly. We are just friends. And we're not having sex," Hanna reiterated, leaving off the *yet*. "So it doesn't matter."

Sara nodded, her lips pursing as she mulled over a laminated menu.

"Great. This week is definitely not going to blow up in your faces."

"No! It's fine."

Sara and Hanna exchanged a wide stare, both fully aware she was full of shit. Hanna's phone buzzed as Sara ordered for them.

> ALWAYS ANSWER
> My apartment smells like you.

> HANNA
> Sorry.

> ALWAYS ANSWER
> Wasn't a complaint, Arizona.

Hanna puffed out a sigh, her cheeks warming. It was already blowing up in her face.

SARA FOLLOWED her through the market as she plucked ingredients off the shelves for her favorite pasta dish

A meal Sara was very familiar with.

She raised an eyebrow when they got to the cheese aisle, but didn't poke at her. Hanna was certain Sara bit her tongue the entire walk home.

"Hanna!" Logan leaned against Milo's door, his arms

folded over his favorite interview suit. Hanna squeezed her eyes shut. She'd hoped to avoid him at least for the day.

"Call me if you need me," Sara whispered, squeezing her hand before crossing the hall into her apartment.

"Got a few minutes?" Logan asked.

"Hold this," Hanna said, shoving her grocery bag into his hands and fishing out Milo's keys. He'd left for the office about an hour before Sara's fitting, mumbling something about an emergency before pushing a kiss into her forehead, the heat of it still lingering on her skin.

She cracked the door open, expecting Logan to follow.

"I don't think Milo would want me in his home."

She scrunched her nose. "Well, it's my home for now, too. He's not here anyway."

Logan hesitated at the door, but ultimately decided to follow her in and set the bag on the counter. He watched the ingredients as she unloaded them.

"Are you making penne alla Lisa?"

Hanna shrugged. "I'm making dinner."

Logan turned over a block of parmesan. "God, I haven't had that in forever."

"Same," Hanna mumbled, organizing the produce. She searched Milo's kitchen for a pot and a cutting board, but nothing was where she expected it to be.

"So, he's getting the full Hanna experience this week then, huh?"

Hanna stopped, casting an irritated scowl at him. "What does that mean?"

Logan's shoulders bounced as he reached for the back of his neck.

"You only ever cooked for me on birthdays and anniversaries."

"That's not true," she protested. "Not for the first five years, anyway."

"Let's not add another thing to the list of shit we're fighting about," Logan grumbled, handing her a cheese grater from the drawer behind him.

"Fine by me."

"I want to talk about her," Logan said, his tone soft, but his words bricks.

Hanna held her breath, waiting for the wave of angry tears to crush her. It stung, but didn't sear.

"Okay," she whispered.

"Okay?"

She nodded. "Okay. But I can't look at you while I do it, so I'm going to keep cooking."

Logan seemed to accept this. "Why didn't you call me? You must have been out of your mind, Hanna."

She concentrated on sliding her knife through crisp emerald herbs, the sound offsetting the sniffling building in her nose.

"Of course I was."

"But you never thought to talk to me? I could have come home. I could have helped."

She tossed him a sorrowful look, unable to hold his blue eyes.

"And Sloane would have been fine with that?"

"I wouldn't have cared either way," he said. "I didn't even find out she was sick until after she was gone, Hanna."

Hanna filled the pot with water and dumped an ocean's worth of salt into it, twisting the knob on Milo's stove to high.

"I know," she sighed. "It was fucked up. And it's one of my biggest regrets, okay? I thought about calling a million times, but every time I pictured hearing Sloane in the background, I just couldn't do it. I was so hurt, Lo. And besides that, I was drowning in my mom's treatment. We had surgeries and radiation and chemo and ER trips and it took up two hundred percent of my brain capacity. And then it was—" she swallowed, her throat constricting. "And then it was over."

She grated the block of cheese, pushing the anxiety twisting at her nerves into the metal. Logan rested a hand over her shoulder.

"I'm so sorry," he said. She could not look at him. She knew he was crying. She always knew when he cried. "For all of it."

"I'm sorry, too," she managed. "For most of it."

Logan laughed, sputtering beside her, the release enough to bring their heads above water.

"I worry about you, Hanna. I don't know how you managed all of it."

"Not well," she admitted, adding a handful of red pepper flakes to her pan. "I'm trying to untangle my life now, but to quote Milo, I'm a fucking mess."

Logan frowned. "He's probably helpful with all of this, huh?"

She nodded.

"That's good. Well, not *good*. I wish neither of you had to go through it. But it's good you have someone to talk to."

Logan fell silent for a moment while she worked on her sauce.

"Is that... all you're doing with him?"

She froze, the tingle of anger flickering back to life. So *close*.

"Is that *any* of your business?"

"I guess that's my answer," Logan snorted.

Hanna rolled her eyes. She should never have let her guard down with him.

"Milo and I are just friends, not that I owe you an explanation."

"Just... tread lightly, Hanna. Okay?"

She reached behind him, pulling salt and pepper mills from the back of the counter.

"What the fuck does that mean?"

"It means what it means," he said, gesturing broadly.

"Insightful," she muttered. "Leave it to you to have an opinion on my friendships."

"I'm just warning you. I've known Milo a really long time." He ducked his eyes to hers, holding them for a beat too long.

She waved her spoon at him. "Your concern is noted, but unnecessary, okay?"

"Okay," he relented.

"I'll see you later?" It was the easiest way to dismiss him.

"Uh, yeah. Sure." Logan didn't move right away, debating something. He leaned over, pulling her into a lightning-quick hug, so fast she hadn't even processed it by the time he released her and dipped out of the kitchen.

The front door opened, but too many sets of footsteps shuffled around one another.

"Oh," Milo said, surprised.

"Sorry," Logan mumbled. The door slammed shut as Milo rounded the corner.

"Smells good," he said, pointing to the stove. "Everything okay?"

Hanna turned to look at him, and she could see he was braced for one of her meltdowns, his muscles poised to grab her. But for once, she *didn't* want to break into pieces.

"Everything's fine," she forced out, holding those green eyes with hers. She wanted to tackle him to the floor and fuck him into oblivion, but she didn't want to feel him inside of her for the first time between boiling pots and timers. She wanted to savor it.

Milo seemed to read her mind. In a flash, she was up against the counter, the edge of it cutting into her lower back as he gripped her neck and hauled her mouth to his. His tongue danced over her lower lip, driving any remaining uncertainty planted by Logan away.

She sighed, relaxing under his touch as his hands kneaded her chest. Something popped and sizzled on the stove.

"Ah, shit," she said, pushing him away, the pasta boiling over. He grabbed a towel and laughed to himself as he pushed the pot to the back eye of the stove, cleaning up what he could before she shooed him away. "Get out of the kitchen before I burn dinner."

He grinned and tapped her hips as he squeezed by her again.

"I got stuff to set the table anyway. Let me know when you're capable of being in my presence."

It took her another twenty minutes to finish the meal, the sun slipping between their buildings as she plated her mother's signature recipe. Milo pulled a record from his shelf and dropped the needle over something smooth she didn't recognize. She darted out of the kitchen to Milo's tiny dining table, set with another teal mason jar full of sunflowers and a hand-labeled amber bottle.

"Looks amazing," Milo said, sliding into his chair with two rocks glasses. He popped the cork from the bottle and poured heavier than she would have. "I'm not sure if this is the ideal pairing, but I think you'll forgive me."

"I'm sure I can be convinced," she said, settling across from him. He leaned forward, a gorgeous smile unfolding for her.

"I cannot remember the last time these dishes were used, so thank you for feeding me."

"You're saving me from shacking up with my ex for the week, I owe you."

"I like it better when you thank me on your knees," Milo said, curling the pasta around his fork. He closed his eyes as he took his first bite. "Actually, I'm not sure that I do. This is delicious."

"Lisa specialty," she said. She hadn't made it since her mother died, and she didn't think she ever would again, but if anyone would appreciate it the way it deserved, it was Milo.

Lisa had made it for dinner when she brought Logan home to meet her, she'd made it when she graduated from ASU, when she got the offer on her first big girl job... she'd lacked reasons to make it for too long.

"Thank you for sharing it with me," he said, sipping his whiskey. "I'd make you something my dad was known for, but the man never lifted a finger in the kitchen. Mom cooks everything from scratch." He lit up at the mention of his mother.

She smiled as she swirled her glass. "You really admire her, huh?"

"I hate to do this to you, because you're already clearly so enamored with me, but my mom and I have a great relationship. Not one of those weird mother-son relationships either. We text daily, and we get lunch every Wednesday. Sunday night dinners. The whole nine."

"You have to stop talking," she said. "You're funny, close with your mom, spend more time in therapy than out of it, communicate clearly, you're *very* good with your hands... your only flaw is that you don't want to bestow any of that on someone long term?"

Milo nodded slowly. "No one can be perfect."

"What a waste," she laughed.

Milo folded his arms. "I did date when I was younger. I dated a lot. But you'll find that it's really hard to be with someone who doesn't *get* what you're dealing with, and it's even harder to be with someone who does. You can't hide from them. I know you and Logan were together for a long time, and I'm sure he cared about your mother, but it's not the same for him. He lost someone he cared about, but you lost *your origin story*. It's a whole piece of you that's just gone."

Hanna held her breath as he spoke, counting all the pieces of her that vanished in an instant.

"I've tried dating non-members of the Dead Parent Society, but I need someone who can actually sit with me in the hard moments. I'm sorry to tell you this, but even fifteen years later, it'll still punch you right in the goddamn face. I had girlfriends who didn't understand why I prioritize my family the way I do, or why I struggle to get out of bed when spring rolls around. There aren't a lot of people our age who have been through it."

Hanna nodded, taking another bite of pasta. She missed the noodle and nipped her tongue, a sharp pain jolting her as she found herself trying to escape his point.

"And even if I found someone who did get it, then this whole other side of me starts to panic. What if I made someone love me and then just die and leave them?"

"A fourth therapist might be able to crack that," Hanna said.

Milo scoffed. "Maybe."

"So what you're saying is, you're just healed enough to function, but still ridiculously fucked up."

"Yeah," he nodded. "That."

"Fascinating."

Milo watched the sunset over her shoulder, pressing his lips together.

"People fear losing their loved ones, but people like us know that's not the scary part. There's nothing to it. They're here and then they aren't. It's finding yourself after that's truly terrifying."

Hanna considered this. "I think that's why I'm so stuck." She took a long sip of her drink, the slow burn just enough feeling to push the rest of her thoughts out. "I start to see a version of myself that's less exhausted, and I shut it down. If I'm not a falling-apart mess, if I can wake up without immediately wanting to go back to sleep..." Her throat swelled around the next thought. "Moving on feels like signing the papers to stop treatment again."

She swallowed, his eyes softening. The worst part about Milo was that he understood the darkest paths in her mind. He saw the pain, and he didn't judge it, but he didn't let her hide it either.

The tears started slowly enough, but then they hit all at once, choking her as the sob she'd been suppressing for months ripped through her chest. Milo did not hesitate to stand and pull her into his arms, wrapping her in a tight hug while she let it all go. It came in crashing waves, the breath in her lungs fighting to break through the crush.

"I'm sorry," she gasped.

Milo smoothed her hair. "I'm not." He let her cry in his arms before he eventually moved her to his bed, curling around her while she shattered into a thousand pieces until she finally passed out.

When she woke up the next morning, the dishes were done and the sunflowers had moved from the dinner table to the coffee table with a hot latte and a promise to see her soon.

She was halfway through the latte when she got a text.

ALWAYS ANSWER

I've never seen someone sleep as hard as you did last night.

HANNA

I don't think I've slept for more than three hours at a time in a year.

ALWAYS ANSWER

You can cry yourself to sleep in my arms anytime.

Sorry I had to leave early this morning. Got called in for an emergency.

HANNA

That's okay! I'm going to take the day off. Maybe go for gold and cry in public.

ALWAYS ANSWER

That's my girl.

She stared at her phone, the last three words doing something to her stomach she knew was a red flag, wrapped in caution tape, steeped in misery.

And yet, she smiled.

Stupid, idiotic, so very dumb.

THIRTEEN

"It's the oxygen."

Her favorite hospice nurse, Shannon, had just started her shift when she woke Hanna, who was slumped sideways in the chair beside her mother.

Lisa had been silent for two days.

"What?"

Shannon's lips twisted, a sunburst of wrinkled wisdom emerging around them.

"It's basically life support at this point, love. If you took her off, it would only take a few hours, maybe less."

Hanna wished she could go back to sleep.

"I just thought you should know that's what's happening. Knowledge is power."

Shannon had repeated that to her a few times. Knowledge was power. Funny how it seemed to drain her of any.

"What would you do?" She sat up in the chair, stretching her neck, unsure if she'd ever sit properly again between the weeks spent on hospital floors, cancer center chairs, and air mattresses. "If it were your mom?"

Shannon laid a hand on Hanna's shoulder, her eyes saying everything she needed to, but she affirmed it for her anyway.

"If the only thing keeping her here is a machine..."

Hanna nodded, the weight pressing down on her chest building quickly. It was that thing again, that goddamned anger she couldn't escape. Anger that this happened. Anger that the surgery hadn't worked. Anger that the chemo only made her worse.

Anger that she'd been staring at her lifeless face for two days, desperate for it to be over but unable to say it out loud.

Anger that she had to be the one to call it.

Her lungs squeezed against the responsibility. Who could possibly make that kind of choice? She reached for her phone—it was muscle memory.

But who the fuck would she call?

Hanna woke with a start, her fingers threaded through sheets that didn't smell like her, sweat pooling at the back of her neck. Her breathing was stilted—it always was after one of her hospice nightmares.

"Hanna?"

She couldn't focus her eyes, her lungs pushing against her ribs with shallow gasps.

"Hanna, it's okay."

The evening sun streamed into his bedroom, painting the blacks and grays in a soft amber. She must have fallen asleep waiting for him to get home. Milo's hand pushed against her chest with a soft insistence, finding the right pressure to force a breath to catch.

"You're okay," he whispered.

She closed her eyes, letting the pressure pull her back into her body. When the fire in her muscles finally burned out, she covered his hand with hers, staring at the face of the clock inked on his arm.

"You were screaming."

"I had a nightmare," she managed, still unsure when she'd even laid down. Milo brushed her hair away from her face, his body flush against hers as the room fell back into focus.

"I won't make you tell—"

"I was in the hospice home again, having to make the call to kill the oxygen. It, uh, it's just a recurring dream I have." His lips fell into a sorrowful tilt as he moved to lift his hand, but she pinned it. She wasn't ready to give up the anchor yet. "Sorry I was screaming."

"Don't apologize," he insisted. "I'm just glad you're okay."

"I'm okay," she repeated.

She risked a glance at his eyes, filled with all sorts of thoughts he didn't share. His lips parted, but before he could ask her if she really was okay again, she silenced him with a kiss, shifting his hand lower. She'd caught him off guard with her tears the night before—once the dam broke, she couldn't get it back. But she trusted herself a little more, believed that she could bend and not break, even if only for a little while.

And if she didn't trust herself, she trusted Milo.

She felt the resistance bubble against his lips as she ran her hand across his side. She pulled away.

"I'm supposed to go to dinner with Matty," Milo mumbled. "I was just coming back to change." He pushed forward, enveloping her completely, his leg wrapping around hers and tangling them into his blankets.

"Won't take long," Hanna said in the space between them.

Milo glared, his hand wandering over her neck and cradling her.

"Thanks for your vote of confidence, Arizona."

It felt so fucking good to laugh into him.

"Please?" In most situations, it was the magic word, and this was no exception.

Milo flicked his watch over and groaned. "I had it all planned out for when I got home."

Hanna hooked her fingers through his belt loops, pulling his hips into her as she sighed and sank her teeth into his neck. The rough stubble against her lips brought her mind back from wherever it'd wandered. She crawled her hand lower, brushing over him, breaking his plans in half.

"Fuck, okay. You make a good argument," Milo muttered, reaching under her to scoop his arms around her back. He rolled so she fell over him, her messy curls tickling the edge of his jaw as she giggled. She was still righting herself as her dress came off, his hands rolling the hem of it over her back with a flourish.

He pulled at the clasp of her bra and slipped his tongue between her lips, a low rumble in his chest the only sound as his hands cupped her. Hanna tried to concentrate on his belt, but her senses shot into overdrive as his mouth swirled across her skin.

He slid his hand to her hip, pushing down on her so she could feel every inch of him.

"Why aren't you naked?" she asked, bouncing over his lap. He laughed, pushing her away and standing to strip off his work clothes. She lay across his bed and watched what little show they had time for while he fished in his nightstand for a condom. It landed beside her on the bed as his knees settled into the mattress. He reached forward, stroking her back lightly before pulling back on her hips so she landed in his lap, her knees spread over his as he kissed the back of her shoulder.

Her head fell back onto his shoulder, baring more of her neck to him as she weaved fingers into those dark curls. When she looked down, she could only see skin and ink, his hands covering as much of her flesh as they could, his hips pushing against hers.

Milo reached forward, dipping his hand between her legs. Her breath hitched, but there was no alarm, no panic. Only pleasure as he circled her and nipped at her ear.

"Goddamnit, Hanna," he hissed into her skin. "You want it so bad."

She nodded, pushing her hips into his lap, grinding against him with zero regard for playing coy. They could play games later.

He twisted her mouth toward his, consuming her in a kiss so smoldering she struggled to see straight as his fingers moved faster. He clutched at her throat, the pressure sending her onto another plane, where nothing bothered her at all. The shift in her moaning must have registered with him.

"Fuck, are you going to come for me, Hanna?"

She nodded, whining against his hand.

"Keep going, oh my *god*, don't pull away from me," he ground out, pushing down on her hips and forcing her to sink into the blinding pleasure. "Stay right here with me. You can do it, Hanna. Shhh," he whispered, pressing his fingers into her chest. "You don't want Sara and Matty to hear you scream my name, do you?"

She cried out against him, her vision exploding into white bursts of light as he pushed her beyond the edge and straight out into the icy Bay, her entire body seizing against his touch. He pulled her chin toward him and kissed her, but she could hardly feel anything as her cells rearranged and merged into a new version of her body, one that now knew what it was capable of with the right encouragement.

"Come back to me," Milo whispered, laughing into her shoulder. "I need you present for this part." Hanna fought the haze in her head, finding where her mind and her body met and attempting to bridge the two. As he nudged her knees further apart and felt him pressing against her, the line snapped, her two halves fusing back together. He ran his hand up her spine and pushed her forward onto the bed, dragging his fingertips back down to her hips and digging them into her soft curves, teasing her.

Milo tore at the condom, the foil wrapper floating to the floor as she braced herself.

It wasn't *regret* she felt as Milo Galantis, the too-hot, too-unavailable groomsman she'd had at the top of her stay-the-hell-away-from list ran his hands over her back, curling his fingers into her skin before he fucked her into absolute oblivion. No, she'd never regret knowing what it felt like to wrap around his thighs or have his hands crawl her ribs, or knowing what he sounded like when he raced toward a climax she'd been dreaming about for months.

It was, in fact, a grief all its own.

She'd have to mourn the doubt she'd clung to about what it would be like with him. She'd have to lay to rest the plausible deniability that he was all talk and tease. She'd have to grieve the sick hope in the back of her mind that maybe—someday, somewhere—they'd be more than whatever this was.

"You're so quiet," Milo said, squeezing her hips. "You okay?"

Hanna swallowed and kicked herself for missing out on a good thing for no good reason.

"Sorry," she gasped, arching her spine more to make room for him. But Milo moved away, nudging her so she rolled onto her back. He fell over her, like a favorite blanket, and leaned in, gripping the back of her leg for leverage.

"What's wrong?" he breathed, nipping at her jaw. Hanna's hands ran over his back, her nails dragging lines into his skin. He hesitated moving against her, the uncertainty in his muscles somehow the hottest thing he could have done.

"Nothing's wrong," she insisted. "That's what's wrong."

His weight collapsed as he laughed. "I *really* wish I didn't understand exactly what you meant." He landed in a heap beside her.

"Are we fucking stupid?" Hanna said, folding into his arms and wrapping her leg around his hips. She ached for him, her entire body screaming to forget about logic—a twist of her hips and he'd be hers. He snagged her lips between his teeth as his hand rested on her ass, kneading her skin slowly, carefully.

"Yes," he whispered, not caring that it was the truth. "Do you want to stop?"

"No." She answered too quickly. He squeezed harder, his mouth more insistent as he grazed her collarbone. "Do *you* want to stop?"

"Does it feel like I want to stop, Arizona?" Milo pushed against her thigh, her heart racing. She reached for his face, tangling her fingers into his hair and pulling him to her neck. If they weren't stopping, she might as well enjoy his mouth on every inch of her.

"You taste so fucking good. So good," Milo murmured, wrapping his arms around her tighter. There were too many truths swirling in the depths of his gaze. Hanna turned away, sighing and closing her eyes at the waves of sizzling heat clinging to her skin. She held her breath, twisting her hips to give him access to her.

She swallowed, the swell of him against her stealing any lingering doubt she might have held onto.

"Mi—"

"Milo! Yo!"

Hanna jolted and he froze, the sound of the front door slamming ripping them away from what they both desperately needed.

"Fuck," Milo hissed as Hanna crawled away from him, off the bed and across the room before he could blink. She searched for her dress, her entire body flushing a deep shade of pink.

"Milo!"

"One sec," he yelled back, his voice cracking. "Just getting dressed!" Milo slammed the bedroom door shut, his jaw clenched as he disappeared into his closet.

Matty called out, "Hanna!"

Milo leaned out of the closet, eyes wide as she adjusted her dress to cover her red-splotched chest. The ghosts of his fingertips haunted her.

"Hanna! Are you home? Sara's looking for you!"

"She's not home!" Milo yelled, yanking his shirt over his head. He walked out of the bedroom, his voice echoing off the kitchen as Matty helped himself to a drink from the fridge.

"Sara thought they were having dinner." Her nose scrunched. Reality slowly came back to her—she had agreed to dinner.

"I'll just check her location," a third voice said, a low one she hadn't anticipated. Her entire body caught fire, and not in the way Milo had just had it burning.

"You still have her location?" Milo asked.

The irritation in his voice did nothing to help fade the red splotches across her chest in the shape of his palms.

Logan mumbled, "Yeah, she probably doesn't even remember she shared it with me. It's been years. I guess I should have checked it before coming out here," he said, a bitter laugh following.

Hanna fought the urge to poke her head out and say something antagonistic. Had he been staring at her unmoving face on a map as it rotted in her house for the last year? She looked for her underwear, but wasn't even sure when they came off.

"Says she's here?" Logan said.

"She might be doing laundry upstairs," Milo mumbled. "You guys ready to go?"

She could see the way Matty tossed his arms up in her mind by the way he sighed.

"Yeah, I'm fucking starving. You were supposed to come over fifteen minutes ago, diva."

"I just need my keys," Milo said. He slipped back into his bedroom where Hanna was pressed against the wall. He shut the door behind him. "He still has your location?"

She whispered, "He's not going to after tonight!"

Milo grinned. "You're so fucking hot when you're flustered." Milo scooped his work pants off the floor and fished for his wallet and keys, tucking them into his back pocket. He snagged her by the neck for a barely breathing kiss so quick she nearly missed it.

"When I get home, we're finishing what we started," he said, pressing his lips to hers once more.

"Okay," she said, swallowing.

"Turn off the location sharing," he whispered against her cheek, releasing her, though she felt the heat of his hold for far too long after.

"THERE YOU ARE!"

It took Hanna twenty minutes to get her heart rate down before changing and crossing the hall. Sara looked at a dozen different floral arrangements, swiping back and forth on her laptop.

"The third one," Hanna said, plopping next to her on the couch. "The drape on the lilies? Gorgeous."

Sara closed her laptop and crossed her legs.

"Do you have something to tell me, Hanna?"

Hanna held her breath—had she heard them? She'd been vaguely conscious of that being a problem, but she could only be so silent when it came to Milo.

"Do I?" Hanna countered, too smart to fall for the open-ended question.

"I just got off the phone with Taylor. *She* said that we're not staying at The Flamingo anymore."

"Oh!" Hanna laughed, sinking back into the couch. "No. We are not."

Sara's eyes narrowed. "Where are we staying?"

"It's a secret!" Hanna made a mental note to text Taylor later and reinforce the surprise nature of their plans—Sara *loved* ruining a surprise for herself, but she deserved to have something planned just for her.

"Ugh," she sighed. "Fine."

"What are we doing tonight?" Hanna leaned her head on Sara's shoulder. "Seating chart? Vows? Table settings? All of the above?"

"None of the above!" Sara pointed to a package on the kitchen counter. "I got face masks! We're relaxing for once. I figured the extra stress of our surprise guest might be getting to you."

Hanna sighed. That *did* sound nice, though she debated telling Sara just how *not* stressed she was feeling after a few days with Milo. She cracked the top on a sparkling water Sara had set out with some snacks, the satisfying *shhh* reminding her too much of Milo's shushing her to stay quiet. Her face heated.

"A perfect evening!"

"Right?" Sara stood, crossing to snag the bag from the counter. "And then, when you're glowing from fucking Milo's brains out for a week straight, you'll have an excuse!"

Hanna choked on the water, the carbonation burning against her throat.

"Sara—"

"Oh my god, I was kidding, but you're ten shades of red right now!" She tossed Hanna a brightly colored foil packet, the woman on the front looking much more at ease than she was. She couldn't stop the vision of their wasted condom wrapper floating onto the floor beside her.

Shit, that wasn't helping with the red face.

"You can't tell Matty," Hanna said. "He'll get *so* weird. And we haven't technically had sex," she added.

"Believe me, the last thing I want to do is tell Matty. He's never really loved the Logan-Milo dynamic, and this? This ratchets that up to eleven."

"Yeah, what *is that*?" Hanna had noticed the strange looks between brothers, the hesitations to interact with one another.

She shrugged. "It's none of my business, that's what it is. None of this is *any* of my business, as long as you all show up to the wedding."

"Perfect," Hanna said as she tore the packet in two. "That is the plan."

Hanna's phone vibrated against the counter.

ALWAYS ANSWER

I cannot concentrate on Vegas logistics.

HANNA

Oh? And why is that?

ALWAYS ANSWER

Probably the insane blue balls I'm sporting
under the table.

HANNA

Boooo. That's a myth.

ALWAYS ANSWER

Oh yeah? You seem super locked in on
whatever you and Sara are doing.

HANNA

Hey, I got mine.

ALWAYS ANSWER

Lot more where that came from.

"None of my business... but... is it at least making you feel alive again?"

Hanna set her phone down and stared out Sara's window, dreading the fact that it made her feel many, *many* things again, the worst of them being fully alive.

FOURTEEN

When Milo got home, she'd been asleep for hours.

She didn't register him slipping into the bed behind her, but when she finally did wake, drowning in his warmth and yesterday's cologne, dread pooled in her stomach.

It was a bad day.

It wasn't that she thought a new city, or even Milo, could stop the bad days entirely, but without even realizing it, she'd let herself hope they could stave them off for at least a little while.

Hanna's heart sank as each breath felt harder than the next.

"Morning," Milo mumbled, half asleep. She rolled in his arms and tucked her head into his chest, his shirt smelling so deeply of him she wished she could wrap herself up in it without tipping him off that she was a pathetic moron. "Sorry we got home so late."

Hanna didn't respond. She only buried her face further into his chest.

"I could make it up to you," he said. Milo's hands found her beneath the blanket, slipping under the hem of her shorts.

She only had to hesitate for a second for him to snap awake, his voice tightening from half-asleep to deeply troubled.

"You alright?"

Hanna sighed. "It's just one of those days."

His hands retreated immediately.

"Sorry—"

"Nope, we don't apologize for that shit." Milo slipped out of bed and pulled on his jeans from the night before.

"Where are you going?"

He shrugged, searching for his keys. "You need a bagel and to stay in bed."

"I'm fi—"

"Banned word." Milo pulled back the curtains. "Look, even the Bay thinks it's a down day." The sky drizzled gray over Brannan Street, blanketing it in a foggy haze that felt completely appropriate for the storm developing in her chest. "I'll be back in twenty." He dove back onto the bed, shoving his hands over the blanket to tuck it around her as she giggled.

When he returned with coffee, bagels, and a bouquet of sunflowers, her heart felt less like an anchor and more like a balloon, bobbing happily along between electric lines and branches, as if she'd be able to dodge them indefinitely.

"WHAT ARE YOU READING NOW?"

Milo flopped onto the couch next to her. He'd been on calls all day, and she'd been avoiding hers with the second installment in the series Sara got her hooked on. She held the cover up so he could see the title.

"Enemies to lovers? Age gap? Shadow daddy? Why choose?"

Hanna held her place with her index finger as she twisted to face him.

"Who taught you these words?"

Milo grinned. "Girl I used to hang out with read a book a day. *Loved* acting scenes out."

She tried not to let the pang of jealousy show on her face, but she worried it pinged so loudly off her chest that he heard it. *Just friends*, she reminded herself.

"It's none of the above, actually," she said. "It's a cozy fantasy—more steam, less spice."

Milo's head tilted, a wickedness flashing across his face.

"Getting your other needs met, then?"

She looked up from the page, glaring. "I'm at a really good part."

Milo backed away, holding his hands up in surrender. He hopped off the couch and crossed the living room to a stack of books she'd borrowed from Sara when they'd moved her stuff over. She tried not to watch as he scanned the spines, but the concentration on his face was hard to ignore. He plucked one from the middle of the stack.

She battled a smile as he reclaimed the spot beside her, laying his head in her lap and cracking open the first book in the series. His eyes flicked from the page to hers.

"So, just to set my expectations correctly, no knotting in this one?"

Hanna giggled. "Not so far. There are two other books, though."

"Here's to hoping," he murmured.

She turned her focus back to her book, the weight of him an anchor as she let the sweet romance sweep her heart away. She rested one hand on his chest, absently fiddling with the buttons on his shirt. Her mind wandered back to two years ago, nestled next to Logan on the couch, when she'd crawled her hand over his thigh to reach for his. She'd just missed him as he moved to answer an email from work.

Milo shifted under her touch. She pulled her hand back, realizing that it wasn't very *just friends* of her. He caught her fingers and pressed the back of her hand to his lips before returning it to his chest.

They both stilled.

"Jesus," he said as he waved the book in the air. "These really *are* a bad influence, you know that? No wonder they try to ban them." He set the book on the coffee table and reached for his phone, reading through the notifications. "Ah, shit, I gotta deal with something."

"Family okay?" she asked, her heart still beating too quickly.

"Fire at work," he mumbled. "I'll see you later?"

"Mmhmm," she said, her eyes glued to the book.

He pulled on a hoodie and took off, and she made it three more pages before she found herself wandering across the hall.

"Well, well, well, look who came up for air," Sara whispered as she pulled Hanna into the apartment. She braced herself for Logan, but it still hit her when his cologne drifted across the kitchen as he stood in front of the fridge.

"Hey!"

"Hanna Hanna bo banna," Matty chanted, grabbing her shoulders. "Where's Milo?"

"Work thing," she said, waving her hand. "You guys wanna go grab dinner?"

Sara and Matty exchanged a glance as they waited for Logan to answer.

"Uh, yeah," he said. "Definitely."

IT REALLY SHOULDN'T HAVE SHOCKED her when a bouncy redhead chirped her name from two tables over halfway through their dinner.

And yet, Chloe caught her off guard. She leaned forward and said something to the man she was with before hugging him and sending him on his way.

"I'm *so* glad you guys are here," Chloe said, pulling a chair up to their table. "That was, hands down, the worst date I've ever been on."

"Oh, no!" Hanna said, moving a basket of chips closer to the end of the table.

"I keep telling myself I'll stop dating finance bros, but here I am," she said, laughing as she reached a hand across the table toward Logan. "Hi, I'm Chloe."

He winced and shook her hand. "Finance Bro," he said.

Chloe tossed her head back, cackling as Hanna patted her arm. "Chloe, this is Logan, Matty's brother. Logan, this is Chloe, she works with Milo."

Sara snorted beside her. Hanna didn't need her to say it out loud. She knew it was the most politically correct introduction ever made.

"I'm sure you're not one of *those* finance bros," Chloe offered.

Logan shrugged as Hanna sipped her margarita. "I've had mixed reviews."

"Everything's okay at work then?" Hanna asked.

Chloe pursed her lips. "I... think so?" Confusion laced her answer.

"Oh, I just, uh, Milo has had a few emergencies pop up. I guess I thought you'd be involved."

Chloe pulled her phone out of her purse, checking her messages.

"I would be. But no, everything seems fine."

Sara leaned forward. "He might have meant at the bar?"

"Ah," Hanna breathed. "That makes sense."

She didn't have much to offer the rest of the meal.

IT WAS NEARLY eleven when Milo returned.

She'd gone to bed in the guest room, unsure of the kind of night he had in mind. She listened as his footsteps traced a path from the front door to his bedroom, and back toward the living room. The stairs rumbled under his weight before he knocked on her door.

Hanna slipped out from under the blanket and hardly had the door open before she was against the wall, her face caught in his hands as he parted her lips with his tongue. Her heart slammed against her ribs in the dark, lightning pulling at the edges of her vision as he dropped one hand lower, searching for skin beneath her t-shirt. She thought about stopping him for a second, just to at least say *hey, how ya doing*, but Milo was not a man who wanted to be stopped.

She could feel it in the threads of his muscles, tightening as he pulled her legs around his waist—he needed something from her, and she was happy to give it to him.

Hanna gasped for breath when he finally broke from her mouth, moving to her neck.

"Are you okay?" she asked.

He didn't answer, save for a brief glance, something pained in his eyes that she wished she hadn't recognized.

She threaded her hands in his hair, matching his fervent movements, giving herself over to the strange mania. His shirt disappeared, along with hers. Milo blurred around her, hands everywhere, mouth everywhere, setting little fires along her body until the entire room filled with smoke.

"Milo?" she asked, somewhere between the bed and the door. He was so quiet. Too quiet. "Milo."

"I'm *fine*," he growled, breaking away from her. He wiped at his mouth, the ink of his tattoos stretching and twisting as he breathed. "I'm fine."

"One more and I'll buy it," she whispered.

He hung his head back, the anger he'd been battling back simmering just under the surface.

"I'm sorry."

"It's okay—"

"It's not. I'm sorry, Hanna. It's just... it's a bad day."

She swept her shirt off the floor, snagging his and tossing it to him.

"I'm the queen of bad days, Milo."

He perched his hands on his hips, glancing out into the hall as he drew another deep breath.

"It's late," she murmured, pulling her shirt on. "You should sleep."

"Yeah. Yeah, okay." Milo nodded, exhaling. He stepped out of the guest room, but paused at the top of the stairs. "Are you coming?"

Hanna shook her head, trying to clear the thousands of thoughts taking hold. Her mind still swirled from the rush of him.

"Yeah," she said. "Of course."

MILO WAS GONE before she woke up, but after her last call of the afternoon, her phone buzzed against the coffee table.

ALWAYS ANSWER

That Oakland distiller I told you about is bringing some new shit by the bar this afternoon. Want to come taste?

Hanna stared at the text. She'd been frustrated all day, unsure what to make of his behavior the night before. She held her breath and hit send on the kind of message she would have sent twenty-four hours prior.

HANNA

You or whiskey?

ALWAYS ANSWER

Both if you ask nicely.

She exhaled. Fine.

HE WAS WAITING at the door when she rounded the corner and slipped into the bar. He locked the door behind her.

She felt it as she brushed by him—the shift between them. She'd let him see the most vulnerable pieces of her over the last few days, and it hadn't scared him off. She'd cried, laughed, and sat in silence with him, and they'd all felt survivable.

In four days, she'd be back across the hall, and this would all be fodder for her vibrator.

But it was there, lingering in their chests. Something far worse than grief.

Hope.

The bar was quiet, only Frankie and a delivery guy hanging at the edge of the cherry-stained oak. She took a moment to really examine all the photos on the walls. There were shots of family trips to Disneyland, the beach, fishing somewhere. He looked *so* much like his dad, the same dark curls and knotted bridge in his nose.

The same green eyes.

"Oh god," Milo laughed. "All the cheesy photos." He hovered behind her, pointing to one of him and Frankie, she assumed, in their early teens, soaked and laughing at whoever was behind the camera. "My dad pushed us both into the lake because we couldn't stop arguing over something. I can't even remember anymore, but it stopped the fight."

"You wouldn't share the Gameboy," Frankie rumbled from behind the bar.

"It wasn't *the* Gameboy, it was *my* Gameboy. I got it with the money I saved cleaning the bar all summer."

"So you do remember," Hanna said, arching a brow.

"I'm Frankie, by the way," Milo's brother said, waving and resting a hand on his hip. Aside from the patches of silver beginning to form at his temples, he could have easily been mistaken for Milo in the dim lighting.

"Hanna," she said, returning the wave.

"The girl from Phoenix," Frankie said, nodding. Milo stilled behind her as she turned.

"I'm *a* girl from Phoenix. Not sure about *the*." Milo's fingers brushed against her hip and her cheeks warmed.

"There's a distillery down in Tempe that we like," Frankie went on. "I try to make it out there every few years."

"On University, yeah?"

"She knows her stuff," Frankie said to Milo, who might have been, for the first time since she'd met him, flustered.

She didn't get a chance to tease him before the Oakland distiller uncapped several bottles, walking them through the tasting notes as they tried four seasonal blends. She *loved* the sour cherry infusion, the tart pinch of her taste buds a perfect distraction from the way Milo licked his lips after a sip.

Without even asking, he popped a bottle from the case into her purse.

When the distiller left, Frankie followed, reminding Milo to lock up before they went home. The door was barely shut before she twisted on her heels.

"Your brother knows about me?"

"Don't let it go to your head. He saw you here, remember?" Milo ducked behind the bar, fussing with the register.

"*The* girl from Phoenix," she hummed.

"You know what? I have nothing to hide," Milo declared. "I have mentioned you a few times at family dinners, okay?"

She leaned over the bar, just inches from him. "Do they hate me for stealing you on Father's Day?"

"No, of course not."

She inhaled. "I don't want whatever we're doing to come between you and your family time."

Milo stopped his work on the register and looked her dead in the eyes.

"Yeah, well, if they knew how good your head game was, they'd understand."

Hanna rolled her eyes, leaning forward over the bar. She dropped her voice, softening her tone.

"Are you feeling better today?"

"I'm feeling better after seeing you bent over in that dress," he muttered, his eyes quickly flashing to the neckline draped lower than she realized. She straightened her back, irritated. Milo stopped whatever he was doing with the register and sighed. "I'm sorry, Hanna."

"For what?" she asked. He stepped to the side, leaning across from her. His hand dropped over hers, tapping the edge of the glass she'd been sipping.

"I know I'm okay being a distraction for you, but I tried to make you a distraction for me, and I shouldn't have done that without talking about it first."

Hanna nodded, processing. He was only a tiptoe away from her, making it difficult to form a coherent thought.

"It's okay, Milo. You have your own shit too, and I know I trigger that. Plus, the work stuff."

Milo winced. "I didn't have work stuff."

She tilted her head.

"I, uh, I was calling my therapist."

Hanna sighed. "Have you ever felt something without analyzing it?" she asked.

Milo huffed a sigh, tapping her hand. "No."

She bit the inside of her cheek, trying to ignore his throat flexing just inches from her lips.

"What if you just did what you wanted for once, and not what you thought you should?"

She'd hardly gotten the thought out before the thread snapped and Milo closed the distance between them. Whiskey still lingered on their tongues as they swept across one another. It wasn't enough pressure, enough heat from where she stood. Hanna climbed onto the bar, pushing him back as she sat on the edge and parted her legs around him, begging him to fall into her. He didn't miss a beat, sliding his hand along her thighs and gliding the hem of her dress higher.

It was a completely different kiss than the night before. Deep and thorough, not starved and scattered.

She yelped into his mouth when his fingers slipped the buttons over her chest away, giving him access to her soft skin. The sound drove him to squeeze harder, grab more of her.

"Milo," she groaned, her head falling back as he moved to her neck. He lifted her, setting her feet on the ground behind the bar and pushing at the lace of her underwear, rolling it down to give him access.

"Fuck," he whispered, finding her more than ready for him —as if she hadn't been his to mold however he wanted all damn week. He kissed her again before pushing her forward, draping her over the bar. His belt hit the wood and a foil wrapper hissed in two.

"How old is that wallet condom?" she asked, laughing.

"Got a fresh box the night you flew in," he rasped as he leaned over her back, gripping her neck and pushing into her slowly. The pressure as he took his time filling her sent a shock-wave over her hips, manifesting in his name slipping from her mouth as he moved within her. They'd gotten so close so many times, she'd been brought over the edge by him so many times she thought she knew what it might feel like.

She'd woefully underestimated how good Milo would feel inside her, and that was one of the less fortunate truths of her life. One she'd have to contend with later—god, the time she'd wasted.

She pushed her hips back, searching for more of him.

"Easy now," he spat out between moaning her name.

"Good time, not a long time," Hanna panted.

Milo's grip tightened on her hips. "You," he gasped. "I need you *so* much closer." He pulled her up and she whimpered at the loss of him. "How opposed are you to fucking on the floor of a bar that I swear was cleaned this morning?"

His hands dug into her ass and wrapped her legs around him, pushing against her as she fought for breath. In that moment, Hanna didn't give two shits if the floor had ever been cleaned. She only wanted to feel him inside her again.

Milo attempted to sink them gracefully behind the bar, but as soon as his knees hit the floor, he fell back. She caught herself between the wall and the backstock lined beneath the bar top, giggling as he repositioned himself to sit against the wall. He leaned at an angle, yanking her down to him and guiding her hips gently over his lap.

She rolled her hips forward and he grabbed both sides of her face, kissing her slowly, reverently. It wasn't a distraction or to get a rise out of her. It wasn't teasing or playing a game.

It was genuinely enjoying being with her, being claimed by her.

His hands glided over her sides, setting a rhythm that had her lost for words and well on her way to only being able to rasp sounds. She wound her hips in circles, her mind so full of him she couldn't think of anything else as she inched closer to oblivion. One hand crawled up her thighs, pushing her dress up. She leaned back, shoving the fabric over her head so he could get to more of her, sink his teeth into her flesh.

He picked up the pace, fingers digging into her hips as they both stopped forming words. Hanna pulled away from his lips to breathe, but he was having none of it, hauling her back to him and biting at her lip, moaning into her mouth.

When the low thunder became her name, she damn near lost her mind.

"Don't stop," he whispered, his jaw clenched. "Keep going, baby."

The silence that followed was short-lived, but said so very much.

She tried not to let the word mean anything. Tried not to let it soak into her skin or tickle her ribs. Tried not to blush as she broke apart around him, her climax definitely not attached to the thrill of being his baby, if only for a second.

Milo was right behind her, his face buried in her hair. If they both stayed completely still, they could pretend it didn't happen. If neither of them looked at the other, they'd never have to admit how right it all felt.

Hanna leaned her head into his shoulder, her eyes fixed on the shelves beside them as she caught her breath.

"What's that?" she asked, pulling at a piece of paper sticking out from between the wood of the bar and the drywall. An old Polaroid broke loose and she flipped it over as he brushed her hair over her shoulder with his eyes still closed.

"Is this your mom?" she said, a faded old image of a young woman standing in front of the bar, her hair falling in long dark waves, teased to hell and back. Milo snagged the photo from her hands.

"It is," he laughed. "Dad must have stashed it back here."

Neither of them pointed out the bright yellow sunflower emblazoned across her cropped shirt as they sat in the silence for another moment.

FIFTEEN

"So, about tonight," Milo said over his eggs and bacon at the cafe.

They'd spent most of the night in his bed, watching old movies, and then *not* watching old movies.

Her ears perked up. "Sara texted me this morning, she confirmed Logan is going to the Giants game with us."

"That's okay. I can keep my hands to myself for a few hours. I figured I'd work from the office today and let you have the apartment to actually get some work done." He smiled, and she giggled. They were both severely behind on their respective projects. "But maybe we could sneak away for a nightcap after?"

"That works for me," she said between pancake bites.

"Great. And then tomorrow night I made a seven o'clock reservation for dinner." He didn't look at her as he said it.

She set her fork down.

"Don't panic, Arizona. Just go with it, okay?"

She tried not to shake her head at the risk of alerting him to the spiral he'd ignited. It was just sex. All of it was just sex.

Until it wasn't. In the bar the day before, they'd stayed together, frozen in a loaded silence, for far too long. It was all she'd thought about and, approximately every thirteen seconds, his voice rang out against her skull, whispering *baby, baby, baby.*

And if she spent one more second wondering about whatever was between them now, or where their time box stood, she *was* going to freak out.

"I gotta go." Milo pushed his plate toward her, knowing that she wanted his fruit, and leaned forward to kiss her quickly. The boldness in public sent a thrill down her spine. "I've got a closet full of Giants shit if you want to borrow something."

"Bye," she tried to say casually as he leaned in for another kiss, but nothing about it was casual.

A moment after she watched him leave, her phone buzzed against the pink table.

> **DO NOT ANSWER**
> Hey, you at the cafe this morning?

It took everything in her not to respond that it was none of his damn business where she was, but it was decidedly easier for her to be nice after a night of panting against Milo's neck.

> **HANNA**
> Yes?

> **DO NOT ANSWER**
> Can I come by?

She only responded with a thumbs up and tried to spend the next few minutes breathing slowly. She was in no mood for round five of Logan versus Hanna, but she had to admit, she was curious what he wanted.

They'd mostly avoided each other after he'd popped by

Milo's, and the brief times they'd been forced together, they had found some sort of neutrality.

"Hey," Logan said awkwardly, sliding into the booth, replacing Milo's broad shoulders. They took up space in such different ways.

Logan was dressed for his last day of interviews in a shirt, a belt, and shiny shoes he used to reserve for weddings. Now she imagined they saw plenty of action in office buildings with equally glaring floors.

"Morning," she said, careful to assume he was there with good intentions, as much as she didn't want to.

She stared, waiting for him to speak.

"How's your week been?"

"Not bad," she said, and she wanted to tell him it was fucking incredible, but that would be selfish of her. Cruel even.

"I'm really sorry," he started. "I know that half our conversations lately have started with me apologizing, but I feel like things are so weird between us, and I just would *love* it if we could patch them up before I'm back in New York."

"I know," she sighed. "And I also know that I haven't exactly made things easier for either of us." Logan's face softened with the relief that she was willing to take on even one iota of the blame. "I don't want to watch Sara and Matty get married across from someone I hate."

"I don't want that either. At all. The last few days have been hard. I didn't realize how much I missed the four of us together, you know?"

"I do. We used to have a great time."

Logan winced. "I hate that I ruined it all."

She chuckled a little. "Yeah, me too. But for the record, I think it was the right thing to do. We had so much growing up to do."

Logan nodded. "Hanna, I have to ask you something, and I

need you to just be honest with me." She knew what he was going to ask before his lips parted. Jealousy sizzled between them like lightning before thunder. "Is there something happening between you and Milo?"

"No," she said. "I told you. We're just friends."

Which *would be* the truth, as of Sunday morning, even if she'd just kissed him goodbye before work like they were three years of marriage and a kid on the way into a relationship.

"Okay," he said. His eyes darted across the diner, searching for anything but her.

"Okay," she shrugged.

"It just seems like you guys have a thing."

Hanna hung her head forward. "Do we really need to do ten more rounds of this?"

"You're right," he said, reaching for her coffee. She slapped his hand away. "I'm sorry."

She couldn't help herself. "How's Sloane, by the way?"

Logan looked out the window. "Fine."

"Great!" Hanna chirped. "Was there anything else?"

"No," he said, flipping a menu down from the end of the table. "You down to grab breakfast? It would be good civility practice for the wedding."

"Fine." She rolled her eyes. Logan and Matty were so similar sometimes—they couldn't go fifteen minutes without food. She'd already eaten with Milo, but she could attempt to be a grown up with Logan.

"You wanna tell me more about New York?"

He winced. "Are you sure you want to hear about it?"

"Yeah, I do. I've never been," she reminded him.

"Well," Logan started. "It loses the 'wow, this is just like the movies' charm pretty quickly, but the food is incredible."

She listened to him talk about all his favorite places to eat for the next forty-five minutes, and then they went their separate ways, and she only felt a little guilty about lying to him.

ALWAYS ANSWER

You know what's hot?

> HANNA
>
> This fucking stadium.

ALWAYS ANSWER

Yes.

And knowing that I'm only three innings away from tearing my own shirt off of you.

> HANNA
>
> Hmm. That's awfully presumptuous.

ALWAYS ANSWER

Says the woman who woke me up with her mouth around my dick this morning.

> HANNA
>
> What was I supposed to do? Wake up with your morning wood in my ass and not do something about it?

ALWAYS ANSWER

I was dreaming of you.

"ALWAYS ANSWER?" Sara hissed next to her.

"Shit," she muttered, jumping as she shoved her phone in her pocket, suddenly *very* interested in the line for the bathroom.

"Hanna!"

"It's nothing, just a bit of flirting," she muttered.

"Are you guys *sexting*? At a baseball game?"

Hanna forced a laugh as she pulled her hair into a ponytail.

"Is it my fault if America's pastime gets me going? It's the pants. So tight!"

Sara picked at her nailbed. "I know it's not my business and we're being very *cool* about all of this, but—"

Hanna held up a hand. "Ask yourself if you want to be the secret keeper here."

She considered that for a moment as the line moved two steps forward.

"Maybe not."

"Okay."

"Okay," she agreed. "But is Always Answer as good in bed as I think he is?"

Hanna blushed again, miserable, but unwilling to lie to her the way she'd lied to Logan.

"Better."

"Damn, Hanna."

She swallowed. "I know."

Sara scoffed. "Best of luck, babe."

"YOU GUYS WANT ONE MORE DRINK?" Matty asked, stumbling down the street after what felt like forty-five innings.

"Let's do it," Milo said. He grinned like a kid who just over-heard their mom suggest eating out.

"You're going to hate yourself tomorrow," Hanna laughed. While he drank often, he never really drank heavily, and seeing his eyes clouded over amused her.

"I could do one more," Logan muttered, pushing past them.

Matty led them into a small, crowded bar and came back with a myriad of things, some of which they ordered, some of which they didn't.

"Cheers," Milo said, clinking his glass against hers.

"What are we toasting to?' Sara asked.

"To releasing the old," Milo slurred, sloshing beer over the edge of his cup. "And... embracing... whatever, you guys get it."

"Can we get a pitcher of water, please?" Hanna asked the server as she scooted by.

"Good idea," Milo mumbled. "You're so smart."

"And you're *so* drunk," Hanna said, leaning across the high top and patting his head. His eyes narrowed, and she knew she'd tripped a wire. She shook her head. Not there. Not feet from Logan. "Down, boy," she whispered.

"Don't do that," he said, not nearly as quietly as she needed him to. "*That* is a gateway drug."

"You're pathetic."

"Don't act like you're not into it," he laughed and leaned a little too far back, slipping off the barstool.

"Jesus," Sara huffed under her breath. She tossed Hanna a warning look.

"Okay," Hanna sighed, pulling his forearm. "I think it's time to get you home."

He shook his head. "No way! I'm fine. But you should stop spinning. It's a little disorienting."

She squeezed her eyes closed, trying not to laugh. "Aw, buddy."

"Do you need help?" Matty asked. "I just ordered wings."

"Wings sound so good," Milo whined.

Hanna shook her head, her ponytail swinging as Milo tracked it.

"I will get you food. You need to get up four floors before you need to be carried."

"Will you please text me when you get home?" Sara asked, wrapping her arms around Hanna. "If you have time."

Hanna rolled her eyes but dropped a kiss on her cheek

before turning to Milo, who seemed to be in a constant state of swaying.

"Come on, big guy."

Milo stumbled next to her for two blocks before the evening breeze reinvigorated him.

"I'm sorry," he said, still soft around the sounds. "I don't usually get drunk. I try not to anyway."

"I owe you one." Hanna fell back to that dive bar in Phoenix, trying not to get lost in those dimples.

Milo smirked. "True. You were *so* mean to me that night." He bumped his shoulder into hers under the streetlight.

Hanna protested. "Only for the first few minutes!"

"No one can resist my charms for long, Arizona."

She laughed as he pulled on the end of her ponytail. "Diner coffee and pie, or cold leftover pasta?"

Milo stumbled over a crack in the street. "You pick."

"Pie," she said, leading him into the diner. The server appeared next to their favorite table with two glasses of water and a fresh pot of coffee.

"Can we get a slice of the French silk and... a..." She looked over the list on the handwritten menu above the counter. "Ah, lemon meringue."

"Be right back," she said.

Milo leaned his head against the laminate table. He mumbled from under his elbow.

"You study me, too."

"You ordered the lemon last time we stumbled in here with Chloe."

He was silent for a second, and then whispered, "I think you like me a little more than you wanted to."

Hanna's face heated, completely caught off guard. "Um—" It wasn't that she was surprised. The feelings didn't sneak up. But she was surprised to hear him acknowledge it.

"Don't make it weird. I *definitely* like you more than I should."

"Can you at least look at me while you drunkenly confess shit?" He picked his head up off the table, and no, no, he could not look at her. He couldn't even locate her. "Oh, god, you're a goner."

"Nothing pie can't heal."

"Let us pray," she groaned as two plates hit the table.

The lemon meringue did some heavy lifting. Halfway through his slice, he was at least able to look her in the eye, though he still wasn't fully online.

"I want to go home, lie next to you in bed, and pass out so fucking hard, Hanna."

"Done and done," she agreed and paid their tab, dragging him across the street and into the elevator. When the doors closed, he slumped against the wall, half asleep as they raced toward their floor.

His floor. Not our floor, she reminded herself.

He reached for her, a gesture she wasn't about to ignore, and she leaned into him.

"I mean it, Arizona, I like you too much."

She nodded against his chest, the dread of the sentiment all too familiar.

"I know."

"And you like me too much."

"I do," she whispered.

They stayed quiet as they stripped off their shoes and jeans. She flopped into his bed in just his Giants T-shirt and he fell over her, nuzzling into her neck.

"You should wear that sundress on our date tomorrow," he mumbled into her skin. She twisted so his arms draped over her, and she lay flush against him. "The one you wore at the engagement party."

177

"Anything you want, Milo."

SIXTEEN

"And then he asked you on a date?" Olivia asked, her infuriating pen moving far too quickly across the page.

Hanna had been determined not to mention Milo during her therapy session, but her mind couldn't find anything else to talk about.

He occupied every space.

"I think?"

Olivia *hmm'd* as she looked over her notes. "And you're... feeling okay about that?"

Hanna snorted. "No!" She rested her forehead on the guest room desk. "It's an insane idea."

"How so?"

"He's not available. I'm not available. We're just friends!"

Olivia remained silent, her signature move.

"I can't lose someone else," Hanna whispered. "And I feel like this is careening into losing a friend very quickly."

"Let me ask you this, Hanna," Olivia said, her beige office even flatter over the webcam. "If you could survive losing Logan, and losing your mother, what makes the thought of losing Milo—whom you've known for a few months—different?"

Hanna leaned back against the chair. What *did* make it different with him?

"I hate when you do that."

"My job?" Olivia asked.

"Yeah," Hanna sighed.

SHE WRAPPED the last few straight pieces of her hair around the curling iron, counting to ten as her heart tied itself into knots. She was still arguing with Olivia in her head when three sharp knocks on the front door interrupted her rebuttal.

She waited to see if Milo answered, but she didn't hear him downstairs. Thinking about it, she hadn't actually heard him come home.

Three more knocks sounded on the door and she skipped down the stairs to see who it was. Glancing through the peephole, she burst out laughing at the sight on the other side.

Milo waited in the hallway, dressed in slacks and a buttondown with the sleeves rolled up, the top buttons undone enough to see the edge of his tattoos. He had one hand behind his back, and she already knew he had a bouquet of sunflowers.

He was going to be the death of her.

She pulled open the door and he lifted the bright yellow bundle, the petals like rays of sunshine hitting his face.

"Hey, gorgeous."

She'd already decided upstairs that whatever happened that night, it would live separately from any other facet of reality. After this weekend, she would never be on a date with Milo again, so for the next several hours, she was going to take advantage of it.

In the spirit of this decision, she threw herself into his arms, the paper wrapper around the flowers crunching into her back as he hit the wall outside of the door.

"You missed me," he mumbled, kissing her softly. The chastity of it somehow felt more intimate than anything else he'd done to her, sending butterflies racing around her stomach.

She giggled against him.

"Maybe." Hanna leaned her weight into him, enjoying how it felt to touch him outside of their little bubble, even if only by a few inches, dressed up for a date.

She wanted to distill that feeling into one of his empty whiskey bottles and draw little hearts on the label like a lovesick teenager.

Jesus Christ, Sunday will be sobering, she thought.

"Let's go, I don't want to get stuck in traffic!" Sara yelled.

Sara?

Sara!

"Fuck."

She wasn't sure if she or Milo said it, but he pulled her into his apartment in a blur, the door slamming behind them. For a second, neither of them moved, but Sara had heard someone and, of course, wanted to say hi. Sara knocked on the door and Milo stared at her, eyes wide. He did not make a move to answer it.

He'd sacrificed her. The monster.

Hanna gestured to her dress, and he shrugged, but Sara ultimately decided for them by tapping on the door again and yelling, "Hanna! Was that you?"

Just then, Hanna heard Logan and Matty's voices bouncing off the hallway walls too. It was getting worse by the second. Hanna opened the door, putting on her best breezy act.

"Damn, what are you dressed up for?" Sara stared at her

like she had four heads. Milo tucked himself behind the door, trying not to breathe too loudly.

Hanna frowned. "I was just on my way over to show you this option! Narrowing down my final Vegas selects."

Sara pressed her lips together tightly. "Oh. Yeah, I mean, you look hot as fuck. Is this for the first night or the second?"

Hanna struggled to think of a single plan they'd made. "Second."

"Oh, perfect! I need to up my game. I'm wearing way too much fabric."

Logan stepped forward. "What are you doing tonight? We're going to visit Mom and Dad, I'm sure they'd like to see you."

Sara and Hanna looked at him with the same mystified glare. His eyes switched between them rapidly.

"I think I'll have to pass on that, Logan."

Sara broke the awkward silence. "Where's Milo?"

She shrugged. "No idea."

"He's not home yet?"

"Mmm, if he is, he's being very, very quiet." At least that was the truth. Sara peered into the apartment, more than suspicious, but she wasn't about to say anything in front of the boys.

"Well, definitely don't let him see you in that, he's an ass man," Sara joked. Matty groaned and rolled his eyes. Logan looked like he had just been kicked in the gut.

Hanna forced a laugh. "Alright well, on that note, give Tom and Marcia all my love!"

"I will." Sara turned to the guys and shooed them forward, looking back down the hall at Hanna as she rounded the corner. She mouthed before she was out of view, "Use protection."

Hanna slammed the door closed. "Oh my fucking god."

Milo let out a breath, a smile playing at the corner of his

mouth. He grabbed a handful of her, slipping his fingers under the hem of her dress and tickling her thigh.

"She's right, though. I am an ass man."

Hanna pulled at his collar. "Yes, you've made that very clear."

"I will not apologize." He held her for another moment before heading toward the kitchen and pulling a mason jar out from under the sink. She watched as he arranged the flowers into a perfect golden halo.

He looked her over. "You ready? Or do you need another minute?"

"I just need shoes!"

She headed back upstairs, finding her heels in her Vegas bag and fastening the straps. On her way back down, she had to stop just to admire the sight of him leaning on the kitchen counter next to her flowers, looking like a damn dream. Olivia's question echoed in her mind once again—what made him so different?

Shit.

"I've got a car coming," he said, looking at his phone, blissfully unaware of the very dangerous yearning she was experiencing from the stairs.

She grabbed her purse and followed him out to the elevator. As soon as the door closed, she made her move.

She pressed him against the wall, wrapping her arms around his neck and applying pressure to his hips.

Milo groaned as they came to a stop. "Easy, Arizona. We've got all night."

The door rolled back and she marched ahead, knowing full well he watched every step.

He caught up quickly and then did something she never expected, catching her as off guard as he'd been in the elevator.

He held her hand.

"THIS IS QUITE THE VIEW," she said over a glass of Johnnie Walker Blue—her pick—staring out the nineteenth-floor window of a gorgeous restaurant in Nob Hill.

From the low-lit table, she could see all of San Francisco, the city lights framing the blue Bay. They were several shared plates in and she was already buzzed from the scotch.

Milo raised an eyebrow over his drink. "Want a fun fact?"

"You have fun facts?" She smiled. He was having more fun than she expected. *Too much fun.* The entire ride over, he kept a hand on her knee, chatting away about any and everything, a levity to him that was totally new to her.

He tilted his head sideways. "Lower your expectations. I have one singular fun fact. So, back when World War II broke out, soldiers would ship out from the Bay, but first, they'd come here to Top of the Mark and toast to the bridge for good luck." Milo winced. "Actually, now that I'm saying it out loud, I realize it's less fun, more sad in the greater context of every-thing. I would like to amend it to an interesting fact."

She shrugged and stabbed another bite of steak with her fork.

"I guess if you have to say goodbye, this isn't the worst place you could do it." His smile twisted a little and she realized he'd taken what she'd said personally. "No hidden meaning, I promise."

"Have I mentioned how incredible you look tonight?"

"You have not."

He grinned. "I'm a stupid, stupid man."

"You know, I've always said that about you." She smirked and he laid a hand over hers. It was funny how intimate such small brushes of his skin had become in the light of Date Night

Milo. But there, where people could see them, and against both of their better judgments, it felt wilder than any of the other encounters they'd had.

He squeezed her hand and then brought it to his lips, gently brushing them over her fingers. She wondered how quickly they could get the check.

But Milo was enjoying the evening, and she was determined to enjoy it for him too.

"Hanna," he said after his last bite, clearly thinking long and hard about his next few words. "I have to tell you, I can't stop thinking about the other day," he finally confessed. "In the bar."

"Which part?" She wiggled her eyebrows at him.

Milo dropped his gaze to their hands. "I'm serious, Hanna. Something changed. I've never really felt like that before."

"Never?" It shocked her a little. She hadn't considered that a man like Milo had anything *but* insanely passionate encounters.

He shook his head, drawing a little circle on the back of her hand.

"Never. There's something that happens between us I can't describe, it's crazy."

"I know. Milo—"

"I know what we said, and I promise you that, come Sunday, I will get my shit together. But can we just pretend for now that we're not on a deadline?"

He looked so earnest and she wished she'd never suggested the time box in the first place. She hated the fact that he was feeling bound to it.

She nodded and soaked in the view.

He was right, they could still enjoy their night. Everything could wait until Sunday.

THE UBER BACK was filled with the kind of tension that only existed when she'd already figured out the ending of a movie, but not quite how they get there.

It wasn't the will-they-won't-they, Ross-and-Rachel shit. It was *when*, not *if*, and the way Milo crawled his hand up her dress, the answer was sooner rather than later.

His finger traced paths on her upper thigh, dancing dangerously close to the point of no return. Once he crossed that line, it was on, and he knew it. So he stayed just to the side of it, teasing and touching, giving her the dirtiest fucking look he could as she debated whether or not to give the driver a free show.

He dropped them off just a few blocks from the loft and Milo pulled her into a loud bar, buzzing with the Friday night crowd.

They headed to the long countertop at the back of the room, watching the bartender take care of a few others before Milo ordered for them—two bourbons—but she couldn't focus on what he was saying. He pressed her into the bar from behind, his body enveloping hers.

While they waited, he took one hand and dipped it around her hip, reaching for her inner thigh. She pushed into him, arching her back in what she hoped was a subtle enough way that no one around them raised an eyebrow, but she could tell it made him reevaluate how far he wanted to push it with an audience.

"Take me home," she pleaded. She loved the way he teased, but she needed more. He shook his head and put a little distance between them, taking a deep breath.

"One more drink," he said, handing her whatever he'd

ordered. She slammed it back, which was no small feat. It was a rough motherfucker.

Milo burst into laughter. "Okay, okay, loud and clear."

He sipped his whiskey intensely, and way too slowly. She ran her hands along his stomach, flicking the stupid buttons on his stupid shirt. She wanted them gone.

"Hanna, as much as I love this enthusiasm, I'm having a really great night with you. I promise the moment we're back in the apartment, I'm going to do every depraved thing you want, but right now I'd love to just enjoy this."

She sensed that he almost said "before it's over," but it died on his tongue.

She took in a sharp breath and sighed loudly. "Okay, fine. You want Date Night Hanna? You get Date Night Hanna. Buy me another drink and I'll behave," she promised.

SHE HUMORED Milo for another hour, answering his questions about her favorite movies, books, and songs—everything he could possibly want to know, he asked.

And she had questions too.

She wanted to know his nieces and nephews' names, the first girl who'd ever hurt him, and which tattoo had been the most painful.

"You know," he said, his words running together. "Tattoos are strikingly similar to grief."

She swirled her glass, one finger tracing the black line of the clock on his forearm.

"Painful?" Hanna asked.

He nodded, his head tilting. "Well yeah, that." He leaned forward, pressing a kiss into her hair. "But the ink, once it's injected, your body panics, right? And it sends all these little cells that attack foreign substances, macrophages, to the site to help fight off infection and get it the fuck out of there. They ingest all the ink, but they can't break it down, so it just stays there, frozen, trapped in your skin. It fades over time, sure, but it never goes away—it just becomes part of you. Millions of little black moments, caught in these well-intended cells that can never get rid of them, but... from far enough away, it's art."

Hanna swallowed, her fingers stuck on the edge of the clock, unable to move as she considered it—the beauty in being trapped. The poetry of ingestion.

She dipped her head, pressing her lips to the edge of the black lines, hoping one day hers might be art too. Her eyes fell on the final drops of liquid in her glass and she wondered if maybe losses like theirs were not so different from whiskey, either.

Undrinkable on day one—but smoother as the years dragged on. Milo was proof she could build a tolerance, wasn't he?

She tapped the glass rim, wondering what notes her mother would carry—the soft vanillas still living in a nearly empty perfume bottle she couldn't bring herself to throw out, a strange blend of unlabeled spices that never had a name but Lisa used it in everything just to cover her bases.

For not the first time, Hanna's mind landed on a question she'd avoided since they met.

If she did manage to give up her vice, would they have anything left between them?

EVENTUALLY, he decided he'd collected enough data on her. He pulled her from the bar, swinging their hands between them as they walked home.

"So," he said, rounding the corner onto Brannan. "You're moving back to Matty's on Sunday, but I thought that since you'll wake up at my place that morning, you're still *technically* in the time box until midnight..."

"Okay," she stared at him, already trying to figure out how she'd tell Olivia about the time box without sounding fucking stupid.

Milo looked incredibly nervous. "What are your thoughts on joining me for dinner Sunday night?"

"At your mom's?"

"Yeah," he mumbled. The confident Milo she'd been with all this time was completely gone. He pulled at her fingers, cracking the knuckles.

"I think I'd like that," she answered, a little confused about what he was asking. "Do you introduce your mom to all your friends with benefits?"

She stopped in front of the building and dropped his hand, prepared to run, perhaps. Anxiety pooled in her stomach— she'd managed to avoid it for so long, but the dread built by the second.

"No." He shook his head, searching her eyes. "I don't."

"Okay," she said softly, smiling as he held the door open to the apartment lobby. He trailed behind her to the elevator, his hand on the small of her back as they got in and hit the fourth floor.

Before the doors even closed, he was on her, one hand in her hair, the other up her dress. He pushed his tongue into her mouth, wasting no time making good on the promise he'd made back at the bar.

It was different from the last time he'd had her pinned against an elevator wall, something more than just sparks between them.

In the hallway, she pressed herself against his back while he tried to get the door unlocked, running her hands over his chest from behind. She kissed his shoulders through his shirt, taking every piece of him she could. The door gave way and he walked forward, throwing keys, wallets, purses, and shoes down in little piles on the way to the living room.

She barely let him get his pants off before she ripped at his shirt, buttons be damned. She pulled at her dress, but he stopped her, his voice low—a far-off storm—but coming for her all the same.

"Leave it on for a bit. We're not rushing this."

Milo pushed against her in his underwear, his skin warm under her hands as he kissed her slowly, controlled. It was not the desperate, messy kissing they'd gotten used to. This was intentional, much more like at the bar.

It was how he would have kissed her if it was a real date and he was dropping her at her doorstep, instead of standing there half-naked.

Part of her was terrified. Part of her wanted to lean into that reality for as long as she could, unwilling to give up the dream. She reached for his face, stroking a thumb along the line of his stubble.

Every inch of her connected to somewhere on his body, and he slowly walked them toward the couch, where he laid her down, settling on top of her. His hands moved from her back to her legs—caressing the soft skin of her calves as they wrapped around him—and back up again, finding a spot just under her breasts to rest while he moved from kissing to sucking on the skin next to her ear.

"Tell me what you want," he whispered between kisses. "I'll do anything for you."

She'd promised herself she would thoroughly enjoy him while she could, and she had been keeping a few ideas in her back pocket. She cycled through places they hadn't gotten to in the apartment, but she was too distracted by his touch to concentrate.

He worked one hand under her dress, slipping a finger inside of her before she could focus on coming up with an answer, enjoying the wave of pleasure that radiated from between her hips into her chest. She let out a moan when he added a second finger, picking up his pace.

Hanna ran her hands over his back, tracing the cluster of tattoos that flowed along the top of his shoulder. She reached one hand to his jaw and pulled his face to hers, staring him in the eye. She felt him between her thighs, just under his hand, and she rotated her hips to create more friction.

His fingers quickened and he ground against her. Her breath came in spurts, her eyes rolling back.

"That's right, Arizona, come for me," Milo whispered against her neck, and she was gone.

She tightened around his fingers and cried out, her back arching off the couch, pushing him even further into her. He kissed her chest, her neck, her jaw, letting her ride the wave until she came back down.

"We don't need this anymore," he whispered, tugging at her dress and stripping off his boxers. He sat back against the couch, pulling her over him.

She yanked the dress off over her head, letting it hit the floor as he traced a line from her ear to her tattooed arms with his fingertip, his eyes searing into her skin. She wanted to stay in that moment forever.

She sank onto him, his voice catching in his throat as he whispered, "You feel so good, baby." She froze once more—there was no ignoring it that time.

But... what if?

She *could* be his baby.

That would be fine, wouldn't it?

That would be *more* than fine.

God, why did it have to be more complicated than that?

She moved her hips against his, his smile spreading over her neck while she gently stroked his hair and shoulders, slowing down her pace to get the most out of him.

He leaned his head back and bucked his hips into her, holding onto the eye contact they typically avoided at that point. He watched her lips part as she lost control.

Neither of them had the presence of mind to hear Matty's keys in the door.

But they sure as shit heard Logan yell, "What the fuck?"

Everything happened in a blur. Milo hauling her off of his lap and scrambling to find her dress, Sara trying to calm down a very drunk Logan whose string of angry opposition only grew louder.

Milo fumbled with his clothes while Hanna pulled on her dress, trying her best to avoid eye contact with everyone in the room while Matty turned away and Sara stared with wide eyes.

It was over.

It was goddamn over.

Whatever had shifted, whatever was changing, it was gone in an instant, the consequences raining over them.

Milo stood between her and Logan in an attempt to slow him down as he pushed past Sara and stormed toward Hanna, yelling. His eyes were wild and the smell of beer seeped across the room.

"Logan, calm down," Milo said, but that just made things worse.

"Don't fucking talk to me, Milo. Of all the—"

"Guys," Matty groaned, rubbing his forehead.

Logan's eyes burned a hole through her. "You swore there was nothing happening between you two, I asked you point-blank yesterday, and you fucking lied to me!"

He stood between all of them, slurring and waving his arms, but everyone pieced together what he'd said just fine.

She tried not to look at Sara, who was standing next to Matty with her hand over her mouth while Logan continued shouting.

"Logan, you're drunk. Go home," Hanna practically spat. She could not believe she was right back to Logan ruining everything good in her life once more. "Go back to Sloane!"

"I might be drunk, but at least I'm not a fucking liar!" He glared at her and then at Milo, who looked as bewildered as she felt. "And you. After everything we've come back from, you motherfucker!"

"I told you the truth at the time," she insisted. "Okay?"

"Oh yeah? Is that what 'just friends' looks like to you?" He emphasized *just friends* with air quotes that felt like a slap in the face.

Logan stopped yelling long enough to look her in the eye, and she could see that it wasn't just a drunken ex ranting. Logan thought she meant she was holding space for him.

"Logan, when we talked, I thought you were trying to smooth things over. I didn't think—"

"You should have told me you were fucking him, Hanna."

"Why the *hell* would I tell you that? Why do you think I owe you anything?" She was yelling then too, and it felt like they had an audience for what should have been a private conversation, but they were on a roll and she couldn't stop herself. "Who do you even think you are? You show up here completely unannounced, and pry like you're entitled to anything about me. I let you in, I even talk about my mother with you, I give you what you need, and you take that little tiny crack in the window as a door wide open. Who I'm fucking has nothing to do with you!"

"Nice," Milo mumbled, clearly offended. She couldn't fight

a two-front war. Her head was spinning and she was just trying to stay upright.

Hanna drew a sharp breath. "I can't fight both of you right now! We haven't talked about what we're doing, so why would I talk about it with anyone else?"

"So what, you guys have just been fucking this whole time and sneaking around?" Matty asked, his unshakable demeanor falling away.

Milo didn't look at her. She tried to explain, "Yes! Yes. We've been hooking up, but..." she trailed off, not really sure what else to say.

That got Milo's attention. "But what, Hanna? But it means nothing? But we're just fucking friends?"

"No, that's not what I'm saying. Jesus, can I get a second to think?"

Milo ignored her. "When did you see Logan?"

Three sets of eyes bounced back and forth between them, and Hanna seriously considered walking outside to the balcony and throwing herself off of it.

She stepped toward Milo instead. "He came by the cafe yesterday."

Milo scoffed. "So, I kiss you goodbye, and five minutes later, you tell Logan nothing is happening?"

She opened her mouth to protest but she was sick of defending herself to an audience. She was sweating. Her bones hurt as they stretched around her lungs, hyperventilating.

She mumbled, "I didn't know—I wasn't sure what was happening. You don't date, right?"

"We should go," Sara said, sensing that they'd hit a wall. Logan was still muttering to himself. Matty yanked him by the arm and dragged him out of the apartment.

And for two seconds, it was the kind of quiet that consumed entire nights.

Hanna's head exploded with thoughts, everything rushing in at once. She fought for breath, the silence leaving room for all of the fears she'd had about losing someone else to materialize. She shook her head, unsure of what to say.

Milo slammed something around in the kitchen. The sound clattered against her skull, driving the thoughts further into her blood.

She thought she heard her name, but she was too far gone. She darted up the stairs and ran toward the bathroom. She needed to cool the fire within her, and when her panic attacks were at their worst, a cold shower could bring her back to her body. She opened the tap to the shower, battling the zipper on the back of her dress.

"God," she hissed. "Shit!"

Two hands pulled at the zipper, Milo's tattoos gently pushing her dress over her hips. He snagged one of her clips from the bathroom counter and wrestled her hair off her shoulders as she struggled to get her breathing under control. He stayed while she stood under the cold water.

It hit her skin like needles.

But it helped.

It brought her back.

When her breathing finally slowed, she turned off the water. The silence was still grating, but tolerable. Milo leaned against the vanity, his eyes focused on the floor.

"You okay?" he asked.

"Fine," she whispered.

"So, no."

"No," she answered.

"I'm too drunk for this conversation, Arizona. I'm going to put some coffee on."

She exhaled, wrapping herself in the towel he held out to her.

"Okay. I'll change and come downstairs."

THE SMELL of coffee flooded the apartment as she hovered at the base of the steps. Milo sat at the dining room table with two mugs in front of him.

"Hey," she said, hesitant to sit down.

"Hey." He laughed darkly, rubbing his temples.

"I'm so sorry, Milo—"

He held up his hand and the face of the clock tattoo stared at her, a declaration of truth she wasn't ready for.

Time's up.

"I've decided we're idiots," he announced.

"What?"

"I really care about you, Hanna. And I know you care about me. But we set boundaries around this for a reason, and it was unfair of me to push them."

She tried to hold herself together. "Oh."

"I knew what this was."

"But—" *But what?* Things changed? Maybe they'd only changed for her.

He continued, "Logan is going home tomorrow. We have Vegas in a few weeks. I don't want to push it further and then lose you as a friend, Hanna. I can't—" There it was. The truth. It caught somewhere between his throat and his lips. "I can't lose you, and I let shit get blurry. That's on me."

"Okay," she sighed. "I hate that you're right."

His lips folded into a frown. "I was kind of hoping you'd tell me I wasn't."

She leaned back, running her hands through her hair. "I wish I could, Milo."

He sipped his coffee. "I know."

"So, what do we do now?"

Milo finished his coffee. She felt him sift through a thousand different thoughts before he spoke again.

"I'll tell you what I want to do. I want to take you into that bedroom, and I want to finish what we started tonight. I didn't know it was going to be the last time I heard you moan my name, and I didn't get to appreciate it the way I should have.

Then tomorrow, we're going to wake up—and probably fuck you one more time because I have zero self-control when it comes to you—and pack your shit, and walk you back across the hall, and try to forget what you taste like before I have to see you in that fucking dress again. How's that sound?

Hanna bit her lip. "Like a really bad idea."

He sighed just as she stood from the table, walked directly to his room, and climbed into his bed. She was ready to let him claim any of the pieces left of her before morning—when their time really would be up.

SEVENTEEN

When her mom died, she could lose three weeks in a blink.

She'd wake up one day, check her calendar, and be absolutely floored to find that another month had slipped away.

The three weeks between walking out of Milo's bedroom, and seeing him in her doorway as she tossed the last of her Vegas necessities into her bag had crawled by—and no amount of blinking had hurried the days.

"Oh Jesus," she gasped, unprepared to see anyone watching her from the door, but especially him.

They'd run into one another twice since Logan had left, and both times were so excruciating that she had heavily considered going back home and telling Sara that their twenty years of friendship had been great, but she was simply going to pass away.

Seeing him in the doorway, his dark curls still wet from the shower, was no different.

"Arizona."

"Hey," she murmured.

"You look like you're dreading this as much as I am."

198

"I'm not dreading seeing you," she whispered, all too aware that Sara was clinging to every errant phrase she could catch from the living room. "I'm dreading seeing Logan. But you, I know you'll at least be nice."

"Have you talked to him?"

She laughed. "What do you think?"

Milo sighed and folded his arms. "He sent me some choice words a few days ago."

"I'm so sorry, Milo. I figured with Sloane, he'd gotten over whatever feelings he had for me. I don't know, it was all really confusing. I hate that I made things weird for you guys. I never wanted to come between friends."

Milo's lips fell into an odd twist. "I wouldn't worry too much about that one."

"Hanna!" Matty called from downstairs. "Did you print a boarding pass?"

She leaned out of her room. "Oh shit, is this flight leaving from the nineteen hundreds?"

That got a laugh out of Milo, a sound that tore a hole in her chest.

Matty called back, "What if your phone dies?"

"I'll use yours. You packed, what, three extended batteries for a two-hour flight?"

Matty mumbled something, and Sara shushed him.

"Airport Dad is anxious," Milo said.

"Airport Dad is not confident in his best man, groomsman, or maid of honor's abilities to be cool, baby." She shot finger guns at him and he dramatically brought his hands to his chest, throwing his head back with each hit.

He leaned against the doorframe. "We're cool! We're so cool. I just saw all the slutty underwear you're packing and I'm barely thinking about the way your breath hitches in my ear when you—"

Matty yelled again, "What about your ID? Do you have it in an easily accessible pocket?"

"Yep!" she yelled back, turning to Milo. "Is this what you want, Milo? To go back to the dirty-talking and teasing?"

He dropped his eyes to hers, pushing her back against the wall.

"It's easier for me to be a sleazy jackass, Arizona. Hurts less than being real. But I can shut it down."

She pressed her lips together. She could understand that. And frankly, get behind it.

"I suppose I do miss your bullshit."

"Great! And if I push it too far, just tell me to go fuck myself."

She crawled her hand over his chest, slapping him gently on the cheek as she rolled her carry-on by him.

"And you would, like the good little boy you are."

Milo glared, took her suitcase, and hauled it over his shoulder.

"Don't be mean to me, I'll come."

She was officially down one awkward former lover.

One to go.

"OKAY, YOU CAN OPEN YOUR EYES!"

Sara stepped forward, pulling the silver *Bride to Be* sleep mask off her face as the rest of her bridesmaids exploded into a chorus of giggles.

"Oh my god, you guys!" She spun around a glittering penthouse suite at The Cosmo, the noisy Vegas strip bustling below.

"Surprise!" Taylor yelled, her ponytail bouncing as she pulled Sara into the room. There were balloons, champagne bottles, and rhinestones *everywhere*.

"This is amazing," Sara cried, touching a banner that read *Lucky in Love*. "Oh Jesus," she giggled at the bucket of penis straws.

"Your mom sent those," Hanna informed her.

"We'll tell her we loved them."

Hanna popped the cork off a bottle of rosé and handed it over.

"Welcome to your bachelorette weekend! You've got a glam squad in the bathroom, we're having pre-dinner cocktails at Ghost Donkey, dinner at Vanderpump, and then we're going dancing at Marquee with the boys!"

Sara's eyes welled. "This is the *best,* Hanna. Thank you."

"Go get in the chair! Yell if your glass gets empty!"

Sara disappeared into one of the bathrooms, and the rest of the girls milled about, snapping selfies with the suite decor and snacking as they got ready for the night.

"You outdid yourself," Taylor said, pouring a glass of champagne. "How ya doing, sunshine?"

She looped an arm around Hanna's shoulders and leaned her head into her. Hanna hadn't seen Taylor since she'd moved to Boston after school, but she'd been so kind when her mom was sick, checking in daily for the first few months after until she was confident Hanna wasn't going to completely lose it.

"I'm fine. Great, actually. I've been staying with Sara and Matty out in the Bay.

"Good change of pace?"

"Definitely."

"Helps that the man across the hall is hot as hell," Maricela, Sara's cousin, said with brows arched, popping a grape into her mouth. She turned to Taylor. "I met him at the engagement party. Dreamboat."

Taylor's eyes snapped to Hanna's. "You holding out on me?"

"No," she laughed, even though it crushed her to say it. "We're just good friends."

If the girls knew just how good of friends Hanna and Milo had been a few weeks prior, they'd never let it go

"I need pictures," Taylor demanded. Hanna pulled up Milo's Instagram on her phone and handed it over. Taylor scrolled for a solid minute before glaring. "Oof, good luck."

"I mean it. It's platonic. We decided to just stick to being friends after we—"

She realized at the same time they did that she had said too much.

"Spill," Maricela said. Taylor leaned in, still scrolling through Milo's feed.

"Nothing," Hanna said, shrugging them off. "We hooked up once, immediately regretted it and decided to drop it."

"Idiots," Taylor mumbled, zooming in on one of Milo's arms. "You two are *idiots*." Hanna's phone buzzed and Taylor's eyes flickered between whatever she saw and Hanna's face. "Miss *ma'am*." Her cheeks flushed and she tapped the screen, holding it up to Maricela.

"Hanna!" They giggled as she lunged for the phone.

"Give me that," she muttered, panicked.

> ALWAYS ANSWER
>
> We just left the airport bar.
>
> You drunk yet?
>
> Or do you need a bad influence? 😈

"No, no, okay, that's not what it looks like." She blushed a thousand shades of red. "I mean it, we decided to just go back to our harmless flirting to keep ourselves from going crazy this weekend. It's a long story."

"Whatever you need to tell yourself," Taylor snorted. "Can't *wait* to watch that play out with Logan this weekend."

You and everyone else, Hanna thought.

"This weekend is about Sara and Matty, okay? Not my bullshit."

> HANNA
>
> You're going to love what I'm wearing tonight.

ALWAYS ANSWER

Bet I'd love it off you more.

> HANNA
>
> Are you that bored with your friends?

ALWAYS ANSWER

I'm not bored. I'm tense. Just picked up
Logan.

> HANNA
>
> Ugh. What's the vibe?

ALWAYS ANSWER

It's not great, Arizona.

> HANNA
>
> Tell Logan I say, 'Fuck off.' He'll know what it
> means.

ALWAYS ANSWER

Easy, hotshot.

Did you get my gift?

> HANNA
>
> No?

ALWAYS ANSWER

Check the bar.

She left the bathroom and beelined for the bar in the kitchenette, several overpriced bottles glittering under the hotel lighting.

But one amber bottle sat to the side with a yellow ribbon around the neck and a card tucked beneath a round flask, a silver sunflower carved into it.

"What's that?" Taylor asked, peering around her shoulder. She snagged the card out of Hanna's hand before she could read it.

"Arizona," she read. "You can be nice to anyone for three days. But if you can't, here's some emergency bourbon to take the edge off. M."

Taylor threw her head back in a cackle. "Oh yeah, you two are *totally* platonic."

Hanna stared at the note and felt a bubble of panic rise in her chest. She grimaced, pulling the cork from the bottle and taking a swig before filling the flask, grasping for the breathing exercises Olivia had taught her.

"Just don't judge me this weekend, okay?"

BY THE TIME Sara left the suite, blown out and blurred, she was a bottle of champs down and ready to *party*. Hanna's thirty-year-old back twitched. She rocked in the elevator in her heels, already certain they'd be slung in her hands by the end of the night.

As they descended a thousand floors, she pulled at the hem of her skirt, acutely aware of how short it was. Her phone buzzed in her clutch, rattling against her new flask.

DO NOT ANSWER

Excited to see you tonight!

(3) MISSED CALLS ALWAYS ANSWER
ALWAYS ANSWER

You update my name in your phone to
sometimes answer?

HANNA

Sorry, was busy squeezing myself into the
world's smallest dress.

ALWAYS ANSWER

Logan and Sloane broke up.

HANNA

Oh.

Jesus.

Is he a mess?

ALWAYS ANSWER

He's being alarmingly chill about the whole
thing.

"What's going on?" Sara asked.

"Sloane and Logan broke up," she murmured. The elevator stopped and they poured out into the casino.

"What! What happened? Is he okay?"

"I'm not sure. All my intel is coming from Milo. He says things seem okay?"

Sara tilted her head. "Huh."

"I know, I wonder what happened."

"No, I mean, *huh*, Milo hates drama. Wild that he's even involving himself. Or that you two are even talking at all." Sara's brown eyes settled on hers.

When was the last time Hanna had even looked Sara in them?

"I think he just doesn't want me blindsided."

"How thoughtful," she said, eyes narrowing.

Taylor inserted herself between them, grabbing Sara's hand and twirling her toward the nearest cocktail bar.

"What fruity little drink am I buying you first?"

ALWAYS ANSWER

Are you fucking kidding me?

HANNA

What now?

ALWAYS ANSWER

We're at The Chandelier and I just watched you walk by.

Along with every goddamn man in this casino.

And several women.

HANNA

Come play.

ALWAYS ANSWER

I'm not coming within a ten-foot radius of you until I get some food in my system.

She tucked her phone into her clutch and took another swig from her flask, determined not to think about anyone but the girls in front of her for the rest of the night.

"THIS WAS SUCH A LOVELY DINNER," Sara said, glowing under the low lights in her white dress. "Thank you girls, so much!"

"I'm ready to shake some ass!" Maricela shouted over her seventh margarita.

"That's our next stop," Hanna laughed. She pulled out her phone to send the obligatory Venmo requests, but damn, her vision was already blurred. "What's twenty percent of whatever this number is?" She held the bill out to Taylor.

"It's eighty-three," a low voice boomed over her shoulder. She jumped in her seat, surprised to hear Logan in her ear.

"My love!" Sara threw her arms around Matty's neck, four tall figures slinking around their table, each a ticking time bomb by the looks in their eyes.

Hanna twisted in her seat, throwing Logan the half-smile she'd practiced all week.

"Thanks, Finance Bro," she said, signing the receipt.

He pulled her to her feet and wrapped her in a hug while everyone watched. Hanna felt the eyes of every bridesmaid on them and adjusted her face, smiling warmly despite the image of Sloane's perfect highlights in her mind.

"Hannyyyyyyy," he laughed against her. "It's so good to see you."

"Is it?" she asked, sober enough to be confused by the lilt in his tone.

"Of course it is!"

Milo appeared behind Logan and reached for her clutch that sat behind her on the table. He leaned in closer, his heavy eyes dropping to the sliver of black lace peeking out from under the ridiculously low neckline of her red dress.

"What's up, Arizona?"

"My eyes." She adjusted the dress, pulling as much of the fabric over her cleavage as she could. His lips spread into an absolutely evil grin as he retrieved the flask from her bag.

"You like?" He took a swig and tucked it back in.

"Yeah, what is it?"

"Local shop. My brother works with them from time to time."

Hanna pushed her chair back in and he handed her the

clutch. He wore all black, a look that did something absolutely tragic to her nerves.

"What are you drinking?" Logan asked.

She waved her hand. "Bourbon, you wouldn't like it."

"And you would?"

"She's broadening her horizons," Milo said, his syllables slipping and sliding.

Two hands landed on the small of her back at the same moment. Milo and Logan both pulled their hands away as if they'd touched a hot stove.

"Oh, good fucking lord," she muttered.

"SO LET me just understand the lay of the land here," Taylor screamed at her over the thick bass of what might have been the seventh Pitbull song to play since they'd arrived at the nightclub. "Logan is single and clearly trying to make nice. Milo is single and definitely trying to fuck you. And you're over here with me when you could be grinding up on either one—or both—of them?"

Hanna nodded. "Nailed it!"

"Okay, two things. One, I am so proud and also so disappointed. And two, they're both heading this way."

Taylor turned her back and ordered another drink at the bar, but Hanna knew she would be listening to every word. Milo squeezed behind her—tapping her hip as he did—and landed next to Taylor against the sleek black bar top.

"What do you want to drink?" Logan asked, his messy blonde hair longer than she'd ever seen it before. *Definitely single.*

"Don't buy me a drink," she insisted.

"I want to! A peace offering."

"That's sweet, Lo, but we don't need it. Let's just agree to be friends, okay? No more rehashing the past."

Milo dropped a glass of something on the rocks over her shoulder. Logan's eyes slid from the drink in her hand to the drink in Milo's, and whatever math he did, he didn't like.

"Friends?" Logan asked.

"Yes, Lo. I'm tired of being enemies."

"Fine! Okay. But friends dance, right?"

"Oh," she said, glancing frantically at Taylor.

"I'll hold your drink, babe! Go nuts!" Taylor grinned and collected glasses from them like trading cards, lining them neatly in a row on a high-top table. Hanna loved her, but in that moment, she could have strangled her.

"You too, big guy!" She pushed Milo—who seemed a little *too* pleased—in their direction.

Hanna followed Logan toward the dance floor where Sara and Matty had been circling one another for at least thirty minutes. The only person who loved drunk dancing more than Sara was Matty.

Sara spotted Hanna and pulled them to the middle of the floor. The other bridesmaids surrounded them and the boys bopped around behind.

They danced and sang until they were covered in sweat, and for the first time in a really, really long time, Hanna was just having fun. Not worrying about anything—or anyone—else.

That. That was exactly why she'd been looking forward to that weekend. She needed to move her body and shake off some of the shit from that past year. She didn't even care that Logan tagged along, or that Milo watched. It was just for her.

"We need to get you laid!" Sara yelled over the thumping speakers.

Hanna rolled her eyes, the alcohol settling in. "We really don't!"

"Please," she laughed. "Where else do you have a pick of guys who won't bother you after tonight, and who aren't at risk for homicide if someone else touches you?" Sara's eyes flashed over Logan and Milo, who were at opposite sides of their circle, both intently watching them.

"What about him?" Sara yelled, tilting her head toward a guy dancing a few feet away.

He was about as boring as a Vegas club rat could get, but he was dressed nicely and didn't have a girl clinging to him. And besides, maybe Milo and Logan both needed a reminder that she didn't belong to either of them.

"Hanna! Come on! Do it for me. When was the last time you even tried to pick someone up?"

She tossed her hair as she danced. "College?"

"Let's fucking go, Hanna!" Marciela yelled. "What happens in Vegas stays in Vegas, baby!"

Before Hanna could stop her, Maricela shuffled her into the guy behind them, his glazed eyes lighting up at the attention. He wasn't bad-looking at all—the tall, dark, and handsome type—but he also appeared to be on another planet.

Sara gave her a pleading look, desperate to see Hanna have some fun after watching her mope around those weeks leading up to the trip. She gave in, rotating her hips in his direction, letting him wrap his hands around her shoulders as he pulled her toward him, booze-soaked breath against her neck.

She would not pretend that the contact wasn't enjoyable. But more enjoyable was the look on the two shocked faces across the dance floor.

While Logan looked decidedly miserable, a spark of something she didn't recognize in Milo's eyes intrigued her.

She reached an arm up and touched the face behind her,

holding eye contact with Milo the entire time her hips were drifting into the stranger. His hands gripped her thighs and she was sure her dress was riding up, but she didn't care.

"What's your name?" he yelled over the DJ.

She shook her head, spinning around to face him and touching both arms as she twisted to yet another remixed pop hit.

"No names," she said, his eyes widening.

"You're hot!" he yelled.

"I know!" she yelled back, laughing as he tried to comprehend what game she was playing. She spun again, grinding against him.

"Where are you staying?" he asked against her ear.

"I guess that depends," she replied, wrapping her hands around his neck. His mouth instantly covered hers. Sara and Marciela both screamed behind her, thoroughly satisfied, but she knew from the second his lips touched hers, it was over.

His tongue slipped into her mouth and it sent her reeling backward.

Shit, is kissing ruined forever?

"Hey!"

"Thanks for the dance," she called before winding her way back toward Sara, where she was greeted with more screams and laughs.

"What the hell?"He yelled from behind them. Her new friend was definitely not amused with her teasing. She turned back around and shrugged.

"It wasn't for me," she said.

"That's fucked up," he grumbled, standing over her.

"You'll get over me, babe. I promise," she sighed, rolling her eyes.

He moved closer, reaching for her, and she backed up, shocked at the aggression.

"You got a problem, man?" An arm snaked around her shoulders in a motion he'd pulled thousands of times over the years. She glanced at Logan, who towered over the drunk asshole. Even though she knew for a fact he couldn't throw a punch to save his life, he still pulled off moderately intimidating.

"Yeah, your girlfriend is a whore." He tried to puff his chest out a bit, but he looked like a child compared to Milo, who popped up on the other side of her.

"What was that?" Milo asked.

He glanced between them and made the smart choice.

"Whatever, man," he mumbled, disappearing into the crowd.

"Are you okay?" Sara asked.

"I'm fine. Hardly a first," Hanna said, shaking her head.

Sara grabbed her hand. "Do you wanna go?"

"You stay here! I'm fine. I'm gonna get some food." She glanced at Milo, his fingertips already grazing her back.

Logan yelled, "I'll go with her!" at the same time Milo rumbled, "I got her."

Sara pitched forward, hugging Hanna tightly. "If you have a threesome with them tonight, Taylor owes me fifty bucks."

"Oh my *god*, Sara!"

"What? I've got a honeymoon to pay for," she giggled and kissed Hanna on the cheek.

"Come on, Arizona," Milo said, wrapping his hand around hers and pulling her quickly.

She leaned against his back as he stopped to let someone pass him by, praying Logan didn't see the way she melted into him.

EIGHTEEN

"I might tap out," Hanna said, standing at the base of the bridge they'd just crossed. "I just want to lie down."

"If you don't eat before you go to bed, you'll be dead by morning," Logan mumbled, his hand resting on her elbow as he ushered her forward. "White Castle is like a block that way, you can do it."

"It's actually that way," Milo pointed in the opposite direction.

She thought she saw Logan roll his eyes, but she was having a hard time even making out faces.

"I know where I'm going, man. It's right there," Logan said, gesturing in no definitive direction.

"I think we're all a little drunk," Milo tried to pacify. "But I can promise you, it's right there, *man*," Milo hissed the final word, imitating Logan.

"Whatever," Logan muttered.

Milo dragged them into White Castle, which was exactly where he'd said it would be. While the thought of eating anything made her want to die, a greasy slider might have been the only thing standing between her and the bathroom floor.

They waited in line silently.

Though she was convinced that the lighting inside the White Castle had been designed to make everyone look as horrible as possible, she was standing between two of the most handsome men she'd ever met—and she had no words to contribute. She tried to think of something funny to say to get them talking again, but every second between her and food grew riskier and riskier.

So she kept her mouth shut and nodded enthusiastically when Logan ordered sliders. Somehow she made it to one of the cheap plastic booths, unsure of when they'd even left the line.

She inhaled three of the burgers before Logan or Milo had even gotten through one, and then laid her forehead down on the table, trying not to wonder when it had last been sanitized.

God, this would have been brutal in her twenties. But at thirty? She wasn't going to make it through the weekend.

"You good, Hanna?" She managed to lift her head and look at Logan, smiling to signal that, while she was certainly not good, she *was* still conscious, which was a win in her book. "Oh my god, I haven't seen you like this since college."

"That's not true!" she protested. "Remember your mom's sixtieth birthday party when your dad made that... ugh, what was it? Some sort of punch that got us all trashed?"

Logan erupted with laughter, and she couldn't help but join him.

"Shit, I forgot. You sang Happy Birthday to Marcia like Marilyn Monroe."

"So I'm told."

Logan turned to Milo. "It would have been super hot if she hadn't thrown up in the lake immediately after."

Milo didn't respond.

Hanna only knew she was yelling because both Milo and Logan jumped when she defended herself.

"Okay, but at least I made it into the lake and not all over the back seat of my brand-new car."

Logan held a hand over his chest. "We agreed to never speak of that night again."

She muttered, "I don't remember putting anything in writing."

Milo ate his food and looked out the window toward the strip. She fished for something else to talk about so they weren't isolating him, but even she had to admit, it was nice not fighting with Logan for a few minutes.

"You know," Logan said to Milo. "This girl right here drank almost my entire fraternity under the table senior year."

Milo chuckled, watching her face. "I have no problem believing that."

"You guys make me sound like a fucking mess."

"You're not a mess," Milo said, his eyes hardening as they rested on her face.

"Although," Logan started. "That kiss back there wasn't exactly... clean," he laughed, but Hanna blushed.

Milo added, "Poor motherfucker, he thought he'd hit the jackpot for all of ten seconds."

"I gotta piss," Logan declared, slinking away from the booth.

Milo watched him cross the lobby and then leaned over the table.

"Are you trying to kill me, Hanna?"

"Yes," she grinned. "Jealous?"

"Nah, I saw how quickly you clammed up after that guy slipped you some tongue. If it were me, you'd have been on your knees in a second."

She tilted her head. "Is that where you like me best, Daddy?"

Milo's face turned a delicious shade of violet. "I don't mind watching you grind on some fucker in the club, Arizona. But I gotta tell you, I don't think I can take three days of watching Logan drool over you without doing something stupid."

"He's not—"

Milo's expression shut her up. He was very, *very* serious.

"I'll talk to him." She frowned, her eyes misting over with exhaustion. "If this is too much for you, Milo, we can dial it down."

"No."

"I mean it. You know how much our friendship means to me. The last three weeks have been hell."

He nodded. "Let's not worry about it, drunk in a White Castle, okay? That's flight home shit." Logan slid into the booth beside her, draping his arm along the back, and she saw it.

The agony on Milo's face, living in the tick of his jaw.

She hit her hands on the table. "As much fun as this is, gentlemen, if I don't get to my hotel in the next twenty minutes, you're going to be carrying me across the strip."

They both laughed, but something in the slur of her voice made them take her seriously. They all fell into an Uber within minutes.

"Longest legs up front," Milo quipped to Logan, who begrudgingly took the passenger seat.

The strip whizzed by in swaths of light and color as Milo's hand drew circles on her knee, the impact of which she wished she was sober enough to feel.

"I'll walk you up," both men said when they exited the Uber at the entrance of The Cosmo.

They all exchanged glances, and she awkwardly mumbled, "The more the merrier!"

They weaved through the casino toward the Chelsea Tower elevators. The silence was deafening in the elevator with Milo on her right, Logan on her left, and her brain running a mile a minute trying not to say anything that would make things weirder than they already were.

She battled a threesome joke into submission multiple times.

When they got up to the penthouse suites, she stumbled toward their door, and Logan fished through her purse for her key card while she leaned against the wall and tried to think sober thoughts.

The door swung open and she wrapped her arms around Logan's neck—muscle memory—and hugged him goodnight. Then, because she hated herself, she forced Milo into the same drunken embrace.

His hands splayed across her back and she realized just how thick he was compared to lean, lanky Logan. He lingered longer than Logan liked and, even drunk, she could see the disapproval pursed on his lips.

She could still hear Logan's internal screaming as she stumbled into the room, her phone buzzing before she even got her heels off.

ALWAYS ANSWER

Meet me downstairs in ten? I'm going to the old strip.

HANNA

I'm going to die.

ALWAY ANSWER

No more drinking, I've got a buddy with a new tattoo shop and I promised I'd stop by.

Hanna stared at her phone, weighing the repercussions of walking out of the hotel with Milo. She snagged a bottle of water off the countertop and chugged as much as she could before she swapped her shoes and stumbled back downstairs.

THE CAB RIDE WAS QUIET—*TOO* quiet.

Hanna hated hearing him breathe so steadily when she felt anything but. They hadn't been alone since the night Logan walked in on them. She swallowed, her heart circulating sheer panic through her system.

"Jenner opened this place a few months ago. He did most of my work."

"What?" Her head swiveled as the cab wound down a street behind the glowing lights of old Vegas, gliding to a halt outside of a shop with a neon sign that read TATTOO. Milo smiled and got out of the cab, rounding behind it and opening her door.

"I was saying that Jenner did almost all my tattoo work." He held a hand out for her and she let him pull her out of the cab, the counterbalance nice as her head continued swirling.

He didn't drop her hand until he pulled back on the metal door of the tattoo shop. The receptionist's head snapped up from their phone, their bright pink hair catching and holding the lights that danced across the street.

"Jenner around?" Milo asked.

"Ink or jewelry?"

Milo glanced at Hanna. "Just catching up with a friend."

"Jenner!" they barked over the counter, eyes gliding back to their phone. "Hot guy here for you!"

Jenner, all six-foot-five of him, burst out from the back of the shop to the lobby, his amber eyes searching over the few lingering faces before pulling Milo into a warm hug.

"I thought you were coming by two hours ago," Jenner boomed.

"I got distracted."

Jenner's eyes fell to Hanna. "Can't blame you."

Milo reached for her hand, a gesture sober Hanna might have resisted, but drunk Hanna found quite enjoyable.

"It's a great space," Milo said, gesturing to the walls claimed by black paint and framed tattoos in a dozen different styles.

"Thanks, man. You still looking for something?"

Milo tilted his head toward Hanna. "You mind?"

She shook her head, happy to sit with him. She followed them back behind the dimly lit lobby and down a hallway punctuated with black doors.

"Each artist gets their own private studio," Jenner explained, tapping one of the open doors. "Sup, Javi?" The artist in question leaned over his tablet and waved as they walked by.

"Are we still doing the bouquet you sent me?"

"Yeah," Milo said, dipping behind Jenner and into the last door on the right. He pulled his shirt off and tossed it onto a chair in the corner, pointing to one of the few empty spaces on the back of his arm.

Jenner held out his fingers, measuring the spot.

"Let me go print a few sizes. You want anything to drink, Milo's Plus One?"

"Hanna," Milo said, leaning against the table. "And she needs water."

Jenner smiled, his lips pierced with two sterling silver hoops that glinted in the overhead fluorescent lights.

"You can sit," Milo said, pointing to the chair. She scooped up his shirt and laid it over her lap, a plume of his cologne flooding her lungs and dominating her senses. He stared at her for a moment, and if she couldn't already hear Jenner's heavy footsteps returning down the hall, she might have asked him what he was looking at.

"Alright, I've got two options. Let me do the bigger one first." Jenner wiped Milo's arm and placed the thin stencil down, peeling it slowly and pointing at the mirror across the room.

"Hmm," Milo hummed, lifting his arm and looking at it from a few angles. "What do you think?" he asked Hanna.

She stood and crossed the space, standing next to him in the mirror. Between a whiskey barrel and a cowboy hat, a purple outline of a vase and some wildflowers nestled in neatly.

"Flowers, huh?" she asked.

"All my mom's favorites," Milo said. "Don't get too excited."

Hanna blushed and Jenner sucked air through his teeth.

"I think the smaller one," Hanna mumbled.

Jenner wiped the space clean and reset it with the second stencil, which left a little breathing room around the petals of the roses and lilies.

"Better," Hanna said.

"Where are we doing the second one?" Jenner asked, holding up a singular sunflower, the size of a silver dollar.

Milo shrugged. "That's for her."

Hanna's nose scrunched as she looked between them.

"Me?"

"Yeah, if you want it." Milo's green eyes caught hers. "No pressure."

She leaned toward Jenner, the petals sloping gently around his massive hand. It was delicate, the lines soft, and it *would* look pretty on her. Bastard.

"Where would you put it?" Hanna asked Milo.

He smirked, sliding his hand over her stomach and landing against her sternum, just below her breasts.

"Just one idea," he mumbled as her breath hitched. "If

you're comfortable with it. If not, the shoulder could be cute? Ankle?"

"Fine," she said, his lips falling into a frown. "But like, actually fine."

He laughed and laid down on his stomach. Jenner wrapped fresh tape around his needle and laid out the ink. Hanna moved to sit back down, but Milo's hand caught hers.

"You're not going to hold my hand? What if I'm nervous?"

Hanna snorted, her eyes falling over the dozens of pieces he'd collected.

"You're a problem."

"I know," he whispered, squeezing her fingers. She dragged the chair over and sat beside him opposite Jenner, who could not have cared less about the weird dynamic he was an unwilling participant in.

"What percentage of those did you do?" Hanna asked as Jenner rounded the vase's mouth.

"Hmm, probably ninety? Few new ones since I left the Bay, it looks like."

"You're prettier, don't worry," Milo said.

"Don't flirt with me, you know you aren't my type."

Hanna folded her arms. "And how many flowers have you tattooed on his plus ones?"

Jenner snorted, wiping away a bead of black ink.

"This is a first," he said.

"Really?"

"I didn't know Milo spoke to women in public until tonight," Jenner said, switching the needle to a shading tip. "But he's full of surprises."

That, Hanna could certainly agree with. Milo turned his head to lay on his free arm, sinking his stare into hers. The silence while Jenner worked wasn't comfortable, but it wasn't intolerable. She could handle it.

That was progress, wasn't it?

Jenner wiped away another pool of ink and leaned back to examine his work.

"Alright, brother. You know the drill." He stretched a piece of plastic wrap over the flowers, taping the edges down. "Go sign her release forms while I reset."

Milo slowly pulled his shirt over his fresh tattoo, following Hanna back to the lobby. He pointed toward the receptionist and asked for a release form, handing over a wad of cash.

"I can pay for mine," Hanna said.

"Nah." It was all he had to say.

Hanna scrawled her name across a tablet and handed it back to the receptionist. She turned to Milo.

"When did you send him the sunflower?"

"Few weeks ago," he mumbled, flipping through one of the flash binders on the desk. "I was going to tell you, but then... well, you were there."

"Right," she whispered, following him back to Jenner's studio.

"Figured I'd feel out the vibe once we got here."

"And it has nothing to do with a certain blonde—"

"Don't," he said, pressing a finger to her lips. "None of that. This is just for you. You want me to come in with you?"

Hanna thought about that. He'd already seen everything, but it had all gotten so strange.

"Do you *want* to come in?"

"Obviously," Milo said, grinning.

"Fine," Hanna said, changing her tune when he frowned. "Great."

She sat on the table as Jenner showed her the two sizes he'd printed—she opted for the larger of the two, so the petals would brush against the curves of her.

"Pasties, tape, or freeballin'?" Jenner asked, pulling out a drawer of adhesive covers. "I'm gay as shit, if that factors into your decision."

Hanna looked at Milo, who only laughed.

She rolled the top of her dress down around her waist, tossing her bra at Milo. Jenner had her lie back and gently pressed the stencil against her skin.

"Check the placement for me."

Hanna sat up, staring at her torso in the mirror.

"What do you think?" she asked Milo.

He swallowed and she could practically see his throat tightening around a response as his eyes swept over her.

"It's perfect." He leaned back in the chair, running his hands through his hair. "You're perfect."

She wasn't sure it was a compliment, the way the words soured on his tongue.

NINETEEN

Before Hanna even opened her eyes the next morning, she knew the room was spinning.

She rolled over and peeked at her phone, dreading any social media tags that might have popped up.

SARA

Hannaaaaaaaaa!

Hanna.

HANNA

Where'd you go??

Okay, you must be having a wild threesome with M and L to not answer me.

Just kidding.

(Unless you are, then in that case, can't wait to hear about it)

Actually, please don't be fucking Logan.

DO NOT ANSWER

Last night was nice. I think I really needed to
just laugh with you again. Thanks for letting
me tag along.

ALWAYS ANSWER

Drink a gallon of water before you even think
about leaving that hotel room today, and
don't take that bandage off.

Jesus Christ, her head was going to implode.

She took Milo's advice and headed to the kitchen, where she slammed as much water as humanly possible before jumping into a long, hot shower. Girls were passed out everywhere, so she did her best to be quiet.

Once she felt somewhat less caked in smoke and glitter, she decided that, instead of tiptoeing around the room, she should go downstairs in search of breakfast and, more importantly, coffee.

She settled on a spot around the corner with a little patio right on the strip and tucked herself into a table. She ordered a black coffee and a pitcher of water, plus whatever had the highest protein content.

Hanna snapped a photo of her coffee and water and sent it to Milo, who instantly started typing.

ALWAYS ANSWER

No hair of the dog?

HANNA

We're spending all day at the pool, pacing
myself.

ALWAYS ANSWER

Want some good company?

HANNA

Why, you know a guy?

She sent him her location and tried to forget what she looked like. Not having planned to see anyone so early, she hadn't put on a drop of makeup, but she supposed that was nothing new to Milo.

He arrived at the same time her server dropped the omelet chosen for her at the table. He was wearing those black basketball shorts she could still feel against her thighs, plus a t-shirt, and a baseball cap with the emblem of what she guessed was an artisanal whiskey brand.

She did her best not to fixate on the shorts.

He sat down across from her and the server took his order—coffee and a breakfast sandwich.

"Can you get her some toast too? Thanks, boss."

"Hi," she mumbled through her food.

He scooted his chair closer and assessed her face. "How we feeling?"

"Oh, you know," she said over her sunglasses. "Like I might never drink again."

Milo rolled his eyes. "Uh-huh. We still have a whole day and night to go."

"Vegas should have a twenty-four-hour maximum."

Milo laughed, took his coffee from the server, and ordered a Bloody Mary.

"Oh god, how can you drink this morning?"

"Hanna, don't take this personally. *I* was drunk last night, but *you* were obliterated. I thought you sobered up by the time we left the tattoo shop, but you were practically asleep when I dropped you off."

"How bad was I?"

He sighed. "Not the worst I've ever seen. Definitely

surprised me when you were already out and about this morning."

"Ugh, I know. I need to sleep, but I'm an early riser. Always have been, my mom used to call me her own personal rooster." Milo arched a brow and she glared. "Do I want to know?"

"Just picturing you screaming cock-a-doodle-doo."

"I hate you."

"Yeah, yeah, yeah," he muttered, reaching for a slice of her toast. He shoved it into her mouth. "Soak it up, hotshot."

"I *love* when you talk dirty to me," she laughed.

He leaned back, taking her in.

"So, you and Logan seemed to get along better last night."

Ah, a portion of last night screamed back to her. She could still taste the vodka on the stranger at the club.

"He was on what I would consider to be his best behavior, I suppose."

He nodded. "That's good."

"It's fine. Neutral," she offered, hesitant to call anything about Logan good after one night without incident.

"Can I ask what happened there? I feel like I only have Matty's version, which was essentially 'They broke up. It bad'," he said, giving his best caveman imitation.

Hanna chuckled, the bones of it amusing to her.

"Oh, sure. Uh, Logan got a job with a big FinTech start-up in New York, which obviously I wanted him to take if it made him happy." She took a moment to drink some coffee. She really hadn't ever admitted how everything went down to anyone. Not even Sara.

"So he moved, and we decided to do long distance while he got settled. I was just starting a new job back in Phoenix and didn't want to try and make a cross-country move work with two new jobs. I think he met Sloane a month later. They worked in the same building and, from what he told me, it was love at first sight or whatever."

"Interesting," Milo mumbled.

"Yeah. I mean, I respect him for being honest right away. He was really torn up about it. I know it wasn't easy."

"Still, it's a little brutal."

"Oh, it was. I'm being very brave about it right now, but that shit happens. You can't predict it."

Milo stayed quiet for a second, piecing together all the timelines.

"And then your mom on top of it all."

"Yeah. Not my best year."

She finished her coffee and moved to the water, pushing the last third of her omelet onto his plate. Her stomach finally settled.

"How sick do you get of people telling you that you're so resilient?"

She thought about that for a moment. Her strength was something she admired about herself but, lately, she'd started to wonder why. Why did she have to take all of this and make it a story of triumph? Couldn't she just be sad and then fade back into normalcy?

"Really sick of it, actually."

"Me too. I hated it when I was younger. It's not like I got a choice."

"Right, it kind of feels like congratulating me for surviving? I don't know, people say all kinds of insane shit." That was why she loved hanging out with Milo—aside from his marvelously talented fingers. He just got it, and she didn't have to tiptoe around how shitty it was to exist after someone you loved ceased to do so. "My dad told me like two months after she died that I just needed to 'change my perspective' about it."

Milo choked on his coffee. "Wow, that's incredible. Why didn't I think of that?"

"Well, you were too busy being so strong, Milo."

He cracked a smile. "And focusing on the happy times we had."

"Of course. I'm just grateful she's no longer suffering, you know, because being here and alive with me was just so awful."

His eyes lit up. "That's one of the worst ones. Man, I fucking hate people."

"Not all of them," she countered. "There are the Saras of the world."

"Matty too. Always so easy to go to. I met him just before the accident, actually. He was one of the few friends I had who didn't bolt."

She nodded with understanding. It was hard to maintain friendships in general, but when shit hits the fan? Circles get small, fast.

Milo settled his gaze on her, the stare a little too intense for her hangover.

She leaned forward, tapping him between the eyes.

"You got a lot going on up there, California." He laughed, but it didn't last. "Come on, therapy king. Let's hear it."

"You don't want to hear what I'm thinking."

"I always want to hear what you're thinking," she sighed. "It's actually incredibly annoying."

"I'm thinking..." He drained his Bloody Mary and leaned closer to her, his fingers twitching against the table. "I'm thinking that I'm the one who needs distracting this weekend."

She swallowed. "What?"

"We weren't thinking about the Vegas of it all. We're really going to spend all weekend drunk in Sin City, and I'm just supposed to pretend I wasn't staring at your perfect tits all night? Seems ill-informed."

"This doing it for you right now?" She gestured to her yoga pants and bare face.

Milo closed his eyes. "You have *no* idea, Hanna."

"Really?"

He pulled at the soft fabric of her pants. "These aren't nearly as bad as the green pair you wear at home. They're light enough that, when the sun hits, I can see every incredible dimple in your ass, and then I can't help but think about how it would recoil if I—"

"Okay!" She drained her ice water. "So, what? You want to fuck all weekend like we're both not going to be absolutely miserable Monday morning?"

"I don't know. I don't know! I feel like a psycho, Hanna. I'm not this guy, but seeing Logan touch you, and then having to sit next to you naked... I'm an idiot."

"Milo, the last time we had sex, we both cried for an hour after."

"Crying is healthy, Arizona. I've been telling you that. "

She rolled her eyes, astonished that he would press it.

"You're possessed."

Milo tapped the back of her hand. "Probably."

She squeezed his fingers, annoyed at how naturally they fit over hers.

"For one second, I need you to set aside all the things you've learned on a beige sofa."

A smirk emerged as she twisted his fingers in hers.

"Went out the window right around when your flight landed in the Bay. Go on."

She pursed her lips and waved her hand. "I'm already heartbroken over this. Have been for weeks. It's not like I'll be extra devastated, right?"

Milo perked up. "That is just stupid enough to work." He grinned. "Send me pics from your pool day?"

She leaned over his chair and ran her fingertips over his inked forearm.

"Not for free. I'm sure you'll think of something to trade."

Milo whipped his head to the side and snagged her lips in a sharp kiss, catching her completely off guard. It sucked the air out of her lungs—nothing like that sloppy random from the night before, not even in the same realm.

He broke the kiss and ran a thumb over her swollen lips.

"If my room wasn't filled with hungover assholes right now..."

"It's okay," she whispered, letting his thumb linger. "We have all weekend."

THREE HOURS LATER, she was sprawled out on a pool chair, religiously applying sunscreen and sipping on margarita number two.

She'd packed plenty of swimsuit options for the trip, but none of them covered her new tattoo, so she opted for a black and gold bikini with a cover-up she hoped would obscure the bandage enough. Sara was in the matching white version and lying next to her, frantically chasing her hangover with tequila.

At their feet, Taylor and Maricela propped themselves on the pool deck, sipping over-the-top cocktails with skewers of pineapple bobbing up and down.

She was not just thinking about the way Milo's lips had felt against hers that morning. She was *fully* fixating.

"This is literally heaven," Taylor said. "Exactly what we needed after last night."

"How late were y'all out anyway?" Hanna asked.

Taylor looked at her over her sunglasses. "Oh god, girl. I

don't think Sara was ready to call it until like three this morning."

"Oof," she groaned.

Sara brushed them off. "I was on a roll! Weddings are expensive. Speaking of." Sara pointed to Taylor. "Which one of us won the bet?"

"What bet?" Hanna snapped.

"You were obviously too drunk to remember, but I told you! If you had a threesome with Milo and Logan, I get fifty bucks."

Hanna slapped Sara's arm and flipped Taylor off. "Looks like the open bar budget just took a hit."

"No!" Sara giggled. "I was so hopeful. Milo was looking at you like you were something to eat. Where did you three go anyway? That must have been awkward."

Hanna slammed the rest of her margarita, Taylor's baby blues burning into her from her perch on the edge of the pool.

"I was truly blacked out. Logan and Milo took me to get some food and then back to the hotel."

Sara jerked upright next to her and she pulled her sunglasses off.

"Did they talk to each other?"

"A little, I guess. It was definitely uncomfortable."

"I bet," Sara said. "They've never gotten along, but after The Incident..."

Hanna rolled in her direction. "Is that true?"

"Oh, babe." Sara sipped her drink, taking a bite of a pineapple wedge. "They've had a weird rivalry for *decades*. Logan stole a high school girlfriend or something. I can't remember, but Matty knows."

"Huh," she breathed. "We talk about Logan a *lot*, and he never says a word about him."

"That's Milo for you, though. He's so well-therapized I'm not sure he actually has feelings, just thoughts about them."

Hanna sat up. "Okay! I say this to him all the time. He's *too* chill about everything."

Taylor threw an ice cube at her. "Sounds like you two do a whole lot of *talking*."

"Yeah well, a lotta good it's done me. I don't know a damn thing that's going on in that head of his."

"If anyone can crack him, it's *you*, Arizona."

Hanna blushed as Taylor slipped into the water, cooling off her shoulders.

Sara cocked her head to the side. "Arizona?"

"You haven't picked up on that yet?" Maricela asked.

"Is Milo nicknaming you?"

"I guess," Hanna laughed.

"God," she scoffed. "He's in *deep*. I mean, I personally witnessed how deep he's in physically, but emotionally... if he takes you to the bar, it's officially over for him."

"His dad's bar?"

Sara set her glass down. "Hanna Stevens. Have you been to the bar?"

She hesitated. "Yes?"

Sara blinked slowly. "I'm too stunned to speak."

"What?"

"Hanna, I have spent half my week with that man for five years, and he hasn't even brought *me* to the bar. I've only heard the rumors. Matty has been like ten times in ten years. Have you met his mom?"

"No, that I haven't done. But he did invite me to dinner with her before the whole Logan thing."

Sara's jaw dropped. "He didn't let me meet her until I was engaged to Matthew! Oh my god, my brain is on fire right now."

Hanna waved her hand. "It's the hangover!"

"It's *not*."

She laid back, thoroughly embarrassed and also tempted to tell her more.

"Sara?"

"Hanna."

"I think I'm in trouble," she whispered.

Sara snorted. "I *know* you're in trouble."

Hanna's phone vibrated against the pool deck beneath them. Before she could grab it, Sara snatched it from her.

"How mad will you be if I read it?"

"Light mad. Heavy embarrassed," she groaned.

"Is that him?" Taylor screeched.

"Hanna. Grace. Stevens," Sara muttered, her lips falling open as she read the text.

Hanna squeezed her eyes shut. "How bad is it?"

"It's been three hours and I can still *taste you?*" Sara fanned herself. "*Ma'am.* You better fucking spill what happened this morning *now.*"

"This morning was boring," she smirked. "Just a kiss over breakfast. What you really want to hear about is the time we had sex at the bar."

If Sara could have evaporated Hanna with a stare, she'd have been dust in the wind.

"I need another drink. Someone help me. Oh my *god.*" Sara sat on the edge of her pool chair and looked her best friend in the eyes, her face bewildered. "I want to hear every filthy detail. But first, you *have* to let me take a picture of you to send to him."

Hanna panicked. She could explain away a lot of things about Milo, but a tattoo?

"Wait! Get her wet!" Taylor pushed herself out of the pool, pulling at Hanna's cover-up.

"I—"

Sara rolled her eyes.

"Oh come *on*, Hanna! It's just a bit of fun!"

Hanna sighed. She'd already exposed more than she'd planned—what was one more thing? She pulled the cover-up off and laid back on the chair. Sara's eyes immediately darted toward the black splotched ink beneath the clear bandage.

"The *fuck is that?*"

Hanna tried to fight back the grin, but it was too late.

"That is... a new tattoo. That Milo paid for last night."

A chorus of *oh my gods* exploded before Maricela got them back on track.

"Use the engagement ring balloon to reflect gold onto her. It'll make her look tan," Maricela spouted as she rushed around the cabana and grabbed the massive ring inflatable. She held it toward the sun to cast a warm reflection over Hanna.

"Cross one leg over the other like, yep, you got it," Taylor said. "Okay Sara, how's our angle?"

"I need more titty," she said, squatting and standing, trying to find the right vantage point. "Move your arm. There they are!"

"Take it in portrait mode!" Maricela shouted, stretching to get more sunlight on the balloon.

"I got it! Okay. Oh my god, yes, this one," Sara said, tapping and adjusting something before she flashed it to Hanna for approval. Hanna's head spun, but her tits *did* look great, despite the peeling plastic beneath them. "Sent!"

"Wait, what did you say with it?"

Sara balked. "Nothing. What man wants to read an essay with their tittygraphs?"

She reached for the phone. "Milo does. He cares way more about the mental game."

She typed out a message and fired it off while Sara read over her shoulder.

> **HANNA**
>
> Hope you're wearing something sturdier than those goddamned basketball shorts or Brendon is going to start getting ideas.

ALWAYS ANSWER

Did Sara take that?

> **HANNA**
>
> Maybe, why?

ALWAYS ANSWER

Noted.

Sara cackled beside her. "Milo just Venmo'd me a hundred bucks with an eggplant and prayer hands emoji."

> **HANNA**
>
> Your turn.

ALWAYS ANSWER

I don't think Logan is going to snap a studio-lit dick pic for me. Do you accept selfies?

> **HANNA**
>
> I'll take Morse code at this point.

"God, you two are insane. No wonder the sex is so hot."

Hanna mumbled, "It's unreal. The last three weeks have been so painful. But this morning we decided maybe Vegas doesn't count."

Sara looked at Taylor, who looked at Maricela.

Hanna sighed. "I *know* it's dumb, you don't have to figure out how to tell me. Oh! He just texted back."

Sara turned away. "You can keep whatever photo he sends to yourself. I still have to look the man in the eye."

"Speak for yourself," Taylor mumbled, leaning in to see, but Hanna held her phone to her chest. "I'm kidding, I'm kidding. Your nudes are all I can handle anyway."

Hanna glanced at the screen, but immediately set it back down to take a breath.

Sara sipped a fresh drink, courtesy of Maricela. "That good, huh?"

"I'm in so much trouble," Hanna muttered.

She braced herself and flipped the screen again, greeted by Milo in the hotel bathroom, gray sweats hardly concealing anything below his waistband. He sent a second without any pants at all, and every drop of blood in her body drained south.

HANNA

I cannot believe you gray sweatpants-d me.

This message was sent from the bottom of The Cosmopolitan pool

ALWAYS ANSWER

Don't drown, I have big plans for you later.

HANNA

Don't flatter yourself. Slightly above-average plans.

ALWAYS ANSWER

Don't make me come over there early

HANNA

Aw, it's okay, buddy. Happens to lots of guys.

ALWAYS ANSWER

I'm going to fuck the smirk I know is on your mouth right off tonight, Arizona.

HANNA

Promise?

Sara gasped as she glanced back over Hanna's shoulder again.

"Hanna!"

"What? It's just what we do. We fuck with each other and

then he hangs out with Chloe, or I hang out with... myself. It's just fun."

ALWAYS ANSWER

On another much less sexy note, how are you feeling about the Logan stuff? Still okay with our deal? I don't want to be in the way.

"Oh my *god*," Sara sank into the chair next to her. "Hanna. You cannot tell me this is just fucking around."

She shrugged. "As far as I know, it is."

"That man is in *love*," Sara chimed.

Hanna scoffed. "That man is jealous."

Her phone buzzed again.

DO NOT ANSWER

Hey, Hanna. Can we talk before dinner tonight?

"A new bombshell has entered the villa," Sara whispered.

Hanna sighed. "Oh, please."

HANNA

We're all good, Cali.

And then swiped over to Logan.

HANNA

Coffee in twenty?

"You're not going to tell Milo you're talking to Logan?" Sara asked.

Hanna rolled her eyes. "Can you just uninvite the groom's brother? It would really help me out."

Sara laughed, signaling the waiter for another round of drinks.

"MEDIUM DARK ROAST for me and she'll have..."

Logan rocked on his heels, glancing at her.

"Water," she said.

"Just water?"

Hanna chuckled. "I'm three coffees and four margaritas deep, Logan. You need me to drink water."

"Fair enough."

She plopped into a rickety chair in the corner of The Cosmo and waited for Logan to get his daily dark roast, the acidic smell bringing back dozens of mornings at the coffee shop on campus, studying for finals or mentally preparing to head home for breaks between semesters.

This morning, however, they were hungover, studying completely new versions of one another, and were mentally prepared for absolutely nothing.

"So," Logan said, leaning back in the chair. "You sold our house."

Hanna choked on her water. "I sold *my* house. Did Matty tell you?"

He conceded. "Your house. And yes. But he thought I knew. When did you sell it? Did you at least get a good deal for it? Who helped you list it? You know, you really should have called me."

Hanna hung her head back. "I didn't need you! I made a decent amount off of it and bought a fixer-upper downtown. Investment property."

She tried not to wonder if that investment was crumbling under the Arizona sun in her absence.

Logan sipped his coffee, his eyes unfocused. She'd seen that look before—calculating.

"Bungalow?"

"Yes."

"Roosevelt?"

She blinked slowly at him. "Yeah."

"Exactly what you always wanted, huh?"

Her face fell. "In a way."

They'd spent years talking about renovating one of the historic homes downtown. Her mom was going to help decorate.

Hanna had gotten what she wanted, but what was the point if everyone she wanted it for was gone?

"Sloane and I broke up."

Hanna put on her bravest face. "I heard."

His brows knit together. "Oh? Did I, uh, tell you last night?"

She opted not to rat Milo out and stoke whatever weird feud they had.

"You wouldn't be sitting here right now if you were still together."

"I accepted an offer in San Francisco."

Hanna smiled. "I think that's great, Lo. But why are you telling me all of this?"

"Because I think I hit rock bottom, and I don't know what the fuck to do about it."

She finished her water. "You come to me—the resident disaster—to soothe your ego?"

"No, Hanna, that's not—" Logan reached for her hand and she leaned away. "I *miss* you."

She scoffed. "You don't miss me. You miss who you were with me. And those are two drastically different things."

"No," Logan said, shaking his head. "I miss *you*, Hanna. I miss you all the time. I miss my best friend."

He squeezed her hand.

"I miss these hands..."

She pulled back, the haze in his eyes crystallizing into something else. Something angry.

"Oh," he breathed.

"Oh, what?"

Logan's lips twisted around his name. "Milo. You guys are still fucking then?"

Hanna stood, her face red as she tamped down the desire to slap him.

"Of course, the only possible reason I could resist the man who broke my heart would be if I was under another one, right? Couldn't be that I have a litany of reasons to never even speak to you again, let alone *be* with you."

He sighed. "You didn't answer the question."

"Aren't you *tired* of this? We're adults, Logan!"

"Hanna—"

"I gotta go," she sighed. She exited quickly, a familiar ache opening in her chest. Her lungs felt like they were collapsing from the bottom up. She pulled out her phone, tapping his name before the hyperventilation took over.

"Hanna?"

"Hey," she managed, trying to sound okay.

It was all he needed to hear.

"I'm sending you my room number." Milo's voice faded from the phone. "You gotta find somewhere else to be, Brandon."

MILO PULLED THE DOOR OPEN, still in his gray sweatpants, a crime against her quickly unraveling brain.

She pushed through him, throwing herself onto the red leather couch at the front of his suite. He closed the door and snagged a bottle of water from the minibar, cracking it open and handing it to her.

"I don't need twelve-dollar water," she laughed.

He sat on the coffee table across from her, their knees touching. His eyes slid over her, assessing. Always assessing.

"What do you need?"

She swallowed the feeling that gnawed at her, but her chest didn't listen. Shuddering, she fought to hold onto a breath.

"I don't know."

"You're upset. Mom stuff? Logan stuff?"

She shook her head, leaning into his hand on her knee.

"How long until Brendon gets back?"

"He went with Matty to the pool with the girls." He stood and flipped the security bar over the door. "I imagine they'll be there for a while longer."

"They have the cabana until two."

Milo checked the time on his phone and sat across from her again, resting his hands on either side of her face.

"I can get a lot of distracting done in ninety minutes, Hanna."

"Okay," she breathed. He ran his finger lightly over her sternum.

"Are you sore? Are you sure you don't want to talk?"

She leaned forward, drawing a line from his knee up his thigh.

"You know what I *really* want to do?"

"Tell me." He trailed his nose along the line of her jaw, her heart racing as his fingers skimmed her sides.

"I *really* want to take a nap."

Milo let a low, rumbling laugh loose from his chest.

"That's the sexiest thing you've ever said to me, Arizona."

He popped up and tossed his wallet onto the table, resting

his hat next to her purse. He pointed to the neater of the two beds and she crashed onto it, sliding under the covers.

"I'll set an alarm," Milo muttered to himself, tapping his phone and then setting it on the nightstand. He tugged at her arms and rolled her over so she wrapped around his back.

"I didn't peg you as a little spoon."

"Not into pegging," he said, snuggling back into her.

She brushed her thumb over his arm, finally feeling the weight of the previous night's lack of sleep. But there was a small piece of her—one she kept on a very tight leash—that felt that his all-consuming warmth was something she could get used to.

She was *so* fucked.

TWENTY

ALWAYS ANSWER
Blue or green?

HANNA
Context?

ALWAYS ANSWER
Getting dressed. Which suit?

HANNA
Green.

ALWAYS ANSWER
K.

HANNA
Black or purple?

ALWAYS ANSWER
Dress?

HANNA
Thong.

Hanna rolled her eyes and tossed her phone onto the hotel bed, a flurry of noise pouring out from the bathroom.

"Half or full lash?" Sara poked her head into the room.

Not nearly as sexy of a game.

"Full. If we're going to do the damn thing, we might as well go full glam," she said.

"How's your not-boyfriend?"

Hanna sighed. "Which one?"

"Oh god, Hanna. What did Logan do?"

"Nothing," she huffed, folding into herself on the edge of the bed. "He's lonely and miserable. He just wants something familiar."

"I hope he gets his shit together. Matty won't want to have to play babysitter."

"Correct," she agreed. "I am determined to keep the peace tonight, I promise."

Sara fanned a strip of lashes in front of her face. "Just don't wear something low enough to show off the new ink. Imagine explaining *that* to Logan. As soon as these are on, we can head downstairs."

Hanna pulled on a pair of much less aggressive heels than ones from the night before and re-read her last few messages from Milo.

Fuck it, she thought, and slipped her underwear off, leaving them behind in her suitcase.

The moment she spotted Milo across the casino, leaning against a slot machine as Matty tried his luck, she regretted her decision to go commando. He was dressed in an olive-green suit, his shirt unbuttoned low enough to see his tattoos.

He didn't go out of his way to greet her when their groups

merged, but he did slide into the seat across from her at dinner, flashing a smile they both knew meant something sinister.

His smile faded the moment Logan plopped down next to her. When the server arrived, Logan ordered first.

"I'll do a gin and tonic. Hanna, you want a mule?"

Hanna started to respond, but Milo interjected. "They've got a really nice scotch selection if you want me to recommend something."

She could hear Taylor and Marciela both squealing internally, glad that Sara was at the other end of the table.

Logan looked her over. "That's right. You're a scotch girl, now." His face was unreadable as she dug deep to smile politely.

"Finer things," Milo said flatly.

Playing Peacekeeper was not going to be as simple as she'd thought.

"Actually," she said to the server, who clearly wanted no part in whatever they had flowing between them. "What do you think of Pinhook's high proof?"

Relief washed over the server's face when he realized he didn't have to mediate a weird, contextless argument.

"If you like something a little different with a bit of a burned-caramel finish, you'll be into it."

She flashed a grateful smile. "Rocks, please."

The server moved on and Logan found something to talk about with Brendon a few seats away. She could see in the way he held his shoulders that he was irritated.

From across the table, Milo returned his attention to her.

"Have you seen what Pinhook is doing with their vertical series?"

"I tried their first five releases. It's a cool concept. Haven't had this year's." She turned to Taylor, who looked at them like they were speaking French, and explained, "They're releasing small batch bottles of the same bourbon every year from four to twelve years-old, so you get to experience the entire aging journey."

Taylor clapped her hands together. "Love that for you two."

It was the most she could offer, and Hanna just appreciated that someone else was there to witness the very odd situation she'd found herself in.

Milo continued talking to Taylor about the nuanced flavor profiles that developed each year in the maturation process and she tried very hard to keep up, but Hanna knew that Taylor hadn't been sober since ten that morning, so it was a Herculean effort she was putting forth just to maintain eye contact.

Hanna's phone buzzed in her purse.

SARA

Okay, hate that I'm sitting at the end of the table because it looks like shit is getting interesting down there.

HANNA

I think I'm in the middle of a weird pissing match between Logan and Milo.

SARA

Wait, are you officially in a love triangle?

HANNA

No.

SARA

I think you are.

HANNA

That would require either of these idiots to be in love with me, which they are not. But I think we're in a territory dispute triangle.

SARA

For the record, I'm Team Hanna.

HANNA

I think you're the only one.

SARA

I expect updates. Tonight will be
veeeerrrryyyy interesting.

She set her phone down and Logan turned to her.

"Work stuff?"

She loved it when people lied for her. "Yeah, nothing major. Done now."

He rested his elbows on the table, staring her down.

"So, you moved to a new house and you're a bourbon aficionado now. What else have I missed out on?"

She didn't expect the question to knock the wind out of her, but it did. Logan was, once again, woefully out of touch with the reality she'd been functioning in for an entire year. It hurt to realize just how much they'd grown apart, and how little he understood.

She swallowed hard, trying to calm the anger welling up inside of her. *What else has he missed out on?*

Oh, just months of being too depressed to put on anything other than the same two pairs of yoga pants and old shirts of his. A few mental health crises. One particularly bad weekend, where she considered checking herself into one of those fancy facilities that out-of-control celebrities go to just to have someone else who would take care of her for a while. She considered telling him he'd missed thousands of dollars worth of paying someone to listen to her cry about him.

He'd missed memorials, insurance arguments, and estate sales.

Paperwork. He'd missed a fuck-ton of paperwork.

His face fell right about the time she finished tallying up

just how many of her therapy sessions were dedicated solely to his bullshit.

"I'm sorry, Hanna. That's a loaded question, I realize that." Logan had always been somewhat self-aware, but was never great at apologizing. She welcomed the change.

"Thanks," she forced out, pushing more air into her lungs, so as not to suffocate.

She was grateful when the server arrived with a tray full of drinks. Logan raised his gin and tonic over the table.

"To Mr. and Mrs. Debrune!" He clinked his glass against hers, and she took a sip, her eyes falling across the table to catch Milo's as he drained his scotch in one go. That's when she saw it.

It was there, swirling in the pained greens of his eyes, written in the crease of his forehead, as he realized it too.

They were never going to be just friends, and there was no amount of therapy that could save him.

That could save either one of them.

AFTER DINNER, they watched Sara play roulette and win four hands back-to-back.

Hanna was a terrible gambler, but she loved to watch. Sara dominated the table in her white minidress and silver cowgirl hat with a bachelorette sash that earned her frequent free drinks, well on her way to another blackout.

Hanna waited at the edge of the table for the boys to reconvene after they'd scattered for some post-dinner gambling. She wasn't as drunk as she wanted to be, which became more of a problem with every glance Milo shot at her. His stare rippled through her nervous system in ways Logan could never touch.

She decided to find another bar with Taylor, their arms linked in the way drunk girls were legally required to do when in Las Vegas, no matter how far away they were from twenty-one.

They walked through a smoky hallway, the lights and chimes of slot machines blaring, their heels clicking against the scuff-marked linoleum. She could see a bar just a few feet from them when suddenly she was no longer linked to her friend, but spinning off the ground, two very strong arms squeezing her tightly under her ribs.

"Haaaannnnaaaa!"

She pushed away from her assailant's chest and immediately flushed with embarrassment.

The only thing standing between her ass and the rest of the world was a very thin layer of black silk, and Logan's stupid arms shifted her skirt.

"Logan," she said, thoroughly annoyed. "Put me down!"

"Aww, you're no fun." He set her down and she yanked at her skirt hem, half her ass out, the top not faring much better.

They'd only been separated for an hour since dinner, but it was clear he'd put in work at the bars.

She reset her face. "Where's everyone else?"

"They're, uh, they were right behind me..."

Great.

She scanned the casino and saw a few familiar faces at various tables, spotting Matty and Milo at the bar. She reached for Taylor's hand and took off again, this time with Logan in tow.

Hanna would have preferred to be as far away from him as possible to avoid another poke at her insecurities about their relationship, but she had to admit, there was something tempting about him crawling back to her. Even if she'd never take him up on it, the more she drank, the more she liked the idea of making him squirm.

Matty threw his hands in the air and yelled a non-verbal greeting as they approached. She leaned over the bar and ordered a whiskey sour and a vodka cranberry, plopping the pink drink in Taylor's hands.

"How are you holding up?" Hanna asked Milo, who'd clearly become the group babysitter. He held a plastic cup of beer in one hand, nursing it while he watched Matty scream again as he hit on black at a roulette table.

"Fine," he sighed. "These motherfuckers are going to get themselves killed tonight. I guess last night wasn't exciting enough."

"Vegas, baby," she replied sarcastically.

Milo pointed over her shoulder at the sight of Logan falling over himself talking to Maricela who could not have been less interested.

"I see you're already well aware what state your boy is in." Logan fell over himself talking to Maricela, who could not have been less interested.

"He's not my boy."

Milo's face twisted into a sinister smile. "You're goddamn right about that."

"Milo," she warned.

He leaned closer, dropping his forefinger over her bare shoulder.

"Which color did you go with?"

She mirrored his expression. "Neither."

He let out a breath, polishing off his beer. "I look forward to verifying that later," he mumbled, a hand tugging at the hem below her ass. She wanted to lean into his touch, but there were too many of them around.

"How's Matty?" She changed the subject, desperate to take her mind off of his hands.

"He won twelve hundred dollars and is working on a grand

plan to convince Sara to marry him at the Taco Bell Cantina, so I would say he's enjoying himself."

Hanna shrugged. "I'd be cool to get it all over with tonight, especially if there's a Chalupa at the end."

Milo moved closer and she braced for whatever depraved thing he had on his mind just as an arm draped over her shoulder.

She drew in a sharp breath, already irritated.

"Hanna! What are we drinking?" Logan slurred.

"*I* am drinking a whiskey sour. *You* should probably drink some water."

She slipped out from under his arm, only for it to land around her waist.

The bastard never learns.

Hanna glanced at Milo, trying to read his face, or at least send a distress signal, but he only ordered another beer.

"Can I get two glasses of water?" she asked the bartender, who was quick to make it happen. She handed one to Logan. "Drink."

"Don't be so boring."

Her lips pressed together, his complaint hitting an inflamed nerve.

He'd used that word once during an argument when she hadn't wanted to book a last-minute trip to New York for a weekend visit. Not because she was *boring,* but because she had been stressed with work and hadn't wanted to lose three days.

Now, of course, she realized he was projecting. Sloane was *just so spontaneous.* One of the many reasons he'd cited for thinking she was the better fit.

"Yep, that's me," she bit. "You wanted someone more exciting, right? How's that working out?"

They had Milo's attention again, his eyes sliding back toward them. The muscles in Logan's neck tensed.

"Sloane was a mistake," he said, his words slipping together like wet clay. "She just didn't get me. Not like you do."

"Of course, it's all *her* fault. That checks out."

Hanna shoved his hand away and stomped off, eagerly on the hunt for Sara and the rest of the bridal party. Logan called after her, but someone must have stopped him from following because he stayed put.

Milo, however, did not.

"You know what's boring?" he asked, catching up and herding her toward a blackjack table. "Watching me lose a couple hundred bucks in record time."

She laughed, shrugging. "Can I have your free drinks?"

He nodded his head and slid into the last empty chair at the table.

"You can have whatever you want, Arizona." He wiggled his eyebrows as he threw his chips down.

She sipped on a complimentary Jack and Diet while he played five hands, winning all but the last. She finished her drink as he collected his chips.

"Where to?" he asked as they wound through flashing lights and clouds of smoke.

"We should probably find the rest of the crew," she said. "Don't need any more side-eye from the bridesmaids."

Milo laughed. "Please, those fuckers are all so blasted they can't keep track of themselves, let alone us."

He had a point.

"True, but I should find Sara."

Milo smiled and pointed toward the massive chandelier in the middle of the casino.

"I spy a silver cowgirl hat."

"Yeehaw," Hanna mumbled.

Milo went his separate way as soon as he knew she had her target locked, going around to enter the bar from the other side of the casino.

Because he'd heard what she'd said about the bridesmaids watching their every move, she realized. And he'd listened.

Imagine that.

"Where were you?" Logan asked when she rejoined the group.

She shrugged. "I went to play blackjack."

"You don't gamble," he lilted, turning to Brendon. "She doesn't gamble."

"You don't know that," said sharply, also turning to Brendon, who looked like he may not have been present with them any longer. "He doesn't know that."

Logan held his hands up. "Okay fine. Hanna, the whiskey drinker. Also, the gambler. What's next? Ripping lines off a Vegas toilet?"

"Night's young."

"This isn't you," he said, shaking his head. "This is *him*."

She tapped her fingers angrily against the bar.

"Excuse me?"

"You heard me. This has Milo written all over it. You're hardly his first project."

Hanna glared, a rush of venom pooling on her tongue.

"Project?"

"Yeah, Hanna. A project. He can't fucking help himself. He loves a damsel in distress who he can psychoanalyze, smooth talk, and have crawling all over him at his beck and call without ever committing, while claiming it's something he 'just can't do.' I've known the guy since he was a kid, Hanna. I've watched him play the same game for fifteen fucking years."

Her chest tightened, the room's temperature skyrocketing

with each word. She folded her arms around herself, a prickling at the back of her neck sending shivers down her spine.

I'm a fucking moron.

"You know I'm right," Logan murmured.

"You're drunk."

He arched his brows. "Doesn't mean I'm wrong."

She bit down on her tongue. "You don't know what you're talking about."

"I know exactly what I'm talking about," he said and threw back the rest of his drink. He gestured to the suited-up figure drifting toward them. "Go ahead, ask him how I know."

"Logan," she warned.

Milo set his whiskey on the bar and Brendon looked nervous, tapping Matty on the shoulder to call his attention to what was about to happen.

Logan could barely hold eye contact with Milo.

"What's going on?" Milo asked.

"Does Hanna know about Michaela?"

Milo's eyes widened at the name, but he recovered smoothly, looking at Hanna.

"I don't think your brother's bachelor party is the time to rehash ancient history, Logan."

"Typical," Logan muttered.

Milo moved toward him, his hand out to de-escalate the situation, but Logan—blasted—read it as aggression. Milo lowered his voice in an attempt to get Logan to back down.

"I'm not trying to get into anything with you right now, Logan. You're drunk and you need to back off." Milo turned to Hanna, lowering his voice even further. "I'll tell you anything you want to know, Arizona. It's not a secret."

Logan shook his head, stepping closer, just a few inches of distance between them.

"Cut the therapy bullshit. It's exhausting. We get it, you're better than us."

"Lo," Matty said, his lips pursed in irritation.

"Great," Logan snorted. "He steals my girlfriend, he steals my brother, he steals my *other* girlfriend," he ranted, gesturing to Hanna.

Milo's fingers twitched. "You know, Logan, there's a common denominator in all these relationships falling apart and it's not me."

Hanna couldn't keep watching the flames roar back and forth, she had to intervene. She slipped between them, facing Logan and resting her palms against his chest.

"Just let it go, Lo. We should be celebrating Matty and Sara tonight."

"He'll crush you," Logan said, eyes locked over her head on Milo. "You'll get attached, he'll get bored. Lather, rinse, repeat."

"Alright, Logan," she growled. "That's enough."

A hand landed on her shoulder, Milo's cologne washing over her.

"Oh," Logan scoffed, his glare flashing between Milo's eyes and hand on Hanna's shoulder. "It's too late for you, huh?"

Milo moved his hand, but Logan had already come unglued.

"I'm disappointed, Hanna. I thought you were smarter than that."

She saw red. "I haven't been, historically."

"You should go back to the hotel, Logan," Matty suggested. "Sleep it off, okay?"

"I'm good," Logan forced through clenched teeth.

"You know what? We'll go," Hanna shrugged. She reached for Sara's hand and pulled her away, Taylor and Maricela close on their heels.

"That was kinda hot," Sara said, giggling. "You okay?"

"Never better," she muttered. "I need a shot and a dance floor."

ALWAYS ANSWER

You okay, Arizona?

I'm sorry about Logan.

Happy to talk as soon as you're ready.

Drop a pin if you want.

"HOW MUCH LONGER ARE YOU gonna torture this poor man?" Taylor leaned over a spread of tacos, Chalupas, and Mexican pizzas with her spiked Baja Blast.

"No more Milo talk," Hanna declared, working her way through a dozen different combinations of the same four ingredients. "What we *should* talk about is the rehearsal dinner and what we're wearing. Sara, we need a rundown."

Sara dutifully pushed them onward. "Okay, the rehearsal dinner is next on the list, but we should *really* talk about the welcome party." She clapped her hands together. "I know we said no more Milo talk, but I actually managed to convince him to let us use the bar's rooftop for our welcome cocktail party. Matty swears it has a great view of the skyline at sunset, and Janet said she can hang some string lights across the roof to give it that really romantic glow."

Hanna wondered for a moment what Janet was like, if Milo got his softness from her or his dad.

"Hanna and I were thinking peonies, but I just saw the most gorgeous hydrangea setup in this magazine on the flight out here. When we get back to the hotel, I'll show you all."

HANNA

You don't owe me any explanations, Milo.
We're just friends, remember?

ALWAYS ANSWER

We're not just anything, Hanna. Please let me
send an Uber for you. We can go grab
something to eat and hash this all out.

HANNA

i'm designing centerpieces. Crucial. Can't
miss it.

ALWAYS ANSWER HAS SHARED HIS LOCATION.

She rolled her eyes and sipped her boozy slushie, but she still tapped the dot on the map.

Seven minutes away.

"Matty has his own room," Sara mused. "I could disappear for the night."

"I don't know," she admitted. "I don't know what to do."

Sara leaned in close, bumping her shoulder into Hanna's.

"What would your mom tell you to do?"

"Are you set on hydrangeas? Because when I think fall, I think something like this," Maricela chirped, flipping her phone toward them.

A cluster of glowing sunflowers nestled between dripping greens and soft pink peonies cast a yellow glow on Sara's face.

"Well then," Sara smirked. "I guess I'll see you tomorrow."

TWENTY-ONE

Hanna perched on a sofa that smelled deliciously like smoke and whiskey in the Baccarat, trying to breathe like a normal person. The previous two days had caught up to her.

Milo stood at the bar, waiting for drinks—not that she needed any more fuel on the fire. Logan's accusations had been circling the drain of her mind, running down her spine and settling in her gut.

Was I just another project?

"I grabbed a cigar too. I don't know if it's your thing, but I can get you one."

He set their drinks down on the glass table in front of them and sat next to her, careful to leave her plenty of space.

Goddammit, why does he have to be so considerate?

"I'll try yours and let you know. I don't think I've ever had one that didn't come in a fruit flavor from a gas station."

He laughed and struck a match, lighting the end. Hanna ran a thumb over the wrapper he'd left on the table. She had no idea what she was looking at, but it was embossed and felt nice to give her hand something to do.

She watched him take a slow drag, admiring the sight despite herself. She knew smoking was problematic in theory, but she also believed that living until ninety would be its own kind of torture.

Besides, her mother never smoked a day in her life, and look what that had gotten her.

Milo leaned back over the couch, his arm extended toward her, fingertips just a few inches away from her shoulder. She could have easily leaned a few inches in, just to see what he'd do, but she was cautious.

Instead, she grabbed the sweaty rocks glass from the table, not bothering to ask what it was. She knew it would be great and was beyond any ability to parse out delicate notes anyway.

She sipped, the amber liquid hitting her in the back of the throat with a thick, peaty punch. A scotch, probably?

"You like it?" he asked, smoke billowing out of the sides of his mouth. "Port Charlotte. It's just about the heaviest peated scotch I've tried. Thought you might want something different."

Something different, indeed.

She cleared her throat. "It's like drinking a campfire... but not in a bad way?"

"Here," Milo said and passed her the cigar. She held it between two fingers and tried not to look like it was her first time. She took a puff, holding it mostly in her mouth, afraid to cough like an amateur in front of him.

She didn't hate the way it stung as it mixed with the scotch. She exhaled slowly, his curious eyes watching her every breath.

"I get why people enjoy this."

She handed it back to him and let her head fall against the couch, stretching her neck and enjoying the lightheaded rush that came with a slow exhale.

They finished their drinks and Milo put out the cigar, a

loaded silence settling over their chests as he offered to walk her back to her room.

The elevator doors closed.

Hanna could feel him watching her face, and she wondered if he could hear the questions rolling around in her head.

"So, we gonna talk about it?" His mouth was set in too sharp a line. The floor felt as though it was falling out from under them as it shot to the top of the casino.

"About what?" she deflected, buying herself time.

She stepped toward him and dragged her fingertip from his chest to the top of his suit pants, at war with herself. He straightened, a hand traveling across her back, pulling at the fabric of her dress.

"Hanna," he whispered, lips just brushing her neck, and it set her soul on fucking fire.

She had questions. She wanted answers. She was sure he did too. But she knew that the moment they started the conversation, it would be game over. All the fun, all the distraction, all the heart-stopping touches and mind-melting texts.

They'd disappear. The thought of losing them a second time made her bones ache.

She fell forward, letting the entire line of her body press into his, his heart racing against her chest.

He leaned his head against the wall, eyes closed as she drifted a hand lower, her fingertips lingering just close enough to where he wanted her.

"Can we make it a problem for the flight home?" she asked.

The elevator stopped. The door opened.

"Fuck yeah, we can."

"WHERE IS EVERYONE?" Milo asked between starved kisses and pulling at pieces of his suit.

"I don't know," Hanna gasped, breathless, kicking her shoes off.

He looped his arms around her waist and pulled her toward him, sliding both hands to her face and shoving his tongue between her lips in a way that made her knees wobble.

"Sara is staying with Matty tonight."

"She's a *really* good friend," Milo murmured, his jacket and tie landing on the couch. "Which room?"

She turned him toward the main bedroom of their suite. No lights were on in any of the rooms, so the other girls were either asleep or still out. She fished for her phone.

It was a little after midnight. There was no way they had made it back yet.

"Eyes on me," Milo said as he plucked her phone from her fingers and tossed it onto the pile of outfits she'd passed on while getting ready. He locked the bedroom door and turned back around, stumbling through his pants until he was down to just his boxers.

Hanna reached behind her, desperately trying to undo the zipper at the back of her neck. Milo sat on the edge of the bed and twisted her around, the room blurring. He yanked the zipper down in one fluid motion and just as she went to shimmy out of the black silk, his hands stopped her.

"You know, I'm supposed to be at a strip club."

"Sorry," she mumbled, throwing the dress into the corner. "I need you inside of me *now*."

He flashed a wicked grin, his hand splaying across her stomach and gently running along the curled edge of her bandage.

"Let me feel how badly you want it, Arizona."

His hands reached around her back and pulled her into his lap, spreading her knees over him. He didn't even give her a second to catch her breath before he slipped a finger between her legs.

"Oh my god, what would you have done if I said no?"

She pointed to her suitcase. "Same thing I've done every night since meeting you—drain a set of AAs and try not to scream your name so loud you could hear me."

She leaned over him and pressed her lips to his, slowing down a beat so she could fully enjoy the way his hands explored her body while she tasted every inch of him.

"Get rid of these," she whined, snapping the waistband of his boxers.

"Yes, ma'am," he said, lifting her off of him and tossing them to the side. There was no doubt how badly he wanted her too.

Milo pulled her back over his lap, holding her hips and pushing them in circles over the length of him, the most delicious bass notes rolling from his throat as she sucked on the stubbly skin beneath that laser-cut jaw.

"Hanna," Milo said.

"Please, don't change your mind," she pleaded.

"As much as I *love* hearing you beg, we have a problem."

She leaned back, resting her hands on his chest. "What?"

"All my condoms are in my room."

She rolled her eyes. "Did you think Brendon was putting out this weekend?"

"Brandon," Milo corrected. "And I planned on taking you back to my room when the guys took off for the club! I hadn't factored Logan's bullshit into the night."

Hanna rolled her hips forward, a slow friction sparking between them.

"Am I an idiot if I say I don't give a shit?"

Milo grinned against the side of her face. "Totally your call, Arizona."

"I'm on the pill," she amended.

"Aligned," he chirped, digging his hands into her hips and lifting them over his lap. He hesitated for a second, the silence between them painful.

She twisted her fingers into his hair and pulled so his eyes caught hers. She could see all of the same thoughts that plagued her mind reflected in his half-lidded gaze, the same dread that pooled in her stomach.

They could fool themselves all they wanted into believing they could just be for the weekend. Just be there. That the heartbreak would be the same, so it didn't matter.

She ran a thumb over his cheek.

"It's already too late for us," she whispered. "We can't fuck ourselves out of it, Milo."

It was the closest she could come to saying how she felt out loud.

His eyes closed, and he pushed into her palm, one hand crawling her back and tangling into her hair, still half-up from dinner.

"Flight home problem," he mumbled, guiding her hips over him. The tension in her back melted as he claimed his space, sliding so far into her she gasped.

"I'm sorry for how fast this is about to be," he said, his voice strained. "I promise I will make it up to you."

His hands pushed her hips again, setting a pace that stopped any lingering thoughts that might have been rolling around in her head. She stretched around him, soft sounds slipping from both their throats.

It wasn't the distraction she needed.

It was a whole new set of devastating problems.

It was a perversion of the highest order, a total betrayal of all their agreements.

It was—

"Where'd you go, Arizona?" Milo murmured. He reached up and tapped her forehead. "Get out of there. Get under me."

It was *so fucking good.*

He twisted and rolled her onto her back, pulling the hotel quilt out from under them and shoving it toward the end of the mattress. He didn't untangle his arms from her back; he didn't put space between them or whisper something filthy in her ear like she expected. Instead, he wrapped her up in an endless kiss, moving against her slowly, edging her toward oblivion in ways she'd never pictured with him.

In ways she'd never *let* herself picture.

"Milo," she gasped, his hips crashing into hers. She hooked her ankles behind his back, needing him as close as possible. Wanting him as close as possible.

"Let go, Hanna. Let me have it," he said between biting her ear and sucking on her shoulder, the skin puckering under the pressure. "I'm not going to take it, I need you to give it to me," he mumbled, fingers curled into her skin, leaving their marks.

She nodded, the pressure building so quickly she couldn't get her head around what he was asking for. He could ask for the deed to her fucking house, and she'd sign it over.

She ran her hands over his shoulders, anchoring herself in his tattoos before she was lost to him completely. He covered her mouth with his, inhaling the rapidly increasing breaths she tried to control, but the second he dipped his tongue between her lips, she shattered.

She was gone.

She was his.

She was so *fucking* fucked.

"God, Hanna, keep going," he said through gritted teeth. "I'm gonna—"

He coiled around her so tightly she thought she might suffocate, but the pressure brought her back into her body to fully enjoy the marvel that was a Milo Galantis climax and the unholy sound of him moaning right into her ear.

For a second, she thought that maybe they'd managed to freeze time. Maybe they had an eternity to spend twisted up in one another.

No talks to be had.

No consequences.

"Well," Milo sighed, his chest heaving as he sprawled out across her bed. "That was just as bad as I thought it would be."

"Terrible," she gasped.

"It's a good thing it wasn't that great," he said through stilted breaths, rolling to his side so he could face her. "Because I was worried we were making a huge mistake that we could never come back from."

"Exactly," she said, staring at the ceiling, unable to look at him for fear of what she might find gathering in those eyes. "I've actually already forgotten your name. So."

"That's alright," Milo said, patting her shoulder. "I'm sure the next suite over can tell you."

WHEN SHE WOKE up the next morning, she realized two things simultaneously.

1. She was naked, and Milo was curled around her on Sara's side of the bed. He was also naked, which was something she'd have liked to spend more time observing, however

2. Someone was on the other side of the door knocking,

which meant Sara was back, and she was done sharing the space.

"Fuck, fuck, fuck," Hanna whispered, shaking Milo.

"Say please," he mumbled.

"Milo," she said. "Sara is back."

He shot out of bed and she watched ten different things process over his face at once. She frantically searched the floor for his clothes, tossing his shirt and pants over her shoulder. She reached for a t-shirt and shorts in her suitcase and pulled them on while hopping toward the door.

"Milo! Are you in there, man?"

Oh my god, is that Matty?

Milo and Hanna exchanged a glance, sharing the same spiral of thoughts from across the room as he shoved his leg through wrinkled suit pants.

"Your jacket is out here, asshole. It's too late. Sara needs her contact solution!"

Hanna wiped at her eyes, swollen from falling asleep with her makeup on, and pulled the door open. Matty waited in the doorframe, thoroughly irritated.

"I'm so sorry," Sara cried from the couch. Milo's jacket lay in a heap on the floor, along with their shoes. "I tried to hold him off, but he wanted to see the suite. You know how much he loves fancy bathrooms!"

Matty entered the bedroom and Hanna bolted out to the kitchen. Milo's muffled voice traded shots with Matty, but neither of the girls was brave enough to move closer.

"Is he mad?" Hanna asked quietly.

"Poor guy," Sara sighed. "He's just got a lot of big feelings about all of you. He works too much, he's missed all of the sexual tension, and I think he's still just blindsided. He's been caught in Logan and Milo drama before."

Hanna swigged the water. "You never told him you thought something was going on?"

"You said it was just sex," she said, shrugging.

Hanna winced. She had a point.

Milo sprang from the bedroom and snagged his things from the floor, pulling his shoes on before throwing the jacket over his arm.

"We're not done talking about this!" Matty called from the bedroom, appearing with Sara's contact case.

"Neither are we," Milo said quickly, leaning over the kitchen island and planting a searing kiss on Hanna's cheek.

"Step away from the bridesmaid, Galantis!" Matty bellowed, clapping a hand over Milo's shoulder and pushing him toward the door.

"I'll text you," Hanna mouthed.

Milo winked, dipping out into the hallway as Matty launched into another series of harsh whispers.

Sara rested her hand on Hanna's arm.

"It'll all be fine, Hanna. They've been friends for like two decades. Your vagina is hardly going to be what does them in."

"Wouldn't be so sure about that," Taylor said, slouching her way through the mini-fridge. "That vagina sure put in some work last night."

"Oh god. I'm so sorry, you guys. We thought you were out still."

"We were," Maricela said, cracking open a bottled iced coffee. "Caught the finale though."

Taylor slapped Hanna's ass as she slid past her.

"You'll have to share your secrets. I've never made a man moan like that."

Sara's eyes lit up. "I need a play-by-play."

Hanna shook her head. "I need Advil first."

Taylor laughed, "For your wrecked pussy?"

"For my hangover!" Hanna stretched a little, her lower back tight, the space between her legs swollen. "And the tattoo. Okay, and maybe for my pussy. Goddamn."

Sara waved at the living room. "Sit! I need dramatic reenactments. Diagrams. Fan casts."

Taylor plopped onto the couch. "Florence Pugh. Brunette wig. Little Women accent, duh."

Sara arched an eyebrow. "And for Hanna?"

Hanna threw her head back and cackled, grateful that this was the reception she got when Milo was probably getting his ass handed to him by Matty.

"Who was that Greek actor in that thing we saw last month?" Maricela snaps her fingers. "Nicolas whatever."

"I think that guy's Russian," Hanna mumbled, scrolling through a litany of texts from Logan. She ignored them all and tapped over to Milo's thread.

HANNA:

T-6 hours until the flight home.

How we feeling?

ALWAYS ANSWER

Like we're going to need to book a redeye to untangle this mess.

HANNA

Is Matty mad?

ALWAYS ANSWER

I think just stunned. Doesn't buy the 'we're just friends' thing.

She typed out a message and then erased it, and then she did that a few more times, finally settling on something easier than the truth.

HANNA

Well, we ARE friends. Not sure what the
appropriate suffix is.

ALWAYS ANSWER

Gimme 6 hours. I'll come with a
recommendation.

Her stomach did a little flip, and then it flipped back the other way. She realized that no matter what he suggested, she was terrified of fucking it up.

TWENTY-TWO

"You're a back-of-the-plane girl?"

Milo shoved his carry-on into the overhead compartment and slid into the last row with her, flipping both the armrests up to make more room for him. Sara and Matty had landed somewhere in the middle, definitely out of earshot.

"Not typically."

He followed her gaze toward Sara's bright red headphones.

"Ah," he mumbled. "Reading more dragon porn?"

She rolled her eyes, holding the cover-up. "No dragons. Fae, though."

"The fuck is a Fae?"

Hanna sighed. "I think we have more pressing topics to cover."

"We haven't even taken off yet. We're still in Vegas!" Milo pointed out the window at the tarmac. "Wanna join the twenty-foot club?"

"Milo."

"Okay," he relented. "I know you've been outlining your talking points for hours now, so have at it."

"No talking points," she said, turning in her seat to face him. His hand instinctively landed on her thigh, a spark in her belly derailing her entire list of questions. Her eyes dropped to his hand, and he removed it, muttering a half-hearted apology.

He watched as she formulated a coherent thought.

"Just ask me, Arizona."

"I'm not entitled to any of your story. I know that. But Logan got into my head last night. He said you like projects. Broken girls you can fix, but never have to commit to. He said you make it their fault for you not being in a place for a relationship, or that you hide behind being friends with benefits, so you come off like the good guy."

Milo took another long breath. "And what do you think about that?"

"I think it feels familiar."

He nodded, taking it in. "I understand why. *And* I understand why Logan sees my history through that lens."

He flagged a flight attendant and grabbed two bottles of water before they took off. He broke the seal on hers and handed it over.

He swallowed, seemingly battling back a wall of feelings that he'd normally have funneled into a too-direct string of perfectly curated 'I' statements. But they were beyond therapy. He took another sip of his water.

"Logan was right in some ways. I do have a type. But it's not because I seek out broken women who I can take advantage of. It's because I can't fathom being in a relationship with someone who hasn't had to hold their dead parents' hand and tell them they'd be alright when they're fucking terrified, or stared at oncoming traffic a little too tempted, or lost days, maybe even weeks, of their lives to a wave of grief they didn't see coming."

She scooted closer to him, his voice wavering as he spoke. The fasten seatbelt sign clicked on, causing them both to flinch.

"I've told you that before. I can't be with someone who isn't willing to share that pain with me because it isn't going anywhere. It'll sit right under my skin until I let that final breath out and I can bitch about it to my dad's face. It will be there with every 'I love you,' 'Will you marry me,' 'I do,' and 'That's my boy,' and I know you know that. And I'm *sorry* you know that. But Logan doesn't, and I sincerely hope he's old as hell before he has to confront all of these shitty realities. Most people I've dated have carried that expectation that I'll just get over it one day. That I'll move on. But I've realized that that's not possible.

This version of me, this semi-healed Milo that you put on a pedestal all the time? Relatively new. I've hurt a lot of people, good people, to get to where I am now, and I'm not sure that it isn't just part of the process."

Hanna dropped her gaze to his hands, nervously fidgeting with the cap of his water.

"I'm assuming Michaela is one of those people?"

"The first one on a pretty long list, yeah." Milo closed his eyes and pushed at an invisible bruise on his chest. "You're two years younger than Logan?"

She nodded.

"Okay well, Matty and I graduated together, but Logan is a year ahead of us. I told you Matty was one of my only friends after everything that happened, but Logan's girlfriend, Michaela ,was our age too. When he went off to ASU, we still hung out with her quite a bit. She lost her mom when she was a kid and I think she took pity on me. We got close. Logan got distant. I was seventeen and mad at the world and didn't care who I hurt as long as they ached like me.

She still made the choice to cheat, but I played just as much of a role. I think that's why Logan is so fucked up over Sloane—he did everything right. Exactly the way he wished Michaela and me would have done it. But we were kids. Look at how hard the last year has been on you, and you're a grown woman. Two teenagers with no regulation skills? Gasoline and fire."

Hanna took that in. She knew Logan had a serious girlfriend before her, but not much else. He didn't talk about her at all, and it was becoming clear why.

"I hurt Logan. It hurt even more that Matty was understanding about it. But he met you, he moved on, and we got to a somewhat civil place, and I never expect him to be anything more than that. It was more than fine for both of us."

"Until me."

"Until you," Milo groaned, leaning his head back and wiping his face. "I was being genuine, Hanna, when I told you I didn't mind being a distraction for you. God knows I had plenty of them over the years. And I was being genuine when I said I knew it couldn't be more than that, and that I didn't plan on dating ever again. Because if I didn't set that expectation from the get-go, I knew I'd let you set my entire life on fire. Fuck, I'd hand you the matches."

"Oh," she managed.

"Yeah. Oh," Milo said. "You're just over the first-year mark, Arizona. You haven't even touched this shit yet. You're going to go through things in years two and three and four that will completely change who you are as a person, and I know you think you're fine, and you tell everyone who asks as much, but I lied like that for a decade. Half the time, I think the heartbreak would be worth it just to be with you for however long you'll have me, but I'm not twenty-five anymore, Hanna. I don't know if I can survive being one of the bridges you burn on your way to the other side, but I can't seem to stay the fuck away from you either.

So I flirt, and I send you dirty texts, and I pray that every single time I touch you, it's the only thing you can think about for days, but I can't give you more than that because I'm fucking terrified of what happens when I'm no longer enough to keep the pain at bay."

"Milo—"

"I've lost people I can't get back, and I've survived them all, but I don't know if I'd survive you, Hanna. Last night," he dropped his voice, leaning closer to her. "Last night... you could see it all over my face, couldn't you?"

She frowned, nodding.

He laughed. "And I know I'm not alone in that."

She glanced out the window, the Vegas Strip rapidly disappearing behind them.

"Yeah."

"Yeah," he huffed.

She wanted to tell him that he was wrong. That he could survive her. That she wouldn't hurt him. That she was doing better, and maybe with a little more time...

But she would be lying to him and, perhaps worse, to herself.

It was already bubbling in a slow-moving panic attack in her throat—she wasn't there.

"Can I be honest with you?"

Milo's lips twisted. He already knew what she was about to say.

"I'd rather you didn't."

"I know."

Milo rested his hand on her knee, and this time, she left it.

"I'm a fucking mess," she whispered, everything in her scattering to the walls of her chest as though a bomb had gone off. "You make me feel like maybe that won't be the case one day. But today, it's the truth."

"Don't get your hopes up too high, I'm not feeling particularly put together right now."

"But whose fault is that?"

"Not yours." He shook his head and pushed a lock of her hair behind her ear. "I knew I'd feel like this in the morning, and I still did it."

"Regardless, the only reason I even wanted to stay with Matty and Sara was for a distraction. I needed to escape and I did. And trust me when I tell you I enjoyed every second of it. But at some point, I have to confront reality again. I have a house to deal with. I haven't talked to my therapist in weeks. Things with Logan are worse than ever."

She took a break to chug her water. She knew she would end up in the airplane bathroom soon enough, which she despised, but she also knew she would need a second alone or she'd end up hysterical and being dragged off the plane with a dozen phones in her face.

"I need to get my life together, Milo. And I won't do it if I'm across the hall from the one thing that makes me forget about all of it."

"Damn," Milo said under his breath. "This is exactly the conversation I knew we'd be having, but it really sucks to hear it out loud."

"Being an adult fucking blows." She watched as he sighed twice, both times equally agonizing. "What are you thinking?"

"I'm thinking I wish we'd had this conversation in the last fifteen minutes of the flight and not the first."

She couldn't help it. The tears started rolling, peppered with laughter that came from somewhere she couldn't identify.

"Baby," Milo whispered, wrapping his arms around her. He

pressed her face into his T-shirt and she inhaled slowly, all too aware that it would be the last full breath she took for a very long time.

"SUNFLOWER GIRL!"

Hanna rolled her suitcase into the floral shop bright and early, her knees still aching from walking in heels all weekend.

She waved, feeling a little stupid.

"Oof," the woman said, noticing Hanna's puffy eyes. "Going through it, huh?"

Hanna sputtered a laugh, her heart aching with every breath.

"That obvious?"

"Not a lot of gals come here with packed bags and tear-stained faces."

She leaned against the desk, folding her arms over an emerald-green apron that matched the stone in her wedding band.

"I'm heading back home," Hanna said.

"Leaving behind something good?"

Hanna sucked her lip between her teeth, biting back the wave of tears that crashed against her ribs. She was plagued by them now, unable to hold any of it back.

"I was hoping you could do me a favor," she said. "Can I get weekly deliveries of sunflowers to this address? On Wednesdays? I can put my card on file."

The woman took the sticky note that had Sara's address scribbled across it. She didn't know why she needed to do it. It wasn't like Milo was going to forget her, but she liked the idea of still being present at wing-and-movie night.

"Whatever it is you're leaving, I hope they regret it," the woman said quietly, ringing up the order.

"Not as much as I will," Hanna said back, her throat tightening.

She flicked her eyes over Hanna's face, softening at the sadness she found there.

"It'll come back to you, honey. Love always does."

TWENTY-THREE

It was too hot in Phoenix.

It wasn't a new observation, but it was a new point to add to the list of reasons she no longer thought of Arizona as home. Home was eight hundred miles north, probably two whiskeys deep, forgetting about her.

Hanna dropped her suitcase in the living room and looked around. Her sublet had cleared out and things were tidy, it was almost as if she'd never left. She walked through the house, mentally cataloguing all of the projects she still wanted to accomplish, and stopped in front of the bathroom mirror.

"Shit," she whispered. She'd really cracked through rock bottom and discovered an entirely new subterranean city to explore.

She flopped onto her bed, the cicadas outside singing a dilapidated hymn, and pulled out her phone to fire off a text— the first item she needed to cross off of her very long to-do list.

IT TOOK everything in her to get out of bed and take a real shower, not just a passable one. Even with clean hair and a washed face, she barely looked like herself in the mirror.

She was just so tired.

For the first time, Hanna didn't fuss with her makeup or hair to convince Olivia that she had her life together. Instead, she pulled on the cleanest pair of leggings she had at her disposal and Milo's flannel. As she slid it over her head, she was back standing in his apartment, her suitcases packed, saying a tearful goodbye on the promise that she'd be back eventually.

For what, neither of them had an answer.

She threw her hair into a bun and found some sunglasses. While she may have been ready to let Olivia see her like that, she didn't need her local barista to ask questions.

An iced coffee and a good cry in the car later, she sat on Olivia's plush beige couch.

"So," Olivia said, holding a pen to her lips. "*This* is the real Hanna."

"What do you mean?"

"In all the time we've seen each other, you've only ever been perfectly put together."

Of course, Olivia clocked that immediately.

"I didn't have it in me today."

"That's okay! It wasn't a criticism. I'm thrilled you've taken such a good step!"

Hanna scoffed, adjusting the cuff of his shirt around her wrist.

"This is what a good step looks like?'

"For you? Yes. Now, you want to tell me what happened?"

Hanna inhaled, letting the breath fill and expand all the places she hid her scary thoughts, forcing them to float to the top. The last time she'd seen Olivia was at the peak of her week in Milo's home—god, she'd been so recklessly stupid.

Hanna talked a mile a minute, including all the sordid details that made her sob. She told Olivia about the bar, about the panic attacks, about the dinner she'd cooked for him. She told her about Vegas and Logan. She told her about how she'd cried in front of Milo.

When Hanna finally got to the final conversation they'd had on the plane, Olivia stopped her.

"Do you think he was right?"

"What do you mean?"

"Well, *do* you think you'd burn him on your healing journey?" She gave Hanna one of those looks, *"Hey, you dumb bitch, you better have a big breakthrough here or you're wasting two hundred bucks!"* and Hanna stared at the coffee table in front of her, filled with self-help books that she probably needed to read.

"No."

"All the therapy in the world can't make a man unafraid of love, Hanna."

Hanna rolled her eyes, but really only at herself.

"I should have pushed."

"Well, you had a good point too. You have unfinished business with a lot of pieces of your life. You won't have room for something new until you handle them."

"Damn, Olivia." Hanna recoiled a little. Didn't she pay her to make her feel better?

"I know, the truth can be a little painful sometimes. But in all the time we've been talking, you've had a pattern of immediately backing away from anything that pushes too hard on your emotions. I think that's what happened here."

"I mean, yes. That's true. But like, what else am I supposed to do? Just keep letting people hurt me? It's been a hell of a year for that. Shouldn't I be avoiding things that are only going to make it harder to keep my head above water?"

"I know it feels like that," Olivia said softly. She said everything softly, even when she was landing a lethal dose of observation. "But we don't get to choose what happens to us. We only get to choose what we do about it."

"God, that sucks."

Olivia smiled, and for the first time in a few weeks, Hanna did too.

"What do you think your mom would have done?"

Hanna flinched. She hated that question. Mostly because, while the answer always came to her quickly, she was never sure if it was truly what her mom would have done, or if it was projection. There was a grief between those layers all their own.

"She would have never been in this mess to begin with," Hanna laughed. Lisa hadn't had patience for men in general.

Olivia tilted her head. "You said he was close with his mom. Do you think that was a blocker for you?"

"With him, it never felt like a big deal in relation to my mom because I know he gets it. It would have been the same if I had introduced him to my dad, you know? I don't know. Maybe there's a part of me that saw how close he is with his family and I was afraid to fall in love with, and potentially lose, even more people."

"Mmm," she said, which was Olivia for *say more about that.*

Hanna frowned. "Maybe I'm afraid it feels like cheating on my mom. A little."

"And if you were to find a maternal relationship like that, what's the worst that might happen?"

The tears stung. She couldn't say it.

"Everyone leaves," she whispered.

"You've endured a lot of trauma and a lot of abandonment over the last year, Hanna. What I often see with clients like you is that the story becomes about how you deserve these things to happen, almost like a self-fulfilling prophecy. Does that make sense?"

Hanna sat with that for a moment.

And another moment.

And on the third moment, the one that really sold it, she cried harder than she'd ever cried in her entire life.

She cried so hard, in fact, that Olivia canceled her next session and let Hanna babble at her for another hour, soaking through every last tissue in the office. She cried about her dad. She cried about her mom. She cried about an unfortunate haircut in high school that she'd gotten teased about for weeks. She cried about Logan. A lot.

And Milo even more.

And when she was done crying about all of them, she cried about herself, because—as Olivia had pointed out—she deserved the same amount of mourning as everyone else.

And when she finally ran out of people to cry about, she felt like a different person—empty, but in a relieving way.

"You've been holding onto that for a long time," Olivia said when she felt Hanna had safely wound herself to a stopping point.

"I guess so."

"So, what are you going to do about it?"

"Well, for starters, I'm going to hydrate."

Olivia didn't laugh, but she blinked, signaling that she was not going to let Hanna sweep anything under the rug with a joke.

"I have some calls to make, I think."

"Let's reschedule again for next week?"

She could tell Olivia was never going to let her out of her sight again.

Hanna agreed and left the office, deciding to stop at the hardware store on the way home.

It was time for her to get to work.

"WHAT ABOUT THE EMERALD?" Cami asked, holding up a patterned tile beneath a myriad of lighting fixtures. "With the bronze hardware?"

"Oh," Hanna said, taking the tile from Cami's hands. She sipped on her iced coffee, trying to ignore the pang in her chest as she assessed how far off the shade of green was from a pair of eyes she'd spent a good amount of time not thinking about. "I love it."

"Let me see the faucets again," Cami said, slipping her reading glasses on. It was a move Hanna recognized, one her mother would have done too. She took a deep breath, letting the moment hurt and then pass.

Hanna swiped through the photos she'd collected in her camera roll as the shipments had arrived and found the section dedicated to bathroom fixtures. She handed the phone to Cami who held it up to a few other tile samples and clicked her tongue.

"I think it's the emerald," Cami reaffirmed. "Oh! Sara's calling."

"You can answer it," Hanna said, squatting to the bottom shelf and reading the labels on buckets of grout.

"Hola, mi amor!"

"Mom?" Sara asked over the speaker. Cami held the phone closer to Hanna.

"Hi! Your mom is helping me pick out tile for my bathroom!"

"So you *do* know how to answer calls," Sara quipped. Hanna took the phone from Cami.

"I know, I know, I'm sorry."

Sara laughed, a gentle reassurance that she understood.

"I was just calling to confirm your flight details for the wedding. The itinerary you sent doesn't have a return flight."

Hanna drew in a slow breath. "It doesn't?"

"Maybe you only sent the first half?"

"Maybe," Hanna said. "I'll check and send you the rest of the info when I'm home! Your mom and I have big plans with a bucket of grout."

"Is it pathetic that I'm actually jealous?"

Hanna laughed as Cami wiggled a black and white patterned tile at her. Hanna shook her head and pointed back at the emerald they'd started with.

"You should be, we're having the best time. Berty might even bring the weed whacker over later, and then it's a real party."

"Good, you two need to be supervised."

Hanna smiled. "FaceTime date next week?"

"Really?"

Hanna tried not to flinch at the excitement in her voice. She'd been too quiet since she'd been home.

"Yeah! Text me your availability. We have a lot to catch up on."

"We *do*," Sara said. "Hey, Hanna?"

"Yeah?"

"Hug my mom for me."

"Deal," she said. She hung up the call and pushed her phone back into her purse.

"She doesn't know you're putting the house on the market?"

Hanna swirled her coffee, watered down in the late summer heat.

"I didn't want to excite her just yet. I could still chicken out."

Cami wrapped an arm around Hanna's shoulders. "Lisa didn't raise a chicken."

LISA DID NOT RAISE A CHICKEN, but she did raise a girl who, at the end of the day, was pretty bad at grouting tile, but not too bad at interior design.

She agreed to a tacit ceasefire with the sponge and set it in a bucket, wiping her brow as she admired her work.

It was only one of the two bathrooms, but it was progress. She still had flooring to install in her kitchen, cabinets to paint, and a few windows to replace, but her list got shorter with each passing day.

Hanna reached for her phone as she fell back on the cool tile floor.

SARA

Wednesday, 3PM. I want the full story, top to bottom.

I feel like I only caught a third of what was happening.

HANNA

It's not that interesting. You got the good stuff.

SARA

I want notes. Diagrams. Screenshots.

Receipts, woman.

HANNA

Does it count as a wedding present?

SARA

Throw in a gravy boat and you've got yourself a deal.

> HANNA
>
> I'll craft you one myself.
>
> I'm a handy lady these days.

She snapped a photo of herself sprawled out on the floor, surrounded by buckets and stacks of tiles.

> SARA
>
> My mom said you seemed to be doing a lot better.

> HANNA
>
> I'm a very brave girl.

Sara sent a photo back, sitting in the middle of her living room, which was filled with small bags as she assembled wedding favors. The edge of a foot caught Hanna's eye, a shoe she recognized.

He was sitting right there.

And all at once, she was acutely aware that she had not fixed things, she'd only patched over them.

TWENTY-FOUR

"Okay, so this was all really bad, we've covered that," Sara said about an hour into a brutally honest phone call.

Hanna had confessed multiple sins and talked her through every timeline, as well as her revelations from the previous few weeks.

"And we've examined the missteps. But I think you're holding out on me."

"Sara!"

"I know, I know. You feel like a mess and everything is sad and believe me, I respect that and get it, but you can't tell me all of this heart-wrenching shit without telling me about the romantic parts too. There's no way you and Milo would be this miserable right now if you weren't close to cracking into something real, right?"

Sara moved dishes around off-screen. Hanna assumed she was making dinner and, for a second, her heart ached thinking about having someone to make dinner for.

Sara leaned over the camera and grabbed a bottle of something or other, gathering a few utensils and propping Hanna up on the back of her stove so she could see her while she cooked.

Hanna asked, "Is he?"

"Is he what?"

"Miserable?"

Sara frowned, "It's not great." She left it at that, which was fair. Hanna knew she was trying to respect their friendship, and she could understand that. "Anyway, I just feel like you didn't even get to enjoy any of it, you never got to gush about all the flirting and flowers and shit."

"And by 'shit' you mean..."

"The sex. I want to hear about the sex," she said dryly as she twisted at knobs on the back of the stove.

"My god. You really are your mom, you know that? Fine. I'll tell you. What do you want to know?"

"Everything, Hanna. I've been with the same man for, like, a decade, I need to live a little. You two were *really* into it when we walked in."

Hanna flopped onto her couch and propped her phone up on the end table, hoping Sara wouldn't notice that she'd become a hermit in Milo's shirt.

"Yeah, what am I telling you for? You got the full show."

"I want to hear about the bar."

"Sara. It was crazy. I've never felt anything like that before. Don't tell Logan."

Sara's eyes widened. "Shit."

"Girl," she blushed just at the thought of Milo naked. She'd effectively banned him from her brain for the month she'd been home. "There was one time—"

"Hold on, hold on, hold on," Sara grabbed her phone and shoved Hanna in her pocket. Matty boomed in the background. It made sense that she wouldn't want him to hear their conversation.

"Hey Sara, what's up?" a second voice said. It was cruel how soothing his voice was to her, even from a state away and garbled through Sara's pocket.

Hanna wished for just one moment that Sara had held up the phone, just so those green eyes could skewer her one more time.

"I told Milo and Chloe they could hang out for dinner, that cool?"

"That's fine," Sara said, her voice tight.

Hanna sighed. It was what she deserved to hear, really.

"Anything I can help wi—" Sara mercifully ended the call before she had to listen to Chloe bespell everyone in the room.

SARA

Omg, I'm so sorry, I had no idea they were coming over.

HANNA

He's seeing Chloe again?

SARA

He is. I'm sorry, Hanna, I wasn't sure if you'd want to know.

She stared at the ceiling, tracing the drip stains in the corner that she really needed to do something about. Her ribs ached, damn near bruised from all the crying she'd done.

She rolled over and sat up.

It was time for the next stop on her apology tour.

"HELLO?"

He sounded like he'd just woken up, and immediately a wave of guilt crashed over her. Just the thought of bothering him wrecked her, even after all the hurt he'd caused her.

Hanna hesitated, but finally managed a nervous, "Hey."

"I didn't expect to hear from you anytime soon."

"I know, and I'm sorry for calling out of the blue. I probably should have texted first."

She heard shuffling on his end, and it hit her that he was getting out of bed. It was nearly midnight in New York.

"Annnnnd I should have considered the time difference. God, I'm so sorry."

"It's okay," Logan sighed. "I'm actually glad you called. I've been trying not to bother you, but I feel awful about what happened. All of it, I mean, like the whole last year, but especially my bullshit in Vegas. I don't know what the fuck is wrong with me, Hanna."

"I'm in the same pit of self-loathing if it helps. Logan?" She was afraid to ask him, afraid to crawl out onto a ledge and get knocked off one more by those piercing blue eyes. "I have something big to ask of you, but I think it will help us both."

"Okay, shoot."

She tried to picture him sitting on the edge of the bed, his hair disheveled and his t-shirt clinging to his back. She wondered if he still slept on the left side.

"I need you to come home."

"To Phoenix?"

"Yeah, I need you to help me with something. I just need you to trust me, okay? I think it'll be worth the trip."

He was silent for a while, but eventually replied, "I'll think about it, Hanna."

She released her breath. It wasn't a rejection.

"That's all I ask. Let me know in a day or two?"

"I will. Thanks for calling."

"Goodnight, Lo."

"Night, Hanna."

IT TOOK Logan two days to answer her.

By Saturday morning, he was sitting in her living room, fresh off a red-eye, sipping coffee from a shop down the street where they used to spend their weekends. It was very strange to see him sitting in the house she'd bought specifically to forget him, but it was important.

"I always loved this neighborhood," Logan said, reaching for a pastry from the pink box she'd snagged when his flight landed.

Hanna shrugged. "Yeah, it's been nice here. It's not New York, but it does the job."

"Eh," he took a massive bite, crumbs falling over his polo shirt. "New York is overrated."

"Ah yes, that's what they all say," she teased.

"I mean it, I'm not going to miss it when I move back to the Bay. I miss being around family, you know?"

She nodded. She knew.

"Anyway, not to be so to the point, but I'd love to know why you needed me to get my ass on a cross-country flight so suddenly."

"Yes, that." She folded her legs beneath herself, biting at the edge of her coffee cup, trying to recall the speech she'd practiced in her head for two days. "I've been re-examining a lot about my life lately, and something that keeps coming up is how I treated you when Mom got sick."

It was like she'd thrown a brick. Logan winced, the pain he'd been harboring rushing to the surface of his skin. She'd forced herself not to see it before, to believe it was unearned, but she'd been wrong.

She continued, "I really regret cutting you out like that. I had my reasons, but... they were wrong. I know I can't go back and fix any of it, but what I can do is include you in how I want to move forward."

His apprehension was understandable.

"I appreciate that, Hanna. Really."

"There's something I promised my mom I would do and I've been dragging my feet on it for over a year." Her eyes swept over the black box on her coffee table, the one she'd kept in a closet, haunting her with each passing milestone. "I was wondering if maybe you'd come with me to spread her ashes at the Grand Canyon."

Logan's eyes widened. She couldn't tell if he was horrified or honored, maybe both. But she also knew that he understood how much it took to ask him to be part of it and, despite all the bullshit, they were always going to be two people who had been in love.

That was worth something.

If she closed her eyes, she could hear the voicemails she'd deleted—frantic, begging her to tell him what was going on with her mom and, in her anger, she forgot that Logan had that piece of him too. He might have been a major asshole when it came to Milo, but he wasn't a monster.

A year's worth of hurt shed from his skin in a moment. She watched as the weight of her request settled over him.

"When do we leave?"

AFTER STOPPING at a gas station to stock up on snacks and caffeinated beverages, they hit the road. It was a little under a four-hour drive, which left plenty of time to dive into all the things they'd left unsaid along the way, one of the biggest appeals of taking him with her.

Hanna was done stuffing all of her feelings down. She was ready to purge them.

She let him lead, not wanting to force him to process at the same rapid pace she'd chosen to keep since getting home.

"Can I ask you about him?" Logan floated as the Phoenix skyline faded in her rear-view mirror. He gripped the steering wheel, falling into the same pattern they'd always kept. He drove, she DJ'd. "Or is that off-limits?"

She desperately wanted to keep it off-limits, but that wouldn't help either of them move forward.

"Nothing is off-limits today. That's the point of this."

"Okay, good to know. Are you guys..." Logan trailed off, unsure what descriptor was appropriate to use.

"Together?"

His teeth sank together against a slow bassline as she shifted away from a playlist that reminded her a little too much of green eyes and whiskey.

"Yeah."

"No," she whispered, struggling to admit the next part, "I haven't spoken to him since I left."

Logan was shocked by this. "At all?"

She opted to fuck with the aux cord instead of looking at him.

"Not a word."

"I find that hard to believe, I gotta say."

"Why is that?"

She could sense his discomfort discussing Milo. He was likely trying to shove down the parts that made them both sweat.

"Hanna, there aren't many guys who would jump in to

defend a girl who they didn't deeply care about the way Milo did for you, repeatedly. He was willing to take a punch to the face if I hadn't calmed down. I've known Milo for years and, even though we aren't exactly buddies, especially after what we've put him through, I just assumed you guys were leaving Vegas as a couple."

"Oh," she sighed. For some reason, it hurt even more that Logan saw it too. "He told me about Michaela."

Logan frowned. "I shouldn't have brought that up, we were kids—"

"It actually helped your case. I thought you were just being a possessive asshole, but I understand now there's some lingering shit up there."

She reached over and tapped his temple. Logan laughed, a sound she had not heard in far too long. It released a cord in her chest, unfurling a parachute behind them.

Logan glanced over as he switched lanes. "So, what's stopping you from hopping on a plane right now?"

"He's seeing someone else," she deflected.

Logan, despite a good portion of her inner monologue's accusations, was not stupid. He knew that was yet another trauma he'd contributed to.

"I'm sorry."

"It's my own fault. He was willing, I think, to actually give it a shot, but I'm a *fucking mess*. He deserves someone more available."

She paused to stabilize her breathing. The Milo of it all was the one thing she still hadn't unraveled. He'd texted her a few times when she'd first gotten home, but it only made things harder. They could both sense it.

"I know I said nothing was off limits, but maybe we could circle back on Milo after we settle some of our shit?"

"Fair enough," he conceded. "Where do you want to start there?"

She laughed, just enough that it gave him permission to join her.

What a fucking mess they'd made.

"I guess we could start with Sloane. I know we've covered what you *think* happened, but I feel like we've only ever scratched the surface."

"Ah. I don't know," Logan sighed. "I think if I'm being really honest with myself, that I had been unhappy with us for a while and was just too much of a pussy to admit it. And then I met Sloane, and she was just so different, and not just from you, Hanna. From me, too."

Hanna was surprised by that.

"You were unhappy?"

Logan shrugged. "Maybe that's the wrong word. I was... content. But... neither of us was misting up at the airport when I left for New York, you know? I'd seen you cry harder saying goodbye to Sara after the holidays."

Hanna's chest cracked with the memory. She'd dropped him off and hadn't even gone inside.

And he hadn't asked her to.

Her own tear-stained face staring back at her in an SFO bathroom flashed to her mind, the thought of leaving Milo shredding her from the inside out.

Maybe they were unhappy. If she stepped back and looked at it objectively, they were comfortable at best.

"I guess things weren't, like, amazing. I actually wasn't that shocked when you found someone else, you know that? I was mostly just shocked that you told me."

"I'm a dick in a lot of ways, but not that one," Logan muttered.

"I know! I know. But you just don't expect a call from your boyfriend to ask if it's cool if he's in love with someone else."

Logan barked a laugh, "That's not how that happened."

"It's not far off!"

The tension between them simmered under the laughter, but it wasn't overwhelming. Hanna didn't feel the need to hang up or run away or ignore it. She could sit with it. She had a passing thought that Olivia would be proud of her.

"But I think that's why it hurt so much. I couldn't even be mad at you. You did everything right, so it felt like I wasn't allowed to be crushed the way I was."

Logan chewed on his lip. "I hated hurting you. I still hate hurting you. You know it kills me that I fucked so much up for you, right?"

She believed him then, but a month before, she wouldn't have been able to. Another thing she couldn't have done was apologize back.

"I know. I hurt you too, and I know that I wasn't fair to you."

"I really miss your friendship, Hanna. More than any of the other stuff. I mean that."

Despite her best efforts at exhausting every tear she'd ever produced in the month she'd been home, more still prickled at the back of her eyes.

"Maybe that's why it was so hard to talk to you about Mom. You were my best friend, and then you were gone, and she went right along with you." She took a breath, grasping for the thoughts before they dissolved into the hot tears stinging her cheeks. "It was like I lost everyone all at once, and I needed you to be dead to me too."

Logan reached over and placed a hand on her knee.

"I'm so sorry, Hanna. I never got to tell you that. Lisa deserved so much more, but so did you."

"Thanks." A silence fell between them, laden with all the things she didn't know how to say, but waited patiently for the disparate pieces to fall into a sentence. "I just felt so abandoned by you both that I started assuming everyone would leave me. It's why I was so mad that you tried to come back into my life after so many miserable months, and why I keep fucking things up with Milo. I'm trying to unpack those things and relearn them, but it really sucks."

"I have to ask one more thing about him."

"Fine," she steeled herself, though the more they talked, the better it felt to hear his name. It meant she hadn't imagined it all.

Logan braced himself on the steering wheel.

"Let's just be really, brutally honest, I guess. Obviously, I got the full show, even if I've done my best to repress it... you *never* sounded like that with me."

She had to laugh at that, mostly because he was right, but also because it was just like him to be worried about that when her mom's literal ashes were rolling around in the back seat.

"Don't take it personally," she said, waving a hand as he groaned. "I don't know how to say this to you, Logan, so I'm just going to rip the band-aid off. What Milo and I had in that department was just on another level. I can't even describe it—"

"And I would prefer you didn't."

"Fair. It had nothing to do with you. I always enjoyed things with us, I promise."

"So I'm not terrible at sex?" Logan laughed, but he was serious. "I've had a bit of a complex since that night."

Hanna patted his arm. "You are not terrible at sex. And I'm really, really sorry you had to see that. We thought you guys were gone for the night and never would have imagined one of you would walk in. I actually never even found out what Matty wanted."

"Oh god," Logan sighed. "He was actually coming to invite Milo out with us. Ironically, he wanted to test the waters between the three of us before Vegas. It's been a long time since Milo and I had to be in the same room together. The last time I really spent that much time with him, we were kids and he was a fucking disaster, understandably, but I never gave him a chance after all the shit with Michaela happened."

"Oof," she groaned. "Well, I can confirm that of the three of us, he's the mature and well-adjusted one. Painfully well-adjusted."

Logan snorted. "So well-adjusted that he fumbled you?"

"He didn't fumble me," Hanna insisted. "I fumbled myself."

"Regardless, I'm sorry. I hope you guys can work it out and I mean that, sincerely."

She waited for the shift in his tone, or even a sneer, but his lips held steady. He really did mean it.

"Thanks, Lo."

He released her knee and turned the volume up.

"Now let's take Lisa on one last road trip."

WHEN SHE'D BROUGHT her mother to the Grand Canyon once she'd stopped treatment, Hanna had been acutely aware it would be the last thing they'd ever do together.

She'd felt it in her bones, the same way she'd felt that something was wrong when her phone rang in the middle of her workday.

The same way she'd felt her mom whispering through golden petals as she chased sunflowers across San Francisco.

There were some truths about death that couldn't be explained, only survived.

When she sat beside Logan on a bench on the South Rim, a black box tucked between them, that familiar knowing crept over her—this would be the last thing they'd ever do as the versions of themselves they clung to.

On the drive up, they'd worked through just about every argument they'd ever had, peeling back the layers of where they'd gone wrong, and what they'd each leave as an offering in the canyon's red dust.

She shuffled the box between them. It was heavier than she'd expected, but also didn't seem as heavy as it should be.

"Are you ready?"

She chuckled. "No."

"I think you are," Logan said gently, and that was enough to spur her on. She stood, leaning against the safety rail, and pulled the top of the box back. A small bag sat at the top, at her mother's request, which she'd denied long enough.

Logan stood beside her as she unwound the metal closure. She handed him the box with the rest of Lisa's ashes and tried to think of something profound to say, but she'd learned over that last year that death was never as poetic as she wanted it to be. The meaning was there all the same, whether it was carried in stanzas or early fall breezes.

"To Lisa," Logan said, the wind scattering the particles over the cliffs below.

"To Lisa," she repeated, her lips wobbling on the soft sound of her mother's name.

Logan's arms wrapped around her shoulders. She leaned into the touch, like driving by a childhood home, searching the yard for new blooms in the planters, the windows for different curtains.

This was finally releasing her. Releasing the version of her she'd been when her mother was only a call away. Releasing the pain, and the anger, and the pleading for all of it to have been a bizarre nightmare.

All of it floated out into the ether, no longer Hanna's to carry.

The sun caught the ashes as they drifted downward into the canyon, glittering as they went. Lisa would have accepted nothing less.

Sweet as hell, bites when necessary.

THEY MADE it back to Phoenix in time for a late dinner at one of their favorite pho restaurants before taking a walk around their favorite park.

When Logan pulled her into a long hug on the front porch, it settled into her skin. Neither he or the house were home any longer.

She searched for her keys. "Want a nightcap?"

"No, actually, but maybe some coffee? I, uh, I gave up drinking for a bit," he admitted.

"Wow, look at us, growing," Hanna joked as he followed her inside and into the kitchen. She pulled a Sun Devils mug from her cabinet for him, the one he used to take onto their patio in the morning before work while he scrolled through the news.

"I really needed today," Logan said. He leaned against the kitchen counter, his arms crossed, but not to keep her out.

"I told you it would be good for both of us," she said and popped a pod into the coffeemaker.

"It was. Thank you."

"Thank *you*," she said, settling beside him with her own mug.

She rested her head on his shoulder the way she always

had, but the gesture between them felt entirely new. They sat like that in a comfortable silence until the time difference eventually dragged him down.

Hanna walked him to the door and leaned against the frame. As he passed her, she realized just how much his face had changed. He stopped in the doorway and looked confused when he caught Hanna staring. Shifting toward her and sinking his shoulders inward, he dropped his face closer to hers and focused his bright blue eyes on her lips.

Despite having kissed him a thousand times in her life, the brush of Logan's mouth against hers felt so *foreign*. She jumped backward, pushing at his chest.

He laughed awkwardly, hanging his head back against the doorframe, his neck turning bright red.

"That was so dumb," he gasped. "I'm so sorry!"

"Why, why, *why?*" she asked, her face hidden behind her hands. "We were having such a nice day!"

"I'm an idiot!"

"You're an *idiot*," she agreed, the panic dissolving into a fit of giggles. "Oh my god!"

"Did we *ever* have chemistry?" he asked, his face still flushed with embarrassment.

"I think we've officially closed the loop on Logan and Hanna."

"They're so over," he agreed.

Hanna snorted. "May they rest in peace with Lisa."

"Oh god," Logan groaned, pulling her into a warm embrace, any underlying doubt gone for good.

Milo would have laughed at her joke.

The next morning, when Logan was halfway across the country and she was alone once again, her phone lit up.

Hanna didn't even have to look to know it was him—yet another infinite truth. She opened the message, her stomach tightening into a knot as a photo loaded. Someone had painted an entire field of sunflowers down by the wharf, spraying the Bay with bright yellows and oranges.

Her fingers reflexively touched the ink running along her sternum, the black petals finally healed over.

She didn't know *how* Milo knew she was down to her last stop on the apology tour, but she wasn't surprised that Lisa had something to do with it.

TWENTY-FIVE

Hanna's phone buzzed in her hand as she tapped her foot against Olivia's plush rug.

"I just want to respond to this real quick," she said, holding up a finger in the middle of a thought. "I'm trying not to let texts sit these days."

LOGAN

What time does your flight get in?

HANNA

Early, I have back-to-back salon appointments with Sara all day.

LOGAN

Let's grab coffee when you can, want to game-plan our speeches.

ME

Sounds good! I'll see you tomorrow.

"You seem like you've made a lot of progress in the last few months," Olivia said over a mug of tea, and Hanna no longer doubted that she was right. She felt fine, but *actually*. Handling things with Logan had freed up a lot of her capacity to take care of herself.

She was still struggling to sleep, but she hadn't had a panic attack in nearly eight weeks. She'd spent those weeks grouting tile, painting walls, and teaching herself to lay wooden flooring.

She'd taken up yoga.

She'd called her dad twice.

But in all the progress she'd made within herself, there was a certain Greek god she still hadn't worked up the nerve to confront.

She'd responded to his photo, but nothing else came of it. She knew he was giving her space, that knew he was waiting for her to set the tone, and she'd settled so many scores.

Surely she could face one more.

"How are you feeling about the wedding?" Olivia asked.

Hanna knew what she was really asking—*how many times have you thrown up thinking about the fact that you have five days of Milo ahead of you?*

"Anxious, mostly. I'll be spending a lot of time around Milo with nowhere to go. And things are weird because we left on somewhat vague terms. I still have so much to apologize for, but I also don't want to make Matty and Sara's wedding about my shit."

"That makes sense. Do you think there will be a time, maybe beforehand, that you can sit down and just make your apology without expecting anything other than him hearing you out?"

Hanna sighed, knotting her fingers together with a tassel on one of Olivia's soothing beige pillows.

"Yeah, I'm sure there will. That's a good idea. Just kick the weekend off with a little groveling."

"Your word choice, not mine," Olivia smirked.

"Yes, sorry. I mean a constructive conversation during

which I'll own my responsibility for our distance, and then leave room for him to react however he needs to."

Olivia tapped her pen against her lips. "I told you twice a week wasn't too much. Look at you."

Hanna thought her bank account might have a dissenting opinion about her habit, but her emotions couldn't deny the impact.

"Yeah, yeah."

Hanna picked up her bag, but Olivia stopped her before she left.

"I think your mom would be really proud of you, Hanna," she said.

Six months earlier, the comment would have sent Hanna spiraling. How could someone who'd never known that her mother's hair smelled like paperwork and Dior J'adore, or that her right shoe always wore down faster than her left, know how she'd feel about anything?

Hanna smiled, not even attempting to hide the tears as they flowed.

"Thank you."

"YOU'VE RETURNED!"

The floral shop glowed in shades of amber in the early autumn sun. Hanna propped her suitcase against the desk.

"I've returned," she said. "And I've come to cancel my deliveries."

"Aw, that's too bad," the owner murmured, flipping through her ledger. "My delivery boy thinks your friend is cute."

"She is unfortunately taken," Hanna laughed. "But I'm only canceling the delivery portion. I'll be around to pick them up in person for the time being," she chirped.

She hadn't told Sara that bit yet, but she figured it would be best saved for a wedding gift. She'd just gotten off the phone with her realtor before walking in—all that eat-pray-love shit had earned her a more than decent offer on the house.

"Oh!" She beamed at Hanna, her green eyes sparking behind her purple glasses. "That's great news, right?"

"Hopefully," Hanna mumbled, glancing at the top of the desk, its wood stained with years of watermarks from spilled vases.

"He get his act together, then?"

Hanna choked on a laugh, her eyes grazing the florist's.

"It was me, actually."

"Ahhh," she hummed. "You know, my husband used to tell me he was never wrong, I was just always right."

Hanna shook her head. "The one who thinks diamonds are boring, right?"

"Yes," she laughed. "Well, thought."

"Oh, I'm so sorry for your loss," Hanna said. "Actually, no, I hate that I just said that."

The woman's eyes narrowed, her mouth parting in confusion.

Hanna corrected herself. "I don't hate the sentiment, I just... I hate how hollow it sounds, you know? I lost my mom not too long ago and I hate when strangers apologize as though they had something to do with it."

Hanna knew she was rambling, but she still took a moment to pat herself on the back for being able to confess that out loud without breaking down.

"I knew I liked you," the florist said, a soft smile pulling at her lips. "Grief is a real bitch, huh?"

Hanna's nose scrunched as she laughed, taken aback by the shift in tone.

Mom would have really liked this woman.

The wound of the thought stung, but it did not bleed.

The florist scribbled a note on her ledger and set her pen down.

"Alright then, honey, I'll just have your arrangement available here every Wednesday morning. You know, you're back just in time for peak sunflower season."

Hanna smiled. That much she did know.

"Actually, do you have something small I can pick up now? I hate to show up empty-handed."

"Let me take a look."

She ducked into the back of her shop, leaving Hanna to brush her fingertips over the bottles of wine and ouzo on the shelf in the window. She returned a moment later with a small bouquet of sunflowers and crisp, white dahlias.

"I have a big wedding this weekend and I've been playing with the dahlias and sunflowers together. I thought they'd be too dense beside one another, but I don't know. I kind of like them."

She held up the stems, rotating them to get Hanna's opinion.

"What if you added something with a softer petal between to break up all the lines?"

She considered this, reaching for loose stems of velvet-soft greenery, the smooth planes falling between the petals for a nice break.

"Oh, I love that," Hanna said.

"You know, whoever sent you packing is lucky you came back."

Hanna's face heated. She wasn't so sure about that.

"I mean it, honey. You and I both know better than most how short life is. It's good you didn't waste too much time."

"You're so kind," Hanna mumbled. "I just hope he feels the same way."

"Well, if he doesn't, his loss." She reached for Hanna's crossed arms, leaning in with her sparkling eyes.

Hanna's heart swelled at the gesture. It was the same feeling as when Cami hugged her—an impossible nostalgia for a version of her mother she would never get to know. She'd have to find Lisa in the curves of mothers who did not share her blood, but shared her burdens. She'd have to look for hard-fought wisdom carved into the smile lines of women in flower shops.

"Oh, honey," she said, pulling Hanna into a hug.

"I'm fine," Hanna protested, despite her eyes welling with tears.

"You deserve to be better than fine," the florist sighed, patting Hanna's back. She released her from the hug, but held onto her arms. "And don't forget that."

Hanna wiped at the corners of her eyes.

"Now," she said, tucking a curl behind Hanna's ear. "Go show whoever didn't follow you wherever the hell you ran off to, exactly what he missed."

"OH MY *GOD*," Sara screamed as Hanna stood in her doorway. "We're getting married!"

Hanna threw her arms around her friend's neck, the bouquet of sunflowers and dahlias releasing a sweet aroma behind her head.

"These are gorgeous," Sara said. "Almost makes me wish we did dahlias."

"It's not too late," Hanna said. "I've got the hook up."

"Hmm," Sara said, arranging the flowers in the teal mason jar she'd kept on the counter for Hanna's weekly deliveries. She snapped a photo. "Maybe I'll shoot her a text."

Matty sighed beside her. "Stop torturing our vendors!"

"I'm not torturing anyone!"

Matty snagged Hanna's bags and disappeared upstairs, but not before dropping a kiss on her cheek. "Room's still yours for however long you want it."

She bit back the urge to take him up on that offer. She needed to wait until she saw *him*.

That would be the determining factor.

"We have a stacked day," Sara said, scrolling through her calendar as though she hadn't already sent Hanna a painfully detailed itinerary the week before.

"I'm ready to be beautiful," Hanna said.

"After manis, we have spray tans, blow outs, lunch with Cami, and then back home to get dressed for the welcome dinner. Taylor and Maricela will help the guys set up."

"Am I your security bridesmaid for all of these appointments, or are you keeping me away from a certain groomsman?" Hanna asked.

Sara arched a brow. "First of all, two things can be true at once. Second, sorry, did you want to see Milo in your sweats and running around with string lights, or did you want to walk into the welcome party tanned, tweezed, and tucked into two pairs of Spanx, and ruin his fucking life?"

Hanna pursed her lips. "I don't want to ruin his life."

"Not even a little bit?"

"No," Hanna insisted.

Sara set her phone down. "Wow, that was a test. Olivia really is worth every penny."

Hanna tossed her hair. "I'm telling you! I'm a whole new bitch!"

TWENTY-SIX

Half a day and several hundred dollars later, Hanna stood outside the loft, spray-tanned, blown-out, micro-dermed, and acrylic-nailed to the high heavens.

She'd caught a glimpse of her reflection in Logan's car window and she thought that maybe she'd get lucky and Milo wouldn't even recognize her.

"Whoa, look at you!" Logan exclaimed when she slid into the passenger seat of the same car he'd been driving for years. "If I didn't know any better, I'd think someone was trying to make a man see what he's missing."

She rolled her eyes, "Will you ever move on?"

Logan laughed, rolling into the San Francisco traffic.

"Milo has been a wreck all day, if it helps take the edge off. Snapped at Brendon—"

"Brandon," Hanna corrected.

"Brandon. Anyway. Told him to get fucked just for breathing too loudly. Man is on the edge of a breakdown for *some* reason."

She hated the rush it gave her.

"You should pull your hair back a little. You have a really sexy neck."

Hanna balked. "I didn't know we were at the wing-man stage of our breakup."

"I've literally seen him inside of you, Hanna." He winced, the memory weighing on him.

"Okay, okay," she hissed. He wasn't helping her nerves. "I need you to have my back tonight. Do *not* let me get drunk, do *not* let me smoke anything anyone hands me, and do *not* say anything else about my neck."

Logan saluted as he rounded a corner.

"Thank you. Now, tell me everything about the rest of your trip. You haven't updated me since somewhere in Nebraska."

"Oh god, corn. Corn for hours. It was brutal, but at least Matty drove half of it."

Logan wound through the city streets, regaling her with stories from his big move. He'd been living just a few blocks over from Sara and Matty for a month while settling into his new job.

They found parking a block down from the bar, and she must have sat for a moment too long because Logan turned and rested a hand on her knee.

"Whatever happens, I need you to remember that you deserve good things, Hanna."

"Thanks," she whispered. She knew it was true. And not just when he, or the florist, or Sara said it.

She pulled her dress down as she stood, smoothing the emerald-green silk over her knees. Logan stood behind her and reached for her hair as she brushed it over her shoulder. She swatted his hand, but she knew he was right.

She did have a nice neck.

The bar door was propped open with a sign framed in

bright orange, red, and yellow florals, dripping in sunflowers and roses. Maricela had won Sara over in Vegas, it seemed.

Logan trailed her up the stairs at the back of the empty lounge, the party in full swing on the rooftop. It was good he was behind her, pushing her forward so she couldn't linger at the downstairs bar, thinking about the last time she'd been there.

He rested his hand on the small of her back as she stepped gingerly over the threshold of the stairs. The amber sunset washed the city in a soft glow, the overhead string lights catching the final dregs of the sun.

Frankie poured glasses of Prosecco behind a makeshift bar in the corner, his eyes lighting up when he recognized her face.

"Arizona! How are ya?"

She flinched at the moniker. For a second, she wondered if he knew she'd ruined his brother's life over the summer, but as he flipped a rocks glass over and flicked his eyes toward hers, she could see it.

He was well aware.

She forced an apologetic smile. "I'm okay, Frankie. How have things been?"

"Great. I think this is the first time the bar's ever been used for anything other than a bunch of fat old bastards arguing over their tabs."

Hanna laughed, even if the sound didn't fully translate. Logan hovered beside her, trying to look busy with his phone.

"Your dad would probably hate all the flowers, huh?"

Frankie shook his head. "Nah. Dad had a thing for flowers. What are you drinking?"

"I got her," Milo said, appearing over his brother's shoulder with three more bottles of wine.

Hanna swallowed, her mouth suddenly filled with sand.

She'd neglected a crucial factor in all of the rehearsals she'd run through in her head—she'd been on a tolerance break. Seeing Milo after three months of *not* seeing Milo hit so much harder than she'd anticipated.

Frankie scooted behind him to mix drinks for Taylor and Maricela who were desperately pretending they weren't listening to every word.

Hanna stared at the tattoos peeking out from under Milo's button-down, a pathetic voice in her head screaming, "*Say something, you stupid bitch!*"

Logan slipped toward the end of the bar, giving her space when, for once, she didn't want it.

Milo pulled a bottle off the back of the bar and dropped some ice into a glass, inches from her as she rocked on her heels. He held up the bottle, flashing a burgundy label with two small rabbits on the side.

"Dareringer from Rabbit Hole. Takes four years just to make the barrels. They finish them with sherry before casking, super interesting flavor notes. You'll like it."

His hand tipped the bottle forward.

"Just a single," she said.

Tilting the glass upward, she sipped it slowly so she could really taste the notes, and goddamn if it wasn't one of the most unique whiskeys she'd ever had.

"Wow," was all she could manage. The scent of his cologne mingled with the top note of the whiskey, sending her head swirling.

"We just got our hands on a few of their bottles last week. I'm heading out to Kentucky next month to tour their distillery, and a few dozen more if I have it my way," Milo smirked. They both knew he always had it his way.

She took another sip and tried once again to think of something that wasn't *kiss him, kiss him, kiss him*.

"Hey, Milo, I just—"

"Hanna!"

Her head whipped around as Chloe's arms wrapped around her shoulders, squeezing tightly and undoing three months of healing.

"Oh my god, it's *so* good to see you!" Chloe chirped.

Hanna couldn't decide which was worse—the tightening in her chest, or the rage that followed the realization that it was, indeed, good to see Chloe.

"Uhhhh yeah! You too!"

Chloe spun Hanna in a twirl, admiring her silk dress that fluttered in the evening air.

"You look so gorgeous in that dress. Milo, doesn't she look incredible?"

Milo looked about as dead inside as Hanna felt.

"Yep," he mumbled as she grew redder by the second. Sara and Logan clocked the pixie at the same time, but Sara beat him to her.

"Hey, all the girls are going to take a photo together!"

"Oh, I can take the photo," Chloe chimed. Sara glanced at Hanna, defeated by Chloe's inability to stop being the perfect girl's girl. She lined up the bridesmaids at the far side of the roof, gracefully recommending poses as she snapped away.

There was not enough slow breathing—or whiskey for that matter—that could get Hanna back into her body, but she did a fine job of avoiding Milo for the rest of the evening.

Not that he sought her out.

"I AM SO FUCKING SORRY," Sara whispered as they tumbled back into her apartment, the door sealing off Milo and Chloe as he fumbled for his keys.

"Milo asked if he could bring a date, like, a year ago and at the time, it was no problem! I just assumed he would have uninvited her."

"It's fine," Hanna said, flicking her hands as she pulled her heels off. "It's honestly my fault for assuming he'd just wait for me to get my shit together, you know?" She dropped the shoes in the hallway, pacing in the kitchen as Sara watched. "Safe to bet she'll be in attendance the rest of the weekend?"

Sara's lips fell into a crooked frown. "I'm not sure. She's still in the seating chart. I can move her to the shitty table!"

"No, no." Hanna pulled her hair into a ponytail, sweating. "Chloe is not the enemy. You know, she sent me flowers while I was back in Phoenix."

She'd called Hanna a few times too, never mentioning Milo, and Hanna was far too stubborn to ask, but appreciated the gesture all the same.

"Fucking Milo," Sara growled. "You spend all this time breaking your own heart open for him, but he's too afraid, so he calls in Cockblock Chloe—"

"She's not the enemy," Hanna repeated.

"I *know*," Sara hissed. "I know. Ugh. What can I do to make this suck less?"

"You," Hanna said, pulling Sara into her arms and stroking her perfectly smooth hair. "Can stop worrying about me. I'm a grown woman, Sara. This weekend is not about me, or Milo, or Cockblock Chloe—solid, by the way—it is about two of my favorite people in the world getting married. I promise you that I can handle this."

Sara grabbed Hanna's face between her palms, squeezing her cheeks together.

"I am just so proud of you, and also a teensy bit nervous!"

Hanna laughed, a genuine thing, not one of the forced responses she'd honed.

"Thank you for your candor, but I swear, Sara. I'm *fine*."

"Okay, okay. I believe you."

Milo wouldn't have.

Sara pressed a kiss into Hanna's cheek. "We should get our beauty sleep!"

"You're going to have to cut me out of these Spanx," Hanna muttered.

They giggled, embracing for one more moment before Hanna headed upstairs and shimmied out of her dress, kicking it off as she began the torturous endeavor of peeling her shapewear away from her body.

She had just flopped back onto the bed and was scrolling through photos from the party when a text came through, sending a lightning bolt straight between her ribs.

ALWAYS ANSWER
Hey

> HANNA
> Hi

ALWAYS ANSWER
You at Matty's?

> HANNA
> Yeah

Milo typed for a minute before stopping, the bubble slipping into the ether. She waited for another minute, desperate for any piece of him he'd offer.

No offering came.

SHE REGRETTED PASSING out in her makeup, but not nearly as much as she regretted not hydrating before bed.

Tolerating a three-hour drive with Matty and Logan was hard on a good day, but hungover? No. No way.

She pulled on the flannel that didn't belong to her and twisted her hair back into a bun to be dealt with later before skipping across the street and ducking into the diner.

She'd missed the acidic smell of lemon scones and burnt Folger's. If she'd been paying less attention to her reflection in the window and more to the man sitting in their favorite booth, she would have had a chance to catch her breath before locking eyes with Milo.

"Fuck me," she muttered.

The night before, she'd been perfectly coiffed. In the cold light of morning, she looked like she'd lost a fight with her mascara wand.

Milo held up his hand in a sheepish wave, and she considered bolting, but New Hanna was better than that.

Or so she told herself as she slid into the booth across from him.

"I was wondering where that shirt went."

A coffee mug hit the table beside her as one of their favorite servers smiled. She poured Hanna's mug to the top before refilling his.

Hanna watched the steam curl into ghosts between them.

"I don't think you were even this hungover in Vegas," he finally said.

"Yeah well, I built up a tolerance when I was hanging out with you. I haven't had much to drink in the last three months and clearly, I'm out of shape."

Milo nodded. "You went clean on me?"

"Most of the time," she said. "I was on an anxiety med that didn't play well with alcohol." She was nervous, the thoughts spilling over themselves. "Still doesn't, obviously."

"Is it helping?" he asked.

"A lot, yeah. That and a million dollars in therapy. I almost feel human again some days."

"Still just the one therapist then?" He smirked, pulling in a long sip of coffee over the edge of his mug.

She grinned, flashing two fingers up. "You'll be thrilled to know I've added a somatic healing coach."

"Not quite the same—"

"She charges two hundred dollars an hour and makes me feel good. It's the same."

Milo leaned forward, but before he could say whatever it was that bubbled against his lips, she held up a hand.

"I heard it." She inhaled slowly, her ribs shaking around her swirling thoughts. "I've been trying to think about how to apologize to you every day for three months."

Milo set his mug down.

"You could have called."

"I could have," she offered.

His eyes softened.

"Why didn't you?"

"I was afraid to jump the gun," she murmured. "I had a lot to process and I just... I didn't want to rush the *you* of it all. You didn't deserve another round of that."

"True," he said.

"Well, at any rate, I *am* sorry. For all of it."

"All of it?" he asked.

"I can provide an itemized list if you want," she joked, her lips twisting.

"Not necessary," he sighed. "Thanks for apologizing."

The tone threw her off—she'd never heard his voice that tight. She started to speak again, but his eyes swept from hers to the blonde beside her.

Logan leaned over the back of the booth, speaking in a hurried tone.

"Hi, so, *so* sorry to interrupt, but you have my keys."

Hanna turned, her vision blurring at the edges as her head throbbed.

"I do?"

Logan pointed to her purse.

"If you don't, we're in trouble."

Hanna sighed, fishing through her bag.

"Is this yours, too?" She yanked his keys and a leather wallet out of her purse.

"Yeah, thanks, okay, sorry, bye!" Logan snatched the keys and wallet, tucking them into his pocket as he bolted from the diner.

"It's good you two patched things up," Milo said, his voice so low she hardly heard him.

"What? Oh, yeah. Yeah, we finally figured things out."

His jaw clenched.

"Was that all?"

Hanna flinched, the chill in his tone so foreign. Her hand came to her chest, pushing on the tattoo shuddering beneath.

"I'll see you guys in Sonoma," he muttered, throwing a twenty down on the table.

"Milo," she huffed, but he was already gone.

She got her coffee to go, her shoulders collapsing under the tension as she crossed the street.

"The fuck was that?" Logan asked as he slid her suitcase into the trunk. Sara leaned against the hood.

"Why's he so *mad*?" she asked.

Hanna shrugged, pulling his shirt tighter around her. She tossed her purse in the back of Logan's car and flopped into the back with Sara as Matty rounded the front and dropped into the driver's side.

"It's his dad's birthday," he said. "Give him a pass."

Sara leaned over, resting her head on Hanna's shoulder, and rubbed her arm.

"He'll come around, babe."

TWENTY-SEVEN

"You look so great," Sara whispered to her on the DeBrunes' sun-soaked patio.

Hanna had missed the sprawling winery's gorgeous views. Marcia flitted around, topping off while everyone settled into two long tables set up for the rehearsal dinner that evening. For lunch, though, it was just the parents and kids.

It shouldn't have been a surprise that Milo was included, but Hanna tensed all the same when he popped out of the house and rolled his linen sleeves up over those fucking tattoos.

She wondered briefly where Chloe was, but pushed the thought aside to focus on Sara who handed her a glass of pale yellow wine and said something, but Hanna heard nothing as Milo sat down directly across from her at the table.

It wasn't really his choice, she realized. Marcia had organized the table to keep all the kids on one end and the parents and grandparents on the other. She could see it, the pain lingering on his skin, like a cut she thought was finally healed, just to move too quickly and tear the scab open.

Hanna swallowed a gulp of her wine. "Okay so, what do

you need from me tonight to help things go as smoothly as possible?"

Sara shrugged. "Honestly, Hanna, I think the staff has everything handled. I feel like we should be more stressed, but it's all shaping up."

She sipped her wine, her eyes landing on Matty. Hanna watched as he made a face and Sara's lips parted again.

"Actually," she continued, "I do need a *huge* favor."

Hanna nodded. "Sure. Whatever it is, I can do it."

Sara watched Matty while she spoke. "When I was unpacking, I realized that I completely forgot to bring my deodorant. Do you think you could run into town and pick some up at that Safeway?"

Hanna could already sense where she was going.

"You can just use mine if you need to?"

Sara frowned. "Is it an antiperspirant?"

"Yep," Hanna said shortly. Milo did not deserve whatever scheme they'd cooked up.

"Is it... unscented?" *Oh god, Sara. Come on.*

"Is my deodorant unscented? That's what you're asking me right now?" Hanna stared daggers into her.

"Yeah, I need it to be unscented antiperspirant. It's a thing. You know fragrance makes me break out and I can't have a rash on my wedding day, Hanna!"

Hanna relented. "Okay, sure," she turned to Logan. "Gimme your keys."

"Sorry," he said. "I actually have to pick up my aunt and uncle from the airport. Their rental fell through."

A coordinated effort.

"Great, you can grab Sara's unscented deodorant—"

"Antiperspirant," Sara corrected.

Hanna clenched her teeth. "*Unscented* antiperspirant while you're out."

"Nope. I can't." Logan said.

Hanna hung her head forward. "Why not?"

Logan's eyes shifted to Matty, who looked at Sara.

"Because," Sara mumbled. "He'll never get the right thing. He's a stupid boy!"

"Yes!" Logan raised his glass to her. "I'm incompetent. You've said so yourself *many* times, Hanna."

Hanna did her best not to let her irritation show.

"Logan, you make six figures a year doing math for a living, you can read a label," she hissed.

"I can't listen to this anymore," Milo finally interjected. "I'll take Hanna into town, because I'm sure I'm also too stupid to read a label on a product that *definitely* exists, and you all can stop the rest of your plotting because that's not why we're here this weekend. Deal?"

"Thank you, Milo," Sara said, smiling and quickly adding, "And while you're getting my unscented antiperspirant, can you also get me a toothbrush, because I actually did forget that?"

"Unreal," Hanna whispered, eating her lunch in a silent protest, knowing that when it ended, she would have to actually face Milo.

She wanted to hold him, to let him break down the way she had so many times, but things were so blurry.

Milo nodded his head toward the house.

"Let's just get this over with, Arizona."

"OUR FRIENDS ARE ASSHOLES," Milo finally said about twenty minutes into their thirty-minute drive.

"They think they're helping."

"There's nothing to help," he sighed. "I told you earlier, we're good."

She crossed her arms, treading lightly. He kept one eye on the GPS and the other firmly on the road. He hadn't looked at her since they'd left the DeBrunes'. She fell right back into his rental car all those months before, slurring her way through their first of many fights.

"They feel bad for how things went down," she said.

"They shouldn't, that was all on us." Milo rounded the car into a little downtown street, pulling into the Safeway parking lot.

"Right." She tried to be patient and remember that this was not the grounded, adult Milo she was running errands with.

This was fifteen-year-old Milo, sitting in a glass office while someone shattered his world, and she was staring.

"Hanna," he sighed. "I really don't want to hash shit out today, okay?"

He parked the car, shutting the door a little harder than necessary. She followed him into the grocery store, trying to keep up with his long legs. He didn't bother to see if she was with him as he made a beeline for the beauty section, searching the aisles for deodorant and stopping at the pinkest shelf.

"Which one?"

Goddamn, she'd never *really* seen him pissy before and resented that she was enjoying how much sharper his jawline looked when he was mad. Leaning toward the shelf, he flicked at the boxes and accidentally knocked one over. He let out a sigh.

Hanna grabbed the brand Sara had been using for a good ten years. Even if it was a ruse, it didn't hurt to be prepared. She jumped one aisle over and grabbed a toothbrush as Milo disappeared into the liquor aisle. She was next in line when he showed up beside her with a bottle of whiskey.

Hanna made a mental note that when the wine betrayed her that weekend, he had a stash. She paid for the deodorant and toothbrush, he paid for the liquor, and they continued back to the car without a word.

She could wait for him.

He drove the opposite direction from the winery.

"Do you know where you're going?"

Milo snorted. "Yes, I know where I'm going."

"So then, you know that the DeBrunes' house is that way?"

She leaned her head to the right, motioning with her thumb.

He muttered, "We're not going back to the DeBrunes'."

"Huh, well," she sighed, trying to maintain a pleasant tone. "I didn't have kidnapped-by-my-ex-boyfriend on the itinerary today, but I guess I've got some time to kill before the rehearsal dinner."

The air between them tightened. She'd fucked up. Any other day and he might have laughed it off.

Milo bit, "Oh. So *now* I'm your ex-boyfriend? And not just your ex-guy-you're-fucking?"

He turned down an old street that was peppered with mid-century facades, all-brick columns, and ornate hanging plants swaying in the early fall breeze. It was all so charming and, if she wasn't being dragged through it against her will, she'd have stopped to enjoy it.

Milo swung the car into a parking lot facing the town square crowned with a lush green park and a perfect little gazebo with blossoming rose bushes.

Milo opened her door. "Are you coming?"

She looked at him, unsure if he still wanted her to tag along.

"Coming where?"

"Just, please? Okay?" Milo huffed. He held out a hand,

helping her out of the car, and pointed across the street, exasperated.

Hanna followed his hand, her chest tightening.

Even the chairs at The Sunflower Café were bright yellow. The patio bustled with late afternoon snackers, a soft and mellow playlist strumming from the open doors.

She'd been to Sonoma with Logan a dozen times, but they'd never wandered this way.

"Milo—"

"I don't want to talk about it. Any of it. I don't need to hear about how much better you're doing, or how you found yourself or whatever the fuck, or how you and Logan are happy now—"

Hanna laughed, unable to stop herself.

"What are you talking about?"

Milo glared. "Logan and you are back together, aren't you?"

Hanna scoffed. "On what planet?"

"On the one where he drove you to *my* fucking bar last night, and had his hands all over you, and you left with him? You had all his shit this morning."

"Logan and I are just friends."

Milo arched a brow. "When we were just friends, we were f—"

"There's that directness I missed so much!" She bit her lip, glaring at him.

Milo sighed. "So, you're not together?"

"Nope."

She gathered all the patience in the world she wished people would have had for her.

He slipped his hand over hers and dragged her across the parking lot. She trotted to keep up with him as he pulled her into the restaurant. They sat on the patio, all sorts of plants blooming around them as plates clinked and the server poured two glasses of water. Milo stared at the menu, unwilling to look at her.

Hanna gave the waiter her best smile.

"Two coffees, black, and a piece of whatever cake you got."

"Anything else?"

"Nope," she said, snatching the menu from Milo's side of the table and handing it over. She'd decided to let him stew for as long as he needed. He adjusted his sunglasses, glancing around the patio in a silence she wouldn't break for him.

When their coffees came, he stared at the cup, lost in his own world. She'd been there so many times, and he'd never once rushed or judged her. When the slice of cake came, she pushed it toward him.

"I'm good," he said.

"Okay," she returned, taking a small bite. It was the perfect level of sweetness—such a harsh contradiction to his attitude.

"Sorry, I want to let you brood for as long as you need to, but you really should try that."

Milo sighed, picking up the second fork. He took the world's smallest bite of cake and set it back down.

"You can quit looking at me like that," he said. "I'm fine."

"Banned word," she whispered.

His eyes slipped from the plate to her. They held it all right there—the agony, the loneliness.

"Have any of your ten thousand therapists ever told you that it's okay to *not* be perfectly okay all the time?"

Milo leaned back like she'd slapped him.

"Okay, you've been in your healing era for, like, five minutes, let's not get ahead of ourselves," he said.

Hanna covered her smile, afraid to scare him back into silence, but thrilled to be teased by him again. He snagged the fork, diving in for another bite.

"It's birthday cake," Hanna said softly, pointing at the plate.

Milo stopped midbite, his eyes closing as he nodded. He inhaled slowly and let the breath back out.

"Who ratted?"

"Your attitude," she said.

He tilted his head.

"And Matty."

Milo finished his bite and set the fork down again.

"How old would Elias have been?" she asked.

"Sixty-four," he said, no hesitation. No need for math. That kind of math did itself, constantly whispering in the back of their minds, marked by missed milestones and new lines carved in faces.

"How do you usually spend today?"

"Pissed," Milo laughed.

Hanna pointed her fork at him. "Okay, checked that one off the list."

"Alone," he added.

She sipped her coffee, the heat of it soothing the wave of emotion in her throat.

"Not this year."

"No." A half smile cracked over his lips.

"Can I tell you something?"

Milo nodded as she set her coffee down.

"Seeing you all shitty like this... gives me a lot of hope."

Milo scoffed. "Hope?"

"Yeah," she said, snagging another bite of cake. "You're still allowed to be sad fifteen years in, but you'll wake up tomorrow and you won't want to stay in bed for two months. There's something encouraging about knowing I can still *feel* it all without wanting to die after, or whatever."

"Or whatever." He grinned.

"Smile still hits," she said, not meaning to say it out loud.

Milo shook his head. "Goddammit, Arizona. I was really trying to have a shit day."

"I know," she whispered. "You still can. I won't say another word."

Milo chewed on his lip. The way his eyes closed reminded her of tucking into him on the plane home, his voice breaking as he'd apologized over and over again.

These were the days he'd been worried about. The days he needed someone who understood. The days he needed to know he was worthy of every ounce of patience he'd shown her.

Someone worthy of the love she thought she might never find a new home for, rotting in her chest.

"We should probably get back," she said.

He only nodded, following her to the car. He walked slowly, like he was dragging something behind him. When he reached for her door handle, she intercepted his arm and pulled him into her, holding a hand on either side of his face.

"This doesn't scare me," she said.

"Hanna—"

"It used to. It used to make me think I'd never breathe again if the mighty infallible Milo still had bad moments, but you'll be fine. We both will."

"I don't wanna be fine," he whispered, his teeth biting down on the next sentence against her hands.

"What do you want to be?"

She stared into those green eyes, convinced she could hear the internal screaming bouncing off his skull.

"I don't know—"

"Yes, you do. You know exactly what you want, you just don't think you deserve it."

Milo rolled his eyes, his arm dropping from the door and wrapping around her back.

"You deserve everything, Milo. You deserve to feel loved

even when you're still falling apart. You deserve to be held together by someone even more fucked up than you."

He laughed against the side of her neck, burying his face, but she could feel his tears on her skin.

"How many therapists does it take to get both our heads out of our asses?"

"Five by my count," she sighed.

Milo leaned away from her touch. "Four and a shaman."

That's when Hanna rolled her eyes.

"I think I still need to be an asshole for a few more hours," he said, sniffling and untangling from her, though she knew he had no interest in letting go. "After the rehearsal dinner, we can have it out. I promise."

"I can handle that," she said.

She slid into the car, trying to hide the smile breaking over her face. She let him drive back in the aching silence he craved, but when they got back to the house, he squeezed her hand before disappearing.

The pressure of his fingertips in her palm was a promise they could solve every last one of the problems she'd brought back to California.

TWENTY-EIGHT

"Hi, wedding buddy," Hanna said, clapping her hand over Logan's shoulder.

He stood on the porch, overlooking an endless sea of fluffy green grapevines as Marcia and Cami issued marching orders to the rest of the groomsmen. She tried not to stare at Milo as he helped Brendon—*Brandon*—move a table, the ink on his arms flexing in the glittering string lights overhead.

"Did you get everything you needed in town?" Logan asked, arching his brows.

"Almost," Hanna said. "What about *you?* What are we doing these days? Apps?"

He laughed, sipping sparkling water. "No. We're doing nothing, at least for now."

Milo set the table down and turned his head, catching her eyes. He lingered, a slight smile forcing its way through his brooding.

"Goddamn," Logan sighed. "Don't take this the wrong way, but I don't know that I've ever looked at someone like that."

"I know," Hanna laughed.

"You know how I know we're fine?"

Hanna twisted toward him, adjusting the cap sleeve of her dress.

"How?"

"I think I'm jealous of you, not him."

Her lips folded into a gentle smile as she touched his arm.

"You're a catch, Logan. Someone will look at you like that one day." She paused, a thought occurring to her. "And if you're into redheads..."

"Chloe?" Logan asked, cocking his head to the side.

Hanna shrugged. "I bored you. Chloe is *anything* but."

"Huh," he said, sipping his water. "I'm going to think on that."

He threw an arm around her shoulders, squeezing her gently before fading off into the vineyard, finding some way to be useful.

Hanna turned back toward the house, ready to face the gauntlet she'd avoided the entire day.

The DeBrunes.

Marcia had greeted her warmly enough, but she hadn't been able to look her in the eye. Tom was worse. Every look he gave Hanna was filled with the kind of silence that deafened. They had flown into Phoenix for Lisa's funeral, which Hanna had appreciated, but they hadn't spoken since.

They'd practically raised her over her decade-long relationship, and now she was standing in their home, pining after another man, trying not to sob.

But Hanna knew she could handle them. She could handle anything, even if it hurt.

"Anything I can help with, Marcia?" Hanna lingered at the edge of the kitchen, holding her breath.

"Oh Hanna, honey, yes! Would you mind helping Tom

take those extra pillows and blankets out to the guest house? We're shoving the boys out there tonight."

Tom's head snapped away from his conversation with an uncle, the dread palpable between both of them. Hanna grabbed a stack of pillows and Tom slung the blankets over his shoulder, holding the door for her as they silently made their way across the vineyard and to the guest house. She nudged the door open with her hip and tried not to tally up all the times she'd fooled around with Logan in the shack at the edge of the vines.

"You look healthy, Hanny," Tom said, dropping the blankets onto the couch. "Happy."

Her lips twisted, the tears nearly instant. When Logan had called her Hanny in the spring, she'd wanted to kill him. But there, after so many months of building up a tolerance, it was a nice reminder of who she'd been to her mother.

"Oh, sweetheart," Tom said, blushing a deep shade of red. He'd never been a man of many words, but they'd always gotten along. He pulled her into a hug, the kind she'd rarely gotten in her life, and she held herself together as best she could.

"You know, we were so disappointed in Logan—"

"No," Hanna said. "No, it's okay. Logan made a choice I was too afraid to make, I think. We just... we had some growing up to do."

"Marcia will never forgive him," he said. "But we're proud of you. I hope you know that."

"Thanks," she whispered.

"Your mom—" Tom's voice tightened. "Your mom would be proud of you, too."

He squeezed her once more and then ran off before she could well and truly unleash, but the tidal wave didn't come.

She would have been angry a few months before, resentful

that someone would have the audacity to presume to know what her mother might think of her.

But in the peaceful dark, she believed him.

She wiped at her eyes, shaking off the strings that bound her chest as she breathed slowly.

"Hanna?" Milo poked his head into the guest house. "You okay?"

"Yeah!" She rolled her eyes, as if she could fool him. "Tom was just being really nice."

"Bastard," Milo said, closing the door behind him.

Hanna laughed, the tears still slipping despite the control she finally felt over them.

"Can I?" Milo held his arms out. She folded herself into them, the relief so instant she almost laughed. He held her face in the dim light, a hint of gold on his shirt cuff catching her eye.

"Are those—"

"I got them before," Milo explained, turning his wrist so she could see the tiny sunflowers better. "I guess I'd just kind of hoped we'd figured shit out by now."

"Maybe we have?" She circled the couch, flopping onto the floral cushions, several decades outdated. Milo sat on the coffee table across from her.

"I've made amends with a lot of pieces of my life over the last few months, Milo. There's really only one loose end I haven't tied up."

"You don't have to make amends with me, Arizona."

"I do," she said, leaning toward him. "You were nothing but clear about what you wanted, even when that started to change—"

"I lied to myself for years and then to you, Hanna. I would hardly say I was clear."

She huffed a sigh. "I just mean that whatever happened or didn't happen between us, it wasn't your fault. If I'd been taking care of myself, I think I would have been better to you."

A silence fell between them. She counted the tattoos on his forearm, following every twist and curve like a map to the melancholic frown on his lips.

"Logan was telling his mom earlier about spreading Lisa's ashes with you."

Hanna smiled. "Yeah. I fucked up so big with all of that, but I thought including him in something would give us both the closure we needed."

"And?"

"And I can very confidently say that Logan and Hanna are a finished book."

Milo nodded as he thought, wrestling with something he didn't want to say.

"I don't know how to be a relationship guy, Hanna."

"Well," she said, resting her hand on his knee. "This version of me has never been in a relationship either, so we could figure it out together."

"You've figured a lot of shit out, but do you really think you're ready for another long-distance relationship?"

"No," she snorted. "Never again. Which is why," she mumbled, scrolling through her phone. She held the screen toward him. "I sold my house."

"You *sold* your house?"

She nodded. "I sold my house. I close right before Thanksgiving."

Milo folded his arms. "So you fixed things with Logan. You sold your house. You're over the whole dead mom thing—"

She flinched. "What? Absolutely not."

Milo leaned forward, his fingers lingering over hers.

"That was a test. You passed," he whispered. "So, you're like, super in love with me, or what?"

Hanna waited in the quiet for a moment, enjoying the way it sounded on his lips. She *was* in love with him. She'd known it for a while, but she'd never let the feeling rise to her tongue, never gave the air it deserved.

"Don't freak out," she said.

A slow smile crawled over his lips.

She grabbed his neck, pulling at the base of his curls and snagging his mouth in the kind of kiss she'd been thinking about for months.

He nipped at her ear and pushed forward, wrapping her in his arms and driving her backward onto the couch, his hands sliding everywhere.

"God, I forgot how good you tasted," he murmured between kisses, pushing the hem of her dress over her thighs.

Hanna sighed, all of those locked-up pieces of her stretching and moving, shaking off the dust as she snapped right back into the version of her who got to be Milo's girl.

He simmered like a tea kettle under her touch, bubbling and begging to pour into something new, something porcelain and precious, but still resilient enough to take the sear of him. The simple comfort of his touch was so much more than she ever dreamed she'd have again. He trailed her entire body with molten kisses, never once losing contact with as much of her as possible.

"Milo," she gasped when his fingers found her, needy as ever for him. He pulled her on top of him in the dark of the guest house.

"You missed me," he laughed.

"Desperately," she breathed.

"Ay! Milo!" Matty boomed from the deck outside the guest house.

Hanna groaned. "No!"

"Jesus Christ," Milo hissed, his hands jumping to his pants.

Hanna jolted off of him, pulling at her dress as Matty barged in and flipped the lights on.

"Ah come on, not this shit again," he whined.

"It's fine—" Milo started.

"I can't do another round of this with you two! I refuse! I need you to look me in the eye and tell me *right fucking now* that this is happening for real, and not just another mess!"

Matty's blue eyes flickered between them, wide with the unhinged combination of several bottles of wine and pre-wedding jitters.

"Matty, relax," Milo said.

"I gotta find Sara—"

"No," Hanna said. "No, we're not bothering the bride. Milo and I are figuring shit out, okay?"

"Not good enough."

He crossed his arms. Milo looked around and grabbed Hanna's phone, flicking through to the screen she'd shown him and holding it up.

"Good enough?"

Matty's eyes bounced from the phone to Hanna's face.

"I was going to tell you guys after the wedding."

"And you're not just fucking around?"

"Well, not anymore," Milo said, grinning against Matty's groan. "I love her, okay? I love her, she loves me, we're going to make a run at this. Logan is cool, everything is fine."

Milo clapped his hands on Matty's shoulders and pushed him out of the guest house.

"You like, *love* love her?"

"Yep," Milo mumbled.

"Sara owes me fifty bucks," Matty said, laughing.

Hanna lingered alone in the guest house, her heart thudding against her chest, not in a panic, but in a full-out sprint toward whatever happened next.

"YOU'RE GETTING MARRIED TOMORROW," Hanna squealed, popping the cork on the final bottle of champagne for the night. Sara giggled, leaning her head on Hanna's shoulder.

"I'm getting *married* tomorrow," she echoed. "Finally."

Hanna poured two glasses, setting the bottle on the nightstand as they snuggled up in Sara's bed. They were halfway through *My Best Friend's Wedding*, fighting the drain on their energy, not quite ready to lay this chapter of their lives to rest.

Hanna muttered through a sip, "Unscented antiperspirant."

Sara threw her head back, cackling.

"I'm *sorry*! But someone had to get you two alone. You're both the exact same kind of stubborn."

"We are," Hanna agreed. "Thank you."

They laid together through the final act of the movie, content to ignore the rest of the world for just a little longer. When the screen flickered back to the Netflix menu, Hanna kissed Sara's cheek and snagged their empty glasses.

"Goodnight, Mrs. DeBrune."

"Goodnight." Sara cleared her throat. "If you *happen* to see Milo tonight, tell him I said goodnight too."

Hanna rolled her eyes, but giggled all the same. She wandered downstairs into the kitchen, setting the glasses in the farmhouse sink. The door to the back porch slid open, several bottles clinking against one another as Milo yelled something to someone out on the porch.

She twisted and leaned against the counter, unable to fight the grin as he turned and saw her. He set the empty bottles on the island and swept her up into his arms.

"You know what I just thought about?" he whispered, her back leaning over the counter.

"Hmm?"

Milo brushed his hands along her jaw. "I get to see that bridesmaid dress tomorrow."

Hanna laughed. "You could see what's underneath it right now if you wanted."

"I'm sharing a guest house with three dudes—"

"Two of them have already seen you inside me, so," Hanna whispered, attempting to be funny, but her cheeks flushed a deep red.

He kissed her cheek. "We should protect Brandon's innocence."

"I've got my own room," she murmured against his neck, her hands wandering under his shirt. "Perks of being the jilted ex-girlfriend of the homeowners' son."

She grabbed his hand and pulled him up the stairs, her stomach fluttering as they fell into her bed, his hands going to work the second the door shut.

"It feels a little sacrilege to fuck you in Logan's house," Milo said, nipping at her jaw.

"Then don't fuck me," she said, wiggling her eyebrows at him. "Make *love* to me, Milo."

She giggled, rolling her eyes. "As if we ever did anything else," he whispered, his hand crawling her thigh beneath the hem of her shorts.

He moved faster as she sighed, sucking the soft skin of her neck between his teeth. He was so warm, so consuming, so *hers*. Her breath caught, the edges of her vision pulling into brilliant white as he brought her over the edge. She buried her face in his neck, running her fingers through his hair as she fought to get her breathing under control.

"You love me," he whispered, grabbing her face to look at her.

"*Desperately*." Hanna laughed. It surprised her—how easy it was to admit. "*You* love *me*."

"Terrifyingly, Arizona."

He reached between them, shoving his sweatpants off and pulling her shorts to the side—there was no show of it, he wanted to be inside her, in any way possible.

"Tell me again," he whispered, taking up space within her as she melted over him.

"I love you," Hanna said, gripping his arm as she sank into his skin, fusing with his veins.

"I love you, too."

He lit her up with a searing kiss and she fell apart over him, crumbling and falling into those green eyes as he followed her, the edge in his gaze from earlier gone.

Not forever—but for long enough.

She collapsed against his chest, pressing her lips to his skin as she stroked his hair.

"Good as you remembered?" he asked quietly, shifting his weight to her side and pulling her against him.

"It was f—"

"I swear to god, Hanna, if you say fine—"

"I was going to say *fucking incredible*," she said.

He pressed a kiss to her temple, frozen in a moment they'd both so deserved, a moment that sent shivers down her spine but, for once, not of panic.

WHEN HANNA WOKE up surrounded by a sea of ink, her heart did not sink like she'd feared it would on such a big day.

No, it held tight, beating steadily against his.

She could still feel the electric current of him as she showered, like a late summer rain washing over her, and she was still beaming like an idiot when she joined the bridesmaids for breakfast.

In fact, the beaming didn't stop throughout the entire day. She'd worried it would crush her to watch Sara marry Matty without her mother's commentary during dinner, or terrible dance moves at the reception. Her heart strained, of course, but it did not collapse.

"Hanna, honey, can I get your help?" Cami darted through the living room with her hair half done. Taylor zipped the back of Hanna's dress, disappointed that Cami had interrupted the prior evening's sordid details.

"The boys need help with their boutonnieres, but I need to get back in the chair. Berty keeps pinning them upside down and the florist is going to kill him."

"I'm on it, Cami," Hanna said, squeezing her shoulder. She darted down the steps of the back porch and out to the guest house, a round of whistles greeting her as she slipped into the French doors. Matty fussed with his boutonniere in the mirror as Berto battled the pin for the third, maybe fourth, round from what she could tell.

"I've come to release you from this torture," she said, tapping Berto on the shoulder.

"Thank god," Matty sighed. "He fucking stabbed me!"

"It wasn't on purpose!" Berto insisted.

"The pin is bent to hell," Hanna muttered, holding the purple-tipped pin between them. "Do you have extras?"

She glanced around the room, uncles and cousins cracking beers, but no florals in sight. Logan appeared from the bathroom, fixing his cufflinks.

"Well, shit," he said. "Milo seen that yet?"

He pointed to Hanna's dress. She couldn't stop the smile from breaking over her petal-pink lipstick.

Logan held up a hand. "That's all I need to know."

"I'm looking for the florist," Hanna said, holding the bent pin up to his face. "Boutonniere emergency."

"Uhh, she's helping my dad," Logan said, gesturing to the deck out back. He pulled open the back door and followed her into another circle of navy suits. "Have you met her yet?"

"No?" Hanna asked. Logan's eyes skipped from Hanna to the florist as she tucked a pin into Tom's jacket.

"Janny," Logan said, tapping her on the shoulder.

The florist spun, her bright green eyes widening and a warm smile pulling at her delicate lips. She looked different outside of her sun-soaked shop and in a cocktail dress—no apron in sight. She clapped her hands together.

"Sunflower girl!" she cheered.

"Oh my god!" Hanna's skin flushed as she pulled the woman into a hug, shocked to see her standing next to Tom DeBrune. "You said you had a big wedding this weekend! I guess I assumed you meant some big fancy city venue."

She patted her shoulder. "No! No, I meant big for me." She reached up and tapped Logan's cheek, squeezing it lightly as she spoke. "I've known these two since they were just boys. Wow, don't you look *spectacular?*" She leaned closer and dropped her voice behind her delicate hand. "I hope whoever that guy was sees you in that."

"You, uh, you know each other?" Logan said, looking between the women.

"Kind of," Hanna answered, giggling as she turned toward him. "Logan, this is my florist."

Logan laughed and dropped an arm around the woman's shoulder. Hanna tried to think through the Rolodex of aunts and cousins she'd met over the years, but she couldn't place her.

"*Hanna*," the florist said, tapping her temple. "*The* Hanna. Of course!"

Logan and Hanna both shook their heads, their eyes widening.

"Not *the* Hanna anymore," Hanna said.

Logan shrugged. "Well, not *my* Hanna, but—"

"Oh," she said, clenching her jaw together. "You know, I think I did hear something about that—"

"Mom, can you help me with this godforsaken boutonniere?" Milo asked, cutting across the deck. "It's crooked no matter what I do."

Logan bit his lip to keep his laughter in as Hanna glanced between them, the puzzle pieces she'd collected falling together quickly. The florist turned her attention to her alleged son, her fingers working quickly to adjust the arrangement.

"Damn," Milo breathed when he caught sight of Hanna, her mouth agape as she watched them move in the same fluid motions. "FaceTime didn't do that dress justice, Arizona."

Janet swatted at Milo's shoulder. "Don't talk to my best customer like that!"

Milo wrapped an arm around her back, pressing a kiss into her salt-and-pepper hair.

"What?" he asked.

"This is one of my sons up for grabs, by the way," Janet said. "Though he's making a terrible first impression."

Logan leaned between them and kissed Janet on the cheek.

"I wouldn't be so sure about Milo's availability, Janny," he said and darted away before Hanna could protest, laughing the entire way back into the house.

"How do you know my mom?" Milo asked, two sets of emerald eyes staring at her.

"Oh my god," she breathed, her eyes catching on Janet's

emerald ring. "I thought your mom was a traffic school teacher?"

"Oh honey, that was decades ago," Janet said. "And really only to pay the bills to get my shop started." She turned to Milo, his face painted in an amused grin. "Wait! *You're* the Phoenix girl. What happened with Lo—"

"Mom, this is Hanna," Milo cut her off. "My girlfriend?"

Janet raised her eyebrows. "Girlfriend!"

"Don't freak out," Milo mumbled, unable to stop the grin from lighting up his face.

Tom leaned forward and squeezed Milo's shoulder as he looked to Janet.

"Don't let *your* son fumble that one. Take it from me."

He winked at Hanna, who was still trying to process being introduced as Milo's girlfriend. Milo grabbed her hand and kissed her cheek.

"Everything fine?" he asked.

Hanna squeezed his hand and laughed.

"Better than fine."

EPILOGUE

"Wait, I have to show you the view from the balcony," Hanna chirped into the phone, holding it out as she ran through the world's most charming countryside home.

She pushed open a set of creaky glass doors, stepping out into the brisk morning air. The hills of Pitlochry, Scotland unfurled before her, a stunning blend of cobblestone and soft green earth.

"Holy shit, Hanna, that's stunning!"

Beneath the balcony, an endless sea of lush greens held onto the early morning dew, soaking into her skin.

"You have to promise you're coming back," Sara said.

"If I can drag Milo home," Hanna said. "He's having the time of his fucking life."

"Where is he?" Sara asked, her voice dropping into a conspiratorial pitch all women knew.

"Showering."

Sara wiggled her brows. "And there's... nothing you wanted to tell me? Or show me? Perhaps a stunning family emerald?"

Hanna threw her head back and giggled, glancing over her shoulder to make sure Milo wasn't within earshot.

"I think he's waiting for the last night. He's been acting a little skittish this morning."

Sara squealed. "I knew it. I *knew* it. You look gorgeous, he'd better do it tonight."

Hanna arched her perfectly sculpted brows and tossed a curl, meticulously styled for a day she knew would change her life forever.

"We're heading out for another distillery tour, I gotta go!"

"Take a million photos!" Sara pleaded.

"Love you."

Hanna took a few more breaths, inhaling as much of the crisp air as she could before heading back into the bedroom and staring at the dress lying over the bed they'd shared for the trip.

She ran her hands over the bodice, eyelash lace tickling her fingertips. She took her time pulling the delicate straps over her shoulders, careful not to snag the train on the ancient floorboards.

"Whoa," Milo sighed, standing in the doorway.

She twisted to face him, the skirt following in a soft swish. "Yeah?"

Milo moved closer, wrestling with his cufflinks. Two tiny golden sunflowers, peeking out from his burgundy jacket. She ran her fingers over them, instantly back in the DeBrunes' guest house. A blush crept over her.

She turned to fix her dress in the mirror, smoothing the front while Milo tugged the zipper to the midway point of her back. She admired the sight of them together, so grateful for all the heartache it took for them to carve out space for one another.

She leaned her head back on his shoulder, placing a kiss on his freshly trimmed beard.

"Sara and Matty won't hate us forever, right?"

Milo laughed. "Not forever, no. Besides, they're about to be so sleep deprived it won't matter."

She touched his hand. "I wish our parents were here."

She didn't mean his mom or her dad, though Janet would surely have a few strong opinions for them when they returned.

He dropped a kiss on her shoulder. "Me too. You ready?"

And she was ready. She'd been ready.

Hanna gathered the train of her dress in her hands, folding the white silk and tulle over her arm as they wound their way out of the house, the Scottish breeze sweeping over them in a soft caress.

"Miss!"

Hanna was almost in the passenger seat of the car they'd rented when Mrs. Blairmount, the owner of their cottage, came barrelling out of the main house, her eyes lit up.

"Miss! I was hoping to catch you before you left. I can't let you two leave without something!"

She disappeared back into her kitchen, the stonework reflecting the sun that peeked out between clouds while they waited. When she reappeared, they both released a heavy breath. Hanna's throat tightened as the woman bustled across the yard, waving a bright yellow bouquet.

"My sister just arrived from Carnie! She brought me a bouquet, and I just can't let you two run off and get married without flowers. Look at 'em!"

She waved the sunflowers into the window, bouncing up and down. Hanna took them and smiled. She felt like she was holding sunshine the entire way to the council chambers.

She knew everyone would flip out when they got home, but there was something to having just one little slice of her life with Milo not on display.

"You alright?" Milo asked, glancing at her as they wound through the rolling hills.

"Fine," she said.

And she meant it.

ACKNOWLEDGMENTS

There are a million people to thank for Fine Fine Fine's existence, and I will get to them, I promise.

But there is one in particular who I'll never get to thank personally, so I owe her some space.

My mother—Cheryl, not Lisa—but just as biting.

There are a few things I need you to know about my mother's death and why it took me nearly five years to be able to edit a book I wrote in less than two weeks.

But before I share, just remember, I've gone to a lot of therapy.

When I say I'm fine—I mean it, unlike Hanna at the start of our tale.

My mother went into the ER with back pain on a Tuesday in March, and eight Tuesdays later she was gone. If you're looking at a calendar... yes, the writers of my life were indeed that on the nose—my mother's last conscious day on this mortal plane was Mother's Day 2019.

And because the writer's room apparently had a personal vendetta against my family, one of my sisters and I were both expecting our first babies.

I know. But remember that I've spent so much time (and money!) on a beige couch.

The last thing Cheryl ever said to me was, "Nothing's going to happen to me today."

And she was right, as mothers so often are.

It took a few more days for us to figure out the magic combination of Flo Rida songs (I'm not kidding) and ex-husband confessionals to convince her to give up.

She was the world's scrappiest woman, so it was no surprise she went down swinging.

The last thing I said to my beloved mother was an accidentally gasped, "You bitch!" after a brutal moment of silence and a second final breath.

Cheryl was funny like that.

I had my daughter three months later, and a year after that my husband lost his father at the height of Covid. In a sick haze of PPD and grief, Fine Fine Fine (then called Chasing Sunflowers) poured out of me in a ten-day stretch of no sleep and a lot of tears. I was still fresh to the grief game, but I was the most seasoned player on the court, so suddenly I found myself in a marriage of two very broken thirty-something kids who'd lost their role models and one of us had to figure it out.

Milo and Hanna are much hotter than us, but there are some truths within their dynamic that I can only attribute to the heaviness our house endured during that time.

I published Chasing Sunflowers in a delusional state and unpublished it just as quickly.

And then it sat on a shelf for five years.

I wrote many other books, went to a lot of therapy, we had another kid, and in 2024, a few months before the release of my debut novel, Rift, my husband got sick.

Sick, sick.

(The writers really need to find a new storyline, okay?)

And even though the circumstances were (are! He's still here!) so very different, the body really does keep the score and I knew that no matter what happened next for us I needed to find a way to channel the impending grief into something meaningful before I lost myself to another five years of grieving.

Between projects one day, I plucked Chasing Sunflowers off my bookshelf and suddenly I could see so much more in the pages than I ever thought possible.

It helped that I knew how to actually write a book too.

Revisiting Hanna's story with five more years of not just grief, but of life under my belt was an incredibly healing experience for me, but more than that it has built a community of grievers that has completely floored me.

The reviews (not that I read them!) break my heart open in the most profound way, and the readers who take time to message me and share about their losses have given me such a gift, I don't know that I'll ever be able to accurately capture my gratitude on a page.

To anyone who took the time to read this story, I'm thankful. It's not the easiest one to get through, but I hope you find it as rewarding to read as I did to write it.

But this book didn't make it into your hands in a vacuum.

The entire Emrae team has held my hand through every step of resurrecting this story. My PR wizard, whiskey buddy, and best friend, Morgan, was a fan even when it was called Chasing Sunflowers, and continues to be my biggest hype girl. Bailey was the first person I confessed I was rewriting this to and the reason the title and theme shifted from chasing ghosts to wearing the mask of being totally fine. Kiersten has so carefully cradled every word to make sure that a story I feel so personally attached to was as polished as possible.

My editor, Erin, has championed this book since day one and meticulously combed through every word to make sure it hit in ways both hard and soft. And long before she was my editor, we sat beside one another in the dark of our respective losses.

That kind of trauma bond can't be broken.

And while all of my friends and family have always been so supportive of all my work, my sister LeAnne deserves so much gratitude. Not only has she been listening to me yap about this damn book for years, but she's read it in every iteration, and is sitting six feet from me working on getting my books into bookstores across the country because she believes in me the same way our mom did.

I know it isn't easy to see your own loss spilled across these pages, and I'm still really sorry that the ARC landed in your inbox the week of Mom's birthday. That was insane behavior, but we both know the timing was inevitable.

Cheryl always makes sure of that.

ABOUT CB WOODS

CB is a romance writer with two romantasy series, The Courts Between and The Living Courts, currently available through Emrae. She writes stories about good women who make bad decisions for the right reasons. Based in Phoenix, she's built her career in writing and marketing and lives with her husband and two kids.

CB is one of the founding members of Emrae—she is hellbent on making publishing accessible without having to hand a portion of her sales to billionaires.

Connect with CB at cbwoods.net

EMRAE PUBLISHING

Emrae Publishing challenges traditional and hybrid publishing houses with a profit-share model. With a focus on direct distribution and partnerships with independent bookstores, Emrae gives authors the flexibility of self-publishing with the support of a team that understands them. Their mission is to keep money in the pockets of creatives bringing stories to life while keeping billionaires out of their business.

Discover new voices at reademrae.com